TH ...

F...

'Scotland's Stephen King' *Sunday Post*

'Donnelly scores with unusually believable characters, well-realized settings and thoroughly researched mythological backgrounds' *Daily Telegraph*

'Exciting and highly readable' *Guardian*

'Joe Donnelly scales the heights of sheer horror ... Not for the fainthearted' *Today*

'Expect to be gripped from beginning to end' *Maxim*

'*Havock Junction* raises Donnelly to being one of the two best horror writers in the UK ... Probably the best horror novel of 1996' *Fantasy Bookshelf*

'Pulse-racing horror ... very satisfying'
Glasgow Herald

ABOUT THE AUTHOR

Joe Donnelly was born in Glasgow and is the author of the highly acclaimed novels *Havock Junction*, *Shrike*, *Still Life*, *The Shee*, *Stone*, *Bane*, *Incubus* and *The Dark Valley* (previously published as *Twitchy Eyes*). A journalist, writer and broadcaster, he has won several awards for investigative reporting, including Reporter of the Year. He is still involved with newspapers and also writes plays for television. He now lives with his family in Dumbarton, Scotland.

JOE DONNELLY

THE DARK VALLEY

PENGUIN BOOKS

For Martin, Nick and Alan.
Boys now men. Now you know some of it …

PENGUIN BOOKS

Published by the Penguin Group
Penguin Books Ltd, 27 Wrights Lane, London W8 5TZ, England
Penguin Putnam Inc., 375 Hudson Street, New York, New York 10014, USA
Penguin Books Australia Ltd, Ringwood, Victoria, Australia
Penguin Books Canada Ltd, 10 Alcorn Avenue, Toronto, Ontario, Canada M4V 3B2
Penguin Books (NZ) Ltd, 182–190 Wairau Road, Auckland 10, New Zealand

Penguin Books Ltd, Registered Offices: Harmondsworth, Middlesex, England

First published as *Twitchy Eyes* by Michael Joseph 1996
Published under the present title in Penguin Books 1998
1 3 5 7 9 10 8 6 4 2

Some of this story is based on events which
actually happened, at different times and in various
places. Boys get into mischief and into danger. Many of the
scenes are set in real locations. The characters, however,
for many reasons, are completely fictional and do not
represent anyone living.   J. D.

Printed in England by Clays Ltd, St Ives plc

CHAPTER ONE

July 27

'His ghost hangs around here,' John Corcoran said. 'I heard it was seen, plenty of times. They say it creeps about in the mist coming off the river. This place gives me the willies.'

'Me, too,' Doug Nicol said. 'I was told he calls out to other kids. He wants to drag them down there.' Doug twisted his face into a snarl and held one hand up in front of his face, fingers clawed but drooping. 'Like the monster from the black lagoon.'

Everybody looked at Doug, who was leaning against the trunk of the old elm tree that sprawled across the grass, an ancient giant that had given up the fight against a winter gale and had dug great gouges in the turf in its dead fall. Doug was running the blade of his knife under the bark, twisting it hard to break off chunks of powdery wood. He nodded as he spoke, showing his big, prominent teeth. The sun was shining through his equally prominent ears, tinting them red. 'He hates being down there on his own.'

'That's rubbish,' Billy Harrison snorted. He blew out a grey plume of smoke and then let two tendrils curl down from his nose. This was a trick he had spent a lot of idle time mastering in the summer, and it made him look like a big shot. Most of the time the smoke rose up and went into his eyes and everybody laughed while Billy spent the next while blinking back sudden tears. This time it worked just fine and Billy raised himself up to kick his heel against the bare root of the toppled elm.

'If he wanted company, he'd drag them up to the graveyard, wouldn't he?' Billy looked round, challengingly. There was a moment's silence while they all thought about it.

'No,' John Corcoran contradicted. (If it had been one of the others, there might have been a bit of pushing and shoving, because Billy was quick off the mark when it came to taking offence.) 'It would be his ghost. They always go back to where they died, trying to get back into the body. I read that once, so it's true. They don't know they're dead for a long time, years even, and that's why they haunt the places where they died.'

Danny Gillan shivered and said nothing. He was sitting up on the collapsed trunk, his feet almost level with Billy's head. Billy nodded agreeably and blew two smoke-rings in quick succession, making his jaw work like a fish's to get the effect. The rings rolled in the air and played hoops with a rootlet before breaking up. 'Maybe that's it, Corky, just maybe,' he conceded. 'I bet you wouldn't come down here at night.'

'Not when the mist comes off the river,' Tom Tannahill agreed vehemently. 'You never know what's in there. It creeps like it's alive.'

'*Gives* you the creeps,' Billy said, and laughed at his pun.

Over at Drumbeck Hill, a mile, more like two, from where the boys were idling, beyond the double hump of the looming rock and the castle ramparts that rose above the flat mud of the estuary firth, a puff of smoke came billowing out from the crater where the quarry had carved a great scar into the side of the hill. Eight seconds later the booming rumble of the explosion came rolling over the town and across the black, fast water of the river.

Danny Gillan shivered again and, though none of the other boys noticed, his eyes had taken on that flat look of someone whose attention is far away.

'Just like when they were looking for the body,' Corky said, running with his story. He was good at that. 'Remember? I thought they were firing cannons from the castle to raise him up. I read that too. They fired cannons over the water when they got a man lost overboard. In *Treasure Island*. The noise brought bodies up to the top.'

'Like, woke them up, you mean?' Doug asked. Corky shrugged.

'It wasn't the quarry,' Danny said quietly, not looking at any of them. His back was turned and he was facing across the river towards the rising plume of smoke and rock dust. Over the distance came the heavy, rumbling thunder of falling stones as the payload slid down the crater. Danny's eyes were now focused closer however, fixed on the quayside on the other bank of the river where the low tide had left a man-high slick of greasy algae and the seagulls wheeled and squalled over something rotten among the mud and old tyres beside the mouldering ribs of some long-dead boat.

'It was a bomb. The one they found in the reservoir up by Overbuck House.'

'What a cracker,' Doug nodded, remembering. 'Smashed nearly all the windows up in Corrie Street, and a big boulder from the dam came right through McFarlane's barn roof like a *meetcherite* comet or something. You should have seen the hole it made.' Doug was grinning, showing most of his big rabbit-teeth.

'They blew it up all wrong,' Billy said. The bomb was an old story, from way back in spring and that was ancient history. A lot had happened since that spring. 'I heard a flock of Barrie's sheep got such a fright they went crazy and took a header off the cliff on the Langmuir Crags.

'An' I heard . . .' Billy told another rumour they'd all heard a dozen times since the spring, but never tired of repeating.

'But Paulie came up, didn't he?' Tom Tannahill asked. 'Just like that book Corky was telling us about. Must have wondered what was happening up here.'

'Yeah.' Doug laughed and held his hands up on either side of his mouth. 'Hey, who's making all the noise?' he said, in a voice that wasn't quite ghostly enough.

Danny Gillan shivered again and not from the cold. The sun was high, beaming through the thick umbrella of leaves on the limes and elms that had weathered the winter gales, and the air was thick with pollen and the sleepy, high-summer buzzing of bees. He lowered his eyes from the skeleton of the boat, and looked down into the black turbulence of the river. The sun reflected bright from the rippling water, spearing right back into Danny's eyes, and in that instant the other boys' voices faded away and he was back in the springtime, on the far side of the river, on a day cold and sharp enough to make your eyes water and scrape the inside of your nose. There had been no leaves on the trees then, only buds still tight-wrapped on stark branches and the blowdown elm showed redwood circles on the truncated ends where the council's park workers had chainsawed the massive branches that had fallen across Keelyard Road.

'Who's making all the noise?' Doug mimicked a dead boy,

and Danny saw the whole scene unreel again in his mind. Who's making the noise? *Who?*

He'd been there when Paul Degman went down into the water, tumbling with the current. Danny was glad he hadn't seen Paulie's eyes, for that would have made the nightmares so much worse, but still he swam and rolled in his dreams, drawn under the surface by a desperately strong hand, clutching for rescue, clawing for life. He'd been *almost* there, almost at that very spot on that very day.

It could have been me! The thought reverberated; a boy's abrupt comprehension of sudden, permanent end.

Paulie Degman was thirteen, just the same age as Danny, and while they came from different parts of town – Danny lived up on Corrieside where the municipal housing scheme petered out against the cleft of the gully and gave on to farmland – they knew each other. Paulie was a down-town boy, who lived in one of the gaunt old tenements that backed on to the river. This had been his playground, the alleys and closes of the quayside, the cobbles and old capstans where boats had tied up when the quay had bustled, back in history. He'd played here all his life and it had killed him, while Danny had come playing here one rare spring day and he'd stayed alive.

Danny remembered the scream. Some other kids had been playing there too, heaving rocks at the gulls they'd tempted down with old crusts from Christie's Bakery. The sound had cut into Danny's consciousness and frozen him in the act of hefting the stone he was aiming at a beer bottle bobbing along on the current. Over the space of the months since spring – and everything that had happened in the town since then – Danny was never sure why that sound had frozen him to the quick. There had been some quality to the cry, some urgency that had snaked into his nerves and set the hairs prickling under his woollen tammy-hat. He'd turned quickly, and the high screech, so like the fighting gulls, had been joined by the frantic cry of a woman, somewhere high up in the sandstone tenement close to Barley Cobble. The stone had dropped from his hand and bounced glassily on the kerbstone at the edge of the harbour.

'*Jesus Christ get back* . . .' Shouts, hoarse and urgent, and somehow riven with shock.

'*Oh mister it's Paulie he's in . . .*' Panic in the voice of a small boy, closer now as Danny Gillan followed the strange and terrible magnetism in the air.

A clatter of feet, segs and hob-nails staccato against the cobbles.

'*Oh sweet mother of God it's my . . .*' A woman's prayer in a voice that said she didn't yet believe.

Big John Fallon the sergeant running the length of the quay-side, leaping over a jumbled pile of bricks from the old boat-shed that had collapsed in the frost of winter. He was stripping off his tunic as he ran, hat flying off to roll alongside him for a few seconds.

Paulie Degman had fallen into the river and he'd gone down in the fast, black current and his boots had got snagged on something.

And that was the worst of it, Danny Gillan knew. Paulie hadn't collapsed and banged his head. He hadn't been hit by a big red bus going hell for leather round the corner from the old bridge to slam him against a wall and kill him stone-dead in the blink of an eye. He'd gone down in the water and he'd got stuck and he must have fought and cried and hauled for breath, and all the black silt had gone down his throat and he must have coughed out all of his air. Of all the million ways to go, all the hundreds of thousands of ways for boys to die, that was just about the worst, with only one exception young Danny Gillan could think of. You could fall off the big fan-shaped cliff up on Langmuir like Neil Kennedy's big brother, who fractured his skull, or you could take a header from the overhang under the castle ramparts down on to the flat basalt slope of Eagle Rock. You could climb one of the high-tension pylons that strode over the hill from the power station to Barloan Harbour and get fried to a *cinder*, so they said, to a *crisp*. You could slip on a rope swing and twist your neck in the noose and be gone before you knew it. You could even die in your sleep like they said in the prayer: '*If I should die before I wake, I pray the Lord . . .*'

But drowning . . .

Paulie had gone down in the river and he'd drowned. In a couple of minutes Danny, casually walking towards Barley Cobble, targeting the bobbing bottle, would have got to where the boys had been chucking stones, and he'd have joined in the fun, making it a team effort, enjoying the company and the contest, the way it always is with boys. He'd have seen Paulie heave his rock, one of the shards from the brick-shed, hurl arm over shoulder, seen him slip on the slick algae at the edge, take a tumble, arms outstretched, a yelp of surprise blurting before he plunged in like one of the big spring-run salmon going up the weir.

Except Paulie was going down . . .

Danny had seen big John Fallon come thundering down, scattering the pigeons feeding on the spilt grain from the distillery wagon. They had gone clapping into the air in a flutter of panic while Danny's heart had been fluttering inside him, and the very air had been charged with a dread tension.

'Out of my way,' the policeman had roared. *Owramawae!* Like some charging clan chief, the words crammed together but as eloquent as any cry and somehow crystal clear. A cart of firewood went tumbling as his boot caught it. John leapt over a cringing dog, reached the quayside and launched himself into the air. Everything about the moment was fixed in Danny Gillan's mind. He could see again the arc of the sergeant's dive, perfect in every way. Arms straight out, his white shirt flapping where it pulled out of his blue-serge trousers. Two rowing boats were anchored just out from the side, a two-man span from the wall. The tide was in, and running high, though the downward current was still fierce from the melt rains, but there was still a six-foot drop to the water. The policeman went between the boats with hardly a splash – and if he'd hit either one he'd have broken his neck for certain. He went straight under and disappeared. Black ripples shivered outwards and the boats rocked on the surface.

The boy saw all this from the other side of the loading stair where the old grain barges used to park in days gone by. Forty yards ahead a crowd had gathered, atoms drawn together by the magnetism of death. Two men came down in a boat, rowing hard to cut across the current, backs bent with strain on the down-push. The screaming woman had reached the bottom of the tenement and she was running down the uneven cobbles, one shoe on and one off. Another splash, this one huge, and there was a second man in the water. John Fallon had disappeared under the surface. Danny knew him. The policeman sometimes came round the school if there was ever an accident, or maybe a spate of shoplifting at Woolworth's – the kind of thing that always peaked before Christmas (and wasn't it an amazing thing that mothers always lost the knack of arithmetic when they unwrapped presents pocket money could never have bought?). Fallon was a decent enough fellow. His son Jackie was only a few years younger than Danny and the two boys sometimes knocked around together.

A clock inside Danny's head was ticking off the seconds.

Another man jumped in, red-haired and red-faced. It was Paulie Degman's Uncle Peter, who drove the cleansing wagon that hosed down the drains and sucked up the crap inside them.

Come up, come up. The words came of a sudden, with their own beat, like a metronome. It was for the boy and for the policeman both.

The water erupted. John Fallon came splashing up, heaving for breath, his face smeared with thick river-bottom clay. He gasped once, twice, and then went porpoising down again. A siren came hee-hawing along River Street and its tone changed as it came fast as it could down the narrow scrape of Rope Vennell. Above it, up close to the shadowed back of the old tenement building, on the roof of the outhouses behind Cairn House, something flashed and glinted, a piece of metal or a shard of broken glass, catching the low light of the sun. It sent a white needle of light into Danny's eye and he screwed his eyes tight for an instant against the sudden glare. When he opened them again, the light was gone. Danny stopped and held on to the railing at the only part of the quayside where the council had fixed a safety barrier. Something made him turn away from the scene and look down into the water, where sun glinted on the tumbling surface. The red wall of the distillery vented steam in a shriek of heat, and a cloud passed over the sun. Deep in the water, something white moved. Danny's heart kicked like a mule and his throat clicked in a dry spasm. Something down in the depths rolled over.

It could have been anything. It really could have been anything – a bundle of leaves, a piece of old rag, a discarded newspaper. Anything.

But for weeks after that, for months after that, in the dark of night as spring turned into summer and brought with it its own strange and terrifying days, Danny Gillan saw the bloodless face of Paulie Degman as he tried to claw his way to the surface.

He came up, didn't he?

Danny's day-dream imploded and he came reeling back to the present.

'It could have been the bomb. What a blast. Like that Jap place.' Doug's face was animated.

'Hirohito,' Billy said.

'Naw, couldn't have been,' little Tom Tannahill disagreed, shaking his head. 'That was the atom bomb. It would have knocked the whole town flat. It was one of the five-hunner pounders. They say if it had hit the shipyard, the whole place would have gone up like a rocket.'

'Probably meant for the dummy village,' Corky said. 'That's where most of the bombs went.'

Danny forced his mind away from the river and thoughts of the drowning of Paulie Degman. In a way he too was drowning. In their own way, all of them were, in this town, in this strange and heavy summer. Mention of the dummy village had helped knock his mind off its dismal track.

'They say it's still standing,' he told them. 'Like a ghost town.'

'Nah. Must have been blown to bits during the war,' Billy said. 'It was like *The Dambusters* up there on the moor.'

The war was twenty years gone and done, but it was still close enough for each of them to remember the backlash. *Eat that and be grateful, you couldn't get it during the war*. Austerity of a sort lived on for a while longer.

'Has anybody ever been there?' Danny asked.

'My brother said he and a couple of fellas went up to have a look,' Corky said. 'But the place is guarded. Commandos or somebody. You can't get in, and if you do they can shoot you. It's the law. They've got the right.'

Corky looked at them all, with a grin on his face. 'But Phil's a lying toad. He couldn't find his arse with both hands in broad daylight.'

Billy Harrison had just taken a deep draw on his cigarette. All the smoke came out in a rush with his first bellow of laughter and then he went into a helpless fit of coughing. The others fell about laughing and even Danny laughed so hard he lost his balance and fell off the tree-trunk to land with a thump on the short grass.

That's how it all began . . .

CHAPTER TWO

March

On the same cold spring day that Paul Degman went into the river, on the same side of the harbour though some three hundred yards upriver, close to the weir at the bridge, Neil Hopkirk was watching the commotion from his vantage point on the roof of some outhouses behind the buildings fronting River Street.

Neil was sixteen years old and had lank, dark hair hanging down below his collar and dangling in a straight and somehow imbecilic fringe over the rims of his glasses. He had a dark, pear-shaped birthmark on his left cheek, which earned him the nickname of Mole, a nickname only his best friends, a handful of idlers (including John Corcoran's brother Phil who couldn't find his arse with both hands), could get away with, chiefly because they were as big as, and tougher than Neil Hopkirk himself. Neil had a vicious temper, as many of the smaller kids could testify. He kept a bunch of keys on a long chain hooked to the belt-loop of his jeans, keys he had picked up here and there and which opened nothing, but they sounded good and important as they jangled on their chain, and to Neil they were the trophies that told the world that Neil Hopkirk was going to be the Best Cat Burglar in the History of Crime.

Whenever he day-dreamt of his illustrious future, or occasionally confided to anybody who would listen, those words always had bold capital initials. Ever since he could remember, his hero had been Gentleman Johnny Ramensky, who had been a thief of heroic achievement, grace and style, and whom the Intelligence Service had once sprung from Drumbain Jail to carry out a daring wartime raid behind the lines. Neil Hopkirk had seen that film in the old Regal cinema four times, sneaking in without paying for three of those visits and demonstrating his uncanny ability (all of his abilities were *uncanny*, so Neil was convinced) to pass unseen, like an Indian tracker. In his fantasies he saw himself abseiling into a darkened vault from such a height no one believed it humanly possible, snatching the diamonds, the bag of gold, the trunk of cash, or the secret plans worth a fortune. In those dreams even the cops hounding him across rooftops – where he would slow down just to give them a sporting chance or a cheeky, swashbuckler's wave – had a grudging respect for him. The newspapers would be full of stories of the Black Shadow, a name derived from another of his comic-book heroes, the Black Sapper who would tunnel under the earth in his mechanical mole. They would wonder who he was, and in the Regal cinema he would sit in the back seat, surrounded by the classiest girls in town – Neil was strictly limited in this part of his imagination – smoking kingsize cigarettes and tipping the ice-cream girl a wad of notes, seeing her eyes light up with gratitude and hero worship. All of the guys would be with them, Phil and Cammy and Pony McGill, basking in the warmth of his friendship, while Tina Denny and Corrine Latta hung on his every word.

He would be the best, Neil knew. He'd boasted to the rest of the guys that he'd be a legend and while they'd laughed him down, he knew they'd eat it when he became the Best Cat Burglar in the History of Crime.

And now he was up on top of the old outhouses, lounging on the slates, with one casual arm hooked across the galvanized ridging.

He'd been trying a locked window at the back of the iron-monger's, sliding the blade of his knife between the sash frames to kick the catch back, tongue stuck out between his teeth. Craw-ford's Hardware sold fishing and hunting gear. In the front shop there was a glass case with expensive penknives, including a horn-handled, three-bladed beauty which Neil had been eyeing for some time. They had axes and glass-cutters, all part of the cat burglar's kit, but they also sold shotguns and cartridges. Old man Crawford, who had a large white hearing-aid jammed up behind his ear and the milky, somehow mouldy beginnings of a cataract in his left eye, always kept the guns in a back store, and while nobody ever got into the back room, Neil was convinced that this window was where the gun cabinet had to be, where big shotguns were stacked on a rack, along with boxes of shells. Already his imagination had taken over and he saw himself with a black Balaclava, a figure of imposing menace, while the bank manager (though he'd never actually been in a bank, never mind met a bank manager) pleaded with '*Please don't shoot.*' And the pretty cashier, she'd be eyeing up the tall, masked stranger, wishing he would take her away from this boring, humdrum job, to a life of luxury and hot adventure.

It was all within arm's reach, Neil just knew.

Then, behind the frosted glass, a shape loomed up in front of him.

'*Wah . . . !*' The eloquence that came so naturally in Neil's day-dreams deserted him completely.

The shape leant forward, right up against the pane. 'What the *fuck* do you think you're doing?' a voice roared, losing none of its force, making the glass itself rattle.

Instantly Neil recognized the bull-tones of Donal Crawford, the old man's nephew, who worked Saturdays. He was six foot four and built like a brick shithouse and as tough as steel bolts too.

Donal reached for the catch and shoved the window up with a ratcheting clatter. Fortunately the frame hit the safety lock when the window was only six inches open. Neil backed against the wall at the far side of the alley and hit his head a smart crack on the crumbly stonework, hard enough to hurt but not enough to damage. Donal was yelling non-stop, all the phrases jammed up against each other, and everyone of them promising lasting pain to whoever had tried to break into his uncle's premises.

In the two seconds before Neil turned and scooted down the alley, he saw he had been mistaken in assuming the window led into the storeroom where the shiny shotguns were stacked. Through the six-inch gap, quite clearly, he saw the hairy, spotty thighs of old man Crawford's nephew and he realized that he'd tried to break into the outhouse where big Donal was having a crap.

Neil came skittering out of the alley. There was a broken-down wall where the old boat-shed had collapsed in the storm and beside it a straggle of weeds from last year. Neil went ploughing into the scrub, crashing through the dried heads of dockens and the wood-saw teeth of bramble runners. Behind him Donal was still bawling in fury, and Neil knew it would be only a matter of seconds before the big fellow pulled up his trousers and came barging out of the back door into the alley-way.

Somewhere downriver somebody screamed, high and glassy on the cold spring air. Neil came stumbling through the weed patch when, without any warning at all, a big, dark shape loomed up. Neil whipped round and saw a policeman come running towards him. His heart stopped still and he felt the blood drain right out of his face.

It was big John Fallon. His black boots thumped on the cobbles and his hat went flying off to roll like a spare wheel along the flat. Neil's first instinct was to run, but the sergeant was going full tilt. The boy measured the distance to the corner of Rope Vennell, the next alley which led up to River Street, and he knew he'd never make it and, even if he did, he'd be caught before he was halfway up and the sergeant would give him an extra toe up the backside for making him run.

Neil turned, hands out in a gesture that said he gave in and was ready to come quietly.

Big John Fallon came powering towards him. Neil stepped forward but the policeman simply leapt over the pile of bricks and crumbled mortar from the ruined boat-shed. For an instant the boy thought the sergeant was going to land on top of him, but Fallon's eyes were fixed dead ahead of him. He didn't even notice the cringing would-be burglar.

Amazed, Neil Hopkirk followed his thundering progress. The sergeant was stripping off his tunic. Neil watched him throw it to the side and again his instinct almost took over. There would be a whistle and maybe a pair of handcuffs. Certainly a police warrant card that would come in handy to an international jewel thief. But just then he heard the slam of the service door at the hardware store and knew he shouldn't hang around.

John Fallon was halfway down the quayside. A couple of boys came round the corner, pushing a cart heaped with chopped firewood, and they tried to take evasive action. The policeman's foot sent the cart and all the bundles rolling across the cobbled walk. Neil went up the alley for a few yards, then turned, jammed his hands in his pockets and came sauntering back the way he'd come.

Donal stopped for a moment, his face red and so swollen with anger it looked as if it would burst. Neil nodded as calmly as he could, while thinking to himself that, for such a big fella, Donal wasn't too gifted in the equipment department. In the *hardware* department, Neil thought, and started to giggle. Donal gave him a suspicious look before he turned to run down in the same direction as the policeman. Neil took a left up Fish Pend, the narrowest alley in town, which bore the powerful aroma of the fishmonger's filleting and gutting slabs. Phil Corcoran and Campbell Galt, they'd been with a couple of girls – at least so they said – and they swore blind that when they got wet, they smelt the same way. Neil, who had never got as much as a kiss playing postman's knock, hoped that wasn't the case, otherwise it would make him pretty sick for sure.

He held his breath until he got to Boat Pend, which led to the arched walkway right under the old tenements. There was a narrow niche here and a downpipe on the wall, out of sight of people passing by up on River Street. Without much hesitation, Neil jinked into the space, took hold of the pipe and went up the wall, hand over hand, bracing his feet against the rough sandstone. In a matter of seconds, he was up on a low, sway-backed slate roof. He went over the ridge and slid down the lee, still out of sight. There was an old skylight here, which let a little light through to whatever was below. He wiped the glass with the heel of his hand and peered in. It was some old shed full of rusted machines, though the shadows changed everything and gave them all interesting shapes. The skylight was shut but he could have broken a pane and slipped the catch. He decided to leave it for the moment, at least until he'd swiped a few flashlight batteries out of Woolworth's.

Up on the roof, despite the cold of the spring day, the slates were surprisingly warm. Neil Hopkirk sat in the valley formed by the two slopes between the ridges, completely hidden from view. It was exactly his kind of place. Further down, on the quayside, there were a couple of men in a rowing boat, and people were shouting. From along near Barley Cobble, a woman was yammering something and Neil thought that maybe some-body had fallen into the river. It was too far away to make out. He sat for a while, enjoying the warmth of the old slates, and then he turned to look at the building behind him.

The tenement was in shadow. It was tall and gaunt and the windows were darkened, and for a moment Neil Hopkirk didn't know which particular one it was. They all looked different from the back. Round on River Street, most of them had shops on ground level, Woolworth's, Crawford's Hardware, Christie's Bakery, dozens of shops in a busy town's main street. From the back, they didn't look so good. It was as if the builders knew the only people who would come round here would be fish-gutters and draymen and van drivers. This was the town's *tradesman's entrance*, dirty and unfinished, the hidden backside of a bustling town.

Neil stood up and took his keys out. He was far enough out from the wall to be in the sunlight. He swung them around, letting the round metal dog-tag glitter in the sun while he checked out the windows. The sunlight sent a circle of white, reflected light flashing as it tracked up the slates and then sparked out down the quayside.

The valley of the low roof still afforded cover. The boy followed the line of the gutter and got to the first low window. It was only a foot square, probably a vent from a cellar and completely festooned with cobwebs. A roan pipe came down from the edge of the high roof, a slender tree of metal with chevrons of branch drains going left and right. Without hesitation, Neil scrambled up the pipe, followed the first branch out for five feet, straining to grasp the nearest window-ledge. He reached it, hauled himself up to sit with his back to the window to check if anyone had seen. There were no shouts of alarm, at least none other than those from the turmoil down there where the men were rowing and the urgent yelling of men and women mingled to create a twist of tension on the air.

He felt behind him, got his fingers pressed up against the first panel of the six framed panes and pushed hard. There was a soft squeal of protest, of dry wood on wood, and the window lifted just a little. Neil's heart started to beat faster. He turned on the ledge to look inside. For an instant, his own reflection moved, as if there was somebody else in the dark room, and Neil almost fell down on to the slates. He had to wait until his heart climbed down from his throat before he could get a hand over his eyes to cut out the reflection and peer in. The gloom had cleared, and in that second he knew where he was. It was Doctor Green's old surgery. He'd moved out a couple of years ago and nobody had seen him since. There was some talk of abortions, but nobody knew why he had just upped and left. He had lived and worked here, using most of the third floor of Cairn House. From where he stood on the ledge, the boy could make out a table and chairs. Some cupboards. A bag which might contain a doctor's medical kit, shiny and deadly scalpels, maybe a syringe, or even some chloroform to overpower guards. Neil Hopkirk's imagination was off and running again.

He eased the window up, inch by inch, fearful that it might jam and he'd fail again this day.

The window opened six inches, ten, a foot, a bit more. Enough to let Neil Hopkirk through. He squirmed in, head and shoulders first, feeling the weight on his ribs then his belly. The flat plaque of metal on his key-chain, where he'd had his name engraved in the cobbler's shop, caught the sun and flashed a sparkle of light over the roof and into the eyes of a boy who was watching a tragedy unfold down on the quayside. Neil wriggled some more, pushed forward. His legs were sticking outside when he got to the balance point of no return and started to slide. Unable to stop, he put his hands out in front of him while he slithered down. His shins scraped painfully on the edge of the window and he landed with a thump and clatter.

He was in.

It took a minute or so for his eyes to become accustomed to the gloom and for the hot abrasion-burn to fade from the skinny shin-bones. It was dusty in here, and there was a smell that was worse than the flat and slimy reek in Fish Pend. Neil wrinkled his nose in disgust. It was a sickly stench that reminded Neil of the time he'd reached into the pigeon's nest last summer when he was collecting eggs. He'd reached over the rim and put his hand into the twiggy saucer. His fingers had touched something cool and yielding and then they'd slipped *inside* the small mound. He'd felt the chill wetness and brought his hand back, and he'd almost fallen off the wall under the railway bridge where the street pigeons nested. It had been an abandoned nest. The two chicks had been half grown and now both of them were half rotted. Their innards had the texture of cold custard and their half-feathered skins were thin as wet paper. Neil had brought his hand down to eye-level – to *nose* level – and white maggots had been pulsing in the viscid mess on his fingers, and the stink had hit him so hard he had almost retched. He'd flicked his hand to whip them away and some of the mess had splattered on Cammy Galt's cheek, and he'd been far from pleased about that. Neil recalled Cammy waiting for him gingerly to descend, and then he'd kicked Neil a smart one right up the crack of his arse with those winkle-picker Teddy-boy boots he always wore, and Neil's backside had gone into a puckering spasm that made him feel as if the boot was still stuck up there a full hour later.

The smell inside the old surgery was almost – but not quite – as bad as the foul reek from the dead squeakers in the nest. Neil supposed a pigeon had found its way in and not been able to get back out again. There was an overlying mustiness on the dusty air, a hint of dry rot, stale urine. This place hadn't been used for a couple of years, maybe more. There might not be anything worth stealing.

But he was inside, and that was a part of it, almost the best of it. There was the excitement of just getting inside a building, coming in through a window or down from a skylight into an empty place. *Trespassing.* Breaking and entering. Gaining illegal access. Neil's heart had speeded up and he could feel the delicious tension in the pit of his belly. All of his senses were alert, though he wished his nose wasn't quite so efficient. The hairs on his forearms were standing up as his hands clenched into fists. He was aware of everything – the far-off noises of whatever was happening down at the quay; the muted piping of gulls; the steamy crash of the jackhammer down at the shipyard next to the castle rock. He waited, listening for a few moments. The back room was still in shadow, but the sun glanced off a window of the yacht repairer's across the river and sent a shaft of light straight in, cutting the darkness with an almost solid beam in which tiny dust motes twirled and sparkled. Out on River Street, a big haulage wagon from the distillery rumbled past, shivering the foundations. The door of the room was open, just an inch or two, not much more. Beyond it, the rest of the building beckoned. It tugged at Neil. Somewhere in the dark of the hallway, something small squeaked twice and then stopped. For an instant, all sound was cut off and the silent ambience of the empty building was filled with hollow echoes.

Neil crossed from the window, keeping low. There was a set of drawers which he opened one by one, instinctively doing it right, starting at the bottom so he wouldn't have to close the one above. Inside, there were some brochures about pregnancy and the kinds of things mothers should eat. The bag on the shelf was oddly clean. Inside, there was some clothing, not very clean, and a half-bottle of whisky with little more than a mouthful left at the bottom. Neil twisted the top and drank the dregs, savouring the burn, and he shuddered at the strange taste. He slung the bottle back in the bag and crossed to the door. The whisky fumes were warm on his breath and he was feeling pretty good about this whole thing.

The door opened further with a tiny creak, not much louder and just as high-pitched as the squeak made by the distant mouse or bat or whatever small creature had panicked. He slowly crossed the narrow hallway. Here, on the floor, somebody had smashed a pane of glass, and the shards crackled under his feet like sharp gravel. Three doors led off and Neil knew one of them would lead down the stairs and out on to River Street. As far as he remembered, the whole building was empty, and if he'd read the *Levenford Gazette* he'd have known that a development company planned to convert the whole of it into apartments – but Neil Hopkirk had progressed none since getting the basics and struggled even to read the shiny *Superman* and *Fantastic Four* comics from America.

The first room was the old surgery. It was not big, but laid out with a flat and mouldering trolley-bed with a thin, plastic cover ripped in so many places it looked as if it had been raked with machine-gun fire. The stuffing puffed out like flak-bursts. The desk was plain wood and thick with dust. Neil opened a cupboard door and jumped back in fright as a white shape swung with it. It took a second for his brain to identify the floating ghost as a white overall. It took several seconds more for Neil to get his breath back.

There was nothing in the cabinet by the window, where an old porcelain sink caught a shard of light. It had two neat tap-handles that could be operated with an elbow.

There was nothing here worth stealing. On the wall, a couple of tracts, pages torn from a bible, were white against the peeling, green-floral wallpaper. They held no interest for the Best Cat Burglar in the History of Crime.

He turned away from the wall and sauntered back to the hallway.

Something froze him in his tracks.

Neil Hopkirk stopped still. The hairs on his arms stuck out so high they formed goose-flesh. The hairs on the back of his neck began to crawl and the skin between his shoulder-blades puckered and tensed.

There was something else in the building. He started to turn, got one hand up against the doorpost. His breath had backed up tight in his throat.

A harsh scraping noise came from behind him. In that split second Neil Hopkirk realized it was the sound of broken glass grinding into the floor.

Something, *some*one, had taken a step behind him, crushing the shards of window-glass. Neil completed his turn. A white face came swooping out of the darkness of the corridor, fast, too fast, to be anything more than a blur. A hand came up even faster and slammed into the side of his head, open-handed and hard. Neil's head whipped back in a bright flash of pain and cracked against the doorpost, gouging a gash into the skin of his scalp.

A blurt of panicked sound escaped him. He reeled, instinctively going with the blow in the same direction his reflex had swung him in an attempt to dodge it. The pain flared bright for only a second and then he was moving. Feet crunched on the glass again and he saw a grey motion out of the corner of his eye. He twisted, squirming past the door jamb, fright galvanizing him into suddenly fluid motion. A hand reached for him, almost caught the back of his jerkin and merely slapped him forward towards the stairs.

He hit the first flight running like a startled rabbit, whimpering as he went. All he had seen was a blurred shape and the hand that had swung round to slam into his head. There had been no warning at all, only the abrupt violence.

Footsteps thudded now behind him in the hall. He took the steps two at a time, grabbing on to the old banister for purchase, heading up into the darkness. He skittered to the landing, swung himself round and up again into the gloom. Here there were another three doors, one of them slanted, torn from its hinges. The other two gaped black. Behind him, he could hear the blundering progress of whoever had hit him. He dived to the left, out of sight of his pursuer, got through the broken door and swung right down a very narrow little lobby that smelled of pigeon shit and mildewed paper. He reached a small room with one window boarded with planks of wood. Over in the corner, there was a tall cupboard with no door. The backing plaster was punctured and rotten, and most of it had fallen to the floor in mouldering grains. The room was gloomy, but Neil Hopkirk's eyes were wide with fright and with the burst of adrenaline now shunting through his veins. He crossed quickly to the cupboard, all of his senses straining for signs of pursuit. He could hear the heavy footfalls of someone who did not care how much noise he made, and the coarse breathing. A meaty thud told him a hand was slapping on the smooth wood of the banister. He tried to slow his own breathing to absolute stillness while he crossed the floor, silent now as a cat, to the open cupboard. He crouched, seeing no other avenue of escape, his glasses further dimming the poor light. He turned, pushed himself into the hole where the plaster had fallen away. It had looked deep, as if there were a passage that might lead into the thick wall itself. He pressed further and came to a sudden stop against the crumbling sandstone, jammed half in, half out.

The man's breathing came harsh. He reached the top of the stairs, paused. Neil could envisage him wondering which room to try, and he pressed himself further into the cavity, managing to get his legs out of sight, but unable to pull his head and hands back. He curled himself tight, trying to make himself as small as possible. In this gloom, if he stayed still, maybe the man wouldn't see him. *Maybe.*

A scrape of sound came from beyond the room, much like the first noise that had alerted him, then a motion in the doorway.

His heart thudded in two hard kicks. A man came in, walking very slowly. His bulk seemed to fill the space, shoulders almost touching each side. He came in, stood there, just a fuzzed shape in the darkness, but scarily defined, solid. Neil heard him breathe, fast and slightly ragged, but other than that, he made no sound. He cocked his head to the side, as if listening, turned to go out again.

Mole coughed.

It was as simple as that, a little catch at the back of his throat and a cough that just jumped out unbidden. The man turned, came stalking back into the room with no hesitation at all, pin-pointing the source exactly. He reached, grabbed Neil by the hair, hauled him right out, so violently one of his shoes caught in the old plaster and went whirling off. The world spun as the boy was thrown across the room towards the doorway. He tried to get to his feet and almost made it, too scared to cry out, his whole scalp burning in pain. Behind him the man moved, caught him by the back of the neck, and drew him to his feet, pulling him out through the doorway. He dragged him down the stairs to the lower level, slammed him through the first doorway, feet crunching once again on the glass shards. Neil's glasses went spinning off to the side. All the sharp shapes blurred. The boy went staggering backwards and the man's other hand came up and straight-armed into his nose.

Brilliant hurt blossomed in the middle of his face and in his eyes. Tears simply spurted, just like the blood which blurted from both nostrils. Neil let out a squawk of pain and dreadful fear. The massive shape that had come through the darkened doorway slapped him again and sent him crashing against the desk. His thigh hit with almost enough force to break the bone and this time the hurt was so much that for an instant the room went completely dark, as if the power had somehow failed inside his brain. He went tumbling over the desk and his chin connected with the hard surface of the sink, thumping hard enough to clash his teeth together and strip a slice of skin from his tongue.

Neil was foundering in a sea of pain, shock now powering up so that his brain was unable to comprehend what had happened. Within the first seconds the shock began to overpower the pain, layering and lacquering it with a strange numbness.

A hand clamped on the back of his neck and lifted him straight upwards. The pressure was so great that Neil Hopkirk only felt himself hauled off the floor before everything faded away and a complete darkness swamped him.

CHAPTER THREE

July 27

'I bet we could find it.'

John Corcoran had swivelled on the fallen elm and was clambering to stand up on the massive trunk. He shaded his eyes against the high sun and pointed across the river, indicating roughly north.

'It's up beyond the barwoods,' Corky assured them. 'Up on the moor.'

'I heard that too,' Tom Tannahill agreed. 'There's the bomb craters on this side of the woods. Remember the craters where we used to catch newts and frogs? The dummy village must be up that way, 'cause that's where the bombs fell.'

'I heard it was up at the Blackwood stream,' Danny Gillan pitched in. 'Right at the source.'

'I bet it's not as far as that,' Billy Harrison countered, which was not entirely unexpected. 'That's about twenty miles away. You could never walk that far in a month of Sundays.'

All of them had spent the better part of every summer holiday – except this one, which was different from all the rest – playing in and around the Blackwood stream, which tumbled down a deep gorge beyond the barwoods and meandered to empty itself into the river just north of the town. They had been up beyond Blackwood Farm, and even to the low ridge of heathery hills beyond, but none of them had ever reached the end of the stream. There was a rumour that, like Strowan's Well down in Arden, the water came gushing pure and clear out of a cleft of rock, like the story in the bible, but nobody knew for certain, so Billy's estimate went unchallenged.

'It's pretty far up, I reckon,' Danny insisted. 'It would have to be if they didn't want the Jerries to miss and drop them right here.'

'It would take too long,' Billy argued. 'We'd never get back in time. It would take more'n a day.'

'Who cares how long it would take?' Corky said. He turned

back towards them, spinning quickly and almost losing his balance on the smooth wood where the bark had been stripped away. He pinwheeled his arms for balance, regained it and stood with his legs planted apart. 'We could take the tent.'

Everybody stopped. It was one of those odd moments when an idea is tossed in the air like a shiny coin and just catches everyone's attention while it spins. There was a drawn-out silence. They all knew which tent. Phil Corcoran and some of his pals had dumped it out of the scout lorry after a camp a couple of years before and it had never made its way back to the scout hall. Sometimes Corky and the rest of the boys would set it up on the flat meadow by the Ladyburn stream that wended its way down past Corrieside, and on hot summer nights there would always be a selection of youngsters sitting out under the stars beside the red embers of a stickwood fire, playing three-card brag and pontoon, telling jokes and tall tales, poring over tattered copies of an old *Parade* magazine, getting all hot and bothered if they saw so much as one bare tit.

Not this summer, though.

Since long before the school term finished at the end of June, since April at least, there had been an unofficial curfew in the town that was as tight as any the council could have tried to enforce, and for most of the summer, since the trouble began, no mother in town would allow any of her children to camp out at night. Most wouldn't let their children play out of sight.

'No chance,' Billy said. 'My ma would throw a fit and a bad turn. She'd go *bonanza* if she even knew I was down here. She thinks I'm round at Doug's house reading comics right now.'

'Mine's the same,' Doug agreed. 'I have to tell her where I'm going and when I'll be back. After what happened to Don Whalen she was a nervous wreck. Our Terry isn't even allowed out of the front garden.'

Danny nodded along with them. There was still a nervousness about the town after what had been happening since the spring, and although it seemed to be over now, *seemed* to be over, it took a while for mothers to settle down again. They were like chickens in a coop, still fretful after the stoat has gone, leaving the thick scent of blood in the air. Mothers were instinctive that way. They could still smell the blood. They were still scared in case the next blood they smelt was the blood of their own.

'They would never know,' Corky said, green-grey eyes bright and alive with that combination of mischief and adventure that made him the natural hub of their group. 'We could say we're going along with the scouts. They're doing the weekend camp up at Linnvale.'

That was true and well enough known. The past couple of summer months had meant every kid was kept on a short leash and the community had organized a series of events, summer play picnics and day-trips, just to give the mothers a break and to relieve the boredom of boys who needed to roam. The scout troop were taking groups of boys, sometimes forty or fifty strong, to a camp-site nearly thirty miles outside town and, as far as most parents were concerned in that particular summer, the further away, the better.

'Nobody would ever know,' Corky repeated. 'We could load up with food and just skin out when the scout bus leaves. As long as we get back at the same time, we could still do it.'

'It would be some hike,' Billy objected. 'Could be twenty miles, like I said, even more.'

'But we could be the first. The first ever. Nobody's ever found the dummy village before. Nobody's ever seen it, except Phil, and he's a liar. We could bring something back to show the rest of them, eh? Better than hanging around all day going doo-lally, bored out of your brains.'

'But what if . . . ?' somebody asked, and somebody else threw in another spanner, and somebody else thought they might get away with it, and while they were talking the quarrymen let off another blast up on Drumbeck Hill. The sound of man-made thunder came rolling down on the still air and rumbled across the water. Each of them stopped talking.

'Come on,' Corky said. 'This place still gives me the creeps.'

Billy ground his cigarette out under his heel. Danny picked up a pine cone and flicked it against Corky's head. Doug loaded his little slingshot with a smooth acorn and aimed it at Tom's backside. In a minute they were out of the trees that bordered Keelyard Road by the river and were heading up towards the bridge, the memory of Paul Degman's death fading just a little in the light of the sun and in the heat of the agreement which might have been yet unspoken, but was somehow fixed between them all.

March

Sister Julia Gillies had come sweeping into the classroom in a rustle of beads and a jangle of keys. She was small and round and had a deep, almost masculine voice and an eye that could fix you like a spear when she meant business, which was pretty much all of the time. She had a raised mole on her cheek with three stiff black hairs sticking out, as if her skin had trapped a fly under the surface and it was trying to work its way back out.

She nodded to Matthew Bryden, who was attempting to teach a class of thirty boys and girls the finer mysteries of Shakespeare and, only with a phenomenal amount of luck, getting through to more than a scant half-dozen. Quarryhill School was perched on the edge of an abandoned hole in the ground where sandstone had been blasted and cut to build half the old tenements in the town. It was just like any other school, a place where kids were sent for five days of the week for the catch-as-catch-can lottery of learning. Here, the teachers churned and hashed their furrows, never deviating one year to the next, scattering their knowledge like confetti, or *shite in a field*, as the local expression would have it. It landed on some and missed others completely, and the grey teachers ploughed on regardless. It was up behind the school that something would happen, later that year, in the drop-off at the old sandstone quarry. At this moment, however, the madness that would settle on the town was yet to stoke up. Only one person was aware of it, and he was not going to tell a soul.

The tough little nun who ran the school turned at the table, one hand clenched around the wooden cross dangling from the outsize beads tied at her waist. She swivelled, as if on castors, and scanned the class, eyes flicking from one desk to the next.

'Paul Degman is dead.' No preamble, no softening of any blow, though everybody knew it anyway. In schools and in schoolyards rumours, gossip and truth travel somewhere close to the speed of light. 'He drowned in the river on Saturday and now he is with Jesus.' She nodded her head when she said the holy name. Down near the front, two girls sitting side by side burst into tears and automatically turned to hug each other. Up at the back Billy Harrison and Doug Nicol stopped digging each other in the ribs and leant forward on their desktops.

'As you have often been told, playing by the river is dangerous. By now you will realize why. Remember that, all of you.'

She swept her eyes round them again, somehow catching every one of them, making beady contact.

'It could have been any one of you.'

Danny Gillan felt that cold shiver again. John Corcoran saw the look on his face. 'We can swim like fish,' he whispered. 'Paulie couldn't.'

'The good Lord can look down on you at any time and decide to take you, and that's what he did with Paul Degman, which is why you must always try to be in a *state of grace*.'

'That's total shite,' Corky said, keeping his voice low, and Danny could tell he was angry just by the use of that word. Corky hardly ever swore, no matter how much his ne'er-do-well father and his crazy, jittery brother might curse. 'What's she want to say a thing like that for? He fell in, poor sod. He was just unlucky.'

Sister Julia's voice boomed on. 'So let us hope that Paul Degman's immortal soul was in a *state of grace* when the Lord decided to take him, otherwise . . .'

Otherwise, he'd be in – Danny Gillan closed his eyes – *he'd be in the bad fire*, wouldn't he?

Danny didn't have to hear Sister Julia to know what was coming. He'd lived with the spectre of the bad fire flickering hot at the edge of his consciousness since before he'd even started in the primary school. Four and a half years old and he knew about hell and the everlasting flames that would burn and sear and never stop. *Not ever!* If there was a hell, then it had to be burning flames that went on and on and on and shrivelled your skin and flesh and could never be put out, while God in His infinite mercy and wisdom allowed it to go on. *And on.*

'Remember now, Daniel.' It was always Daniel. Never Danny, or Dan. He'd read about Daniel in the lions' den – and read every other book in the bible besides – and sometimes he felt a strange kinship with his namesake. There were times when he felt he'd been put into a hole and somebody had rolled a rock over to close out the daylight and, down in the shadows, eyes would watch him and beasts would roar. In his imagination, lions prowled in the darkness. Somewhere in the distant blackness, there would be the hint of burning, the smell of smoke. 'Remember, Daniel,' his father never tired of reminding him. 'He can see everything you do, and you don't want to go to the bad fire, do you now? That's where you go if you're bad.'

Always a warning, always a parable, and hardly a laugh along the way. This God business was a serious thing, as the young Daniel Gillan discovered at a tender age, and He was always ready to look down with fire in his eye and give it to you good and proper. No messing about. His heavy hand could come out of nowhere and knock you to the ground. A paternal thing. What fathers were for, especially fathers almighty.

Jesus loves me this I know . . . But good God's getting the furnace stoked and glowing.

When he was three, Danny's sister Agnes had been helping their mother in the kitchen. She had come out with a bowl of bubbling-hot custard and Danny had stumbled against her, sending the bowl flying. The boiling custard had come down in a searing, cauterizing splash to cover his back and his neck, and he'd fallen screaming to the linoleum floor, trying vainly to crawl out of the puddle of scalding liquid. His hands and knees could gain no purchase, and the more he tried the more he slipped, while the skin on his neck and back puckered and blistered. The family had no car then – and still didn't – so it took half an hour to get to the cottage hospital and another hour to be transferred to Lochend General, where he spent three weeks getting the dressings changed twice a day by nurses with kindness in their eyes and ruthlessness in their fingers. At the age of thirteen, Danny could still remember the sear of the pain as the nurse pulled the lint away, taking off the thin slick of blistered skin, while another nurse held his shoulders flat on the bed to stop him squirming. They could not stop him hurting and they could not stop him screaming. That had been bad. That had been excruciating.

But it had been nothing compared to the scalding custard and the shriek of his nerve endings on the day it had happened. That had been the most fundamental experience of his entire existence. The pain had seemed never to stop, while the skin all

27

down his shoulders and back sloughed away and shrank on his flesh while he screamed and shrieked and tried to crawl.

Burning was something he knew about. *Oh, Hallelujah.* And according to Dan Gillan senior, if you weren't in a state of grace when God took you, then burning is what you got. An eternity of it.

All of his life, young Danny had been made aware of the bad fire and, until he was seven years old, his dreams had been fraught with heat and flickering red shadows and the smell of burning flesh.

And the idea of a God who could do that, who knew everything from start to finish and had it all planned in His vast mind, that was a very scary idea altogether. The young Danny didn't want to believe in the kind of God who was so two-faced he would pretend to love you while he knew you would burn for ever. It was a set-up. *It was a fix.*

But as a kid he'd been too scared not to believe. He had prayed at night so that the God of his father would spare him from the flames. He'd prayed. And occasionally his own father would get the priest, Father Dowran, to come round and reinforce the lesson, Father Dowran with liquor on his breath and a strange heat in his stroking hands. They'd all prayed. For a state of grace.

'So tomorrow morning there will be special prayers offered up for the repose of his soul,' Sister Julia was saying. A girl close to Danny and Corky burst into tears, and beside her a boy started to snivel. Danny felt the cold shiver crawl up his spine, and in his mind's eye he saw the pale shape under the dark surface of the river and the strange twinkle of light on the roof of the old outhouse buildings on the far side of Boat Pend.

'Everybody be there at nine sharp.'

Yeah, so we can all pray, Danny thought, *that he doesn't end up in the bad fire*. Danny knew prayers did no good. What a deal for poor Paulie. Down there in the cold water. One minute he was playing on the bank, throwing stones at gulls and tin cans and the next he's down there in the cold and the murk, swallowing river mud, and then we've got to pray so that he doesn't get hauled away to the bad fire by a terrible, vengeful God.

Danny wondered what a boy like Paulie Degman could ever have done to have been allowed to drown down there in the river, what he could possibly have done to be allowed to burn. He couldn't think of *any* reason, any sin that would be bad enough to make you burn for ever. On the curve of his shoulder, just beside his neck on the fine skin on the collar-bone, there was still a flat, puckered scar that had been the mark of the scald as a child. Automatically, his fingers stroked the memory.

'It's shite,' Corky said again, snapping Danny out of his black thoughts. 'Once you've had it, that's it. Finished. Gone and done. That's why you better make the most of it while you've got it, and you only ever get the one chance.' He turned to Danny. 'You believe in all this garbage?'

Danny shook his head. He'd shucked off his belief in an Almighty only a year or so past, but old habits died hard and old indoctrination ran deep.

CHAPTER FOUR

March

On the Wednesday that Neil Hopkirk was finally posted missing, Big John Fallon had been round to have a chat with Phil Corcoran, who answered in slow monosyllables. Danny and Tom had been sitting with Corky under the aluminium shelf that served as a porch when the policeman had come. He'd stood on the step, nodding to them all in his sage and watchful way, letting them know that he saw everything they did and was all right about it so long as they didn't overstep his mark. They all nodded back, even Corky, which came as a surprise to the other two. They'd thought he'd hate the police after what happened to his old man, but Corky made a silent acknowledgement, as if determined not to show any weakness. It was almost man to man.

When the policeman had gone inside, Corky had shrugged off their inquiring glances, and Danny sensed there was more to that simple nod than any of them realized.

'Sit up straight,' Mamie Corcoran chided her son, with a swift knuckle to his shoulder. He grunted a guttural response and through the open window – the three of them sat still so they could catch every word – they heard the policeman patiently try to ascertain Mole Hopkirk's last whereabouts. Phil Corcoran swore blind he hadn't seen Neil since Friday, when they were down at Biagi's snooker hall on Kirk Street. In fact, he'd been with Mole Hopkirk on Saturday morning, testing the locks on the old warehouses at the far end of the Rough Drain, just in case one of them hadn't been snapped shut. Neil had had to go off on some errand and that was the last he'd seen of him. But Phil knew that the 'busy-boys' could be sneaky and, while it was true he hadn't seen Neil for a couple of days, he couldn't be sure that this was all a pretence on John Fallon's part and that he was just trying to draw Phil out so he could pin something on him like they had done to his old man.

The three boys listened to Phil's verbal swerving, grinning

each time he sounded nervous and began to stammer, but the policeman didn't hang around long enough to make him really sweat. The next day it was all round the school. Neil Hopkirk had left the previous autumn, having reached the age of fifteen. He was well known to most of the younger boys. The last anybody had seen of him was when Donal Crawford had passed him in the alley after somebody had tried to jemmy the hardware store's window. Now that Donal thought about it, that person could very well have been Hopkirk, but now it was too late to do anything about it. As far as anybody knew, Mole had gone up the alley and disappeared along crowded River Street.

During the week, a different policeman had come round the classes, introduced by Sister Julia, who would have been better at wringing a confession than a squad of police with truncheons. Had anybody seen Neil Hopkirk? Everybody had.

'. . . And he's a swine,' Doug said when they were out behind the boys' toilets, sheltering from the cold and blustery rain. 'As *crabbit* as a stoat. He tried to kick me in the balls just because he thought I was staring at that birthmark of his. Chased me all down Aitkenbar Hill when we were sledging. I thought the creep was going to kill me. Probably would have and all.'

'Aw, there's nothing to him,' Billy said. 'He just talks big and flashes that bunch of keys about, but he couldn't punch his way out of a wet paper-bag. He's as strong as a dry fart.'

'I suppose you've fought him then?' Danny asked. He'd taken the odd sharp-knuckled punch on the arm, or the occasional dead-leg from a well-placed knee. Mole Hopkirk could be mean whenever he wanted and, with the younger kids, that was most of the time.

'No, I never fought him, but that doesn't mean I *wouldn't* if he claimed me,' Billy asserted. 'He's all mouth.'

'So why did you give him a cigarette down on Rope Vennell last week?' Tom demanded to know. He turned to the rest of them. 'It was the same day Paulie went into the river. Mole came down the alley near the ironmonger's, swinging those keys of his that don't fit anything, and he saw me and Billy smoking. Right away he's in at us for one.'

'I had plenty,' Billy protested, his face reddening. 'It wasn't a big thing. I just gave him one out of the goodness of my heart.'

'Either that or he'd have swiped your face with his keys and taken the whole packet.'

'Yeah, he can be a mean swine,' Danny agreed, taking the heat out of it before Billy got any angrier and felt he had to prove something. 'Maybe he's just left. Moved on.'

'With any luck he's fallen in the river along with Paulie. Couldn't happen to a nicer person.' Doug laughed. 'I wouldn't miss him, I can tell you.'

'Maybe he took on somebody bigger than himself and got a severe tanking,' Billy said. 'Maybe somebody beat the shite out of him and threw him in.'

'Too much to hope for,' Corky said. 'He'll turn up sooner or later. Anyway, who cares about him? He's as thick as shit in the neck of a bottle.'

The bell rang out, muffled only slightly by the drizzly rain. They hitched up their collars and filed across the yard from the old toilet block. The rain was still spring-cold and blustered in up the firth on the west wind. Summer hadn't yet arrived, but it was coming.

In the back room of Cairn House, in the old abandoned surgery, Neil Hopkirk was dying.

It was dark in the shadows, but a slanted beam of light piercing between some boards over the window, white and solid in the dust-laden air at the far end of the hallway, told him it was daytime. The occasional rumbling vibration of a truck passing on River Street confirmed it.

The hurt had faded for now, faded to a burning glow from the intense flame of the last time he had come round, and that had been really bad. Bad enough to make him scream; but no sound had come out and all the screaming had been inside his head.

Mole was dying and he couldn't move. He had come swimming up from the black depths, floating towards the surface of wakefulness, unable to prevent the return of conscious thought. His dreams had been filled with a deeper dark where shadows came lunging from beyond his sight and grabbed at him, and twisted and bent and broke him until he slipped away again.

He had broken through into a dopey wakefulness and after a

while he had been able to open one eye. The other one was clamped shut, and there was a numb sensation under his eyelid that felt like a pulse, but his skin was wet and Mole was no longer sure whether or not his left eye was still in its socket. A slow breath eased out and a jagged shard of pain dug into his back, making him wince involuntarily, again setting up a ripple, a vibration of hurt. With a great effort, he closed his eye and made the motion stop. After a while, he struggled to lift the lid again. It slowly cracked open, with an almost audible squeal of protest, as if it needed oil. The room was twisted somehow, with no vertical lines at all, and even in his state – and at the best of times Mole Hopkirk was never the most eloquent or observant – he realized it was not the room but himself that was twisted to the side. The light from the far window was a silver bar slanting down to the floor, where it sparkled on scattered diamonds of shattered glass.

If thine eye offends thee, pluck it . . .

The memory came unbidden and the horror came on its heels and all of it came rippling back. His breath came ragged, through his nose and occasionally past the obstruction in his mouth. He had tried to get his tongue around whatever it was and force it out, but there was something wrong with his jaw. It wouldn't work properly and, when he did move it, splinters of pain ground inside him so fierce and hot that he had to stop. Every now and again, his nostril blocked, and whether it was blood or snot he couldn't fathom, but when it happened he was convinced he was going to suffocate, and a part of him didn't really mind that at all. His body, on the other hand, refused to go along with it quite as readily, and his frantic breathing reflex took over and convulsed him so violently that he felt he would pass out under the pressure of the pain.

If thine eye offends thee . . .

He had said that. The man in the shadows.

Oh Jesus where is he . . . ? Is he coming back? Oh mammy don't let him . . .

In through the window Neil had come creeping like a mouse, while outside the seagulls were screaming as they wheeled around the chimney-tops and the masts of the old fishing boats, and a woman was screaming and some men were yelling and it was all right because nobody was looking and he was . . . *in*.

And then it had all happened so fast. The white face, just a blur, a ghost high up in the shadows, and then the massive blow on the face, and he'd been running and hiding and the man had filled the doorway. He'd coughed. *Coughed*. That was all, and that had finished it. The man had grabbed him and thrown him and dragged him, flopping and helpless down to the room, and there had been a blurt of hot blood. He had hit something hard and the lights had gone out for a dreadful second when the pain had screeched inside his thigh, and then a grip of metal – it had to be metal – on the back of his neck, hauling him upwards, lifting him like a doll.

He was *in*.

The pain had been there, waiting patiently for him to waken. The axons and dendrites inside his head were reconnecting themselves after the fragmentation of the shock of hurt, and for a while he was cocooned in warmth, numbly aware of low sounds far off, and for one sweet moment he imagined he was in his bed on a Saturday morning, dozing in the mid-morning light of the sun coming through a crack in the curtain. Even as he slowly uncoiled from unconsciousness he was aware of the heat in his nose, a burning throbbing just under his eyes, and another auger screwing into his thigh.

He breasted the tape and came through to the real world, and the fear came exploding up from within as memory came back. He had twisted round, blurrily aware of the light in the hallway, and a scraping sound, the noise of heavy shoes on broken glass, had come in from the right.

'Who comes like a thief in the night?' A man's voice, low and somehow hot, almost wheedling.

Neil was not an academic and he had left Quarryhill School having achieved a proficiency certificate in horticulture (he weeded the shrubbery) and a failure in metalwork and technical drawing. But he was not completely devoid of intelligence, and at that very moment he knew he was in desperate danger.

The feet had crunched on the broken glass again, now louder, now closer, and he had shrunk away from the shadow that came looming to cut off the dim light.

'The first woe is past, and the other woes are yet to come.'

34

The voice had been closer, hoarse and cracking as if the speaker had been breathing the dust.

'Wha . . . ?' Neil had started to say, but a hand had come swinging up and clamped over his mouth.

The shadow came closer, right up to his face. Through the clog of blood in his nose he could smell bad breath and smoke and the flat scent of unwashed clothes.

'Nice and quiet now lad, eh? Nice and easy,' the voice rumbled. The hand still clamped his mouth, fingers and thumb, squeezing so hard on his cheeks that it forced his jaws apart. The other hand started pulling at the narrow leather belt around his waist.

'*What's he doing?*' The question jolted inside his head. The belt buckle jangled, fell free. The hand groped again and yanked at the popper stud. Neil's zipper rasped and cold air tightened the skin on his belly. The hand dived straight in, horny and tough, and everything Neil had shrank upwards reflexively.

'No!' he blurted, though the pressure on his face made the sound come out in a single grunt. He had squirmed away from the probing, groping hand.

'Lie still,' the man had hissed, hot and shivery. He'd leant forward . . .

Time had changed. Everything had changed.

Neil was slumped against something hard that could have been the waste pipe of the wash-hand basin. His right eye creaked open again and every movement set fire to some part of him. How long had it been? He couldn't say. He'd climbed in the window on the Saturday, some time the afternoon and, while it seemed like a lifetime ago, it might have been only a day, maybe two days ago. Some things were hazy in his memory and other things might have been crystal clear, sharp as glass, but for the moment he kept them battened down. The numb sensation under his left eyelid was pulsing again, throbbing in time to the beat of his heart the way a finger will begin to throb if you coil a rubber band around it and let it go from red to purple. Another slow breath let itself out and the sliver of pain came arcing into his back. The puzzling slant to what should have been the vertical lines of the window shutters and the corner of the wall made all the perspectives incomprehensible. The light spangled blurringly on the scatter of broken glass and once more he remembered the footsteps crunching it into the floorboards.

The pain had been intense, unbelievable. It had come burning up into the root of him and he had felt as if he would split apart.

The hand had kneaded between his legs and his panic had taken wing. He couldn't speak, and the force on his jaw had made his eyes water so that the room swam in liquid ripples.

Oh mammy daddy it's a homoqueer . . . it's a BAD MAN.

He'd been turned over, roughly, as if he weighed next to nothing, and the calloused hand had slid across the skin of his buttocks. He felt the skin pucker and he felt his sphincter pucker, and the fear had simply erupted.

Two days ago? Three days? It was far away, a lifetime away, but the pain was here and now. Every movement scattered the anaesthetic effect of dehydration and blood loss. Every motion woke some broken and torn part of him. Down there, where his skin was pressed against the flat of the floor, he could feel a trickle, and he couldn't tell whether he'd pissed himself or shit himself or whether his insides were slowly leaking out on to the boards.

If thine eye offends me, pluck it . . .

A memory was trying to work its way back and Neil tried to dodge away from it because it came scrabbling up inside his head like a scary spider, dripping pain and poison, and he didn't want to see that again . . . oh no!

'Don't look at me,' the shadow had said and by now Neil Hopkirk knew it was the devil talking to him. This was some time on the second day, maybe the second day, so it must be more than two, more than three days now, and Neil knew he would never get out of here. His head slumped towards the floor, making the slanted angles list even further. His arm twisted up his back, but that was only a minor pain, adding little to the rest. He needed a drink and, inside his mouth, where his tongue rasped against some rough fabric that might have been a piece of sackcloth but felt like sandpaper, the memory came crawling and scuttering in.

'Don't you look at me or I'll . . .' Neil had closed his eyes quickly. He had seen nothing except the looming shadow. All his senses were focused on touch and smell. The scent of old tobacco and the metallic cloy of his own blood and the burn of piss down there on the floor.

Then the voice had changed. There had been a silence for a moment, no more than two seconds, and when the devil spoke again, it was in the different voice.

Eye for eye, tooth for tooth and do not resist an evil person. If thine eye offends me, pluck it OUT.

Sour breath blew in at him. The hand on the back of his neck squeezed tight, so tight Neil thought the thumb would come through the skin and into the muscle, popping through his windpipe. His right eye opened involuntarily and something fast flicked up, quicker than he could blink. It hit him in the eye, pecking like a blunt-beaked bird. His head jolted back, and for an instant there was no pain at all inside him. It all flew away, leaving him floating in warmth. His right eye wheeled, panning in a short arc, taking in the shadow and the sliver of light and the other hand pulling away from him. There was a small sucking noise and a wetness trickling down his cheek, and it might have been a tear.

Love your enemy and pray for he who persecutes you that you may be sons of the father.

Neil Hopkirk had floated away on clouds of shock.

Now the shadows were lengthening and the angle of the beam of light was changing as the sun swung, weak and still wintry in the early spring, and Neil knew it would be night soon. The memory had come crashing through, forcing past his defences, and the realization of all that had happened came back to him, but he was too tired now to fight it, too exhausted to react. There was something wrong with his left eye and he didn't know exactly what it was because he couldn't move it and the eyelid wouldn't open but there was a strange feeling there as if something had caved in and he still couldn't really tell whether he had an eye in there.

The fabric in his mouth absorbed all of his saliva and made his throat dry and bleached. Neil felt himself slide sideways to the floor, and the motion blocked off the airway at the back of his throat. He breathed through his nose, or tried to, and found it blocked. For a second the exhaustion claimed him, then he snorted hard, clearing the clotted blood, found another breathing hole and drooped further. One of the hands, tied behind his back, hit against a metal upright, just a touch, but it felt as if a ton-weight had slammed down on it. Another memory tried to come back, one in which a foot stamped down on his fingers again and again, but this time the lethargy was creeping into his brain and it was hard to think.

The hunger was gone and the thirst was so bad it felt as if all the moisture in him had been wrung out, but the tiredness was overwhelming and after a while the slanted light began to fuzz out. From his slumped position, jammed against the old wash-basin, he could just make out the gleam from the bunch of keys and the little polished metal disc as they reflected the light. The sun moved and the glimmer faded away and Neil Hopkirk went with it.

Over in the corner, a shadow remained motionless. It stayed there for a long time, just waiting. After a while, a black fly came buzzing through the door and settled on Neil Hopkirk's cheek.

CHAPTER FIVE

August 1, 9 a.m.

'Here come the tear-drops,' Phil Corcoran sneered, and Campbell Galt and Pony McGill sniggered. 'Snivel, sniffle and bawl.' He winked at his two pals, then turned back to his young brother. 'And who said you could take my tent anyway?'

'*Your* tent?' Corky retorted. 'You stole it from the scouts.'

Phil had been sitting on the gate at the end of the road, where the tarmac petered out when it met the hawthorn barrier of the farm track. In a couple of years all of the hedge would be gone and the road would continue in a wide curve past the cemetery and down to the main road, and the greenery would be replaced by nearly three hundred council houses. It was all a time of change.

Phil stopped working the blade of his knife into the top gate-spar where he'd been carving his initials. 'Are you calling me a thief? Eh? You little shit that you are.'

Being called a thief was a sore point with Phil. Old man Corcoran was banging the Drum, as they said hereabouts, banged up for six months up in Drumbain Jail. He was just halfway through his time for hoisting three hundred in used notes from the pigeon club's cash-box, money which had been set aside for taking all of the club's best birds to a race from Cherbourg in France. Everybody wondered why Paddy Corcoran had ever been voted in as club treasurer. Everybody knew that he hadn't done a day's work since before the war and hadn't had a drink-free day since it ended, even if he was good with the homing birds. Of his three sons, Phil would see the inside of Drumbain in four years' time after several visits to approved school in his later teens, once for a rampage with a broken bottle on River Street in a drunken frenzy. Pat junior was already in an army jail for head-butting a colour-sergeant to his severe injury. Both were cast in the same mould, and it looked to everyone like an odds-on certainty that John, the youngest of them (Corky to his friends), would be unable to avoid the consequences of his natural inheritance. He'd no doubt end up banging the Drum too.

'Are you calling me a thief?' Phil wanted to know, and he wanted to know *now*. They'd called his old man a thief and put him inside over what had to have been a misunderstanding, and according to Phil that was a slur against the whole clan. He came down off the gate and, as he did so, his left hand casually hauled at the black lock-knife he had been digging into the wood. Behind Corky, Billy and Doug saw the glint of metal.

'Let's get out of here,' Doug muttered. He took a couple of steps backwards, pulling at the tent slung between himself and Corky. Billy agreed.

'Yeah. Let's skeedaddle.' Corky turned slightly and they could see the freckles standing out like sepia ink-blots on his cheeks. Billy took up the weight of the old green tent.

'Are you? Huh? Calling me a thief?' Phil came strolling forward, all languorous and slow, arrogance on two feet. He had the same colour of hair as his young brother, the same cow's lick all the Corcorans had, but where Corky was stocky and looked small for his age, Phil was tall and thin as a stick. He threw the knife, spinning it with studied casualness to catch it by the handle again.

'Just saying it isn't yours,' Corky said. 'Everybody knows that.'

'Just put it back where you found it. Right this minute.'

'No chance. We're going with the scouts.'

'Over my dead body,' Phil said slowly. He put both hands on his hips.

'Suits me,' Corky said. Campbell Galt snorted, dribbling beer foam down his chin. Pony snickered like his namesake. Corky turned to the two of them and, while he was pretty sturdy for his size, he was completely dwarfed by his brother's friends.

'What are you laughing at, *plook-face*?' Corky snapped. The sunny day went suddenly quiet.

'Oh, shit,' Billy muttered. He and Doug were edging away and were halfway through the narrow gap in the hedge where the old blasted oak had come down. A blackbird chirped and clucked its liquid panic as they startled it among the nettles. A wasp flew right up against Doug's ear and he almost dropped the tent while batting it away. Corky stood there and Pony McGill's ravaged face looked as if it would erupt from within, into even greater devastation.

Pony was taller even than Campbell Galt, who himself would end up nearly six foot, and he had shoulders that could have shored up a house. He was strong as an ox and would have been a good-looking big man but for the havoc his teenage acne had wreaked upon his face. His skin was angry and livid, rough as pebble-dash.

Face full of plooks and a head full of broken bottles. That was how Danny Gillan had described him after he'd kicked their football down into the stream, where it had burst among the thorns. Corky had convulsed into manic laughter, while thinking that Danny must have some kind of death-wish. That remark had almost cost Danny an arm after Pony had swung his big Toe-tector boot again and clipped the smaller boy on the elbow so hard it had gone numb for the day. The phrase had come back to Corky just then, and it had slipped out.

'*Plook*-face?' An instant surge of blood suffused the big, broad face, reddening in the clear spots but purpling among the acne scars. Very deliberately, he put the beer can down on to the flat top of the gatepost. 'What the fuck did you call me?'

'Come on, Doug,' Billy said, dragging the tent through the thorns and on to the farm track while they were out of immediate focus. 'Let's go.' Doug didn't need a second telling. The pair of them scooted up the path.

Pony came lunging forward just as Tom and Danny came out from the lee of the end house in the gap where the fence had broken. Tom saw Corky, but the other big lads were hidden by the hawthorn hedge.

'Hey Corks,' Tom called. 'Did you forget the tent?'

Corky turned, taken by surprise, and a big, meaty hand came whooping out from the side in a wide arc. Corky must have caught the motion out of the side of his eye, and ducked quickly, not quite fast enough to escape, but sharp enough to diminish most of the force of the swipe. His head was moving back and down, so instead of catching the knuckles on his temple, a blow which would have felled him like a bullock in the slaughterhouse, or at least knocked him arse over tit right into the sharp thorns of the hedge, he went with it. Pony McGill caught him with the underside of his big hand and sent him reeling backwards.

'What's happening . . . ?' Tom started. Corky went stumbling back, whirling as he went, trying to catch his balance. It was then that Danny saw Pony McGill and Corky's big brother, along with Campbell Galt.

'Hey, leave him alone,' Danny bawled before he had a chance to get a rein on his tongue. He'd had run-ins with all of them before – in fact there was no one in the nearest five streets who hadn't – but the words just blurted out when he saw Corky staggering back.

Phil Corcoran spun around. He was walking away from the fence, and the two boys saw the sunlight spangle on the blade of the knife in his hand.

'Oops,' Tom said, and then, quite unaccountably, especially for Tom, he giggled.

'Another couple of tear-drops,' Phil said. 'We've got the complete crying match here.'

'Bastard,' Pony grunted. He'd expected his haymaker to connect squarely with Phil's cheeky shit of a brother, and the force of it had almost thrown him off balance. He spun, moving much more slowly than the smaller boy. The two others had turned to face the new arrivals.

'They will insist on butting in,' Phil went on, shaking his head with exaggerated regret.

'Leave him alone,' Danny blurted again. Corky ducked another hooking punch, quite easily this time, and as he did so, he snatched up a dried piece of hawthorn root from the demolished hedge, which still had a hard sod of earth around it. He swung it against Pony's shin and the big fellow let out another grunt.

'Want to join the party?' Phil asked, smiling that creepy grin of his that somehow made him look like a weasel. He held up the knife and turned it slowly in his hand, the way knife-fighters did in films, making sure it caught the light. As he did so, he let out a beery belch.

'What, play with you three stooges?' Danny's tongue was off and running again, like the day he'd made the remark about Pony's acne. 'Tweedle-dumb, tweedle-dumber and Crater-mess with the pits.'

Pony was spinning around on one leg, lifting his shin up to cradle it in both hands. Campbell Galt, blond hair slicked back into what the younger boys called an old-fashioned Teddy-boy quiff, took his eye off the action and whipped round. Phil Corcoran's grin froze solid.

'Hells bells, Danny,' Tom said. 'I don't think he liked that.'

'What did you say?' Phil's voice was as icy as his grin. For an instant his eyes seemed to flicker, as if a sudden charge of emotion had sizzled behind them, which it most probably had, and in that moment Danny and Tom saw the little craziness that lived inside Phil Corcoran's head. 'What the fuck did you call me?'

Both boys stopped still. Pony was still hopping about, unable to keep his balance. He backed into the five-bar gate at the Aitkenbar farm track and slammed it against the post with a sound like a gunshot.

'Bastard,' he grunted. 'Just wait till I get you.'

Corky danced away from him, swinging the heavy root, unconsciously imitating Pony's hopping jig. 'You and which chorus line, you big jessie,' Corky jeered, his mouth even more of a runaway now than Danny Gillan's ever was. Pony roared like a bull. Phil Corcoran didn't even look; his eyes were fixed right on Danny Gillan.

'Stop horsing around,' he said. 'This fuck-mouth needs shutting up.' He favoured Danny with a wider grin this time and his eyes gleamed. 'Maybe we'll have to make sure he gives us less of his lip.' Phil held the knife up again, and flicked it forward.

Danny didn't wait. He turned on his heel and ran, not before Tom, who was one split second ahead of him. Corky jinked back, swung the root again, but this time it snapped in his hand and the heavy club of root and dirt went spinning away. It caught Campbell Galt just under his ribs and pushed him forward, sending him crashing against Phil, whose hand came slashing down even as he went spinning sideways and the knife went flashing through the air.

Danny and Tom were scooting up between an old wooden garden shed and the side of the hedge, with Tom leading by three clear yards. Danny reached the corner, stuck a hand out to whirl himself around a fence-post, when the knife hit him right behind the ear.

Corky saw it all, virtually in slow motion. The knife helio-graphed the sunlight as it spun black and silver, black and silver, through the air. Then it hit.

It made a small *bonk* and bounced off into the bush.

'*Jesus*, Phil,' Campbell bawled.

'Jesus, *Danny*,' Corky yelled.

'Bastard,' Pony grunted again.

A hot pain blossomed behind Danny's ear and a sound like a gong vibrated right through his head. For a second he thought he'd been hit by a half-brick, but then he realized it wasn't sore enough for that. He didn't miss a step as he whirled round the corner.

Corky watched his pals disappear from view. Then Pony's beefy hand clamped on his shoulder. Without thinking, Corky turned and bit the big man's finger, not hard enough to draw blood, but enough to make Pony think he had. The big fellow grunted again, let go. Corky didn't hang around. He ran for the gate, clambered up the bars and threw himself over into the lane.

Campbell Galt swore comprehensively at Phil, and *he* swore unintelligibly and explosively at everything. It took him nearly half a minute to gather himself and set off running in thundering pursuit. Danny and Tom heard their approach and took off like rabbits. They got to the far end of the field, where the bulldozers hadn't yet churned everything to mud, and angled for the corner where the two thorn-hedges met at right angles. Here, genera-tions of youngsters had broken and worn a crawl-way through to the far pasture. Both boys, panting with the effort, unslung their haversacks as they ran. Tom slung his along the ground at root-level, followed it, and Danny and his bag rolled in behind him. They came out the other side, covered in dead leaves and spiked here and there by hawthorns, but otherwise unhurt. Behind Danny's ear, the glow of pain pulsed. He reached there, expecting to find blood, but there was none.

They ran down the hill and on to the farm track angling across to the gully. Ahead of them, Billy and Doug were lumbering along with the green tent between them. Over the far side of the bushes, curses exploded. Danny and Tom reached the crossroads where two farm roads intersected. A figure came hurtling out towards them and they pulled up in dismay.

'Only me,' Corky said breathlessly. He grinned widely. 'I don't think they're too happy with us.' He giggled, and the other two couldn't help but laugh, despite the fact that Crazy Phil and his crew would come crashing after them in a matter of seconds.

'He's a flippin' nutcase,' Danny managed to say. They were running hard up the hill and he was getting a stitch in his side.

'You're telling me. I got to live with him.'

'What will he do when you get home?'

'Hell knows. You can come to the funeral. No flowers, please. And no priests.' Corky laughed again, almost sadly, as if death was a distinct possibility, then he turned, grinning. 'He's not too bright, so he might have forgotten by the time we get back.'

The boys caught up with the other two and, with hardly a fumble, Tom and Danny each grabbed an end of the tent. They breasted the low hill just as Phil and the others came hammering round the corner. The younger boys went over the brow and down the lee and then, without a word, when they reached the corner, out of sight of the others, they slung the tent and the rucksacks over the three-strand barbed-wire fence into a field of yellowing corn. They crawled underneath the lowest strand, Corky still laughing almost hysterically, and then doubled back for about twenty yards. Here there was a line of saplings which framed the drainage ditch leading down to the Ladyburn stream. They followed this for a hundred yards, came to the brook and followed it up to where they could shelter under the footbridge. For a while, the sounds of the chase had disappeared, but Phil or Pony had figured out that they must have gone into the corn-field and, in a few minutes, the pursuers had trailed them along the line of the ditch.

Under the low bridge, there was a niche, hardly more than a foot wide, where some of the masonry had crumbled. They crawled through into the small service-duct where the water-works engineers had built the valves for the reservoir up on the hill. Billy dragged the tent through and they all sat in the darkness, trying to slow their breathing, listening for the others. This had been their place last summer, since Corky and Tom had found the hole in the wall while fishing for trout in the stream.

Two minutes later, footsteps came thudding on the bridge. Danny put his ear to an arrow-slit vent in the wall. Above the sounds of running water, he could hear voices.

'Must be here some place,' Phil said, breathless and wheezing. 'Little bastard called me a thief. And Gillan, I'm going to wring his scrawny neck.'

'You nearly stuck him like a pig. *Jeez*, Phil. If that knife had hit blade first it would have pinned him. You could swing for that.'

Overhead, the footsteps came louder, then faded as the others crossed the bridge. Down in the dark, they heard Pony shout something and then came a pop and the sound of shattering glass. One of them had thrown a bottle into the stream.

'That's really great,' Tom said. 'Some kid's going to go paddling and get cut to pieces.'

'They should be locked up,' Doug said. He looked quickly across at Corky, whose face was just a pale oval in the dim light of the narrow vent. 'Sorry, Corks. I didn't mean anything . . .'

Corky shrugged. 'You can't pick your family. I sure didn't. And anyway, everybody knows about the old man. Sometimes I wish he was still at home. At least Phil wouldn't be acting so big. He's really off his head.'

He looked at Danny, who was sitting beside the opposite arrow-slit. 'Flamin' hell, Dan, I thought that blade was going to nail you.'

Danny rubbed the tender spot behind his ear. 'I thought it *had*.' The others looked from one to the other, unaware of what had happened.

'Phil threw it at Danny. You should have heard the noise. Just like that xylophone in the school band. The glockenspiel thing.' Corky let out a low laugh that threatened to get louder. He clamped his hand over his mouth until it subsided. Outside the others had moved to the far side of the bridge and then come back, their footsteps echoing down to the dark hollow – *doom-doom-doom* – as they passed overhead. After a few moments they were gone.

'I tell you Danny Boy. You shouldn't have run. Phil's been trying that knife-thrower's trick all summer. Wants to be just like that knife-fighter in *The Magnificent Seven*. He says if he comes across ol' Twitchy Eyes he'll give it to him right in the eyeball. I've been watching him try to stick it in the old man's pigeon hut. *Jeez-oh*, I've never seen him hit the flamin' *hut* yet, never mind stick it in.'

He went off into another convulsion and it was a moment or two before he could speak again. 'Must be your lucky day, Danny. Must be your lucky *year*.'

They all giggled at that, but the laughter stopped soon enough.

It had not been a lucky year, not for any of them. It had not been a lucky year, not since the spring, since the day that Paulie Degman had gone down into the river and Neil Hopkirk had clambered in through the window of the old surgery at the back of the house on River Street. Corky had just touched upon it when talking about Phil's lack of expertise with the knife, which had bounced off Danny's skull.

Twitchy Eyes.

There was a moment of silence, broken only by the hushed sound of running water from the Ladyburn stream, running low and slow towards the end of a dry summer.

Twitchy Eyes. The mad stranger who had slipped into town in the spring.

The silence ran on for a moment longer. Danny rubbed the throbbing spot behind his ear, now feeling gingerly for the signs of swelling, but there were none. Billy leant back against the wall, his face the dimmest of all in the shadows.

'They found her under the other bridge,' Doug said after a while.

'No, the next one down from this,' Tom contradicted. 'It's got a bigger access tunnel. They think he was staying there a while, camping out.'

'God a'mighty. We had a gang-hut there last year before we found this place,' Billy said. 'Imagine we'd come crawling in there and found *him*.'

'As long as we had Phil with us he could have used his knife,' Corky said, trying to lighten the mood a little. 'Then we'd all have been up shit creek without a paddle.' They all had a laugh, though a subdued one.

It had been only a matter of luck.

'They say she was cut to bits,' Billy said. 'They found her in a puddle of her own piss.'

'*Don't*,' Tom barked, and they all jumped, startled.

'Wha . . . ?' Billy started to say.

'Don't talk about her,' Tom said quickly. His curly fair hair framed him like a dim halo. 'Jeez, she's dead, isn't she? It wasn't her fault.'

Billy looked at him, then as quickly looked away. He didn't say anything. Corky stuck his hand out and clapped Tom on the shoulder, the way boys do when they're on the way to becoming men and still have a way to go. Too old to put their arms around each other, still young enough to touch.

'Hey, Tom.' That was all he said.

'It's just that she was just a kid,' Tom said, and his voice cracked a little, a hint of the pressure that was building up behind whatever dam he'd built. Everybody knew he was thinking about his little sister and what had happened in the winter.

'Sorry, man,' Billy said finally, reaching out a hand in the darkness. He took a hold of Tom's narrow wrist and gave it a squeeze. 'I didn't mean anything, you know?'

Tom gave a little snort, like he was sniffing back hard. 'Yeah. It's just . . .' He sniffed again, then hawked and spat out, letting them know he was just clearing the dust from his throat. 'It's just sometimes it looks like the whole place is going crazy.'

'And Phil's leading the parade,' Corky said, doing his best, easing them off this threatening track. He made an effort. 'He's the craziest loony still walking outside Dalmoak. Crazier even than old Annie Monkton and she's so far round the bend she can see herself coming back.'

'But not as crazy as old Twitchy Eyes.'

'Yeah, but he's long gone, and Phil still lives at my house,' Corky said, finally getting a laugh. In the gloom, Danny was the only one who saw that he wasn't smiling.

Twitchy Eyes.

He'd haunted the town for almost the whole of the summer, haunted the hearts of mothers, the dreams of children. He was the bogeyman, the Bad Man, the ogre under every bridge (he'd been under the bridge with little Lucy Saunders, hadn't he now?) and the shadow outside the window in the night-time.

'I reckon the cops caught him and hung him,' Billy said. 'They do that with some of the really bad ones. Just take them away where they can't be found again and do them in.' He crept over to the hole they'd clambered through and began to crawl back out again. 'I'll just see where they are.'

'And make sure they don't see you, or we'll be stuck in here with no way out.'

'They'd brick us up and we'd never get out,' Danny said, 'like in the House of Usher.'

'Jeez, don't say that, Dan. It gives me the creeps,' Doug said. Already he was edging towards the hole in the wall, towards daylight. In an instant, Tom was clambering after him as the idea of being walled up inside the inspection chamber struck him.

Corky and Danny followed them out, neither of them as panicked, but each unwilling to stay alone in the dark after what had been said. Corky started moving and, as he did, his foot kicked against a loose stone which rolled into the corner of the small chamber. It hit something which rustled dryly and, almost simultaneously, a clodden smell of rotting shit came wafting up, accompanied by a frenzied buzzing of flies.

'Oh, for God's sake,' Corky said, gagging at the smell. At the same time, he realized that the five of them were not the only ones to have discovered the inspection pit under the arch of the bridge. Somebody else had been there too. They had all scurried in through the niche in the masonry and crouched in the first chamber, but there was a narrow crawl-way to the sump trap which they had explored weeks ago, using candles to reach the narrow space. It had been dry and dusty and festooned with spiders' webs, which showed it hadn't been touched for a long time. If somebody had found their way in to the first hollow, then they could get through to the back chamber.

They could be sitting quiet in the dark of the back chamber *right now*.

The same thought had struck Danny, but worse, the buzzing of the flies had brought back a powerful memory, an image from late spring, before the real impact of the stranger had hit the town.

There had been flies in the window of the house on River

Street, and that's where Mole Hopkirk had been found dead, with his hair and his fingernails still growing. The flies had pattered against the window-pane like black rain, hundreds of them. Thousands.

Suddenly the smell and the buzzing and the dark all gelled into one enormous, powerful threat.

'Move it,' Corky hissed in a voice that said he really wanted to shout but didn't dare. He shoved at Danny, who was halfway through the hole, and right at that instant Corky felt the creepy eyes on his back and sensed the long, crooked fingers reaching out to grab him and drag him back into the darkness. That was enough to send him crashing into his friend, who stumbled out, rolled off balance and landed with both feet in the stream.

'Bloody hell,' Danny yelled. Billy and Doug turned round, right on cue.

'Shhhhh!' they both hissed, holding their hands up, miming the need for hush.

Tom was up on the bridge, peering over the parapet. Far along the road, the three others were sauntering away, almost out of sight round a slow bend.

'We're safe,' Tom said.

'Good,' Corky retorted. 'You can go back in and get the tent.'

He was thinking of what Tom had said. '*We're safe*.' But he wasn't prepared, right at that moment, to go back into the dark and put it to the test.

Safe. He hadn't felt safe for a long time. Had anybody?

CHAPTER SIX

May

'Come on, Jeff, it'll be dark by the time we get started.' The voice floated up from ground level.

'It'll be the bloody weekend,' somebody else chipped in. From the Irish accent, it had to be Neil Kennedy, who lived in Swan Street. Some time far in the future, Neil would go through the nightmare of losing a son in another spate of madness that would hit the town, but for the moment he was sixteen and had only two cares in the world. The second was to get on with the game of football they had going on the space next to the river where the old barge-loader shed used to be. Its flat base was now an ideal five-a-side pitch.

Jeff McGuire had punted the ball with an uncoordinated foot and sent it sailing over the low roofs of the outbuildings on the corner of Fish Pend, where it had bounced on the slates, landing in the valley of the roof, well out of sight. He who kicked last was obliged to climb for it.

There were some little girls at the far corner, waiting for the end of the shift in the fishmonger's where their mothers worked at the filleting slabs. They were playing a kid's skipping game, chanting the kind of school-yard rhymes that seem to have gone out of fashion.

'Hey, McGuire, get a move on,' Neil Kennedy called up again. 'Shift your arse. Another goal and we've got them beat.'

Them was the River Street team, as opposed to the Swan Street crew, in the days before the heart was ripped out of the town and replaced by a concrete and steel barracks of a shopping centre. Then, on this particular May afternoon, with President Kennedy dead only a few years, Mick Jagger every mother's nightmare and the Beach Boys getting around-round-round in surf city, there were plenty of people still living down by the river and there was always a game going on.

One of the girls giggled. She was holding one end of the rope while her partner spun the other. A whole team of kids, all with pigtails or pony-tails, had lined up to skip in for a couple of fast beats of the rope before dancing out again on the far side in the elegant rhythm of play. When Neil Kennedy shouted up at the roof telling Jeff McGuire to hurry it up, the rhyme instantly changed.

Missus McGuire sat in the fire . . . a tiny girl skipped in, agile as a fawn, kept the beat, feet feathering on the ground before skipping out again.

'Ok, give me a minute, willya?' The disembodied voice floated down. 'Think I'm Spiderman?' *The fire was too hot, she sat in the pot . . . the pot was too wide, she sat in the Clyde . . . and all the wee fishes swam up her backside . . .*

The girls tittered, some of the smaller ones holding their hands up over their mouths at the use of a naughty word.

'Hey, Jeff, they're singing songs about your mother,' Neil shouted up.

Jeff McGuire didn't hear him. He'd just been bending down to pick up the old, tattered, leather football when a motion to his left caught his eye, a shadow at the window just above the slope of the low roof. He put a hand over his eyes to block out the glare of the sun and peered forward.

Some small particles, like grains of sand, rattled against the dusty glass. The shadow changed shape and Jeff saw it for what it was. Flies. There were dozens of them, flying in tight circles or crawling up the window pane. He picked up the ball and threw it over his shoulder. It bounced on the ridge and then down the far slope. Far below, somebody shouted. The thud of a boot against leather followed immediately and the game was back on. Jeff took a tentative step forward and then another, raising his hands to the sill. He put his face right up against the glass.

The room was dirty inside, from what he could see through a pane crawling with big bluebottles. Every now and again one of them would go buzzing off and come hurtling back in a kamikaze dive for the light and freedom, rapping with a chitinous click against the flat surface. Jeff eased himself up along the diagonal waste pipe and got on to the ledge. He pushed against the frame and it squealed up in protest. Five or six of the big shiny insects bulleted out past his face. One of them brushed his cheek with tickly wings and he drew back. Inside the room a swarm of them, spiralling like a miniature tornado, buzzed and hummed angrily in the hollow emptiness.

Jeff climbed in, curiosity aroused now, the way it happens with boys and empty buildings. They attract each other like magnets, with an irresistible pull of gravity. A bluebottle landed on his forehead and he slapped it off. Apart from the flies the room was empty. Outside somebody shouted something which he vaguely heard. The window creaked and slid slowly down on the sash-groove until it almost closed. Jeff edged along the wall, avoiding the dense insect whirlwind, and went through the open door.

The smell hit him halfway down the hall.

'Oh my . . .' he gagged, unable to finish the sentence. There were flies here in the dark of the passage, hundreds of them, maybe thousands. Most of them were crawling on the walls. Right away Jeff knew that something had died in there. Maybe a pigeon or a jackdaw that had come down the chimney and got trapped. Maybe even a cat. The smell was awesome, almost solid in the dusty air, flat, sweet and oily all at the same time. It was even worse than the throat-clenching stink of the dead sheep up on the moor if you got downwind.

In that moment, Jeff knew something was wrong, but for some reason he could not turn back. That gravity of curiosity had him now. He took a tentative step along the corridor and the sound of his boot rasping on the shards of broken glass sent shivers up his spine. Something made him turn to look back into the room and, in that instant, the cloud of flies coalesced, throwing a shadow against the pale light framed by the window. For a moment the shadow looked like the shape of a man and Jeff's heart kicked in a sudden spasm. He backed away, now gulping for breath through a dry gullet, and knocked against the door halfway down the hall. It swung open. Jeff stepped through, still half turned.

A black shape roared and came leaping up from the floor.

Jeff squeaked in utter fright. He flinched back, cracked his shoulder against the door jamb. The thing on the floor came bolting towards him. He raised a hand up to protect his face, thinking that some monster was coming for him. Then it broke up into a cloud of black dots. More flies.

Jeff's heart came down from the back of his throat. He gulped again, still unable to speak, though if that had been possible he would have cursed without repetition for several minutes.

The insects were big and bloated, and where they passed the beam of sunlight coming through the chink in the wooden boards nailed over the window frame, they glittered the green-blue of rare metal. In the swarm they were creepy and scary, but in the sudden relief that they were only insects, only bluebottles, Jeff almost laughed. Flies couldn't hurt him.

Two of them tussled in aerial combat right in front of his eyes, and then landed on his shirt. He swatted them away and just at that moment the stench really hit him.

'Oh my God,' he mumbled, completing the sentence that he'd started in the other room. His hand flew to his mouth. His eyes watered and his throat spasmed. Jeff turned, ready to go stumbling out of the room, when another shape on the floor against the sink snagged his attention.

At first it looked like a pile of rags and sticks jutting out from under the lip of the basin, hidden by the shadows. Despite the sickening stench, Jeff moved forward, brushing flies away with his free hand. They buzzed and hummed, skimming his skin and hair.

The form was crumpled and shapeless. He moved closer, holding his nose pinched tight-shut between his fingers. Something stuck out from the bulk, and for a long moment it didn't register on him. He turned his head, saw an off-white ridged line that reminded him of something. He drew his eyes along it, close to the floor, saw a gaping hole from which something liquid seeped. In that moment of time Jeff's brain seemed to have gone completely numb. He was trying to think, but something inside his head was blocking out all thought. He shifted his gaze down the edge of a ragged piece of damp cloth which covered a series of jutting lines.

Below the lines, where the fabric was ridged and folded, something moved. The cloth heaved. He moved back one step. The thing sticking out from the mass moved too, just above the bent angle. Not a real motion, just a shiver under the skin.

Under the skin.

It hit him then, and the force of it was like a physical blow. He was staring at a corpse. It was bent almost double, face cheek down against the floor and the mouth agape, lips pulled back behind a line of teeth set in black gums. A trickle of some thick stuff had pooled by the head. An arm was hunched behind the body and a blackened hand was just visible, fingers hooked into claws.

The body was naked from the waist down, belly bloated underneath a desiccated and taut parchment surface, and it was slumped in yet another pool of viscid liquid. At the abdomen, just up from the shrivelled crotch, the shirt was moving slowly, as if the thing was trying to take a breath.

'Oh,' Jeff said very quietly, while his brain was yelling frantically at him.

Getout getout oh for Christsake it's alive it's fuckin' breathing!

He felt his knees sag as he stumbled backwards. The scene suddenly leapt into startling focus. The head was down on the ground and a hank of hair was trailing on the old oak boards, growing right along the blackened puddle. The fingernails jutted down like curved talons, half an inch beyond the end of the fingers, like the claws of a monster in a nightmare.

And it was breathing. The belly was moving under the shirt, enough to make the fabric shiver.

A small, pearly-white maggot dropped down on to the stretched skin of the abdomen and rolled to the floor where it pulsed weakly in the slimy puddle.

Jeff reached the door and, just as he did so, all the flies swarmed together and, like a single entity, they alighted on the body. In the blink of an eye it was covered in a blue-black skin, and for an instant it looked like a man made up entirely of insects. At the far end, the filaments of hair grew out.

He backed against the door. It shut with a hard slam, and all the light was cut off except for two slender needles of daylight piercing the cracks in the boards.

Panic exploded. He grabbed for the handle, fingers scrabbling down the dirty surface. A splinter went digging right up under his nail and he never felt a thing. He was in the dark with the body, with its nails still growing and its hair still growing and its belly full of maggots. Behind him the flies buzzed and it sounded like the movement of a heavy body rising from the floor. Jeff's heart almost burst. His hand hit the handle and he hauled. The door opened and he threw himself out of the room. He crashed against the far wall, made it to the back room and ran for the window. In his panic he hit the frame and it shuddered down the last few inches and slammed itself shut.

Jeff whimpered. A dozen or more flies which had followed through from the dark room came smacking against the glass, and the sudden noise was loud in the empty room. Jeff reached for the frame and hit it with both hands. His right fist went through the old glass and a jagged edge raked his skin from wrist to elbow, drawing an immediate line of blood. The terror soared. Behind him the tornado of flies made a feral, growling sound. Jeff pushed desperately at the frame. It gave an inch and then slid all the way up. He shoved himself through, all the time expecting to feel a black and wizened hand, armed with long, still growing nails, clasp around his leg. He cracked his knee on the sill as he threw himself out, jabbering incoherently. A swarm of flies followed him on to the low roof. He went stumbling across the slope of the slates, clambered up to the ridge and slid down the other side.

'Hey, McGuire!' Neil bawled. 'What the hell's been keeping you?'

Jeff went sliding down the slant on the shingles, skittered across the guttering and tumbled ten feet to the ground, miraculously landing on his feet and rolling with the momentum. The impact left him with a hairline fracture in his heel and a badly bruised knee. The blood from the cut in his arm trickled down on to the cobbles. Otherwise he was fine, at least physically.

Both teams gathered round him where he crouched close to the wall. 'Did you hurt yourself?' one of them asked. Jeff's eyes darted left and right. He could see people around him, insubstantial figures in the light of day. In his mind, more clearly than anything, he saw the dripping corpse with the hair growing out along the mess on the floor and the clawed hands with the sickle nails and the shivery motion under the shirt.

'Gha . . .' Jeff managed. 'Gha . . .'

'Hey, the idiot's gone gaga,' Neil said, laughing. 'Come on, McGuire, stop fooling around and get back in goal.'

It was two days before Jeff McGuire spoke a full word and by that time Sergeant Angus McNicol from CID had been up to the empty house that backed on to Boat Pend and he'd found the body of Mole Hopkirk. He later formed the opinion that Hopkirk was the lucky one of the two boys. The shock of it all had such an effect on young Jeff McGuire that he was never quite the same again.

Fatal Accident Inquiry into the Death of Neil James Hopkirk (Verbatim Extract)

John J. Mack, Crown Office: 'So you believe the boy took several days to die.'

Dr Colin Bell, Pathologist: 'No question of it. At least three days. Five at the outside.'

Mack: 'He would have been alive, and conscious for all of this time, and possibly in considerable pain?'

Bell: 'Perhaps conscious for some of the time, although blood loss and shock may possibly have rendered him unconscious for the latter part. Pain? Most certainly he was in very severe pain because of the nature of the injuries, the beating and the bites and the rest.'

Mack: 'So in your opinion, what happened?'

Bell: 'The attack on this young man was designed and deliberate and savage. It took place over a considerable period of time, I hasten to add. If I may venture an opinion, it is almost certain that death was a merciful release.'

Interlude

'First real bad one I had to deal with,' Angus McNicol said. 'And that was the start of it, though nobody knew that at the time.'

He was sitting in the front room of his house out beyond Castlebank Church and sipping a mellow whisky. His eyes were bright blue and frosted under grizzled eyebrows, and his expression said he was way back in his memory.

'I was a sergeant then, just promoted to CID. We had to break the door down. Young McGuire was very disturbed for a long time after that and, to tell you the truth, I think the shock affected the poor lad's head. Understandable, too. John Fallon kicked the door off its hinges and when we got in the smell would have knocked you down for the count of ten. Millions of flies too, not pleasant.

'We found the lad tied up against the sink and I could see

what gave the McGuire boy the heebie-jeebies. There was a fungus growing along the puddle, and it looked as if the boy's hair had grown there. The skin of the hands was pulled back and the nails were sticking up. Old Colin Bell, he was police surgeon in those days, said the nails keep growing for a bit after a death, but that was the first time I'd seen it.

'One of the others was sick right away, but I managed to get a handkerchief up quick enough so I didn't make a complete arse of myself. Hate to have destroyed evidence with my own puke, eh?' The old man grinned and took another sip, finishing his drink. He poured another two whiskies and offered the glass over.

'Don't suppose there's any harm in telling you any of this. It's long gone. Hardly anybody remembers it, but it was a bugger of a summer. Strange that somebody like yourself wants to go digging it up all over again.'

Another sip and he closed his eyes, concentrating. 'That poor bugger Hopkirk had been lying there a long time, ever since March, and the flies had made the most of it. His mother damn near died when we told her, and she kicked up a stink about wanting to see her boy's body. It was all we could do to stop her. She'd never have lived with the sight. Hell. It was hard enough for me.

'The pages were sheets from a bible. An old bible, according to the book expert we spoke to. Maybe one that had been handed down in a family. Some of the pages had been torn out and the killer had wiped his backside with them. Some of them were crumpled up and stuffed in the boy's mouth. They'd been scrunched into a thick wedge and it was no wonder the lad choked to death. Bell was right. When it came, it was a blessing. That poor boy had walked down into hell.

'Whoever did it had been squatting in the old surgery for a while, but at that time, we didn't know a thing about the man you kids called Twitchy Eyes, but I remember getting a really bad feeling. We'd been looking for Hopkirk for a few weeks by then, five or six, as I recall. So we knew then that there had been a killer around a month and a half before. But by then one or two other things had happened.

'There was little Lucy Saunders . . .'

Chapter Seven

May

'Lucy. *Lucy Saunders!*'

The hoarse voice echoed across the Rough Drain, where the run-off from the gully at Corrieside found a flat level that was swampy and crowded with a tangle of scrub willow and twisted alder. The winking of torches could be seen as the line of searchers edged their way along the waste ground, some of them up to their thighs in the stagnant pools. Now and again, a beam would angle up towards the sky, making a pillar of light in the fine, drizzling mist.

They searched all night, teams of policemen, workers just off the back shift at the shipyard. Neighbours from the row of houses at High Cross Road, gardeners and pigeon-fanciers who had their huts and allotments down the west side of the Rough Drain scrub. Every now and again, somebody would shout her name and the call would drift along the flatland. Everybody listened for the reply, the cry of pain, the whimper that would mean little Lucy Saunders was at least alive and, with luck, maybe even well.

They searched all night and they found nothing.

Lucy Saunders was eight years old and she disappeared in the warm light of an early-May afternoon. She had got the bike for her birthday in March, a little fairy two-wheeler, and her dad Charlie Saunders had taken the stabilizers off only a fortnight before, down at the park where Lucy had wobbled her tentative way to learning to ride properly.

'There was a man,' Chrissie McKane told John Fallon. He listened gravely, towering over Chrissie and her sister Janice, who was only six. 'We saw him on the path.'

'What was he like?' John asked. He had a deep and rumbling voice, but despite that it conveyed gentleness and security. He gave the girls a smile and they grinned back.

'Big,' Janice said. 'A great big man and his hair was black like yours. But not short.'

'Good girl. And where was he?'

'At the trees near the allotments,' Chrissie said. 'He was just standing looking at us and then he waved to us. Janice went across, but I said to her to come back. We had to go home.'

'And then you saw Lucy?'

Both girls nodded. 'She said she was going down to the shop. She asked if we would come with her, but we had to go home. She went round by the lane and we saw the man waving to her and then she went across to him.'

'And what happened then?'

Chrissie shrugged. 'We had to go home.'

'He had twitchy eyes,' little Janice said brightly. 'Like this.' She screwed her face into a grimace, narrowing her eyes to slits, and blinked several times in rapid succession.

'Just like that. I think he had something in his eyes.'

Twitchy Eyes.

Tom Tannahill and Doug Nicol had come across the searchers on their way up from the scout hall at Castlebank. Their only concern was that, because of all the activity, they couldn't cut across by the old willow that had fallen across another blow-down, creating a natural shelter. It was one of their places, out of the way of prying eyes, where they and their friends could creep for a smoke or a game of cards, or a fascinated scan of a crumpled, black and white picture from the magazines they would swipe from the top shelf of Walter Dickson's shop.

They watched the line of men trampling through the gloom of the Rough Drain, calling out the little girl's name, one voice louder, more desperate than the rest, and that had to be Charles Saunders', of course.

One of the men passed quite close, and Tom asked what was happening.

'A wee girl's gone missing,' the man said. 'The police think she's been taken away.'

It was all revealed the following day. Little Lucy Saunders' bike had been found not forty yards from the corner where the McKane girls had seen the tall stranger with the dark hair and the twitch in his eyes. The bike had been thrown well away from the track, the front wheel and fork still brand-new and shiny but the back end now covered in slime and mud where it had sunk into the marsh. Somebody spotted the cleat marks of boots on the soft earth beside one of the many tracks that criss-crossed the barren ground and another found an imprint of a kid's sandal. They searched the whole of the wasteland and all the area around it, down past the allotments and the old dye-works. The police tracker-dogs were called in, and they followed the trail of something as far as the edge of the Ladyburn stream, where it took its dog-leg turn down to the castle, and from there the trail went cold. Lucy Saunders was gone.

Danny Gillan's Aunt Bernadette lived only two doors from the Saunders' house, and Danny had listened, sitting quietly doing his homework in the corner of the living room, as she told of the girl's mother's complete and utter collapse and how the sobbing had gone on all night.

'There's no hope now,' Bernadette said. 'Poor wee thing's been taken away and they'll find her in a ditch somewhere, raped and strangled and cut to pieces.'

Bernadette's prophecy was fairly accurate, so it transpired.

August 1, 10 a.m.

'How did you manage to get away?' Corky asked. The other three had fallen behind, two of them struggling with the weight of the tent.

'It wasn't easy, but he believed the scout-camp story,' Danny said, grinning. 'But if he finds out, I'm right up the creek. He said I had to go to mass tomorrow, no matter what, so I'd better find out who the priest is. He's always trying to catch me out. Asks me what the sermon was about or what colour of robes the priest wears. Sometimes I'd be better off just going to chapel. If he catches me dodging, it's me that'll need a priest, that's for certain.'

'Oh, he'll never find out,' Corky assured his pal.

'Well, if he does, it'll be the bad fire for me. He's dead keen on the old hell-fire.'

'Still got it bad?'

Danny nodded. 'You know what it's like. Everything gets round to prayers and the Holy Virgin.'

'My old man never bothered with that. He doesn't like priests. Me neither. But he was always kicking the hell out of me.'

'I know,' Danny said. He'd seen the bruises many a time. 'Same as my dad. He's started using the buckle end of the belt. Says I have to show an example to the rest of them and, if I don't, he'll show me an example. I got a thick ear last night just for not kneeling up straight.'

'That's a real bummer. Having to pray all night and then getting a smack, that's not fair.'

'You're telling me. You've got it made. I sometimes wish my old man was in the jail.'

He nudged Corky to let him know he was kidding. His friend took no offence.

'He'll be back in a month or so,' Corky said. 'With a bit of luck it'll get Phil off my back. He's been acting the hard man ever since my da went into Drumbain. But sometimes the old man's just as bad. Once he gets a hold of a bottle, everybody has to stay out of his way. Sometimes he'll come looking anyway and if you think the buckle end of the belt's bad, you want to see what he can do with the toe of his boot.'

Danny and Corky had grown up together, along with Doug and Billy. Tom had been born two streets away, but his family had moved down south when he was seven and had come back again only two years before, just after they found out Tom's little sister Maureen had leukaemia. Tom had fallen right back into the way of things until the winter when little Mo had died, and then he'd gone quiet, hanging around on his own, and occasionally hovering bleakly in the cemetery, close to his sister's grave. It was only when the spring had turned to high summer that he really started chucking around with the boys again, going down to the gang-hut at the Rough Drain or even to the new place they'd found under the bridge, but he was still silent, still withdrawn. He was taking a long time to get to grips with his loss.

'My ma just said to be careful,' Corky said. 'She's still scared of old Twitchy Eyes.'

'She's not the only one. If my mum found out I was going up the hills, she'd throw a fit.'

'He's gone,' Corky said. 'I heard they think he's topped himself.'

'But they never found a body or anything.'

'Only a matter of time. I just wished he'd grabbed Phil before he went,' Corky said, very sincerely. 'He's a crazy fool, so he is.'

'He who calls his brother a fool is in danger of hell-fire.'

'*Jeez*, Dan, wherever do you get all this crap?'

'That's one of the old man's favourites. It's in the bible.'

Corky laughed aloud, head thrown back. 'Well, I'm in for a right old roasting, Danny Boy. I reckon I've called Phil a fool a million times.'

'Maybe it doesn't work if you're telling the truth.'

Danny glanced at Corky, who looked back, and then they both suddenly burst into a fit of laughter that swept through and over them, doubling them up so hard their sides hurt. It took them a while to chuckle it all out and it was the first real laughing Danny could remember since the spring. The sun was rising high over the oaks bordering the edge of the Corrieside gully as they made their way up the hill in the warmth of the summer day. They were just two boys, only thirteen years old, glad to be out in the sun, glad to be out from under at last.

Behind them, tinny music floated up the slope of the path.

'Billy's brought his radio, silly idiot,' Corky said. They sat down by the grass at the verge, waiting for the others to catch up. Corky leant back and almost put his hand on a wide cow-pat sending a riot of red dung-flies whirling into the air.

Corky bared his teeth. 'Remember the flies in the window?'

Danny nodded. His expression had gone flat, and the bright twinkle of laughter faded from his eyes. 'That could have been us, couldn't it?'

Jeff McGuire hadn't been the only youngster up on the roof behind the house on River Street. Corky and Danny and another fellow called Al Crombie had been on their way home from school when they'd gone exploring up on the low roofs. You could always find a ball stuck up on the slates, or a bird's nest in the eaves, even though it was still early in spring. All of the trouble was yet to erupt, so there was no reason to hurry home. They had gone clambering, pretending they were commandos, up and over the tin ridges and the sway-backed slopes on the roofs. Alan Crombie, who would have been with them on the trek to the dummy village if he hadn't been sent away, for safety's sake, to his uncle's farm at Creggan, had hooked a plastic toy-glider out of a drainpipe.

They'd gone across the roof of the outhouse behind the old building, and Corky had seen the movement in the window.

The flies had been crawling up the pane, hundreds of them, big and black, with that sheen of metallic blue at the edges. The three boys had stopped to look at the swarm on the glass, almost thick enough to cover half the window.

'Worth a look,' Corky had said, but Danny had thought it was really creepy.

'There's millions of them. I read a story about flies that came and choked somebody to death, and it gave me nightmares for weeks.'

Just then, somebody shouted from a window of one of the tenements further along. A man was leaning out of a window and bawling at them to get down off the roof. The three of them had turned and scuttled over the ridge and down the far side, using the downpipe to get to the ground. They had forgotten all about the flies until Jeff McGuire had been a little bit more curious than they had. Now he was up in Barlane Hospital, which was only one step away from being committed to Dalmoak, where the real crazies were kept locked up.

'It could have been us,' Danny said, giving a little shiver, though the day was warm.

'Flipping glad it wasn't,' Corky said, chewing on a stem of grass he'd plucked. 'Old Mole Hopkirk lying there with flies coming out of his mouth and all his hair growing across the floor. That would give you the heebie-jeebies. They say he was there for weeks and weeks, and his nails just got longer and longer.'

'If I'd have seen that,' Danny said, 'I'd have died on the spot. That would have been worse than Paulie Degman in the water, and I had bad dreams for weeks after that.'

Tom, Doug and Billy had almost reached them and the tinny music had swelled. Mick Jagger was growling that this could be the last time.

'Maybe the last time,' Billy sang, well off-key. 'I don't kn-o-ow . . . *oh, no.*'

'Give it a break, Harrison,' Corky told him, quite reasonably. 'You can't sing for toffee.'

'Great song that,' Billy said. 'But not as good as good ol' rock 'n' roll.'

'It *is* rock 'n' roll, idiot features.'

'No. I mean the old stuff, like Bill Haley and Elvis. My ma's got dozens of records. Plays them all the time.'

'So does our Phil. He's got all that old-fashioned crap. He says Jagger's a poof and all the Beatles are big nancy boys.' Corky turned to Danny and grinned. 'Another step closer to hell for me. Phil really is a fool.'

The other three looked at them askance. Danny and Corky burst into laughter again, and the others watched them, wondering what the joke was. Billy waited until the end of the song and then turned the radio off. It was a tiny thing, hardly the size of a paperback, that he'd won by collecting tokens, and you could pick up Radio Christina, one of the pirate stations run from a boat of that name anchored just outside the official limit. Everybody agreed that the pirates were better at music, and their deejays were far superior to anything on dry land. The radio was Billy's pride and joy.

They had reached the edge of the row of houses close to Cargill Farm Road that would take them up parallel to the Ladyburn stream and then up on to the moorland. Here, the self-service general store served most of the families in the area. They came up round the back, still carrying the tent.

'How much have we got?' Doug said. They had pooled their money, not much of it, and certainly not enough for any expedition longer than a day. Corky told him not to worry, as he unslung his haversack and brought out a bundle, something wrapped in an old towel. He half unwrapped it, until a beady eye showed, then a rounded head. It was a pigeon.

'What's that for?' Tom asked. Corky grinned.

'We can get what we want,' he said. 'You wait here and guard the tent.' Billy laughed and Doug showed his big teeth. They followed Danny, who was holding the fistful of coins, into the shop and sauntered up an aisle while he went up to the counter and pointed to the string of big beef-sausages. He checked the price, saw that he could afford two pounds, and asked for them. Mrs Fortucci behind the counter, the mother of Brenda Fortucci, who was a class above them in school and gifted with the most substantial breasts of anybody in the whole school, counted the sausages on to the weigh-plate, wrapped them and passed them over. She cocked an eye up the aisles, checking on the other two. Danny was just handing over the change when the back door opened. He saw a hand push in, quick as a wink, and then the sudden grey flutter.

The pigeon exploded into the air in a panicked clap of wings. A small, downy feather tumbled out and rocked slowly as it fell towards the floor.

'What on earth . . .' Mrs Fortucci yelped. The pigeon came fluttering past her, heading for the window. It got halfway there, saw the grille over the glass, veered, then flew in a tight, frenzied circle around the store.

'Oh, get it out of here,' the woman squawked. She turned to the side and lifted a broom, swung it up into the air and started jabbing at the pigeon. Corky wasn't concerned. It was an old scrag from his father's pigeon loft, one of the street-tykes lured down by the big arrogant cock-bird, and not a real homer. Even so, it was still easily fast enough to avoid the swinging broom-head.

Up in the aisles, Doug and Billy were stuffing tins into their bags. Billy scooped cans of beans and tomato soup. Doug went for the corned beef and spam. He crossed the aisle, grabbed a loaf, stuffed it into his pack so hard that the paper burst, but he didn't stop. He spun and lifted a jar of strawberry jam and a packet of chocolate homewheat biscuits.

Above them the pigeon fluttered in a tight circle, wheeling round the light.

'I'll get it, missus,' Corky cried, running across from the back door. Beside him, the girl assistant was whooping in fright, hands clasped to her hair in the mistaken assumption that the bird's claws would get tangled in it. Corky crossed to the door, opened one side, then reached to swing the other, jamming it back. By now Billy and Doug had gone out the back way. Light shone through the double doors and, as soon as Corky moved away, the pigeon arrowed straight for the gap and swooped out into the summer air.

Mrs Fortucci dropped the broom, face flushed. Danny stood at the counter. She pointed at Corky.

'Come here,' she said, beckoning with a thumb. Corky looked at Danny, wondered whether to make a break for the door, shrugged and came forward.

'I'd never have thought of that,' Mrs Fortucci said. Her chest was heaving up and down, a vast double mound in magnificent motion. 'That was good of you.'

Corky shrugged again. She moved towards him and for a moment Danny thought she was going to hug him. He got a sudden vision of Corky disappearing into the deep valley and never coming out again. Mrs Fortucci passed him, heading straight for the till. She reached beyond it, lifted a large bar of chocolate and handed it to him.

'Can't stand birds in the shop,' she said. 'You go and enjoy it, son.'

Corky almost burst out laughing, but he managed to keep it in until they were halfway up the farm track, and then it all came out in a mirthful explosion. He sagged to the ground, dropping his end of the tent. Danny, holding his belly again, sat beside him. In a second they were all braying like hyenas. It was nearly five minutes before they could speak.

'Want a smoke?' Billy asked a while later, producing a packet. Doug took one and sat down on the rolled-up tent. They were unfiltered, full-strength smokes that smelt like pipe tobacco. Doug inhaled, coughed heartily, as the thick smoke dragged itself down into his lungs, and looked up at them, eyes brimming.

'Far to go now?' he asked through a dry throat.

'Miles and miles,' Danny told him. 'We've only just started.'

'I'm whacked already.'

Billy blew one of his famous smoke-rings and made another one roll through the first. He'd been smoking since he was eight and had spent nearly six years practising the trick, which he thought was just about the neatest party piece you could do.

'Great smoke. My old man used to smoke these in the war before he was killed.'

The rest of them looked away hoping Billy wouldn't start about his war-hero father.

'That's what my mum said. She's got a picture of him in his uniform, and he's smoking a Capstan. Dead casual, like he's never been scared of anything.'

Doug looked at Danny, a quick, private glance.

'When we get up to this place,' Billy continued. 'And if we really find the dummy village, then I'm going to find something to bring back. Something from the war.'

'Of course we'll find it,' Corky said, trying to get Billy off the subject. Billy was fourteen, the oldest of them all, and for most of his life he'd believed that his father had been a war hero, killed fighting the Germans. His ambition was to become a soldier when he grew up, and to go marching off, rifle in hand, to wreak his revenge. It was getting difficult for the rest of them to say nothing. They were hoping that Billy, who might have been the eldest but was academically the weakest, would do some mental arithmetic, some simple subtraction, and come to the inevitable conclusion, and then shut the hell up. Nobody wanted to tell him to his face what he should already know.

'We should get going,' Danny said. He stood up and took an end of the tent. Corky took the other and they hauled it up off the ground. Billy deftly nipped his cigarette and Doug tried the same manoeuvre without success. A red ember flew off the end and landed in the tall grass close to the hedge. Immediately a wisp of smoke spiralled up. Billy stepped in and stamped hard.

'You'll set the whole place on fire,' he said, giving Doug a shove.

Just then, something crackled, like a small branch breaking underfoot. It came from the shadows of the stand of trees on the other side of the track, and they all froze. Something moved again, a heavy object. Dry bramble runners snapped. Everybody looked at everybody else. Billy was about to speak but Corky held a finger to his lips. *Ssssh!*

Another footstep, slow and deliberate. Somebody was in the trees, moving towards them, hidden only by the sprawling hawthorn that lined the track.

'Phil?' Danny asked in a tight whisper. Corky shrugged.

'Have they followed us?' Tom asked softly. 'Sneaky, rotten shites.'

They looked at each other again, all of them holding their breath. Out there in the shadows beyond the farm road, under the canopy of oak leaves, something was moving slowly towards them, using the forest as cover. Danny felt his scalp prickle.

Doug turned on his heel and scooted up the track. Billy was right on his heels and then they were all running, going hell for leather despite the drag of the stolen booty and the weight of the rolled tent. Behind them, the sounds faded as the distance widened, but they didn't stop until they reached the ruins of the old shepherd's cottage at the far end of the lane high above the town.

Tom climbed on to the crumbling wall, right up the gable slope, and craned over the chimney to see back the way they'd come. He scanned over the hedge and saw the black and white cow come shambling out of the trees, munching on the dry grass in the corner of the narrow field.

'It's only a cow,' he called down. 'We ran away from a bloody *cow.*'

The relief was so great they all started laughing again. It wasn't Phil and Pony McGill come to beat the living daylights out of them. And it wasn't anything worse, which all of them had thought of and none of them had mentioned.

Billy said how, if it had been Phil, he'd have pulled his own knife and squared up to him and everybody just jeered that notion to scorn. Billy was tough when it came to talking, but everybody knew Corky was the toughest of them all, and even he would think twice about taking his brother Phil on in a serious square go.

They were still laughing when they turned and squeezed their way through the stile and headed up across the field of gorse, listening to the seeds snap and crackle in the heat of the sun, winding their way through the maze of vicious little spines, heading for the line of trees that separated the high and low pastures, the rugged moorland from the rich agricultural loam of the farms.

They were quite unaware that while they struggled with the tent and the weight of the rucksacks, a pair of black eyes watched them from the cover of the thick plantation high on the far hill.

CHAPTER EIGHT

May

Angus McNicol's boss, Commander Ross, who was head of the county force, made the announcement when Lucy Saunders was finally found. Angus and the rest of the team under Hector Kelso, who headed CID, had worked night and day for two weeks, going over the ground again with the tracker-dogs, asking every boy and girl within a mile, trudging round the doors, asking people a second time if they'd seen anything. At the end of the day, it was the sergeant who pieced together what had happened to the child.

Her body was found under the third bridge over the Ladyburn stream, a fair distance upstream of where it flowed to the sluggish marsh of the Rough Drain. She was lying crumpled and bloodied in a corner, slumped in a puddle.

From the Rough Drain, where the bike had been thrown into the marsh, Angus McNicol, using hindsight, worked out the route the man with the twitchy eyes had brought the girl along – through the far side of the wasteland and up the curve of the stream where it skirted the lower end of the Overbuck Estate, by the Dower house, where old Lady Hartfield had, according to legend, thrown some crazy, equally legendary parties back in the twenties.

He must have carried the child, it seemed certain, because it was unlikely a girl of eight would willingly go along with a man who had thrown her brand-new bike into a stagnant pool. Also, Angus reasoned, she must have been unconscious, or silenced in some way, because to get to the stream they would have passed by the old timber-frame houses still occupied by the estate workers. Somebody would have heard a child crying, or screaming, and would have come to investigate.

But nobody had heard a thing.

What was certain, from Dr Bell's post-mortem report, was that Lucy Saunders had still been alive at that time. For, like Neil Hopkirk, it had taken her some time to die.

Danny Gillan's Aunt Bernadette had been right in her prophetic statement.

It was a matter of luck, if luck could be involved in such a thing, that they found Lucy Saunders so soon. She could have lain under the bridge for several weeks, possibly months, had it not been for George Scott and his cousin Eric, who had been poaching for rabbits on Overbuck Estate in the early hours of a May morning. They had just come down from the hill, using the trees by the stream as cover, because the estate's fields were open and old Leitch the gamekeeper was as wily as a red fox. They came splashing down with the two terriers ahead of them and, when they got to the bridge, both dogs had started sniffing around at the darkened hollow of the metal access door into the water valve. The door had been pushed open and the two dogs disappeared into the gloom.

George had bent in front of the low door, leaning into the shadows, calling on his terriers. They were scrabbling in the corner, both of them growling that low rumble, the way they did when they'd got too close to a fox in its den. Eric pushed by his cousin and struck a match, sending a flare of light into the shadows. The dog's bobbed tails were sticking straight up, white salutes over in the corner. Beyond them, a pale arm stuck upwards, as if waving.

Eric thought it was a doll at first, and then he breathed in the smell. Right away he knew what he'd found. The arm was raised up and out. Below it, a small shape was slumped to the right, head down. The dogs were snuffling heavily, and over the sound Eric could hear the humming of insects. He backed out fast, hissing at the dogs to come away, inadvertently grinding his heel down on his cousin's toe.

George yelped and cursed vehemently, but Eric didn't even hear it. 'It's her, George. That girl everybody's been looking for.'

'You should watch where you're going,' George said. 'Nearly broke my flamin' toe.'

'*Wheesht*, man,' Eric hissed, in the same stage-whisper tone he'd used on the dogs. 'It's that wee girl who's been missing. It must be.'

'What are you blethering on about?' George finally asked.

'Bloody hell, man, would you listen to me,' Eric grabbed his cousin by the lapel, forcing him to stop hopping around in the shallow gravel in the stream. 'It's a dead fuggin' *body*!'

Angus McNicol and John Fallon were up at the third bridge in the space of fifteen minutes from the panicked phone call and, under the bridge, in the square, stone box normally closed to the world by a heavy iron door fastened with a big brass padlock on a hasp, they found Lucy Saunders.

The pale little body was sprawled in a puddle, legs spread-eagled in pitiful invitation, arms outstretched, each one tied by a ripped piece of cloth to pulley-hooks set in the stonework. Her head was thrown back over to one side and her hair hung in rat's tails down on her bare shoulders.

The only article of clothing was the collar of a shirt and a scrap of cloth which hung down on her chest. One of her sandals was in the puddle, but there was no sign of the other.

At first, when the beam of the flashlight swept across the body, Angus McNicol thought, just as Eric Scott had done, that they'd made a mistake and merely found a discarded doll. The girl's small frame looked waxy, almost plastic in the damp gloom. But the smell was unmistakable, the stench of rotting flesh.

Even Dr Bell found it difficult to keep the emotion out of his post-mortem report.

The name Twitchy Eyes spread like a searing brush-fire around the town. Mothers panicked and, down at the distillery, the biggest employer of women, two of the bottling lines had to shut down completely because so many women had taken time off to make sure they were home when their children arrived from school.

Down on Strathleven Street, at the edge of the leafy path that angled down towards the allotments, a telephone-line worker stepped into the shadow of an overgrown privet hedge to relieve himself of the pressure of two pints of beer he'd drunk in Mac's bar over lunch-time. He'd turned round, shaking himself dry the way men do, unaware of the mother and two children passing by on the other side of the street. All she saw was a man looming out of the bushes and exposing himself. She screamed like a banshee and dragged her girls to the nearest doorway – both of them squealing in fear and alarm though completely unaware of the workman's presence – and banged on the door until the householder, who'd been tending his dahlias, came running round the front of the house. A window slammed open and a woman leant out, yelling and pointing an accusing finger. Postman Johnson McKay came round the corner into the mêlée. A car stopped and two men – canvassers for the upcoming council by-election – got out.

All they saw was the pointed finger and all they heard was a gabbled and garbled accusation, and the four men took after the line-worker. The dahlia gardener still had a long-handled weeding hoe in his hand and without any hesitation he took a swipe at the man, batting his hard hat into the privet hedge and knocking him to the ground. By the time the police arrived, the unfortunate man thought the whole world had gone crazy. He'd a lump the size of a pigeon's egg on the side of his head. Two streams of blood were dripping from his nose and one badly blacked eye was closed tight shut. Not only that, but when he'd tried to escape from the four madmen, two of them had grabbed his arms, and out of nowhere a demented, screaming woman had come rushing across the road and kicked him right in the balls and drawn a row of bloody lines down his face with her fingernails. To add insult to this injury, on the following morning, when it was accepted that he was not the crazed killer, he was hauled in front of Baillie McGraw at the Monday-morning court and fined five pounds for committing a public nuisance. After that he refused ever again to work on Strathleven Street.

More unfortunate was the poor Asian salesman who had just come into town to take on a new territory for the Housemarket Supply Company. He had a dark coat and a turban and a glossy black beard and was a pretty exotic fellow by the normal standards of the backwater where he planned to sell his plastic toilet brushes and knick-knacks.

He was on the far side of town, up by Arden Road, and he stopped to ask directions of a group of children. Everything would have been fine, but for the fact that a four-year-old had turned round and seen the dark face under the turban, and the shiny beard, and taken him for a pirate. She gave a wail of fright, which was immediately taken up by her younger friend and, in an infectious wave of panic, a bunch of little girls who had been skipping gaily in the late-spring sun were screeching like piglets.

A group of men playing quoits with old-iron carthorse shoes on the wasteland where the old quarry buildings used to be came running round and attacked the salesman with such violence that he ended up in Lochend General, where he needed a three-hour operation to relieve the pressure caused by a dreadful curved dent in his skull caused by a solid-iron shoe from a Clydesdale horse.

It was that kind of panic, the jitters that sizzled through the town. There was a Bad Man here, a murderer, and while people naturally suspected it must be a stranger, all that was known was that he was a man, tall, with dark hair. And with twitchy eyes.

From the pulpit in St Rowan's on Sunday, Father O'Connor, who ruled the parish, took the opportunity to warn the children of his flock.

'Let us pray for Lucinda Saunders,' he enjoined them, clasping his hands together to show the little ones exactly how it was done, 'who was only eight years old and who met such a dreadful end.'

The old priest, who sported an Italian-style biretta hat and an accent as thick as the bogs of Ireland, was hell on pagans, Protestants and purgatory, along with the devil and all his wiles, who was lurking around every corner waiting to snare a good Catholic boy. And the said devil wasn't above using flirty, teenage, non-Catholic girls to do his dirty work either.

'Yea, though we walk through the valley of the shadow of death,' he began, 'the Lord is with us. This poor girl was not of our faith, children, and because of that she had never been baptized in the cleansing water of Christ's holy Church, and that is a terrible thing, don't you know.'

He peered at them, hands clamped over the ornate, polished-marble edge, marble that would have cost six months' wages in a good-paying foreman's job, and leant forward.

'For that means she was not cleansed of original sin and, because of that, she will be tormented by the purifying flames of purgatory, burning until that sin is purged away and she comes out shining and clean and fit to meet the Lord in all His great glory.'

Danny Gillan put his head in his hands and, as soon as he did so, his father leant over and knuckled him sharply, letting him know he had to sit up and pay attention. This was God's business and He liked straight kneeling. The old priest lumbered along on his theme, purging and purgatory, cleansing fires. Over by the side altar, Father Dowran kept his eye on the unruly boys.

Danny had vaguely known Lucy Saunders, the way all children know the connections. She was the cousin of some of the guys who played football on the spare field at the bottom end of Overbuck Estate and, while he might not have picked her out in a crowd of small girls, she was no different from anybody else. Just a kid.

Burning and purgatory. Just like the bad fire, like hell itself, except that after a thousand years in the shrivelling heat of the flames, you got a chance to get out and go to heaven, and that was something Danny Gillan couldn't fathom out. He just couldn't get his thoughts to hold on to that concept at all.

He looked up at his father, sitting straight-backed in his good Sunday suit, one long-knuckled hand clasped around Danny's little sister's dainty fingers, nodding all the while, as if mesmerized by the truth of the priest's words.

But Danny's thoughts had gone sparking off in a different direction. The kid was no different from anybody else, except for the fact that, when she was small and helpless, her parents hadn't brought her here to the old Italian-marble fountain and had the water poured over her while they renounced Satan and all his works and all his pomps, and because of that – according to old Father O'Connor – she would feel the cauterizing sear of purgatory. After all she had suffered (and Doc Bell's report missed out one part of that awfulness), after having the life squeezed out of her in a puddle of her own piss, she had to suffer some more.

He shook his head at the immensity of it, the complete and utter wrongness of it. His father looked down at him, hunched in the corner of the seat, eyes diverted, and he thought Danny was day-dreaming again. He reached once more and nudged his son's shoulder. Danny automatically straightened his posture, while the priest asked them all to pray for the repose of the innocent but somehow tainted soul of Lucinda Saunders, and he wondered what his father would think if he knew that some of the boys in the Church Legion said that sometimes the curate,

Father Dowran, who ran the boys' club, would take them down to the room under the hall and chastise them for any perceived wrongdoing. And in the dark of the storeroom, he would take their trousers down and . . .

'Daniel, pay attention.'

Danny brought his eyes forward and thought of Lucy Saunders and Paulie Degman and, not for the first time, he thought the whole world was going totally crazy.

Either that or *he* was going mad.

CHAPTER NINE

August 1, noon

'Just climb down,' Billy prodded, nudging Doug with his elbow. 'Quick, before somebody sees us.'

The pair of them were up on the orchard wall, fifteen feet above the ground, and it would have been an impossible climb but for the solid swathe of old ivy that festooned the stone. From up on the top, the thick growth helped hide them from view. An expanse of dead-straight rows of vegetables angled away towards the far wall – thick lines of lettuce, curly red or tight green footballs of new cabbage. There were beans on wires reaching for the sky, stalks of rhubarb as thick as a boy's arm.

They had taken a detour back down to the Ladyburn stream, rather than going up through the barwoods on to the high moor, for no particular reason except that it was a tiring hike up the hill and much easier going down in the shadow of the valley. Old Leitch the gamekeeper might chase boys off if he came across them, but it was hardly likely he was down in the gardens of Overbuck Estate, and so, as long as they were quiet and careful, they'd be in and out again before anybody noticed.

'It's too high,' Doug protested, 'and there's no way back up.' Doug had never liked heights.

''Course there is,' Billy insisted, urging him over the parapet. 'Look over there. They've planted trees against the wall. It's just like a ladder. No bother at all.'

The pear-tree espaliers slanted upwards, hugging the stonework, laden with half-sized, stone-hard fruits. It was far too early in the season for them to be worth stealing, but there were richer pickings on a hot August day and, for the five boys, out on an adventure after the claustrophobic and tense summer months of the school holidays, they were too sweet to resist.

Already Tom, never one for taking huge risks, was crawling along by the wires where the tall raspberry canes nodded in a warm eddy of wind. Beyond him, Danny and Corky were leaning

over the blackcurrant bushes. Billy could see their hands peck out and come straight to their mouths, and in his imagination he could already taste the bitter-sweet juice bursting on his own tongue.

'Well, I'm not waiting around,' Billy asserted. He scrambled along the top of the wall. Somewhere in the distance, in the shadow of the massive conifers, great Californian redwoods that towered over the water garden, a pheasant squawked its metallic challenge, and overhead a woodpigeon murmured softly. Billy gingerly slid his feet over the other side and lowered himself down, tongue hanging out as he concentrated on finding a toe-hold. He dropped down another few inches, and his T-shirt, the kind of thing they used to call sloppy-joe scraped upwards, exposing his belly to the rough sandstone.

Finally, his questing foot found a convenient cross-wire and he lowered himself backwards. Further along the wall, a lead fastener pulled out of its niche, instantly slackening all the tension out of the wire. Without warning, Billy dropped almost a yard before it pulled him up sharp, wide-eyed and heart-thudding. The wire sprang back vibrating like an old guitar string.

'Fu . . .' Billy mouthed, hands scrabbling for the edge of the wall in case the wire snapped under his weight; but, by luck, it held fast.

'Told you it was too high,' Doug told him.

'Oh, don't be such a *crapper*,' Billy shot back. The colour was coming back into his face after the fright. 'Honest to God, Bugs, I never saw a bigger scaredy-cat in my life.'

'Don't call me that, *fatso*,' Doug snapped back. He forgot his complaint and scrambled over the top, feeling for hand-holds. Billy climbed down the pear tree, one step at a time, trying to avoid the support wires. Over on the far side, they could hear somebody talking or singing, but there was nobody in sight.

'Come on, Doug,' Billy cajoled when he'd reached the bottom. After a few moments, Doug carefully turned himself around and got on to a sturdy lateral branch. Whispering loudly, Billy directed his feet, but it was slow going. It took several minutes of prompting and persuasion to talk him down to earth. They finally reached the raspberry patch and found Tom stuffing himself with long, pink fruits, and the two of them tried to make up for lost time.

After ten minutes of pillaging, Tom asked where the others were.

'I saw them down at the far side,' Doug said, his face stained with juice, making his chin as red as his big ears. 'They're getting tore into the goose-gogs, but I think they went through the door in the wall over there.'

'What for?'

Doug shrugged. Billy was shoving raspberries into his mouth like a harvesting machine, making juicy little slurping noises all the while. He was enjoying this.

Danny and Corky stopped just beyond the green door at the far end of the vast greenhouse which took up half the length of the entire orchard wall. The panes had been whitened with the same chalky material that greengrocers used to advertise their prices on shop windows, but there were a couple of clear patches which showed green shadows behind. Corky pushed himself up against the glass to cut off his shadow, and peered inside. He turned and tapped Danny on the shoulder, eyes wide and mouth set into a perfect circle. Danny leant, shaded his eyes, and took in the enormous grapevine stretching from one end of the greenhouse to the other. For a second he saw nothing but a thick canopy of leaves, and then the picture jumped into clear focus. Immense bunches of grapes, great purple inverted pyramids, hung down by the dozen. The grapes themselves looked as big and as succulent as ripe plums.

'I want some of them,' Corky said. Danny nodded. He'd never seen such a wealth of exotic fruit, and he was sure nobody else had. If they were lucky, they'd maybe get an apple to eat in the school-yard, but grapes, they were for rich folk. And nobody came any richer, in these parts, than the folk from Overbuck House.

The greenhouse door was unlocked and they let themselves in, looking apprehensively over their shoulders, every nerve alert and tingling, ready for the shout of rage that would follow discovery. Off to the side, they could see Billy's red T-shirt against the green of the raspberries. Inside the greenhouse the air was hot-damp and just how Danny imagined it would feel inside a jungle in Africa. The vine was festooned with grapes, groaning and sagging with them. They seemed to glow with inner fire under the bloom on the top curves.

'We could take hundreds and they'd never even notice,' Corky said. 'But we'll need something to carry them in.' He went out, beads of sweat already trickling down his temple, and into the dry air outside. 'Find a bag or something,' he said, looking beyond the door. 'Or a potato sack would be even better. We could carry more.'

Danny thought they'd already done pretty well with the raid on the general store. They'd all shared the chocolate, giggling at the reward for mischief, none of them feeling particularly guilty at swiping a few cans from such bounty. Here was greater bounty, rich and lush – beyond their expectations. They went through the green door, following a line of nodding, scarlet poppies towards the yew hedge.

'They must be as rich as sin,' Danny said. The grey, baronial columns of Overbuck House towered over the dark green of the tight-clipped hedge, spiral turrets pointing to the sky.

'Richer than that,' Corky said. 'I read about them in the library. They've got millions and millions. My old man said they made their money out of making gas for the Germans to use, and he says they should be strung up and bayoneted, but the book says it was guns and dynamite, and I reckon that's probably right. My old man doesn't read books unless they're about pigeons.'

He turned, face earnest. 'There was a picture of them from way back, before the first war, in the olden days. There were about a hundred people working in the house, just to look after the family, like make the beds and polish their shoes and even pour their drinks and wipe their arses.'

He grinned. 'They even had somebody to heat the bed up for them if it was cold. Can you imagine that? Having that much dough?'

Corky raised up his hand, as if holding a glass. 'More *cavvy-yarr*, Jeeves,' he said in a fake toff's accent. 'And light me a cigar.'

'You don't smoke,' Danny said, returning the grin.

'I would if I had their fortune,' Corky vowed. 'Great big cigars.'

The wealth of the place was unimaginable, beyond any of their dreams. The boys followed the track down to the stables and crept by the tack rooms, still buzzing with the delicious sense of danger. If the gardener caught them, they'd get a boot right up the backside, just for starters, but it was worth it. This was a fairyland, a film set. No money had ever been spared on Over-buck Estate.

One of the dusty tack rooms was open, filled with saw-horses and horse-jumping fences. In the corner a trunk sat angled in against a horse-box. It was a wide, curve-topped, wooden affair, bound with ornate metal ribs, and looked like every chest ever described in a pirate story.

'Treasure,' Corky whispered. He pushed against the lid and, to their surprise, it creaked open. Corky got it up to head height and flipped it back slowly, letting it settle against the cobwebs on the wall. A shaft of light angling through the window made something glitter, and for an instant Danny thought that they had indeed found treasure, but it was only the top of an old decanter, chipped on one side. It lay on a pile of old books.

'Some treasure,' Danny said, but already Corky was turning them over in his hands.

'*Celtic Myths and Legends*,' he said, leaning over to see the cover. 'Must be about football.'

'No,' Danny said. 'It's Irish stories. They're pretty good. I read some of them – remember I told you about Cuchulain the Hero. He beats Superman any day.'

Corky flipped the book open and a monstrous face, a witch from a bad nightmare, glared out from an old woodcut print.

'The Mórrígan,' Corky read the caption. 'The Irish goddess of destruction.' He turned to the other boy. 'Look at the mug on that. Looks like a really mean old bitch. Look Dan, she's a dead ringer for Sister Julia.'

Danny suddenly burst into a fit of the giggles. The hideous face with feral eyes and the jagged, monstrous teeth looked nothing like the little nun who ran the school, but she looked just as fierce.

'*Wheesht*, man, you'll get us both hung.' Corky stuffed the book down the waistband of his jeans. On the wall, an old, tattered nosebag hung from a nail and he reached to unhook it. They crept back up towards the greenhouse, keeping to the shaded side of the stables and, just before they reached the green door in the wall, Danny heard somebody talking beyond the corner of the wall, where the flower garden sloped down to a shorn-smooth lawn shadowed by trees. At first he almost called out, thinking it was the other three coming. A shadow appeared, just a motion seen through a tear-dropped fuchsia bush, and a man came walking towards them, his head just turned away from them. Corky spun and pulled Danny backwards, yanking him by the collar of his tartan shirt back into a stand of flowering shrubs.

The man was tall and had short blond hair slicked back like an old movie star's, though he was still young. He was dressed like a cricketer, all in white, with a pullover draped casually over his shoulders. It flapped behind him as he came striding up the path, his face sunburn-red.

'Fucking little whore,' he spat, managing to curse in a way neither of them had heard before. It sounded like a dirty word properly spoken. He went loping down the path, feet crunching on the stone chips. 'Dirty, common *slut.*'

Corky started to rise out of the bushes, but this time Danny pulled him backwards, as another figure came tripping round the corner. This time it was a woman, maybe in her early twenties. Like the young man, her hair was that rich golden colour, but it fell in waves on either side of her face. She was wearing a pink shirt and a short tennis skirt. The top was open to her navel and as she moved, both boys saw one breast come swinging out. The motion flared the shirt, exposing its twin, both of them pert and firm and up-tilted. She strode forcefully along the path, shoes grinding on the gravel, golden hair spilling and bouncing.

To Danny and Corky she was the most beautiful thing they'd ever seen.

'Don't you *dare* call me a whore,' she called out in an accent they had heard only in English films. 'At least I know which side of the fence I'm on.' She stamped her foot, petulant as a little girl, and then went chasing down the path after him. Danny thought she looked like Marilyn Monroe, but even prettier.

Much prettier. A waft of perfume drifted towards them, sweet as climbing roses, yet mingled with another scent that none of them recognized, because none of them had ever yet smelt the true scent of a woman.

They huddled by the door, wondering whether anyone else would come through, but there was no sound on the path beyond. They sneaked up to the door in the wall. Corky turned to check on the lawn. He stopped and pointed. Another man was standing beside a slowly swinging hammock. His back was to them and he was tucking a shirt into the waistband of his trousers. He was tall and slim and his hair was thick and grey.

'That was Janey Hartfield,' Corky said. 'What a pair of knockers. Hells bells, she must have been *doing* it.'

'What, right there in a hammock?' Danny was shocked, amazed, strangely excited. He and Corky, they'd both confided in each other that there were a couple of girls who weren't too bad after all. Danny had found that in recent months, Claire Brogan had developed an uncanny appeal. Corky admitted that her friend, Ann Coll, who had jet-black hair and eyes to match, had the best smile ever. In that moment, however, both the girls seemed thick and clodden compared to the slender, hot and prancing grace of Janey Hartfield.

'Looks like it,' Corky said. 'Lucky swine that he is. Look at the age of him. He looks like a colonel in a war movie.' Corky nudged Danny forward through the doorway, but Danny's mind right at that moment was elsewhere. It was the first real breast he had ever seen outside of the tattered pages of *Parade* magazine and he was still stunned by the sight of it. It was the first time he had smelt a perfume just as rich and as heady as that, and the first inhalation of that other special scent. He did not know it, but that smell had affected him more than the perfume. Little hot shivers went juddering inside his belly and for an instant his jeans felt as if they had shrunk. Danny hadn't quite crossed over into puberty yet, but the chemistry was just beginning to happen. He felt as if a warm and soft hand had trailed up the inside of his thighs, making the skin ripple into gooseflesh.

'She's a goddess,' he said in a whispering sigh. 'A film star.'

'No. She's a whore,' Corky said. 'At least that's what her brother thinks.'

'He didn't look happy,' Danny said. In his mind's eye he kept seeing that pink nub of flesh swinging out, followed by the other one, defying gravity, smooth as polished marble, ruby crowned.

'And with all that money,' Corky observed. 'If it was me, I'd be laughing every day of the week. If it was me, if I had all that and I could speak that way, I could do anything.' He winked and held up the old canvas nosebag. 'But I haven't, so come on, put your eyeballs back in again and let's give him something to worry about.'

He pulled Danny's arm and hauled him along the track. Together they went into the jungly heat of the greenhouse. When they emerged, crouched low, five minutes later, the bag was stuffed heavy with the biggest grapes any of them could remember. They reached the pear trees and clambered up to the wall, giggling all the while, Danny still unable to completely cast away the spell of the fair-haired woman, but doing his best. Up and into the waxy ivy leaves, with the release of tension juddering inside them at the thought of almost getting caught and then, winning through, they crawled along the wall. Finally, the giggles subsided.

'Where's Billy and the rest . . . ?' Danny started to ask, when suddenly there was a crash of glass and a loud, hoarse shout.

'Come back here, you thieving little cretins,' the voice echoed across from beyond the wall. A split second later, Tom came streaking through the other door, across the far side of the kitchen garden, the one that led to the majestic main house. Billy came next and went blundering across the cabbage patch. Doug came last, his face white, even in the distance, but in a couple of seconds, elbows pumping, loping with the grace of a startled roebuck, he had overtaken Billy, who was an inch or so taller, but carried more weight. In a moment he was right on Tom's heels. The three boys came racing over the rows of lettuce, sending the leaves flying. Doug hit the wall first and came clambering up the pear tree, no hesitation now. He didn't even see the two others lying in the thick carpet of ivy. Tom followed next, gripping his way up the ladder-like branches, climbing quickly, but missing some holds in his panic. His body seemed oddly stiff. Behind him, Billy was jabbering.

'Come on, *Jeesacrist*! Move, will you!' The fright had screwed

84

his voice up so tight the words were all jammed up against one another. He gave Tom a shove and the smaller boy almost went flying off the top of the wall. He grabbed for a piece of the ivy, felt it rip away, began to fall backwards, a yell blurting out. Then, quick as a snake, Corky stuck his hand out and snatched his wrist in a tight grip.

'You were nearly a goner there.'

'Stupid fat shite,' Tom gabbled at Billy. Doug was halfway down the tangled ivy creeper on the far side. A big, lumbering shape came crashing towards them across the garden. Danny thought he saw a gun and simply threw himself off the wall, using the thin ivy twigs to slow his descent. He hit the ground hard but kept his feet. Doug was running for the trees. Danny followed, with Tom and Billy pounding after him.

Beyond the wall the angry man's voice followed them, but they were safe. They got to the trees and along the beaten-earth path that led down to the stream and splashed over the shallows and up the other side. They didn't stop until they were up on the edge of the woods, sitting on the fallen spruce tree under which they'd hidden the tent and the bags.

Tom was hauling for breath. Billy's face was so red with exertion that it looked as if it might explode.

'Don't you ever call me that again, runt-face,' he grunted.

'Stupid fat shite,' Tom repeated, this time in a grated whisper. Billy's brows came down, visible now under the fringe of black hair. His eyes went dark.

'Lighten up,' Corky said in that reasonable way he had. 'We all got away, and look what we've got.' He held up the old nosebag. Oily-black grapes seemed to be bursting out of the top, spilling out the way Danny had seen in the old paintings in the art gallery. Big and swollen and somehow magical.

Billy's face lightened and instantly he forgot his gripe with Tom. 'Not bad. But you never reached the kitchen, did you?' He turned to Tom and winked. Tom ducked his hand under his shirt and pulled out a bottle that was jammed into his waistband. Now the reason for his stiff-gaited climb was apparent. The wine glowed a deep red in the light of the noonday sun.

'And look at this,' Billy said proudly. From under his T-shirt he produced a rolled-up parcel. He unravelled it and it turned out to be a kitchen towel. Even before the full unwrapping occurred, they could smell the juicy tang of roast chicken.

'It was just lying there and the window was open.'

'*Jeez*, if they catch us they'll shoot us,' Corky said.

'Not if we get rid of the evidence,' Billy replied. 'It's our lucky day.'

'Lucky bloody *year*!'

It was less than two hours after they'd run away from Phil and the others at the gate on the farm road, and they had plenty of time. They hauled the tent out from where they'd hidden it and followed the stream up the hill, beyond the fork where the Ladyburn and the Langcraig tributary met, taking the left branch, which would angle them north and west and up into the hills, climbing all the while. They stopped about two miles upstream at a natural clearing where the trees had petered out and the sheep had grazed the grass short. They fell on the stolen chicken and the grapes, and Billy spent a lot of time with the spike on Tom's old army knife, working the wine-cork free. He finally popped it and took a deep drink, belching and gasping when he finished.

'Great stuff,' he pronounced. 'It's really hot when it gets down.'

Tom and Doug tried it and then Danny took a swallow, feeling his tastebuds leap at the sudden infusion of a taste he'd never experienced before.

'Don't hog it all,' Billy said. 'Finders get first dibs.' He took another swallow then passed it to Corky. 'Here, take a slug.'

Corky shook his head. Billy nudged him with the bottle.

'I don't want any,' Corky said. 'I can get any amount of wine at home.' He caught Danny's eye. 'It rots your brains out.'

'Oh, big, tough Corky. Don't smoke, don't drink and don't swear,' Billy scoffed. 'Just what *do* you do?'

Corky ignored him. Billy pushed the bottle at him again and Corky just hit it with his hand. It went tumbling out and fell on to a stone, where it caved in with a liquid crash.

'Flippin' hell,' Billy bawled, rising to his feet. 'You didn't have to break it.' He reached for the bottle, but the bottom had cracked wide open and all the blood-red wine simply drained into the grass. Danny watched it go with some regret. His mouth still tingled with the tantalizing, rich flavour. He could have used another swallow. He had savoured riches.

Billy sat down again, still complaining, but everybody ignored him. Doug told how a gardener had spotted him under the net of the strawberry beds and how he'd almost got tangled in the mesh in his rush to escape. Billy and Tom had been ahead of them and one of them had put his foot through the glass of a cold frame.

'Could have taken my leg off,' Billy said vehemently, forgetting the wine, and now checking his shin for signs of damage.

'Then you could have really hopped along,' Doug told him.

'And you could save a fortune on shoes,' Tom added.

'And gone in for the hop, skip and *hop*,' Corky said, laughing now.

'Let's go to the hop,' Danny chipped in, shoving himself up from the grass and getting on to one leg. He hopped to the edge of the stream and started to sing. 'Oh, baby . . . let's go to the hop.'

Without any hesitation Tom and Doug followed him, both of them hopping jerkily and singing raucously until Tom lost his balance at the edge of the bank and slid down to land backside foremost, in a couple of inches of shallow water at the edge of the stream. By this time they were all laughing, even Billy. Corky was lying back, holding his sides, and Doug, who had eaten more grapes than he had consumed in his entire life, was almost sick.

They were just boys out on an adventure, glad to be away, glad to be out from under. The day stretched ahead of them, all the trouble and excitement behind them. They fooled around by the stream for a while, then climbed up the slope of the far side of the valley to the last fields, where they hooked out a few pounds of early potatoes and some carrots, adding to their provisions. In half an hour they were beyond the line of the barwoods and, as they straggled up the natural track made by the cattle coming down to drink, a pair of dark eyes watched their progress from the shade of the tall spruce trees.

The eyes narrowed in the glare of the sun reflecting off the water in the stagnant pool. The rays heliographed dazzling white light that made the eyes blink furiously against the glare, but they did not turn away from it. The light flashed sharp spears, fading out the colour of the grass and the thick ferns that crowded down the shoulder of the valley. For a second, the scene was fuzzed in monochrome, in layers of misty grey.

He was out of this time again. He was back . . .

The light was in his eyes, reflecting from the black space in the floating weed. An iridescent blue damselfly helicoptered in on impossibly slow wings, great black eye-spots swinging seductively at the ends where they stroked at the air. The light was in his eyes and the beat of blood sounded like a mill-weir behind his ears.

Dung-fly. Dung-fly.

Somebody had spoken. He twisted round as far as he could but the sound hadn't come from Conboy, who was slumped against the wedged-open door, lying half in and half out of the truck as if he couldn't make up his mind whether to come in or go. The flies were crawling all over Conboy's eyes and he wouldn't do a thing to make them go away. Black flies, humping and bumping, jittering into the air, in Conboy's eyes and in his mouth and in the other eye in the corner of his forehead. Conboy stank and he hadn't said anything for a while, but maybe he would talk some more later on.

The light was in his eyes and the pounding was in his head and he soared with it.

Dung-fly. Dung-fly.

Somebody had called it out. The darkness came and the light went out and he slept for a while and then he remembered the pain. The truck had rolled and bounced and he'd been thrown and now he was stuck under the fallen tree, unable to free himself, and the flies had gathered on Conboy and they were crawling on the deep wound that scored down his own thigh on the leg that was trapped in the mud.

Up there on the track, he heard people moving about, and the chants in that strange, high and bell-toned language where every word sounded like a shout of anger or a cry of pain.

'All of them,' the sergeant-major had said. 'They're all gun-runners and terrorists. Just keep them on the move, and that makes sure the Reds got fuck-all to live on. And don't worry, they don't feel the same as you and me. They don't think the same. Don't feel pain and they don't cry tears.'

He knew that. They were pagan people. Little barbarians. They had no belief.

Up on the track, people were moving beyond the lush foliage, and he shrank back, unwilling to call out, yet scared of the next rain and the water-level of the pool rising up to his chin or higher still. How long he'd been here he could not say. Two days, maybe three. No longer than a week. The pain in his leg came and went and the buzzing in his head ebbed and flowed, and Conboy sometimes looked at him with the flies in his eyes, and when night came he could hear his blaspheming voice accusing him.

'Mad bastard. Mad bloody bastard.' Conboy's voice grated. The way it had done when he had pulled him back by the arm, reaching to grab the still-hot barrel of the rifle.

'Jesus fucking Christ, you crazy shit.' Conboy had been angry and scared then, when he'd come round the side of the hut. Everybody had panicked when the shooting started and a couple of grenades had gone off with sudden concussions, punching into the air, converting two of the little huts to fountains of tumbling chaff. Blood was splattered over one wall, a whole line of it. A flop of bodies lay in the corner, beside an overturned basket of grain or rice.

'No comfort,' a voice said, deep inside him. 'Give them no aid and no comfort.'

'Holy mother,' somebody had whooped. 'Gideon's flipped his fuckin' lid.'

Gideon they called him. Well they might, for Gideon was a warrior for the Lord.

Now Conboy was lying there with his third, ragged eyehole and accusations in his voice.

'You shouldn't have done it, man. Shouldn't have touched the kid.'

Pain pulsed up from his leg and he prayed for it to stop and for Conboy to go away and leave him alone, and he prayed for mercy the way the priests had shown him. But there was no God to hear him and succour him out here in the heat and the steam.

They were down in the valley now. *The valley of the shadow.*

Dung-fly. That's what it sounded like. Over and over, hollow little clucks that sounded like no true language. He heard it again and something touched his cheek. Very slowly he forced his eye to open. The left eyelid was thick and glued and he could feel a fly crawling over it.

He squirmed awake, fighting off the dreadful tiredness. Two children were standing on the far end of the fallen tree. The girl a head smaller than the boy, both of them tiny and very thin, with long black hair and patina skins. The boy plucked another small berry from an overhanging bush and threw it towards him. It bounced against his forehead.

'Dung-fly,' the girl said. She pushed at the boy.

He turned, ignoring the pulses of pain and the ripples in the water.

'Do it, Gideon,' Conboy said drily. 'Get them quick.'

The boy's eyes widened and the girl's face puckered as if she would cry. She pulled at his hand, tugging him away. Conboy's flies spun into the air and the boy started back. He jabbered again, a tumble of hard consonants and nasal diphthongs. They turned quickly and went scampering off the trunk, disappearing immediately into the sea of green with hardly a rustle, but he could hear the girl's high-pitched voice for a while, until it too faded.

The blackness came back.

'They're all head-hunters,' Conboy had said. 'They've been at it for millions of years.' The flies buzzed around him and his sockets opened wide. 'They take the head and eat the brains and that way they get your soul for ever. That's what they think. Crazy little shits. You can't tell what they're thinking, but you know what's in their heads. They put people on spikes and watch them die.'

The humming sensation was back again, a shuddery little vibration that sometimes lifted him out of the pain and up into cool height where his thoughts were clear and powerful. And he knew that God had abandoned him out here, turned his back on him, but he also knew that now he did not need any other. He had the power of life and death. His given right.

The bamboo crackled and he forced his eye open again. The

boy was back and this time there were two men. A third joined them and then a fourth.

'Dung-fly,' the boy said. That's what it sounded like. He pointed. The men stood together. They wore long skirts made of some rough cloth and they all had the *parang* blades for cutting bamboo. They regarded him solemnly and in silence. Finally one turned to the rest and made a short speech.

Out of sight, he lifted the butt of the gun and drew it towards him. The pain was high and glassy and he swooped along it.

They all turned round again. They looked like any of the villagers he'd seen in the past six months and each of them looked the same as the rest. Their villages went up in flames and their rice stores scattered and burned. They were herded into the trucks and taken forty miles up the track to start again, and that made sure they were in no position to help the hordes of godless commies trying to beat the forces of the good Lord.

One of the men lifted his *parang* and spoke. Another raised his blade. He watched them coming, through the half-closed eyelid. They edged across the log, walking warily, feeling for purchase with their bare feet. The darkness closed in again and the rush of blood pounded behind his ears. The black flicked out and he was up in the cold again, and he saw them moving towards him with chopping blades, and there was no chance a slant-eyed little heathen was going to take his head.

'Shoot them,' Conboy insisted from his vantage point. 'I can see them coming. They're coming for you. You should finish what you started, *Gideon*.'

The men stopped, eyeing him warily. He squirmed a hand forward, drawing the gun towards him, skating on the smooth ice-pain.

The men scattered. One second they were creeping towards him and then they were off and his gun was bucking again and they were screaming in terror and crashing through the green. The smell of cordite mixed with the smell of broken leaves and wet sap and the scent of blood.

'That showed them,' Conboy said. 'Kill them all and they can't touch us.' The flies crawled out with the words, crawled back in again. Conboy's silent yell went on and on. His other eye bristled with life. Up the slope, a line of people were moving fast, following a track, and he could hear their shouting and he knew they'd come back again.

'We'll be waiting,' Conboy said in his buzzing, hazy voice, and the darkness began to crowd in again in billows of shadow.

The next time he saw the light he was in a hospital bed with a drip snaking into his arm and a pipe coming out of his leg where the flies had been eating at him, and after a while the major wanted to know who had put the bullet through Conboy's temple. And he couldn't remember anything except the voices and the look in Conboy's eyes as he lay back, talking to him while the flies buzzed.

The sun spangled on the water and the major's face wavered away and the world gave a little *shudder* and he was back on the hillside watching the line of boys moving slowly, following a track up the slope, and he could hear them yelling at each other. The sun was high and it was hot and the buzzing of flies came drowsily down from the trees and he could feel the beat behind his ears again, the surge of hot blood, and the feeling started pushing its way back into him.

It was hot under his shirt and a trickle of sweat rolled down from his armpit, a cold little line tracing its way across his ribs, and he blinked his eyes hard, once, twice, against the glare, and for a moment their cries sounded like . . .

He was going up now, into that cold place where he remembered.

They sounded like . . .

CHAPTER TEN

August 1, 1.30 p.m.
They sounded like . . . the girl.

He watched from up on the hill, listening to them calling to each other. He blinked his eyes hard, once, twice, against the glare and for a moment their cries sounded like her.

. . . 'I have to go home, mister.' The girl had said, clear and high.

She stopped her bike. Here at the edge of this waste ground where the pools of run-off drainage water lay black and deep in places, overhung by fronds of willow and the umbrella leaves of giant hogweed that looked just like jungle rhubarb in the steamy gullies.

'Not far,' he'd said, blinking against the sunlight on the slick surface. 'You'll like it.'

'I don't see a rabbit,' she'd said, looking up at him in quizzical innocence. There was the slightest hesitation in her eyes, the merest flicker of doubt. But they were beyond the low bridge now. Here the pathway was narrow and it forked three ways, and he knew this place from a long time ago.

'Just down here,' he'd told her. 'You'll like it.' He blinked furiously. Under his tongue, the familiar surge of saliva squirted juicily. 'What's your name?'

'Lucy.'

Lucy. Lucinda. *The light*. He remembered that from the priests.

And the light was in his eyes.

He stood back to allow her past and she pedalled forward, concentrating on avoiding a piece of broken bottle. He let her get a yard ahead, then stooped. Quick as a snake. His hand clamped around her mouth and in a smooth motion he lifted her upwards. His right hand shot out and grabbed the seat of the bike. She squirmed, but he was too strong. He turned and slung the bike high over the stand of hogweed. It spun in the air, red and silver, flickering in the sunlight, to land with a splash.

She kicked her heels and he felt her fear sizzling through her, letting it arc into his own body.

Dung-fly. The sound came back to him and fell out of his mouth. He repeated it again and again, just under his breath, as he made his way quickly along the path. No one came. He crossed the water, wading knee-deep through the reeds and iris stalks and then he was past them, reaching the heavy cover of the far side. He travelled some distance, stopping only once to settle her up in his arms to make the carrying easier, and in his head the thrilling vibration was as pure as the hum of a mosquito.

She shuddered, shaking her head from side to side, and the air snuffled through her nose. He glanced down, and saw her eyes roll madly, and the fear was wide and clear in them. After a while he got through the scrub and reached the bridge. In an instant he was under the span. The door swung open with hardly a squeal. He turned, pulled the girl behind him. Her foot hit the ground and a little red sandal flipped off. He hooked it back towards him with his foot, leaving a heavy cleat-mark in the damp clay.

He pushed the door shut. The girl hiccuped, sending a delicious shiver through him. He waited until it passed and then he turned and sat down on the wide metal pipe that carried water down from the reservoir. He loosened his hand from her mouth, confident now. She did not cry. A small groan escaped her but her whole attention was focused on getting air into her lungs. He let her have one or two breaths, great whooping scoops of air, and then he closed her up again.

'Blow,' he said, and all she heard was the deep rumble of his voice in the dark. 'Blow *hard*.'

She blew hard, clearing both nostrils. When he was satisfied she could breathe easily, even though the lungs were bellowing fast as a rabbit's, he reached down and found her foot, tugged hard at the sock until it came off, balled it in his hand and then used his thumb to force it between her teeth. She shook her head with violent desperation and a spasm rippled through her, but he persisted until she made no sound. He could feel the shiver and knew she was beyond crying out for the moment. He knew the fear was running around inside her. It would chase her down into the valley of the shadow and she'd come through the other side, up in the cool place where there was no pain, the place that he himself could reach.

She knew. The certainty of it came off her in waves, like electricity. There was no escape. She would die here.

Whatever thou dost to these, the least of my children, you do also to me.

In the dark, he nodded, and he smiled a sly smile. *My Lord, why hast thou forsaken me . . . ?* His desolation was past now. He was.

I am who I am!

He reached for the matches and lit the little lamp by sense of touch. It flared, sent up a sputter of smoke and then began to glow. He turned to look at her, a small form, pale and shaking uncontrollably, a frightened bird caught in a trap. Her eyes were wide and fixed on him, and in them he saw the knowledge.

Dung-fly . . . The eyes of a child far away, begging him.

The lamp guttered and Conboy's flies buzzed in the shadows and the voice of the priest had come back to him.

'Holy Orders. A gift from God. To make sacrifice to him.'

But there was no God here.

After a while he crossed to her.

Interlude

'We knew, or at least we were fairly sure at that time, that it had to be somebody who knew the area,' Angus McNicol said. 'That was what we thought at first and we pulled in the usual suspects, shirtlifters, flashers, the whole gamut. The Hopkirk boy, he could have been just a one-off, and that's what we thought, until we found the girl. We spent six years teaching men how to kill in the war and there were bad people then, just like there are bad folk now. Look at your Nilsons and that nutcase down in Hungerford. And nutters like the Jonestown mob who think they're doing it all for the glory of God.'

Angus leant back against the thick upholstery of his easy chair and ran his fingers through a thick head of white hair.

'After we found Lucy Saunders we realized he knew that access duct to the chamber under the bridge. But how local is *local*? I mean, it could have been somebody who had been in the town before and moved away. I thought it had to have been some fellow who played around the Rough Drain and up the stream as a boy and knew the paths. But you have to remember *when* it was.

'What I mean is that there were no credit cards or the like. There was more work then, at least more than there is today, and people came to work the bottling lines for the summer and then were off again. There were potato-pickers and dry-stone-wallers, and teams of folk who'd come in to help with the fencing for the Forestry Commission, or digging the drainage ditches up on the Langcraig moors for the plantations. A lot of movement in those days, when you were doing the twist and growing your hair long. Don't think I forget giving you a toe up the arse for breaking that street light over at Station Street.' He grinned again and the eyes twinkled.

'The only thing we had was that people noticed more. If it was somebody who lived in the town, he'd have been recognized, and a stranger would be noticed. That's why that poor Indian fellow got such a beating up by Arden Road. Our man was cunning enough, though he took risks and let himself be seen a couple of times. That made him arrogant and maybe not in control of himself.

'He was a big fellow. Bigger than me probably, going by the weight he put on his Toe-tector boots. And he took a size twelve, which is about normal for a big man. He had dark hair and he blinked all the time as if he had something in his eye, and that's how the name got around. We had his fingerprints, mostly from the old surgery where they found the Hopkirk lad, and they didn't match with anything on CRO files. We could have done with some of this computer technology then. Press a few buttons and you've got it. Then it was all done with files and teleprinters.

'We had casts made of his boot prints and we had pictures of his bite marks that showed he'd a bottom tooth missing. Fabric from his jacket, hairs from his head and his crotch, and we had bugger-all really because Twitchy Eyes, he was a nobody. He just came and he went.

'Oh, we knew he had religion, *Christian* religion, from the pages of the bibles he left. You know this place. We've been murdering each other for years in the name of God Almighty, and there's nothing to chose between them all. This man left the word of God covered with shite and flies, and he was killing as well.

'When I think of what he did to that wee girl under the bridge, I tell you, I still wake up some nights and my hands are clenched so tight the nails are digging half moons into my palms. If I had got that bastard, pardon my language, if I'd got him when I was on my own, I'd have torn his arms off, I kid you not.'

Angus McNicol drained his glass, but he did not smack his lips as before. He put it down slowly.

'I would have done to him what he did to those people. I'd have done to him what he did to that poor wee soul under the bridge, and I'd have made it last. And then I'd have buried him.'

Interruption

Angus McNicol's face had twisted with anger when he described in detail what had happened to little Lucy Saunders in the mud under the bridge, and I believe then that he would have done what he said. He'd have killed the killer. The memory for him was as clear as day, as defined and sharp as if it had happened only yesterday. Some memories are like that.

Here I have to intrude. *Author intrusion.* My editor will scream blue murder and I'll have to explain that sometimes when you tell a story, you have to find your own way through it and round it, and that's just the ones you make up and knit together from the ideas in your head. Maybe one or two of you have read my other books under my pen-name, and you'll know I butt in now and again, but hardly ever. But that's in the stories I make up, or at least the ones which I dragged out of my nightmares to make into horror stories and chillers to help me get rid of the dreams.

Now I know the dreams will never go away because this is where they all live.

Back then. Back in the memory, hunched in the shadows under the bridge like the troll waiting to eat the billy goats, under the bridge like the man with the twitchy eyes. Under the bridge with the smell of rot and the buzzing of the flies.

When I spoke to Angus McNicol I let him have only half the truth. I told him I was researching for a book, but I had no intention of writing one then, not a true *story*. I was asking for *myself*, in the hope that I could find some meaning for all of that, for the monkey that's been hunched on my shoulder, pressing down with the weight of the years. I thought I could find a cure, a magic bullet, that would kill the thing off and rid me of the dreams.

Dreams don't give up easily, and memories don't give up at all.

In the end, I had to admit that part of it was just a need to bring the memories right out into the open and face them in the light of day instead of running away from them. I honestly don't know if it's done me one bit of good.

But writing it down lets me spread it around a little, maybe in the hope that a nightmare shared is a nightmare halved, and I know that might sound a little bit flippant. I am just not sure any more.

Anyway, a little more patience and I'll be out to leave you on your own if you want to read further. I've tried to put the thoughts into people's heads, to express them the way they were thought. Not an easy job, but further along there will be occurrences that explain enough, that gave me hints as to what thought processes – some of them murky and dreadful – were going on.

Also, for many years before I sat down to write my first book, and for some years after that, I worked as a newspaperman, checking out facts, digging in under the surface of things, and I'm still proud of the little card tucked in my wallet that tells me I'm a journalist, a reporter of fact, a life member of a tarnished but still honourable breed, no matter how governments wriggle and twist. Some of the stuff I got from Angus McNicol and some of it I dredged up from my memory, and a few other facts I got from digging around in some old dusty places. Maybe I've taken a bit of licence here and there, but I don't believe I've gone over the bounds. I want to impart some of the *taste*, the bitter apples and hard pears and exotic purple grapes.

But remember also that the five of us boys knew each other, had known each other, and you know what it's like being a kid of thirteen or so, just getting ready for your hormones to kick in, getting set for big strides into that big world up ahead. You can't keep a secret and you try to keep a promise and most of the time a thought's in your head no longer than the time it takes to speak it out, spit it out. Mostly we knew, just at a glance, what each other was thinking.

Five of us.

There was Corky with his drunk of a father banged up in Drumbain Jail, and not for the last time either. There was Danny, and his father who had given up a good-paying job in the ship-yards to start at university and spent all of his time either studying or praying and threatening everlasting punishment from an angry God. There was Doug, whose father was already in Toronto, run out of town by his wife's shame and the need to take his family out from under the cloud. There was Billy and his strange failure to accept his inheritance, nurturing his belief in a father who did not exist, or who lived and battled only in Billy's imagin-ation. There was Tom Tannahill who had watched his little sister slowly die of leukaemia in the front room of their house while his mother was out at the shops, and who walked with the knowl-edge of death shadowing his steps.

Five of us.

And yet despite the storm clouds of those strange and crazy times, we were trying to grow our hair long and get away from those slick-quiffed old fogies who jived to Elvis and Jerry Lee Lewis. We wanted to be different from Teddy-boys like Phil Corcoran and Pony McGill with his cratered face. We wanted to be like Donovan, trying to catch the wind, and we had a ticket to ride. Gil Favor and Rowdy Yates were our heroes on *Rawhide*. Old William Hartnell was Doctor Who, going through time in a police box, and that was the mind-blowing marvel that made adventurers of us all. Woolworth's still had wooden panels on the counters and sold bags of broken biscuits for a penny. And a policeman could still kick your arse and send you on your way to sin no more.

It was a year when everything was exploding and we had no control over it and we knew that Mick Jagger was telling the truth when he strutted up and told us *this could be the last time*.

Because it *was* the last time, and even then, in the warm summer sunshine, struggling up the hill with a bellyful of grapes and chicken, lugging the packed tent and (unsuspected by us) with a strange man's eyes drilling into the backs of our necks, we knew this *would* be the last time.

The world was changing and plans were in the air. In a couple of months, in less than a year, most us would be scattered to the winds. Jobs were hard to find even then and, besides that, other things had happened that set in motion the irrevocable machinery beyond our control.

There was the knowledge of the past season, from spring through to summer, still fresh in our minds, the realization forced upon us that sudden death could come out of the blue, in the cold light of day, whether by accident, or creeping sickness, or looming shadow under the trees on the Rough Drain. There was the prescience of the year to come that would change things for ever.

Maybe it was to save something of it all, keep the essence of us intact, that we went up the hill searching for the decoy target, looking for the dummy village. It was our last chance to find that El Dorado before it was gone for ever.

Maybe even then, we were trying to find ourselves before it all slipped away from us and got lost.

And maybe that's what I set off to do when I began all of this. Who really knows? I don't.

CHAPTER ELEVEN

August 1, 2.30 p.m.
A sound of thunder cracked way over at Drumbeck Hill and the noise of the explosion at the quarry face came rolling over the fields and up the valley. Doug stopped on the brow of the hill, where the dry-stone wall angled back towards the barwoods.

'Houston, we have lift-off,' he bawled in a dreadful American accent.

'Bombs away,' Billy hooted, and the rolling grumble in the air passed them by in a shock wave they could actually feel. Doug clambered up on top of the wall and helped Danny heft the tent over.

'Look there,' Doug said, pointing south and east towards where the tall conifer trees crowded on the other side of the valley, marking the edge of the Overbuck Estate. He shaded his eyes and the others followed the direction of his outstretched finger. 'I saw something.'

'Yeah. The wild larch tree,' Corky said. 'Very rare. That's the last million larch trees in the whole world.'

'No, you daft *baskit*. I saw somebody. Over there at the edge.'

The boys all made visors of their hands and peered under the shadow towards the edge of the plantation. The high trees straggling close to the edge were all in silhouette against the heat haze of the summer. Nothing moved.

'I saw somebody watching us,' Doug insisted.

'It was the cow again,' Billy said. 'It's supercow oh-oh-seven. Trained to search and destroy. Fitted with exploding tits. It won't give up until it's molocated us all.' Everybody laughed, even Doug. Still nothing moved in the plantation. They all climbed the wall and lugged the tent along the bare path worn by the sheep as they moved up on to the moor. The peaty ground was dotted with thick clumps of gorse, wickedly spiked but, in the warm up draughts and eddies, wafting an exquisite scent of coconut and delicate oils into the air. They ambled slowly up the track towards where the line of electricity pylons marched west, trailing black cables under the sky. The quarry blast rumbled again.

'That's what it was like all the time during the war,' Billy said. 'Must have been great.'

'Must have been murder,' Corky said. 'You'd go to bed and never know if you'd wake up again.' He swung his stick and lopped the head off a thistle, watching it go tumbling through the air.

'Wonder if there's any more bodies in the river,' Doug said. 'They'll all come floating up.'

'Jeez, Dougs, give it a break,' Tom snapped.

'I was just thinking about Paulie. Just when I heard the quarry blast.'

'He was covered in all sorts of crap,' Billy said. 'The current took him almost across to the other side of the river and he must have been stuck under the ribs of one of the sunk boats down in the mud. Al Crombie said he was all grey, and stuck like this.' Billy hunched his shoulders and hooked his hands out, mimicking a twisted corpse. 'But the crabs and fish had got his fingers and the toes on one of his feet where his boot had come off. Chewed them all away. His lovin' mother wouldn't have recognized him.'

'Jeez, Billy, give it a rest,' Tom pleaded again. Billy ignored him.

'And they think Mole Hopkirk got his the same day. That's when he went missing.'

'Everybody knows that,' Doug said. They were ambling along, in a ragged line, weaving between the jagged thorns of the gorse, listening to the drying seed-pods crackle and pop open in the heat of the sun. 'That was really creepy. Like old Twitchy fixed it so nobody was looking.'

'No. Mole was off his head anyway. Remember we saw him down at Rope Vennell?' Tom asked Billy. 'When he was cadging smokes? He was always swinging those keys, trying to swipe them down people's faces. He could have put somebody's eye out with them.'

'And then somebody put his eye out. What a horrible way to go.' Billy turned to Doug, who was just behind him. 'You said with any luck he'd fallen in the river. You wished it on him.'

'No, I didn't,' Doug protested. 'And anyway, you said you wished he'd taken on somebody bigger than himself, and that's what happened, so *you* wished it on him too.'

'Listen to yourselves,' Corky said. He was ahead of them on the pathway, just behind Danny, both of them lacquered with sweat and panting. Corky had taken off his frayed shirt and tied the arms around his waist, leaving a tail hanging like an apron. The marks of cleg-fly bites stood out on his shoulders. 'You two would start a fight in an empty house.'

'But he said . . .' Billy started.

'So what? He's a goner, isn't he? He was dead before any of us knew about it, and he was as crazy as a cat with a poker up its arse and all. It wasn't our fault he met up with some loony. He shouldn't have been breaking into houses anyway.'

'Like we broke into Overbuck's kitchen?' Billy asked mischievously.

'That's different,' Corky said. 'They're as rich as sin. And there was no crazy about to grab us.'

'That gardener looked pretty crazy to me. If he'd have caught us we'd have been in real stook. I nearly crapped my pants.'

'I thought you had, from the smell of it,' Corky said, and everybody laughed again.

They got to the brow of the hill and dropped the tent. Doug had taken off his faded T-shirt, revealing a tattered string vest with more holes in it now than when it was new. Billy said it looked like a lot of spaces joined together and Doug admitted without rancour that most of the holes weren't joined at all.

'I want to get a tan,' he said. 'All criss-crossed.'

'You'll look like a chain-link fence,' somebody said, and they laughed some more. They were all in a circle, Corky standing astride the green bulk of the tent, rapping his knuckles on the polished wood of the support poles jutting from the roll. Billy was leaning against the creosoted trunk of an electricity pole which bore three parallel cables down the side of the hill and across the valley. He lit a cigarette and offered them around. Tom took one and Billy lit for both before flipping the match to the side. Immediately a clump of grass started to shrivel and crackle as a flame, made invisible by the bright sunlight, caught the tinder-dry brush. Billy casually stamped his foot and put it out. He lifted the long ash-stave he'd cut in the valley and started peeling the bark back in strips. Danny got his slingshot from his pack and shot some small stones at the glass insulating-plates high overhead, missing with every shot. He was better at throwing. Doug switched on the radio, made it whinge and whine as he spun the little dial searching for a station. For a brief moment, the Righteous Brothers cranked up to losing that lovin' feeling, then they were gone, gone, gone, in a crackle of static.

'You're too near the power-lines,' Corky said. Doug looked up, switching the little radio off.

'There's a nest up there,' he said. They looked up and saw the little tangle of grass and moss out on the arm where the black cables snaked in their loop from one set of insulators to the other. He got up and reached towards the overhead spar joining the two poles. Beyond them, barbed wire set round the uprights offered resistance to temptation and, as an added deterrent, a tin plate bearing a lightning-bolt motif blared in red letters: WARNING: 130,000 VOLTS. DANGER OF DEATH. Overhead, even though the air was dry, they could hear the low, somehow animal, growling vibration of power.

'Not worth it,' Danny said. 'You go near those wires and they'll burn you to a crisp.' He was sitting furthest away from the pole and the trickling buzz of the voltage made him nervous. 'And you can't let go either. It makes you hold on tight and burns you up until there's nothing left.'

Doug moved back from the strut and ran a hand through his straight, fair hair.

'That can't be true,' Billy said. 'Look. There's a crow up on the wire. It's just sitting there, no bother at all, and it's not getting zapped.'

'That's because it isn't earthed,' Corky said. 'Don't you ever listen in science?'

'I don't believe it,' Billy retorted. He jammed the cigarette in the corner of his mouth and hauled himself up, using his stave as a climbing pole. His weight drove the point deep into the earth and he had to pull hard to get it out again. He hefted the straight stick, holding it like a spear as he walked backwards up the hill. They all watched him.

'What's he up to?' Tom asked.

'Damned if I know,' Doug said mildly. Billy got about thirty yards, right on to the shoulder of the slope. Behind him, two lapwings flopped into the still air, beating jerkily while they bleated their distress at the intrusion into their territory and the danger to their nest.

Billy stopped, looked up and then came running back the way he had come. He took ten steps and swung his arm back.

'Geronimo!' The stave soared like a javelin, heavy end foremost, curving through the air. It arrowed above the wires, seen from where the rest of the boys were sitting, and for a moment they assumed it would fly straight over, to land in the gorse beyond. It landed right on top of the wires, fifty feet from the pylon. It made a pinging sound as it slapped across all three of the thick cables.

A red flame flashed across its length.

There was absolutely no warning, no hesitation. It simply flared with a sound of ripping canvas.

'Bloody hell,' Tom mouthed.

'Yee-hah,' Billy crowed triumphantly. The others watched in amazement. The flames crackled across the ash-stave, making it jitter on the wires, twisting like a snake. An explosion of blue sparks erupted where it lost contact with the centre cable and a sound like a road-drill came rattling down.

The five of them stood simply mesmerized.

'Look at it *burn*,' Billy yelled. He was jumping up and down, his T-shirt flapping, waving both hands in the air. A sheet of flame flew off the burning branch, coiled into a sphere and rolled upwards, roaring like an angry beast. Even from where the four nearest boys stood, open-mouthed, they could feel the heat. Another shower of sparks fountained outwards, sparkling like sapphires. The drill noise came rapping across, shuddering through the wires. Then the stave just exploded.

It was a real blast, not merely a disintegration. The white, peeled sapling had turned to black in the space of mere seconds. The flames were reaching up towards a blue sky and then a crack like a shotgun blast punched the air. The stick was there and then it was gone. Burning cinders catapulted into the air, trailing smoke in grey streamers. A piece of charred wood came whirling past, making a *whoop-whoop* sound as it spun, and hit Billy on the cheek, making him yell, though none of the others heard him. They were running to get out from under the falling debris. Doug and Corky reached the tent first and heaved it up. Danny and Tom grabbed the rucksacks.

The punch of the explosion faded away, though it still echoed in their ears.

'Did you see that?' Billy bawled, racing down towards them.

'You're a crazy *baskit*,' Doug asserted.

Just then, the first crackle of flames became audible. Doug stopped, almost pulling Corky off his feet. 'Listen,' he said, holding himself still, head cocked.

'Nearly put my eye out,' Billy was saying, still rubbing his cheek where the piece of charred wood had left a sooty smear.

'Wheesht.' Corky hushed him to silence. For a moment, they were still. Billy was standing with his mouth open and his brows drawn down angrily, about to argue with Doug. Corky had his hand up, telling everyone to hush.

The snap and crackle of fire came from beyond the pylon. They all turned. A gorse bush burst into flame. It was as if burning petrol had been thrown over it, and it just blossomed fire. It growled madly like the flame-throwers in war movies. One second it was thick and green and festooned with golden flowers; the next it was shrivelling under a ten-foot flame. The heat came rolling on the dry air, slapping them like a hot hand. Behind them, another bush roared into flame, like a fiery lion rising from a thicket.

'Christ, man,' Corky bawled. 'The whole place is going . . .'

Ten feet away, a third bush erupted. The fine hairs on Danny's arms twisted and shrivelled in the sudden flare of heat. To the right, two smaller bushes crackled into life.

'. . . out of here,' Doug was yelling, the first words lost in the roar of the flames, but the meaning perfectly clear. He and Corky ran between two reaching hedges, bent with the heavy weight of the tent. Danny followed. Tom and Billy were somewhere behind them.

'Yee-hah,' Billy hooted again. 'Bombs away.' Beyond them, a towering forest of flame reached for the sky, a great red animal clawing upwards. The air all around them danced as if it had been turned liquid in the scorch. It tasted of pollen and charcoal and instantly seared their throats dry.

Something flew round the corner of one flowering hedge and missed Corky by a hair's breadth, in a flurry of whirring wings. The panicked woodcock jinked and headed for the stand of pines further down the slope of the hill. Overhead, two skylarks warbled their distress, while somewhere in the bushes their almost fully fledged nestlings huddled in fear, their instinctive compulsion to freeze now acting against them as the flames licked around them.

A pillar of fire exploded into life to Doug's left and he jinked right, holding a hand up to protect his face. Corky followed, hauled by the tent, stumbling as he went. A gust of wind, sucked in by the powerful up draught, dragged with it a wall of grey smoke. Danny scrambled into it, felt the incredible blast of heat and backed away. Corky and Doug kept on moving. They got twenty yards and came scooting out of the gorse bushes and on to the flat of the sphagnum damplands.

Danny reeled away to the right, smoke in his eyes and searing down his throat. Somewhere close by, Tom yelled something and Danny stumbled backwards, knuckling under his brows to clear the dust and smoke-induced tears. By this time, the heat was unbelievable. A roaring noise thundered close by and he shied away from it, falling over one small bush which stabbed him in what felt like a thousand places. A gorse spine went right up under his nail and a needle of pain drilled into his finger. Danny rolled and found himself in a small clearing. A chance eddy of wind sucked the smoke away. Ahead of him, up the slope, he could see a line of flames, twenty feet high. Behind him, hardly fifteen yards away, a stand of scrub hazel was well alight. He turned, panic beginning to bubble up. A minute before, Danny could have outrun anything except Doug, who could run like a greyhound. Danny was fast and agile and he'd been able to show Phil Corcoran an easy clean pair of heels. But this fire, it *moved*. It ran like a red tiger, chasing and hounding. It had leapt in front of him to bar his way, catching him no matter how fast he could run, no matter how he jinked and dived.

'Danny,' Tom's voice came wavering from somewhere to the

right. 'Help me!' Danny whirled, trying to gulp down the rising terror. He spun again and stopped. Right in front of him, a roe-deer fawn stood quivering, a tiny, spindly thing, no bigger than a mountain hare, balanced on four stick-legs. Its eyes were huge and black. The deer and Danny looked at each other. The animal was shivering so violently it looked as if it might have been connected to the voltage in the black cables overhead. Then it turned. Danny couldn't tell how it had done it. There was no visible movement at all. It stared at him and then its back was toward him, and it flicked, as if by magic, between two bushes. To his left, another wall of flame burst into life. To his right, Tom squealed, high and clear, and there was real fear in the sound. Danny blundered through the small gap, brushing past the spines which dug through his jeans and drove into his knees. His lungs were hurting and the skin on the back of his neck felt as if it was turning crisp, and a dread horror came rippling through him.

He was stuck here. He was trapped in the fire.

The bad fire.

Sister Julia's face came wavering on the heat-tortured air. *The good Lord can look down on you at any time and decide to take you.*

Like he had taken Paul Degman.

You must always try to be in a state of grace.

The fire was all around and the heat was searing his throat and he was stuck in it. Sudden fear almost froze him to stone.

'Danny. Jesus, Danny, I'm stuck,' Tom's cry came from just beyond the next bush. It punched him through the membrane of paralysis.

He fell over the hedge, almost blown over by the force of the heat. Tom was snagged on a hazel branch. He'd been crawling under a natural canopy and a dead branch had fingered down the neck of his shirt and out the tail. Under any other circumstances, it would have looked completely ludicrous. Tom's feet were scrabbling and slipping on dried mud.

'Oh God, don't let it get me,' he babbled. In a flash of reality, he saw the very real possibility that he could die. Panic soared. The awesome finality of death had been with him since long before Paulie Degman had fallen into the river, since little

Maureen had slipped away while his mother had been out at the corner shop getting chicken soup. She'd gone and they'd taken her away and put her in the ground, little Mo, his baby sister, and they'd all had to pray while his parents stood frozen by a deadly graveside, too poor to put up a headstone. Tom had held on to his other kid sister, Marie, held on so tight his fingers bruised her shoulder and as he looked down at that hole in the ground, in the old graveyard behind St Rowan's church, it was like looking into a black well that went down for ever. Nobody who went down there ever came back.

'Danny,' he screeched. 'Help.'

He pushed forward, the way a snared rabbit will, and felt the branch strain against the cotton. He pushed again, felt the fabric rip, pushed some more and was stopped dead. He could not go forwards; he could not go backwards.

'Danny,' he screeched again, voice high, just like a girl's. 'Help me, Danny, I'm stuck!'

He squirmed in a sudden desperate frenzy. He was stuck and the flames were all around him and in that instant he clearly saw the maw of infinity approaching fast. His feet shoved at the dusty hardpack of the ground, gouging out two grooves but gaining no purchase strong enough to break the branch that snagged him or rip the shirt on which it was hooked. The heat of the flames pressed in from the side. A billow of smoke rolled over him and he coughed violently, rasping his throat. Just then something hit him from behind. At first he thought it was Danny pushing him through. Then a soft body squeezed beside him, wriggled past in a shiver of muscle and fur. The little roe-deer, in its panic, hadn't even seen him. It made it through the gap and flashed away. Tom was left stuck.

Out on the far side, Corky and Doug watched the wall of flames. Further up the hill, beyond the line of power-cable, Billy was whooping with unfettered glee, completely unaware of the danger Danny and Tom were in down the slope among the massed tangle of burning gorse. It just hadn't occurred to him that they would still be in there.

'Like a fuckin' bomb,' Billy yelled. He had a bird's eye view of the whole thing, but he couldn't see Tom or Danny were stuck in the middle of it all. The flames absolutely gobsmacking fantastic. They rumbled and roared, snarled and fought, leaping from bush to thicket, a contagion of instant fire. The bushes just splurged into flame. The heat warped the air so much the power-cables seemed to shimmy and dance. Little birds spiralled up through the smoke. Only fifty feet away he saw a yellowhammer come flitting up in its bouncing, undulating flight and then suddenly fall like a stone into the mass of flame below. Two hares came scooting from cover, brown blurs that raced up the slope and swerved just before they reached him, their eyes rolling.

'Christ on a bloody *bike*,' he bawled to himself.

He trotted down the hill a little distance, getting to within twenty feet of the nearest bush, which had crumpled in on itself, thin, grey ash tumbling down in a stream where the spikes of gorse powdered to threatless dust. The fire had eaten and moved on, leaving a bare skeleton. Billy bent and grabbed at a tussock of couch grass, rocking his weight from side to side to free the roots. It finally came ripping up from the ground and, without any hesitation, he jammed it in against the smouldering roots of the burnt bush. The grass crackled and caught. He spun, whirling the turf and grass around his head, then aimed for a clear patch down the hill the fire hadn't reached.

His grenade tumbled in the air, trailing smoke. He watched it level out, then curve down. It landed off to the right, almost due south. Over the screaming of the flames he didn't hear the thud. There was a pause, and then, with a startling *whoosh*, the bush and its neighbour were ablaze.

Billy howled in delight. He saw himself in uniform, just like his father, tossing grenades or hosing liquid fire from the flame-throwers he'd seen in the films. The wavering air and the heat, the smell of burning and the sudden *violence* of it all was incredible. Billy just couldn't believe he'd done all that, all with just one thrown piece of wood.

Out on the damplands, where the sphagnum moss had sopped up the moisture of the pre-summer rains and held it in the seeps and depressions of the moor, Corky and Doug stood side by side.

'Can you see them?' Corky asked. Doug shook his head. His light-blue eyes were ringed with smudges and he used a finger to wipe a trickle of dusty snot from his lip. A twig of gorse had snagged in his hair like a miniature crown of thorns.

'Can't see a thing.'

'I heard somebody. Sounded like Tom.'

'What, in there?' Doug jerked his thumb towards the flames. His face went suddenly pale.

The fire rampaged along. Something came soaring over the smoke and hit beyond them, and another growl of flame started eating at the gorse. It made strange sounds. It roared and rasped and, underneath that sound, it screamed and screeched as the branches and roots twisted and gave off their gases. It sounded as if lost souls were writhing in agony in there, buckling and shrivelling in the heat of the flames.

Corky remembered what Danny had said, his own vision of hell. That's what it would sound like. Just screaming and shrieking, and it would go on and on. He shook his head. It was just fire. It was just bushes. He'd seen the gorse go up before. It wouldn't last long.

But what if . . .

It rustled and whispered, it crackled and it laughed, as if it could read his mind.

'No,' Corky said, more in hope than in certainty. 'They must have gone down the other side. And Billy went up the hill.'

Just as he said that, Billy let out a triumphant holler. They saw a shadow move and he came lumbering through a pall of smoke. He had a dry tussock in his hand and he set it alight before tossing it down the slope, leading the fire on.

'Where's Dan?' Corky bawled, making himself heard above the commotion. Billy shrugged. His face was aglow behind the smudges.

'And Tom,' Doug bawled. 'You seen them?' Billy shook his head. His mind was elsewhere.

Just then a flight of partridges came bulleting out of the smoke on whirring wings, fat, little, propeller-driven birds. They arrowed straight towards the boys, seemed to notice them at the last possible second and veered up and over their heads. Right behind them, the tiny roe fawn came springing out. It stopped on its spindly legs, its tongue lolling. It didn't even see them.

The gorse crackled behind it and it was gone, a brown, little blur, spider-fast, gone and away.

Corky looked at Billy. His eyes were alight and his face was red with excitement. Doug followed Corky's look. Billy was prancing around, throwing the sods of peat and grass into the flames, spreading it further as if it needed stoking.

'He's off his bloody head,' Doug said. The fire squealed as it tortured a briar root into impossible torques.

Inside the burning swathe, Danny found Tom snagged on the hazel branch. His old, scuffed shoes were digging into the soft earth, ploughing up furrows as he frantically tried to free himself. Danny could hear his panicked whimper. The heat was incredible now, searing his cheeks, and there seemed to be no air to breathe. He stumbled forward and tried to break the thin stick with his hands. Tom's hand grabbed his ankle and pulled desperately, almost throwing Danny off balance.

The branch wouldn't break. Without thinking it through, Danny simply bent down and got his weight against Tom's skinny backside, dug his own feet into the ground and pushed with all his weight. There was a sharp crack as the branch snapped. Tom went flopping forward, and Danny fell on top of him, knocking the wind out of the smaller boy's lungs.

'Oof . . .' Tom gasped, and that was a whole lot better than the fearful whimpering. Danny rolled, slipped and fell flat. Tom was up, his canvas bag still slung over one shoulder. He grabbed for the back of Danny's shirt and hauled him first to his knees, then up to his feet. Without a word they stumbled forwards. Ahead of them, the flames danced in orange spires. But then a gust of wind thinned them momentarily. They had reached the edge. Both of them realized there was no turning back. They both closed their eyes and ran for it. Charred twigs and branches crunched under their feet and the dust rose up to clog their nostrils. They barged through, and for a second the heat soared up to an incredible scorch. The whole world seemed to be on fire. Danny hit hard ground first but the smoke was in his eyes. Tom reached for him, got a hand to the strap of the rucksack and both boys came out of the burning gorse like the two hares, running blind, cheeks tear-streaked. Danny went crashing over the ridge of hummock-grass and down the far side, lungs hauling for cool air, down the lee side, missed his footing and started to fall. Tom was right behind him, flipping over, bouncing on the moss, then tumbling in pursuit.

They rolled for fifteen feet past the ridge and then both of them hit the water of the shallow pool at exactly the same moment. The surface was covered in duckweed and the pond was less than two feet deep, a low, circular depression on a flat shoulder below the ridge of the hill. They tumbled into it and immediately the tepid water sucked the heat from their skins.

Tom came up spluttering, coughing water out. It dribbled from his nose in muddy streaks. Danny turned over, trying to push himself to his feet and at first only succeeded in driving his hand a foot into the mud. Finally he managed to get to his knees, then pushed himself up to a shaky stance. His tough jeans, cut-down versions of workmen's denims, complete with the long ruler-pocket down the leg, sagged with the weight of water. Tom was hauling in great breaths and still coughing violently, trying to expel the slimy water that had splashed down his throat.

'Jeez, Tom, I thought we were goners there,' Danny blurted.

Tom nodded, still unable to speak. He opened his eyes and he and Danny shared a look that expressed the words they couldn't say. It had been a close thing.

Corky and Doug came running down the hill. 'You all right?' Both boys nodded breathlessly, chests hitching.

'Flaming hell,' Corky said. 'We thought you were in there.'

'We *were* in there. Nearly singed all my hair off.' Danny held up his arm to show where the fine, white hairs on the side were twisted and curled. He peered closer and saw where the ends were shrivelled. Each had a little dot of melted hair on the end. He closed his eyes, remembering the heat on his face and the back of his neck, and felt the panic try to weasel in again. He shook it away.

Billy came loping down the slope. Behind him the air was thick with smoke. Pieces of grey ash were twirling skywards in the up draught. The fire had crept down for more than fifty yards until it reached a boggy patch where the gorse gave way to a dark patch of low reeds. Beyond the marsh the land rose up again, golden with furze and broom blossom, but the flames could not cross over the reed bed to get to it. Almost as quickly as it began, the fire died, leaving little smouldering patches of charred briar root and the twisted stems of the bushes blackened and skeletal.

'Pure brilliant,' Billy said. 'Fan-bloody-*tastic*.'

Tom rounded on him. 'You nearly killed us, you stupid fat shite. Me an' Danny, we nearly copped it in there.'

'Oh, quit blubbing,' Billy sneered. He took a step forward and gave Tom a push, not hard, but enough to make the smaller boy take a step backwards. 'No kidding, your lip's always trembling. And just watch who you're calling names, *Titch*.'

Tom hit his hand away. 'You're off your head. No kidding. You've got screws loose. You nearly killed us. That fire was . . . it was . . .' Tom's mouth started opening and closing, but his throat and tongue had ganged up against him and refused to let the words out. His eyes filled with tears. Doug and Corky shuffled their feet, embarrassed for him. Tom turned away, and the others could see his shoulders jerking up and down.

'What did I tell you?' Billy started to say. 'Always whinging about something.'

'Leave off,' Danny told him. Billy's eyes opened wide, taking offence again, but Corky spoke up. 'Yeah, Billy, let it rest, eh? You could have killed somebody.'

This time it was Billy's turn to act like a fish. He looked from one to the other, then shook his head in disgust. For a second, Doug thought Billy might have a go at Corky, just because he was all fired up with the excitement. Billy was the biggest of them all, almost a head taller than both Danny and Corky, and he towered over Tom, who looked as if his wet clothes would make him stagger. Danny said nothing. He just looked at Billy without any expression on his face. The confrontation faded. Billy shrugged and walked up the hill to get his old army rucksack.

He stood there while the others waited for Tom. He could hear them mumbling and he assumed they were persuading Tom to come along with them rather than turn to go back down the hill and home again. Finally, Tom wiped his eyes, and the boys started to straggle up the hill.

'Come on, you lot,' Billy called down. 'This ain't a picnic, you know.'

The fire finally died out. Down at the station near Castlebank church, and over at the waterworks post up from Cargill Farm, the smoke and flames had been monitored. It was always a hazard at this time of the year and, in the high summer, hardly a week went past without a brush fire or a gorse fire.

It was what the kids did, part of the tradition. Most of the time, like this time, the fires burned themselves out. When the smoke cleared, the light wind carried the dust high over Langmuir Crags and everybody forgot about it.

The five boys trailed over the brow of the hill and down the lee slope on a slow descent towards the Blackwood stream. Billy was still in a state of high excitement over the violence, and the sudden destruction, and while Tom and Danny could cheerfully have choked him, his actions that day, while they almost killed two of his friends, had a far-reaching effect.

When he'd tossed the stave on to the wires, shorting out the voltage between the cables, a heavy breaker-gate slammed open and shut off the current in the junction station just west of Barloan Harbour, the next village along, near Old Kildenny. All the power in Barloan Harbour winked off.

Down on Barge Street, where in the old days the hauliers would unload their goods from the canal bay, Terry Hughes, an engineer with the sewage department, was inspecting a blocked duct when the lights went out. He had planned to stay down a half-hour longer before coming up for a break. In the dark, he turned, and his cable-light cracked against a rock with a pop of glass. Up in the fresh air, he had a flask of strong coffee waiting. Terry made his way along the duct and reached the up-well. He took off his hard hat and hung it on the hook, going by sense of touch. He climbed the fifteen horseshoe steps set into the brick shaft. Somebody had put the manhole cover down and Terry assumed that one of his colleagues had been playing a practical joke, shutting off the light and then shutting him in. He pushed it up, crawled into the daylight and let it slam down again. He turned to the little canvas shelter where he'd left his flag when the ground shuddered. The manhole cover exploded upwards on a pillar of blue flame, tumbling like a tossed coin. It soared right across the railway line and crashed through the upper deck, the galley and the hull of a neat little ketch down in the harbour basin, taking it straight to the mud at the bottom.

Terry Hughes was knocked off his feet and he suffered a graze to his finger.

Investigators later found it had been caused by a huge build-up of gas in a sump, gas which had leaked from a cracked mains pipe. When the power winked back on, the cracked lamp had ignited the gas and let rip an explosion so violent that it ruptured the entire wall of the sewer duct and caved in a section of road fifty yards long. Terry Hughes' protective hat was found, or what was left of it, a hundred yards away in the fork of a tree. It was split into four ragged shell-pieces that made it look like a blossoming dog-rose. As he told his workmates in the Horseshoe Bar, where he got monumentally drunk that afternoon, if the lights hadn't gone off, he'd have been down there when it happened and he'd never have come back up again.

CHAPTER TWELVE

June

Kids were screaming and yelling. A rough voice cursed loudly and comprehensively and a high-pitched one cried out in sudden pain.

'Let me go, you big swine,' the boy squawked, clenching his teeth so that he wouldn't cry. Up on the hill behind the school, close to the angle-iron fence that bordered the old sandstone diggings, it was a bad idea to let people see you cry. It would let them know you were soft. In Quarryhill School, rough and ready as any, you had to keep your footing.

Further down the hill a crowd of boys broke into a raucous cheer, the kind you hear in a school-yard when kids are up to mischief. A bell rang in the distance and the smaller boy squirmed away from the older one who was twisting his arm up his back.

'I'm telling the teacher,' he yelled. 'You're in trouble.'

Quarryhill School. It stood just off the Arden Road leading out of town on its west edge, and the paved school-yard backed on to the slope known to generations of pupils as the Hump. Here the tall, green-painted, spiked fence formed the boundary of the school land. Beyond it, the chasm of the old quarry, which had supplied stone for most of the old tenement buildings in the town, was a barren landscape of sheer drops, massive tumbled blocks of stone and tangled weeds and scrub. The fence was supposed to keep the pupils away from danger but, naturally, this being a school, nobody ever came up the Hump to check how effective the barrier was. In one section, three of the spars had been torn away, leaving a space a man could walk through without turning sideways. There were other places, closer to the low hill on the far side where the pigeon huts huddled, where the earth underneath the bottom spar had simply been scraped away by years of boys escaping the boredom of classes on sunny afternoons. That part of the fence was not visible from any part of the school building, so for any truant the space under the fence was the ideal escape route. It was used so often that no grass grew there. It was Quarryhill's back door.

At lunch-time, especially on a dry day, the backyard of Quarryhill was just like tribal lands. Down close to the wall, the first-year girls played skipping ropes and a hopscotch game called peever. Smaller boys played tag, though they called it tig. High tig, low tig, ball tig, if they had a ball. Over at the sheds, the second- and third-year boys gathered to play five-a-side, or heading the football on to the roof, taking it in turn, scoring points if they could keep it up without letting it drop. When they tired of that, they might goggle at the senior girls of sixth year who hung around with the older boys who had lost interest in heading the ball and cared no longer about games of tig or kick-the-can.

On the Hump, lower down-slope where the ground was almost flat, teams of boys would mill around with a football, yelling and bawling the way they do, sometimes twenty to a side, everybody chasing the ball at once to kick it between piles of school bags and jackets. Nobody outside the game ever knew how the score was kept, but again, that's the way it is in schools. Further up-slope there was a hollow close to the fence where the fights took place, and that was generally a couple of times a week and an occasion for half the male population and a substantial fraction of the girls, too, to come swarming up to spectate. Some of the fights were particularly violent, though most of them were simply pushing and shoving affairs involving a lot of swearing and name-calling as two reluctant boys squared up to each other, each determined not to be the first to land a blow. In real fights it was different. There were bruises, contusions, broken noses, mud, blood and snot flying. At any time outside class periods, the noise was horrendous. Kids were yelling and screaming, roaring and bawling. The senior boys, all of them smooth and cocky, or so it seemed to the thirteen-year-olds, had their radios turned up to a roar, listening to the Who or Manfred Mann, most of them with Beatles fringes and hair down over their collars, and most of them with bad, florescent acne. The back school-yard and the Hump was like a cluster of galaxies, each group milling around with its own kind, and two groups hardly in contact, kept apart by the reverse gravity of age. Whenever two groups collided, as happened now and again, somebody could get hurt.

The smaller boy with the now-sore arm ran away threatening to tell the teacher, and the older boy, who was strolling up the hill, tapping a ball lightly ahead of him with the toe of his scuffed Chelsea boot, gave him the sign and turned away grinning. He kicked the ball to his friend, who passed it to the third, and then it came back. They were going up the hill towards the fence.

'Got any smokes?' Crawford Rankine asked. His voice was just on the cusp of breaking, going from deep to high and then cracking to a thin, gravelly rasp. His skin was just beginning to erupt in a line of risen weals on the edge of his jaw.

'A couple,' Don Whalen replied. 'But we can club together and get more.' He was a thin boy with fine, crinkled hair, through which his scalp showed pink. He'd pulled his tie off and was trying to whip it against the third boy's backside.

'Chuck it,' Derek Milne told him. Don ignored the warning and whipped the tie, making it crack like a lash. Derek tried to catch it, but failed.

'If at first you don't succeed, fuck it, chuck it, never heed,' Don chanted, mocking his pal.

'Use the boot and then the *heid*,' Derek snarled back in mock threat. There was no malice in it. They were pals. They moved up the hill, skirting the low wall where the huddled groups of gamblers sheltered from the breeze, deftly dealing cards for high-speed three-card brag (deuces floating wild), or rapid-fire black-jack pontoon with double odds for twenty-one and better than that for a five-card trick. Some expert hustlers would be thumbing coins against the brickwork in sudden-death challenges of pitch and toss.

'Deuce is wild,' a high voice complained vehemently. 'That's three aces. A *prile*, and that beats you.'

'Piss off, you lunatic,' a deeper voice countered. 'Jokers don't count.'

'You're the flippin' joker, Caldwell. That's my game. I win.'

Somebody shouted and somebody else yelled back and there was the unmistakable thud of a fist landing on a cheek.

'Fight, fight.'

The words bounced from one group to another. The game of football on the flat grass stopped.

'Fight, *fight*!'

The girls stopped skipping. The senior boys with the acne pushed themselves away from the side wall, craning their heads to see what was going on. Small galaxies spun off groups of wheeling individuals and whirled them towards the gamblers. By now, two boys were rolling on the ground, locked together, each of them grunting and snorting with effort.

'It's a fight,' Derek said.

'No, it's a kissing and hugging match,' Crawford said. 'Look at them. Just a pair of jessies.'

He strolled on and the others followed as far as the fence. Up against the green-metal railings, another group of younger boys had been playing dead man's fall, pretending to attack a machine-gun nest and then being shot and dying in the most spectacular and dramatic fashion. When the fight-cry had sparked from group to group, they had forgotten their little private war and gone trotting down the slope like pups coming down to a kill, heads up, feet fast. The three pals reached the fence. Crawford Rankine threw his bag over the spikes at the top, eased himself down to the ground and limbo-crawled under the deep space where the earth had been worn away.

'Listen,' Derek said. 'I can't go. We got Matt Bryson for second period.'

'So what?'

'He said if I don't bring in that essay today, he'll have my guts. He will an' all.'

'Oh, he's nothing but a big nancy,' Crawford sneered. 'Come on, man. My Uncle Steve said there's a run of sea trout coming up. It's a great day for fishing.'

Derek hesitated. Don urged him to come along, and for a moment it looked like their friend could be persuaded, but he shook his head regretfully.

'Ok, don't say you weren't asked,' Crawford told him. He picked up his bag and started walking on the path on the other side of the fence, heading away from the quarry and down toward the pigeon huts and the shacks where the Quarryhill men kept their lurchers and greyhounds and, occasionally, some fighting dogs. Don gave Derek an apologetic shrug and then scrambled under the fence. On the down-slope, the low rush of sound rolled up the hill, the tense and somehow hungry sound a crowd of teenagers make as they mill around two fighting bodies. Derek turned and walked towards the mêlée.

Don and Crawford skirted the top shacks and followed the natural alley-way between the old wooden huts. Pigeons cooed and mumbled from behind slatted openings. Overhead, a flock of them clapped through the air, wheeling together with such perfect timing they might have been joined together by threads. Here the track, no more than a yard wide, fell away, heading for the old back road that was once the service access for the stone-haulers at the quarry. In this part the yards and small paddocks were bounded by thick chain-link or heavy-duty chicken-wire. Crawford stopped at the corner and Don opened the pack of cigarettes.

'Got a match?'

'Not since Samson died,' Crawford threw back.

'You mean his crippled baby sister, don't you?'

They lit up and drew in deep, then sauntered casually down the hill to where some steps had been constructed with old planks of wood in a rickety descent. Just as they reached the top stair a big, black shape came lunging out from behind one of the corrugated-iron shacks and hit the chain-link with such force that the wire shrieked through the stay-holes. Don drew back with a cry of alarm and dropped his cigarette into the mud at the side of the track. The pit-bull terrier lunged again, a squat and powerful beast with a head twice as wide as any normal canine head should be. Its pinprick eyes were flat black in a grey face wrinkled into a snarl and showing an impossible array of teeth. It growled deep and rumbling in the back of its throat.

'Jee-*fuh* . . .' Crawford gasped. He was further from the fence than Don, but the powerful dog's attack had pushed the wire right out to the middle of the path. The beast growled and slavered.

'Look at the teeth on that,' Crawford said. 'If that got you it would take your bloody arm off.'

The fighting dog launched itself at the fence, massive and muscular, leaping right up from the ground to hit with ugly snout and paws. Specks of saliva splashed on the two boys, who had cringed back to the far side of the track.

'It's like a Tasmanian devil,' Don said, and they both laughed, now realizing they were safe and that the powerful beast couldn't get through the fence. Don picked up a slender twig from a privet that overhung the track and poked it through the wire. The dog leapt up at it, jaws snapping together with the sound of boulders clashing, and Don pulled his hand away. Crawford reached for Don's smouldering cigarette. He drew hard on it, making the end glow brightly.

'Here, poochie-poo, here, boy,' he wheedled. The black dog twisted its head to the side curiously, though the low rumble continued. Crawford pushed a finger through the mesh. Without hesitation the dog lunged. Crawford whipped his finger away, twisting as he did to bring his other hand up. The dog hit the fence and Crawford jammed the lit end of the cigarette against its shiny nose.

The pit-bull terrier seemed to explode. It leapt back in a perfect somersault, howling madly with pain and rage. It landed square on its feet, smooth hair now all spiked and hackled. Its thick neck seemed to have ballooned to twice its previous bull thickness. The howl turned into a slavering snarl and it attacked the fence again, hitting it with such powerful force that one of the staples on the high upright popped out and pinged on the barrier on the other side of the track.

'Flamin' hell, Craw,' Don yelped. The dog leapt at them, pushing its nose far enough through the mesh that the skin beside its snout pulled back so violently that it began to bleed. Its black eyes were rolling wildly, showing a ring of yellow-white all around. It snapped and howled like a crazed beast, which in fact it was. Don and Crawford took to their heels hooting with laughter.

Down to the left a trio of greyhounds started growling. Don and Crawford scampered down the swaying steps past the dog pen, while the pit-bull terrier went beserk behind them, attacking the fence with such ferocity it seemed certain to break through and come after them. The pair darted to the right past the greyhounds, tall, emaciated dogs with arched backs and goitred eyes and long, grinning mouths. They began to bark in chorus as the boys ran past, thrusting their thin noses through the holes in the wire.

Crawford got to the flat just ahead of Don and they ran along the gravel path, past a series of old shacks, and reached the dead end. Here a piece of sheet iron had been set up as a makeshift gate, but it had been peeled back by others in the past and the narrow gap allowed them to squeeze through. This was the final paddock and, beyond it, there was a secondary worn track that led down to the back quarry road. They stopped and got their breath back.

'Nearly shit myself,' Don wheezed. 'And look. My smoke's all wet now. It's like a duck's arse.'

Crawford flicked it out of his hand and ground it into the earth. He passed his own smoke over and Don took a big draw.

'Cured my constipation as well,' Crawford said. 'If that thing got out it would eat you alive.' The danger over, they began to laugh nervously.

'It would eat *you*. I'd be a hundred yards clear ahead of you.'

They finished the cigarette, smoking it down until it almost burned Don's lip, and then they moved through the mass of tall weeds that filled the paddock. The brambles and willow-herb grew higher than their heads, and they had to push the trailing runners away to reach the far side. Here, an old railway boxcar was angled against the barbed-wire fence that marked the east edge of the quarry. Don made to go past it, when he stopped and bent down.

'What is it?'

'A padlock.' Don straightened up and turned to his pal. 'Somebody left it.'

They turned simultaneously towards the boxcar, which was grey with age. A faded number 188 was just visible against the pocked grain of the wood. Any time they had passed this way the truck had been firmly closed. Somebody had jemmied the lock off. Don leant forward and touched the pale gouges where the wood had been chipped off. Crawford moved past him and gave the door a tug to the left. It refused to budge but he got two hands to it and heaved. It gave a squeal of protest and slid back a few inches on its solid runner wheels. He peered through the gap.

'Can't see anything,' he answered the unasked question. He pulled back, and his pal got a grip on the door, and between them they rolled it open enough to let them inside. A pale pillar of light crossed the dusty floor and climbed up the wall, illuminating the centrefolds tacked to the wall.

Crawford pushed his way inside with Don clambering just behind him.

'Look at the tits . . .' he started to say, craning forward to ogle a blonde boasting a stupendous and quite improbable chest. Behind him, Don grunted.

A loud thud shook the goods truck.

He turned round, only curious at that moment. Don came swinging up in front of him, moving fast, his pale, frizzled hair catching the light.

'What the heck are you doing?' Crawford blurted in surprise.

Don grunted again. A tall figure loomed out from the shadow. He had Don by the neck. Crawford got a glimpse, no more, of thick fingers clamped against the back of the boy's head. His friend hit the side of the wagon. Don's bag flew off to the side.

'Donny . . . ?'

The tall figure came lunging forward, his other hand reaching out. It seemed to happen in slow motion. Don went slamming against the side, flicking out of the light and disappearing into the gloom. The pale hand, massive and wide, came expanding toward Crawford's face. It reached the pillar of light. The fingers brightened. Crawford jerked back reflexively, instinctively. His feet slipped and he fell to the floor. The hooked hand clawed the empty air.

'*Ungh,*' Don said. His feet hit the side again. His head was almost at the curved roof of the wagon. Dreadful panic twisted in Crawford's belly. The hand lunged for him again, crossing the shaft of light once more. Crawford rolled. His bag slipped from his shoulder as his feet scrabbled on the wooden boards. He twisted again and, by a sheer miracle, he tumbled out of the wagon and into the daylight.

The man growled, almost as loud, almost as ferocious as the pit-bull. Crawford's shin scraped down the edge of the door runner, burning a sliver of fire up on the bone, but at that moment he hardly felt a thing. The awful sound that had come out of Don's mouth was ringing in his ears, even louder than the growl of the big man who had lifted his friend up by the neck and slammed him, one-handed, so violently against the side of the rail truck that the whole thing shook.

Crawford's foot shoved at the muddy ground, failed to grip. The panic burst inside him and he whimpered in fear. His foot got purchase, pushed him forward. Something heavy – and he knew it was that reaching hand – hit him on the backside. He felt fingers hooking at the flannel of his pants, pulled away from them with a desperate heave. The material dragged away. He shot forward, got to his feet and crashed through the weeds. The man grunted again and snarled ferociously. Crawford reached the makeshift gate where he and Don had bent back the thin metal. They hadn't pushed it back into position and it was still open. He dived through, not trusting himself to squeeze between the uprights quickly enough. His hip hit the ground on the other side, abraded a red scrape into his skin, and then he was up and away.

Behind him, there was a thud of something heavy hitting the side of the wagon. Almost immediately, the weeds and bramble runners snapped, as an even heavier mass pushed through them. Crawford's whimper became a wail of pure terror. He ran along the track, past the snarling greyhounds, pushed himself off a slatted wall to get round the corner and then went skittering down the final track towards the Lochend road, which curved in a long bend past the base of the path. He stopped, head swinging right and left. If he used the road, he had five hundred yards to get to the junction that would lead him back up to the front of the school.

Five hundred yards. Would he make it? Could he make it? His mind was jittering and jerking, not gauging consciously, but working it out none the less.

To the left, the entrance to the quarry gaped, an overgrown and rutted space between two perpendicular faces of stone where the rock had been blasted and chiselled. Between them, a thick bow of steel chain acted as a barrier against people who dumped rubbish or cars on any vacant spot.

The quarry was forbidden to every pupil at the school, which meant that everyone, at least almost every boy, had explored it at some stage, and some of the older girls had made their own teenage explorations there too. There were paths up on the ledges, worn by the feet of countless boys taking a short cut or playing truant.

Twenty yards behind, he heard the growling of the man coming after him. Feet thudded on the track, heavy and deadly. Crawford froze for a second, paralysed with fear and indecision, then he spun on his heel and ran hell for leather for the opening of the quarry. He reached the chain and leapt over it like a hurdler, his shirt-tail pulled out of his waistband and flying free.

The man came thundering down the track, moving so fast that when he reached the edge of the road his momentum carried him clear across to the far side of the road and almost into the line of trees. He looked left and right, much as Crawford had done, then the boy's loose shirt caught his eye. It flashed in the shadow of the quarry like the tail of a startled fawn. He turned and went thundering after it.

Even in the height of summer, the south faces of the quarry never saw the sun. They were covered in ivy and moss and constantly dripped the dampness down into the trenches where the masons had carved the blocks way back at the turn of the century. Jumbled and tumbled piles of stones were covered in willow-herb and wild rhubarb while, close to the sheer face, square blocks of stone, some of them ten feet tall, lay like dice thrown by a giant hand. Crawford ran for the nearest block, jinked round the side and squeezed between it and its neighbour. The narrow defile led to a series of steps which had been cut in the sandstone and he clawed his way up them, breathing hard and fast. He risked a look behind him and saw the big man come rushing in through the man-made chasm. All he saw was a shock of black hair and a flapping coat. He could hear the thud of boots on the hard ground and the angry, almost inhuman growl.

'Help,' he bawled. The cry bounced off the sheer faces of the cut rock and faded to merge with the steady drip of the seeping water.

From higher up, beyond the flat edge, the school-yard shrieks and shouts came louder as he scrambled up the narrow defile.

Below, the man was growling words which were all mashed and jumbled together and made no sense at all. Crawford pushed himself up and through the cleft and on to the top of the first massive stone block. From there he could take a run and a short jump over the yard-wide cleft that would take him to the next block. The sound of the running man's boots came thudding up to him.

'Help,' his voice was getting higher, and the word seemed to squeak out from a dry throat. His heart was thudding and kicking against his ribs and his knees threatened to buckle under him.

Up on the top, where the grass was short and the paths leading away from the fence radiated in all directions, worn smooth by the feet of those years of truancy, there was a hollow depression that had once been the original quarry-works when the stone was first cut out for an ancient farmhouse which stood on the land now occupied by the school. The hollow was bounded on three sides by a tangle of birch trees and overrun by a thick mat of creeping ivy. From the school fence, anyone inside the dip could not be seen.

Brenda Fortucci, a plump and dark-haired sixteen-year-old, whose attractions included a large and pallid pair of soft breasts and the fact that her uncle ran the café and snooker hall along Kirk Street, pushed herself away from Brian Grittan. In a couple of months a group of boys would use a scrag street-pigeon as a decoy while they robbed the store where Brenda's mother worked.

'Did you hear something?' she asked. Brian ignored the question and sneaked his hand back inside her school blouse to the smooth, yielding warmth.

'Sounds like a fight,' he said quickly, in a voice that said he couldn't care about anything outside the hollow, or outside her blouse for that matter. He gently pushed her back down on to the grass and hunched over her to press his mouth against hers. She had a soft tongue and clumps of black hair under her armpits, and Brian tantalized himself with the notion that between her thighs it was the same luscious dark shade. He hadn't risked putting his hand down there, not yet . . .

'Help, oh, please help me,' Crawford Rankine bleated. The words came out all crimped and squashed together.

Behind him he could hear the ragged breath of the man who had lifted Don up by the neck and hit him against the wall. It was much closer now. He leapt over the space on to the next

127

block and angled right up the steep track, hands scrabbling for purchase on the ivy roots.

Up in the hollow, Brenda pulled away again. 'I did hear something,' she said. Brian tried to fasten on to her again, but she squirmed away. 'Sounds like some kid.'

'There's always kids around here.' Brian was seventeen and was about to spectacularly fail in maths, French and physics, because his mind had recently become so distracted from school work. 'Come on, Brenda, the bell's going to ring in a minute.'

Over beyond the fence, a strangely hushed roar went up as the crowd around the fighting pair of boys reacted to the contest.

'Kick his head in,' a loud voice rasped.

Closer, on the other side of the dell, a higher voice called out. Brenda sat up.

'There. That's it again. Don't you hear it?' She began to fasten her blouse, flicking off the dried grass that stuck to the material.

'It's only kids playing games.'

Down below them, Crawford Rankine was climbing for his life. Here, the quarry ascended in a series of man-high steps, most of them covered in ivy runners and bindweed. The boy pushed himself up and through another narrow gap. The man was closer now, climbing fast. The boy felt his sphincter clench and unclench as if he was going to mess his pants. His throat clicked drily. In his mind's eye he saw Don's crinkly, fine hair up close to the roof of the rail wagon, while the white hand floated into the beam of sunlight.

'Ah . . . Ah . . . *AAAAAH!*' No words now, just a wavering, inarticulate cry. He reached the flat of the wide ledge where the birches leaned out of the face. There was a corner here with handholds, maybe twelve feet high. He had climbed it many a time without difficulty, taking a short cut back into school. But he had never climbed it with a maniac chasing him up the side of the quarry. Behind him, the man growled. Crawford launched himself at the corner and began to climb up, moving so fast and so desperately that his foot slipped on the smooth rock. He slid down two feet to the flat of the ledge again and started upwards once more.

Up in the hollow, Brenda got to her feet. She pushed her way through the tall stands of willow-herb close to the edge.

'Watch that, or you'll go over,' Brian warned. He was angry now, frustrated and disappointed both at once, but he didn't want to see her fall.

A hand clamped on Crawford's ankle.

It happened so suddenly that for a fraction of a second the boy thought his foot had snagged on a loop of ivy.

The fingers squeezed so hard on his tendon that a dreadful pain seared up the back of his leg. He thought he cried out but in fact no sound came out of his throat. He struggled away from the grip, managed to raise his foot six inches to the next little ledge.

Then he was down. The grip on his ankle simply jerked him off the corner of the rock. His head hit against a knuckle of stone and a white light flashed in front of his eyes. He came crashing to the flat and hit with such a thud that all of his breath came out in a whoosh of air. Another hand clamped on his neck and lifted him up just as abruptly as he had been slammed down.

'Got you,' the man's voice growled, deep as rocks grinding together.

He was lifted up and turned, as if he weighed nothing at all.

'And he took him up to a high place,' the man said slowly, in a strange, distant tone, as if he was talking to someone else. His dark hair was falling over his brow and his eyes blinked so rapidly it looked like a quick-fire series of tics.

A sudden and deadly knowledge sparked. '*Twi* . . . *twi* . . . *twi* . . .' The boy stammered.

'Call thy angels.' The face loomed close. 'And they will bear thee up.'

Crawford dimly realized that the face had not moved. It was himself who had been drawn down towards it. The face moved away. Crawford felt himself rise up. The hands let go. He was still rising. The sun flashed over the rim of the quarry. He went up into the air.

And then he was falling.

Up at the edge where the brambles hung over the face, Brenda Fortucci screamed. The boy soared out from the cleft. All she saw were the arms windmilling for balance and the legs running in the air. The figure went flying out from the rock and plummeted straight down.

'Oh, look . . . oh, Brian . . . he's . . .'

'What is it?' Brian asked, bulling through the weeds. He reached her side and she turned into him, arms grabbing for his support, breasts pressing into him.

'He fell,' she bawled. 'Oh, that boy. He fell.'

A dull, somehow deadly thud rose up from below.

Brian peered over the edge. Down on a flat rock, fifty feet below, the boy was spread-eagled on a flat block of stone. His legs were shivering violently as if an electric current was running through them. In the space of a few seconds, a stain spread out underneath the boy's jacket, turning the rock dark.

'Oh Brian, he's dead. I know he is.'

He grabbed her by the hand and went running for the fence. Down on the hillside, one of the teachers had pushed his way into the centre of the crowd and was now hauling two bloodied boys out by the scruffs of their necks.

'Help,' Brian Grittan shouted. 'Mr Doyle!'

Brenda made a soft sighing sound and fell in a dead faint at his feet. Suddenly, without warning, Brian's gorge clenched, opened, and he retched so violently his recent lunch sprayed all over the fence and his prostrate girlfriend.

CHAPTER THIRTEEN

'Look at that,' Doug called out, pointing straight ahead. The others reached the low brow of the hill and stood beside him. Down the slope, the four black pools, each of them almost perfectly circular except for the last, which was kidney-shaped, descended in steps. They were evenly spaced and nearly identical in size, as if they had been dug for a purpose.

'Dead-straight line,' Billy said. 'The bombers must have come right over the hills.' He stuck his arms out and made a noise like a fighter plane in a dive, and started to run down the hill zigzagging left and right. He stopped halfway and beckoned to them with a wave of his arm.

The others started to follow him down towards the craters.

The first one was deep and ridged all around its rim where the earth had been thrown up by the force of the explosion twenty years before.

'Just like a crater on the moon,' Corky said. A dragonfly came soaring towards them, buzzing like a miniature helicopter. It banked on clattering wings before it reached them and zoomed out across the still water.

'We must be close,' Danny said. 'If they were dropping their bombs up here.'

Tom shrugged. 'Could still be miles away.' His face was still smudged with dust and ash and streaked with his tears. He had come along with them but he looked more reluctant to stay. Behind them, far in the distance, a pall of smoke still hung in the sky, but it was fading away now, just a veil of grey against the blue. From where they stood, the town, three miles away, was hidden from view by the curve of the hill. The faint sounds of the foundry steam hammer and the clanging from the shipyard down in the distance had all but faded, leaving only the piping of a curlew on the hill and the liquid sound of a lark rising on the hot air.

They ambled down towards the lowest crater-hole, this one

completely round and deeper than all the others. The water was slick and patched with duckweed. Pond skaters slid on the surface, while underneath them, water-boatmen darted in search of prey. They dropped their bags in a heap and slung the tent beside them. All five of them lay on the sheep-shorn grass at the lip of the pond and peered down into the depths.

Danny reached out slowly and dipped his hand under the surface, sending the slick of algae undulating in slow ripples. 'It's warm. You could swim in it.'

He moved his hand slowly, very slowly, only an inch or two above the silt a foot below the surface close to the bank. Corky watched and saw a long, black shape resting on the mud close to Danny's creeping fingers.

'What's that?' he started to ask, but just as he did, Danny lunged and hauled his hand clear of the water. Without hesitation, he dropped the black shape on the grass. It was three inches long and wriggled furiously out of its element, twisting its segmented, coal-black body this way and that.

'Dragonfly,' Danny said and everybody crowded round.

'Can't be,' Billy contradicted. 'It hasn't got any wings. Creepy-looking beastie.'

'It's a larva. It's got to change first. It climbs up a stalk and breaks out.'

'Metamorphosity,' Corky said, knowingly.

'Ugly *baskit*,' Doug said. 'Bet it can't wait to grow up.' They all laughed.

Danny broke a stem of reed and jabbed it close to the insect's bulbous eyes. Immediately the bottom jaw shot out with a tiny *click*. It looked like a long, jointed arm, jagged with grabbing spines. The underslung mandible clawed viciously.

'Jeez-o, it's a flamin' monster,' Billy exclaimed.

The jaw snatched the reed and pulled at it, and they all crowded round to watch the alien, wriggling thing twist and turn, viciously defending itself.

'There's a big water beetle that's got pincers,' Corky said, holding his hands up at the side of his mouth and using his first fingers to imitate the motion of how those pincers worked. 'Big enough to go right through your skin, right into the bone. If it flies into you it can crack your skull.'

'Well, I'm not swimming in here,' Tom said. 'You could get bitten to death. It must be full of creepy-crawlies like that. Probably piranhas as well.'

Billy got to his feet and, without warning, he stamped down hard on the black larva. It crunched against the grass. 'Something that ugly shouldn't be allowed to live,' he said, grinning. Doug made a disgusted sound in the back of his throat.

'How would you like somebody to do that to you?' Danny asked, getting to his feet. The black larva twisted slowly now, broken and burst, its legs clawing weakly at the air. Yellow liquid oozed out from the split in its abdomen.

'Nobody big enough,' Billy said, wiping his foot on the grass. He grinned. 'And I'm not ugly, neither.'

He sauntered round the pool while Danny watched angrily, wishing he hadn't caught the insect, even if Billy was right. It was ugly and alien, something from a nightmare, but it would have gone on living if he'd left it, and some day it would have turned into one of the long, flickering streaks of black and gold that cruised on the summer air, hunting for insects.

Billy hunkered down. Something splashed in the water right in front of him. He reached, made a grab, missed his footing and stumbled forward into the pool. One foot sank into the soft mud.

'Dammit,' he grunted. He reached again and snatched a bobbing shape up from the floating duckweed, then hauled himself out. His baseball boot and the leg of his jeans were red with mud. He shook his foot, then turned and held up the fat, green frog, waving it like a trophy.

'Hello, *froggy*,' he sang, making his voice grate like a juvenile Louis Armstrong's. He brought it across and thrust it in Tom's face. The smaller boy squirmed away from it.

'What, scared of frogs?' Billy demanded.

'No, I'm not,' Tom protested. 'It's covered in slime.'

Billy giggled. 'You can have great fun with frogs. Watch.'

He searched around for a dried piece of reed and broke off a narrow stem, holding it up to the light to see if it was hollow.

'You have to watch for earwigs with these things. They crawl into your mouth and down your throat.' He held the frog tightly while they watched. The creature jerked powerfully in an attempt to escape but Billy had its head in a strong grip. The legs pinioned helplessly.

'See its hole?'

Doug agreed that he could see it. Billy jabbed the reed at it. The legs kicked desperately. There was a little pop sound and the end of the reed disappeared into the frog's vent.

'Aw, Billy,' Corky protested. 'That's bloody awful.'

Billy grinned, and moved his eyebrows up and down. 'Now for the piece of the resistance,' he said, mimicking Gomez Addams. He bent his head, put the free end of the reed in his mouth and blew steadily, puffing his cheeks out with pressure.

The frog inflated. Billy squeezed the free end of the tube to close it and leant back.

'You're lookin' swell, *froggy*,' he sang. He breathed in through his nose and blew again. The frog blew up to the size of a tennis-ball. The sun glinted on transparent skin. The round body swelled so much, the spots on its pale belly had expanded to the size of shirt-buttons. The yellow eyes glared out from a distended head.

'Look at its face,' Doug said.

It was an odd moment of fascination, tinged with disgust and blackly cruel humour. Danny and Corky each screwed up their own faces, but they did not stop watching. Billy blew again and the frog expanded even more. 'I can tell, *froggy*!'

'It's going to burst,' Doug said, shaking his head and taking a step back, and holding his hands up protectively just in case. 'Give it a break, Billy.'

'You're still growin', you're still *growin*',' Billy rasped.

'Oh, that's really rotten,' Tom said, and then, without warning, he burst into horrified laughter. Danny looked at him, feeling the disgust rise inside himself. He turned to the frog. Its eyes were bulging now and it bore a look of complete and mute bewilderment. A hiccup of laughter bubbled up from inside him and he tried to swallow it down, feeling a flush of shame at how hysterically funny he found this.

'Looks like Fat Sonia Kowalski,' Corky said. Doug giggled, then the two of them exploded with laughter. Billy turned and the frog slipped from his hands. It fell off the reed impaling its vent and landed on the water. Immediately bubbles came farting out in a steady stream. Its legs kicked out but it was still swollen to five times its size, and they only paddled against air, hardly touching the water at all. It floated like a balloon on the duck-weed, turning slowly in a little circle.

Billy let out a howl. Tom was holding his sides. Danny and Doug were holding on to each other, convulsing with laughter, and Corky was lying on the ground doubled up. They were completely helpless for several minutes until the hysteria passed.

'God, that was really mean,' Doug said, the manic laughter still in his eyes. He tried to keep his face straight and failed. 'You should be done by the animal inspector.'

'Look at it,' Billy said. 'It's as big as a flamin' football, and it's farting away like crazy.'

'Fat Sonia,' Doug said, remembering what Corky had said, and he was off again, bending over and holding his belly with both hands. 'Oh, stop it,' he pleaded. 'Don't make me laugh.'

'That's really rotten,' Tom said, stifling his laughter. 'It never did any harm.'

'It's only a frog,' Billy said, dismissively. 'What are you worried about? They don't feel pain like us.' He turned, picked up his pack and started walking towards the lip of the valley.

The rest of them looked at each other. Danny felt a flush of shame creep across his face, making it hot and red. It had been cruel, dreadfully cruel, but it had been funny and the frog *had* looked like Fat Sonia Kowalski. The inflated frog was out in the middle, vainly trying to cross a patch of weed. It would die in the heat for sure. The flush of hot disgust, at the frog's torture and at his own laughter, stayed with him.

'He's right off his head,' Tom said with feeling. 'I'm telling you. He's ten cents on the dollar.'

Behind the next ridge of tussock grass, Billy turned. 'Come on, you lot. At the double.'

Doug shrugged, sniffed. They moved on past the ridge of the crater, leaving the algae ripples to settle to silence, and the dragonflies snatching clegs and horseflies out of the air.

It was another hour before they got to the floor of the valley where the Blackwood stream tumbled clear and fast over the smooth rocks. They had followed the contours of the hill, travelling parallel to the flow of the water, walking on the sheep-tracks until they reached the end of the thick forest that covered both sides. Beyond that, single trees and small clumps grew here and there, perched precariously on the steep sides of the valley, hazels and ash and some alders. The stream had cut the moorland into grooves here, deep gorges that fell away down to the twisting flow below. High on the sides, scrubby hawthorns and an occasional rowan clung to almost sheer walls. Branching tributaries bringing the winter melt-water down from the Blackwood hills to the west and the Langmuir crags on the east side, cut the land into chevrons of gullies and fissures. The five boys trudged along the edge, tired and slow now, and ready for a rest from carrying their bags and the increasingly heavy dead-weight of the tent. The valley swooped below them, the steep sides lined and striated with alternating dark bands of thick shale sandwiched between hard mudstone which slashed white parallel lines in layers from the stream bed to the high ridge of the canyon lip.

'It's like something out of the movies,' Doug said. They had caught up with Billy and nobody mentioned the frog. 'Like cowboys and indians.'

'*Treasure of the Sierra Madre*,' Corky said. 'That's what it's like.' He turned to the others. 'We don' have to show you any *steengking* badges,' he said in a reasonable imitation of a Mexican bandido. Danny grinned widely at the impersonation and lopped the head off a nettle with his stick. Billy looked puzzled.

'It's a film,' Corky explained. 'Really good, and scary, too. The baddy gets it in the end. But the book's better. You should read one some time.'

Billy threw him a look that told them all he wasn't interested in books.

'It's like the Grand Canyon,' Tom said. 'I saw a picture of it in geography. It goes down for miles and it's got these lines all along the sides. I've never been up as far as this before.'

'Right up in the wilds now, Tiny Tom,' Billy said. 'Miles from home. Only us mountain men and the wild frontier.'

'There's bears and wolves and sabre-tooth tigers up here,' Doug added, grinning his wide, goofy smile.

'Tyrannosauruses and stegosaurs,' Danny threw in.

'Giant spiders,' Corky said, keeping it up. 'Martians with three eyes.'

'And window-lickers from the special-school bus,' Tom said. He rolled his eyes up and let his tongue hang out imbecilically. 'That's you lot, that is. A bunch of morons if you believe all that stuff. And I bet you do, every one of you.'

They started down the slope, reached the edge where the grass stopped and the steep shale fell away for more than a hundred feet at such a steep angle it seemed almost vertical from where they stood. Doug stepped back from the edge. 'It's high, isn't it?'

'Not really,' Tom said mildly. 'Only from up here. It looks further than it is, I think.'

'I don't like heights,' Doug said. 'I got stuck on the quarry once. Scared the shite out of me. It took me ages to get the nerve up to climb down and I missed most of the afternoon.'

'What quarry, the one behind the school?' Danny asked. 'Where Crawford Rankine fell off?'

Doug nodded gravely. 'Yeah.'

'Got thrown off,' Tom corrected. 'They thought he fell at first, but he got thrown off. Same time as Don Whalen was caught. Brenda Fortucci saw it all.'

Doug shrugged, not caring for the moment, though this was something they'd all discussed, and at length, in the long weeks running up towards the end of the school holidays. He looked down to where the Blackwood stream meandered down there, a silver snake crawling through the steep valley. 'I hate falling. I'd rather get shot.'

'Like my old man,' Billy said. 'He got shot a couple of times. You don't feel it if it gets you in the head. You don't even hear it. He wiped out a whole Japanese patrol, so he did.'

He stuck his hands in his pockets. 'He could have taken Cammy Galt and Plooks McGill and your Phil all at the one time. He could have molocated old Twitchy, that's for certain. No bother.'

Doug ignored him and looked away. They'd all heard it before. 'Can we find somewhere that isn't so steep? You could fall and break your neck here.'

'It's all right,' Corky told him. 'It's not as steep as it looks, and even if you fall you won't go far. Watch.'

Corky took a leap forward. Doug blurted a warning as his

friend leapt off the edge. Corky yelled at the top of his voice and went plummeting down. He hit the slope feet first, sending up a bow-wave of shale, and then went sliding down the scree on his backside, forcing a fountain of gravel into the air, leaving a deep groove of his passing. Danny went skidding right behind him and Doug was encouraged enough to follow. Billy took the rear, bouncing down heavily, leaving wide footprints with every stride. In only a few minutes, they reached the bottom, and followed the stream until they reached a flat part at the conjunction with another of the feeder tributaries that had cut the chasms in the moor slope. The twin gorges angled away from each other, each of them filled with the echoing sound of running water. Danny stripped off his canvas shoes and threw his socks on to the grass. He rolled up the legs of his jeans and waded into the clear stream shallows just down from the deeper pool where the crystal water tumbled through a low cleft. Corky kicked off his old, scuffed boots and followed him in.

'What's it like?' Doug asked, struggling out of his torn denims.

'Magic,' Corky told him. He came out of the water and rubbed the droplets from his legs. Already he was getting some brown hairs on his calves. Danny, who had now stripped off his own denims, looked at them enviously. His own legs were white and smooth.

'Let's get the tent fixed up,' Corky said, still dripping water. 'Then we can light a fire.'

'Bags me to light it,' Billy demanded. 'I can get a blaze going with one match.'

'Yeah, we know that. Just so long as it stays in one place,' Tom said rancorously. 'You nearly killed us the last time.'

'Oh, give it a rest, *Titch*,' Billy rounded on him. 'It was an accident, ok? He pulled his T-shirt over his head, slung it behind him and ran up to the rocky ledge at the side of the pool. Without stopping, he scrambled to the edge.

'Bombs away . . .'

His cry echoed down the valley. He leapt into the air, bunched his legs together and hugged his knees so that he curled into a tight ball and hit the water so hard the impact sounded like a drum in the confines of the pool. An immense splash of water arched out on all sides, soaking the bags and the tent.

Billy came up to the surface, his black hair glistening in the sun. Underneath him the red mud which had dried on the leg of his jeans dissolved in the current and trailed downstream in banded clouds of ochre silt like streams of blood.

August 1, 4 p.m.

He watched their progress from the cover of the thick trees on the other side of the valley, standing very still so that he betrayed no movement at all.

The fire had died away but there was still a musky smell of grass smoke on the dry air, mingled with the aroma of burnt gorse and its perfumed pollen. The hills up beyond the farm rolled away into the distance, barren of trees up this high, covered in heath and heather and thick bracken fronds.

The five of them had followed the sheep-track down to the pools and then they had moved on. He followed for a while, feeling the tide of heat swell inside him. He was in no hurry, none at all. The time was not yet right. There were still things to do, important things.

He hunkered down beside a fallen pine tree that had broken its back as it tumbled, and pulled a piece of dried meat from his pocket, smoked pork from the dry-store next to the farmhouse kitchen. He chewed on it absently, waiting until the troop of boys began to angle down the slope, like a patrol in the hills. If he listened he might hear them call out.

Dung-fly. There was no rush. Up here he had all the time in the world to do what he had to do. There was no hurry for now. He would watch and he would wait. He would let them know, at some stage, when the time was right, who he was and why he had come.

He rose to his feet and went down into the trees, heading back towards the farm, where the others were waiting for him. He blinked several times in quick succession and the world flickered in a strobe of flashes, intermittent light and dark. The boys were going along the ridge at the edge of the valley, where the land fell away sharply in the narrow cleft down to the stream, in a line, just like a troop of infiltrators. It was steep there. Maybe one of them would fall . . .

CHAPTER FOURTEEN

June

In the dark he could hear his own breathing, a watery snuffle. He could feel wet on his cheek and the dull throb that told him he'd been cut, but as yet there was no pain there. Not for now. The memory of pain hovered close in the darkness, but it was hard to remember anything else.

He'd been with Crawford and Derek. No, not Derek; *he*'d gone back on the other side of the fence, gone back to school. Crawford had been there. Where was he now?

He tried to think, but it was difficult. The dark wavered and broke up into small spangles of light when the numb dizziness came swirling in on him again. Going fishing. Taking the day off to cast a spinner in the river and test that big run of sea trout. Down the path, teasing the dogs, then through the sheet-iron fence and past the tall weeds. The door had squealed open and he'd looked in and something – *a man* – had grabbed him. Hit him. It had happened so quickly that he hadn't even had time to react. Crawford had said something. The noise had come from the shadows. An image of balloon-like breasts hovered there on the wall, and then the looming shape coming out of the dark.

The pain had been unbelievable. The shadow had slashed out and hit him right on the side of the head and the whole world had exploded into a fountain of whirling sparks. The pain had punched from one side of his skull to the other as his head smacked against the wooden planks. Another explosion, more fiery, more volcanic than the first, blossomed in a burst of heat and hurt.

'Look at the ti . . .' Crawford had said, and then he'd stopped. To Don he had sounded suddenly far away in the distance.

Something had him by the neck, but there were sparks bursting in front of his eyes and he couldn't see. All he could feel was the pain in his head and the rolling nausea bubbling up inside him. There was a pressure on his neck and he was flying into the air.

He could remember his eyes, blind with the whirling lights, bulging in their sockets, and he recalled the collapsing sensation of his windpipe.

The pain in his throat was coming back now and his head was throbbing. The metallic smell of blood was in his mouth and his nose and when he tried to cry out he found he couldn't make a sound.

Where was Crawford? Had something happened to him?

He tried to move, but his shoulder screeched with pain so badly that the little lights started orbiting in the dark again. Outside, out there beyond the door, the angry sound of dogs barking started up. Somebody yelled and another boy laughed.

Crawford? Were he and Derek coming back? He turned and smeared a trail of blood on the floor.

Somebody rattled a stick along a taut wire, making it jangle. The greyhounds started up their hysterical barking once more.

'Skinny, big buggers,' a boy's voice bawled. Another boy sniggered again. Not Crawford, not Derek. A metal sound, like a tin can banged against something hard, rang out tunelessly. The dogs went into a frenzy. He could hear the thud of running feet and the whoops of schoolboys, sounding just like himself and his pals, but they were out there, running up the track he had come down. They were heading back to school and he was, he was . . .

The pit-bull terrier roared savagely and Don could hear the protesting squeal of wire as it slammed against the fence, followed by the jeering laughter of the boys going up the hill. He tried to call out again but all he managed was a gurgle in the back of his throat.

He shivered involuntarily, smearing blood against the floor again, and a bubble swelled at his nostril before bursting silently. Far off in the distance, he could hear the clamour of kids up on the hill behind the school, like the squalling of wheeling gulls, faint but clear. Here and there he could make out an individual hoarse cry, a higher yell. Somebody screamed like a girl. All the normal noises of school at lunch-time.

The scream came again, high and wavering, distant, but closer than the school sounds. A moment later the bell rang, to tell everyone to line up and get ready for the afternoon classes.

Crawford had disappeared. Don tried to think, but he couldn't remember. Had he run away? He must have. He must have seen what had happened. He would be up there at the school getting help, getting a doctor, calling for an ambulance. Help would be here soon.

He tried to stop shivering, but he couldn't find a way, and the heel of his black school-shoe drummed an uneven rap on the hard floor. His throat spasmed and a sudden dread overtook him that it would lock shut and he would choke on the blood. He coughed and a saw-blade of hurt rasped into his shoulder. Of a sudden, Don Whalen's mind cleared enough to let him realize that he was in awful danger. Very slowly he got a hand to the floor. He could smell the blood and the dismal reek of human shit, and he couldn't tell whether it was his own.

Crawford had gone to get help. That was for sure. Wasn't it? He eased his hand down. It pressed into a wet puddle that could have been anything, and then he gingerly levered himself up from the floor, one millimetre at a time, breath rasping, head pounding, shoulder screeching in protest. He got to a sitting position, still in the dark. The school sounds had faded, though they would have been hard to hear over the gasp of his breath. Don pulled himself to the corner, where he thought the door would be, and he raised his hand to press it against the planking.

His fingers left an almost perfect handprint. It was the full stop at the end of his tortuous two-yard crawl. Another smudge of dried blood showed where the sickness and pain and exhaustion had caused him to slip to the floor. Some time later, he couldn't tell how long, thudding footsteps roused him out of the dizzy stupor.

Don Whalen came almost awake when the door opened and a slender column of light widened to a thick pillar before being cut off again. The floor and the walls of the rail wagon shuddered as the door rolled back on its casters and slammed shut with an awful finality. He still had not seen anything except the brief flash of light.

In the dark he could hear the rough sound of breathing, over-laying his own laboured breath and he knew he was not alone.

'Crawford?' he tried to say, though he somehow knew it was not his friend. He lay there, frozen in the sudden clench of fear. The breathing continued for a while, ragged and effortful, dreadfully close in the dark. Then a footstep shivered the floor and the breathing got louder.

Derek Milne had turned back from the fence, got halfway to the wall, and then stopped and turned back again. He'd an essay to hand in to Matt Bryson, the English teacher, one which should have gone in two days ago, but which he had pretended to have forgotten, though in truth he hadn't even written it. His two friends had gone down the track and in half an hour, he knew they'd be at the Pulpit Pool on the river, casting for sea trout.

Indecision stopped him in his tracks. It was a good June day, late for a run of trout, but last week's rain had raised the river level enough to give a decent head of water and bring fish in from the estuary. The afternoon stretched dismally ahead of him. A dull period of maths and another two, even duller, of English. He walked ten yards, stopped, looked back at the fence. Beyond there, he could hear the yapping of the greyhounds and the deeper growl of another dog, and he knew his friends would be at the bottom of the track by now, heading past the quarry to get the fishing-rods from Crawford's garden hut.

He turned back to the fence, swithered some more, torn between the desire to go fishing and the sense of self-preservation that demanded he get down to school and write the essay for Matt Bryson. Derek even put his hands on the fence, ready to limbo under the bottom bar, when he changed his mind again and ruefully turned back, heading up the hill towards the Hump. He got over the rise and saw the milling crowd that had swelled to three or four times what it had been when he and the others had gone up the hill together. As soon as he crested the shoulder of the hill the noise had hit him like a physical force. Boys and girls, too, were in the crowd, crushed together in a swarm. In the nucleus, from his height advantage, he could see a fist rise up and fall again. The crowd growled, like a single entity, a strange and eerily fierce sound, a mixture of alarm and primitive hunger.

'What's going on?' a man's voice bellowed. Mr Doyle, the junior maths teacher, came hurrying up the slope on short, sturdy legs.

'Stop that this minute,' he shouted, quite ineffectually. Nobody heard him. In the milling crowd, everybody was trying to get a ringside view of the two combatants. Derek made his way down the hill just as Mr Doyle was coming up. He got to the edge of the crowd as it swelled and contracted with a life all of its own, feeling the strange infection of excitement reach and invade him.

'All of you, move back from there,' the teacher snapped, peeved at the lack of response. His face was red with effort as he came up the hill at a trot. A few of the girls closest to him peeled away from the crowd. One of them had lost a shoe and was hopping about trying to keep her white ankle-sock off the ground.

Another fist flew and a sound like a mallet-strike cracked in the air. The mob let out a collective groan of appreciation. A boy yelled, high and vicious. Another cried out, angry but also frightened.

Mr Doyle waded into the crowd, pulling bodies by the scruffs of their blazers and the hoods of their anoraks, shoving them aside as he thrust his way to the nucleus. In a few seconds he was up to his shoulders in the press of pupils, as much part of the crowd as they were, jostled left and right by the wheeling mass. Finally he reached the centre. Derek Milne saw him duck down. He was almost knocked off his feet, but he managed to steady himself and, when he came up again, he had a boy in each hand, fingers clenched on their collars.

The crowd sighed its disappointment and immediately began to fragment as if some physical attractant had been switched off. Derek Milne strolled down the hill past the scattering clumps of pupils. The two boys were still charged up with anger and adrenaline and, despite the dire warnings from the young teacher, they were still trying to aim kicks at each other. Both of them had bloodied noses and their clothes were slick with mud. The taller of the two had a black eye swollen and closed over. The stockier one had a thin trail of blood leaking from his ear.

Derek moved past them, feeling the hot and somehow dangerous elation drain away from him, and walked down, bag swinging on his hip, towards the school.

Just as he reached the wall a girl screeched from the top of the

Hump, up beyond where the fight had been. He turned and saw that Mr Doyle had stopped. The girl screamed again, but from the distance, Derek couldn't make out what she said. Mr Doyle let the boys go and went up the hill. They made good their escape before he had got ten yards. Derek grinned and turned into the doorway just as the bell rang shrill, to head for the maths class where, with some luck, he could sit at the back and write his essay. It was not until the middle of the afternoon that he heard the news.

'Rankine's fell off the quarry.'

Derek stopped in his tracks. He was just coming out of the maths class and about to go up the stairs to Matt Bryson's room to present his delayed and hastily scrawled work when he heard a boy tell another with obvious shuddery relish: 'Broke his neck, so he did. There's blood all over the place, I heard.'

'What's that?' Derek asked, more curious, not sure of what he had heard.

'Didn't you hear? Your pal Rankine fell off the quarry. Took a header.'

'Nah,' Derek said, 'he couldn't have. He was nowhere near the quarry . . .' he stopped again. Crawford and Don had gone down the track to the back road. They would have been only yards away from the old quarry entrance.

'It's true, honest. Brian Grittan and Big Brenda Fortucci saw him. They were up on the other side of the fence. She's down at the nurse screaming her head off.'

'When did . . . ?' Derek started. 'I mean . . .'

The other boys looked at him. Everybody was buzzing with the news, the little horror that had happened to somebody else, all the more shivery and exciting because it had happened to somebody they knew. He got to the top of the stairs where the rest of the class were lined up outside the English room. Everybody was looking at him expectantly.

'Didn't you and Don go up to the fence with Craw?' somebody asked. Matt Bryson popped his head out of the doorway. Derek just turned round and ran down the steps.

'Milne, get yourself back here, boy!' the teacher bellowed. 'And you'd better have that essay.'

Derek threw himself down the stairs and along the corridor,

pushing smaller kids out of the way. He got to the east exit and went out, running hard now, and by the time he got to the top of the Hump, he was gasping for breath. On the other side of the fence, the janitor and two of the teachers were standing close to the drop. Beyond the tip, Derek could see nothing but the blue, winking light of an ambulance reflected repetitively from the damp stone face on the other side.

'Sir,' he called out. One of the teachers turned round. 'Sir, who was it got hurt?'

'Shouldn't you be in class?' Mr Doyle asked.

'Yes sir, but you have to tell me. Who was it?'

The teacher looked at him, considering. The boy was clearly agitated. He gave a little shrug, which conveyed kindly intent more than anything else.

'Crawford Rankine. Is he a friend of . . .'

'Sir, is he dead?'

'That I can't tell you, sonny,' Mr Doyle replied. Derek backed away from the fence, hot tears beginning to swim and blur his vision.

Robert Doyle, known to the pupils as Wee Bob, had reacted very quickly when he'd got to the top of the hill. The two combatants escaped and ran away, and he forgot all about them when he saw the prostrate girl on the other side of the fence. He scaled it with surprising agility and when he dropped to the far side where the boy was kneeling over the girl, he smelt the sour stink of vomit.

'What happened?' he asked. 'Come on, Brian, she's been sick. Has she eaten something? Drunk something?' The boy mumbled, and then he threw up again. For a few seconds Bob Doyle thought they'd both been sick. But the boy wiped his mouth.

'No, sir, she's fainted.' He jerked his thumb over his shoulder. 'It's the boy. He's dead.'

The teacher looked at him, brows knitted together in puzzlement. On the grass the girl moaned. A couple of her buttons had loosened and a large white breast, marbled with blue veins, was trying to pop out under the pressure of its own weight. Bob Doyle drew his eyes away.

'Over there, sir. He fell off the quarry.' The boy's face contorted and his mouth spasmed in a wide, retching gape, but he managed to contain it this time. 'Brenda fainted. There's blood all over the place,' he added.

Just as he said that, the girl's eyes fluttered open and she pushed herself upright. She took one look at Brian and fell back against the grass again. Mr Doyle got to the edge of the quarry and looked down. There was nothing to be seen down there. The base of the old diggings was far below, hidden in the shade and the clumps of brambles and tangled dog-roses. The massive blocks of stone heaped on each other in a series of giant steps leading to the bottom. There was nobody down at the quarry bed, no bloody and broken body.

Brian Grittan came stumbling over to join him, and the teacher grabbed the boy by the elbow, wondering if perhaps he and the girl had been drinking. He began to lean inwards to smell the boy's breath when the lad pointed down and to the left where the thick ivy rooted in a crevice. Bob Doyle followed the pointed finger. The flat surface of a block of red sandstone lay close to the vertical wall. He blinked and everything jumped into focus. It was no red sandstone. It was a red splash on the stone. The body lay spread-eagled close to the edge. Palms up, white face tilted to the blue sky.

'Oh, my God,' the teacher whispered.

He stared at the blood and at the still body for a few moments longer. Then he turned, grabbed the boy by the arm and walked him back to the fence. He told him to stay with the girl and not to let her near the edge, fearful that she might wake up and stumble over the precipice. That done, he clambered over the fence and ran down the hill and into the school. The ambulance got to the quarry in thirteen minutes and, by the time the crew reached the flat rock, Father O'Connor, the school chaplain, who had been giving a religious talk on the need for chastity in these devilish times, had clambered down with Bob Doyle and Jake Denning, the physical-education teacher. The priest was anointing the boy's bloodied head, hoping to speed his soul through the searing, unavoidable, cleansing fires of purgatory.

As it happened, Crawford Rankine was not dead. He was one of the few people who had come in contact with the man with the twitchy eyes and survived. He lost four pints of blood and had a dreadful depressed fracture in his skull. His pelvis and both elbows were shattered and needed twenty-seven pins in an operation described at the time as 'pioneering'. But he was not dead.

It was a surprise to the police that he woke up two days later and was able, despite his injury, to tell them what had happened, up to the point of climbing up the quarry with the man hot on his heels. After that, he could not remember anything. Neither did he know what had happened to his friend, Don Whalen. He thought the man had hit him.

Derek Milne ran all the way to Crawford's place, still unable to believe what had happened, that his friend had been killed in the quarry. He sneaked in through the old wooden gate, hunching down out of sight behind the trimmed privet hedge, and round to the garden hut, knowing that the teacher had got it wrong, and that the rods would be gone, and somebody else, somebody he didn't really know, would be lying dead at the bottom of the cliff.

But the old Greenheart spinning rod and the even older split-cane wand were angled in the corner of the shed.

By now Derek was badly frightened. He hadn't waited around to ask what had happened to Don, but if he had been with Crawford in the quarry, then he was probably hurt as well. No matter what had happened, he himself was in big trouble, because he knew they were dodging off school to go fishing. He had condoned it. If he had stopped them, Crawford would still be alive. (And if he'd gone with them, he too could be smashed on a rock in the quarry.) He went round to Don's place and hung about, scared and guilty. His friend's young sister came home after four and got the key on the string inside the letter-box. She let herself in. Don waited for an hour. Mrs Whalen came, carrying two bags of groceries. Later, Don's father came in, hands still black from the foundry. Derek went home, and his mother, who had been on the verge of calling the police, demanded to know where he'd been. It was at this point that Derek burst into real tears and told his mother that his friend had been killed.

At eight o'clock that night, Sergeant McNicol knocked on the door. The big, uniformed policeman who was with him accepted a cup of tea and dwarfed Derek's father as they sat round the kitchen table, with Derek's pale face between them.

Angus McNicol's face visibly brightened when he heard Derek's story. It was bad, but it could have been worse.

'So the boys were going fishing and you turned back?'

Derek nodded.

'But they must have come back as well, taking the short cut to school,' Angus prompted, and the boy nodded again. 'So with a bit of luck, then the other boy could still be in the quarry?'

Angus slapped the boy on the shoulder. He was grinning from ear to ear because, as soon as he heard a boy had gone missing, he had feared the worst. Now there was a perfectly logical and reasonable explanation. Both boys had scaled the face of the quarry. If one had fallen, it was a fair assumption that the other had been with him. He could have tumbled, fallen into a crevice and, if that was true, the chances were that he'd be hurt too, but possibly still alive. Even if he was dead, McNicol thought pragmatically, it would be better for all, better for the town if he'd fallen off a cliff and died, rather than been killed by the maniac who had taken the lives of Neil Hopkirk and little Lucy Saunders. Most likely, Angus thought to himself, as he admitted many years later, Don Whalen had got such a scare, seeing his pal crash on to the rock, that he'd simply run away and was hiding somewhere, probably still in a state of shock. He'd turn up.

'I've got good news, sonny,' he told the pale and snivelling lad. 'Young Crawford's hurt pretty sore, but he's still alive. You did the right thing not dodging school, especially with this bad fellow around the town, but I hope you've learnt a lesson. You've got to stay with your mates, stay close, and don't be bunking off anywhere out of sight. This man's a nasty piece of work.'

'Don't worry, sergeant,' Derek's father said. 'He certainly has learnt a lesson.'

The police set up floodlights on the top of the quarry and angled them down, bathing the whole workings in silvery light and sending harsh shadows behind every bush and clump of ivy. The lights glistened from the damp sheen on the vertical faces. They brought the dogs in to search all over and a team of divers from the navy base came down in a big, blue truck and searched all night in the narrow shafts that were filled with water. They found the carcass of a black Labrador dog that had fallen in and was now bloated with gas. At the bottom of one shaft they found a human foot, now bare bones, inside a remarkably well-preserved boot, and at first the police thought they had another murder hunt on their hands, until it was proven to be fifty years old. Its former owner, a seventy-five-year-old retired quarrier who stayed with his daughter in the far end of town, had lost it in a blasting accident just after the First World War and the foot had never been discovered until now.

There was no sign at all of Don Whalen.

Two days later, Crawford Rankine woke up and told the police about the man who had chased him – a tall man with dark eyes and thick black hair hanging below his collar – and Hector Kelso, who was in charge of the murder hunt, knew the man with the twitchy eyes had struck again.

'We're looking for a body,' he told the team.

They did not find it for ten days.

Police Superintendent Kelso, using his genius for reconstructing the scene, worked out what had happened. The door of the railway truck was wide open, letting in the bright sunlight. He'd put down folded newspapers where he wanted to put his feet, even after the place had been sampled and dusted by the forensics team. He pointed out where the boy had been knocked against the wood, and where his shoe had hit the other side, leaving a scuff of mud.

'My guess is that the man came back pretty quickly,' Kelso had said. 'Maybe if the boy had had more time, even just a couple of minutes, he'd have found the door, but I don't think he'd have opened it. But he was moving on his own all right. These prints are clean, not smeared, and you can see where he's been pushing himself along. He was hurt, but not dead. You can rely on that.' Kelso looked around at the rest of them. 'But I won't take any bets that he's alive now.'

CHAPTER FIFTEEN

August 1, 5 p.m.

The bird flapped laboriously into the air, a grey shadow rising above the ferns bordering the stream. Without thinking, more an instinctive reaction, Danny threw his stick at the motion, and his aim, quite uncharacteristically for him, was easily six feet wide of the mark. The stick flew through the air, making a whirring sound as it spun end over end.

The slow, whooshing wing-beats pushed the heron forward, the neck curved in a white serpent-shape and its long dagger-beak pointed at the sky. It flew straight into the path of the whirling piece of wood. The thrown stick caught it at the base of the neck and the bird simply stalled in its flight. The branch flipped onwards and landed in a hazel bush. A small, white breast-feather tumbled outwards. The heron dropped to the earth and hit with a thump. One wing flapped madly, while the other was clenched tight in against its body. The beating wing carried the big bird around in ungainly circles, a graceful thing now graceless, clumsy and broken.

'Bloody *great* shot,' Billy whooped.

Danny's heart sank. He hadn't even known what he was throwing at. He had only seen a movement beside the ferns, a rabbit, maybe a hare. He'd lobbed plenty of rocks at plenty of rabbits for many a summer, and he'd never succeeded in hitting any one of them.

Now the beautiful bird was down, its beak opening and closing like a slender trap, making no bird noise, but emitting a harsh and ragged hiss that made him think it was choking. Its head was twisted at an odd angle.

'Didya see that shot?' Billy yelled again. Doug, following behind, still stripped to his string vest, popped his head over the fern tops.

'What's happening?'

Danny ran forward, the soles of his thin canvas shoes pattering on the smooth stones as he crossed the stream at the shallows.

Billy was right behind him, ignoring the stepping-stones, splashing through the water.

The heron flapped madly with its one good wing.

'Kill it,' Billy said. 'Kill it before it gets away.'

Danny froze. The bird was broken. The long and slender legs were stuck out below it as if they were incapable of taking the weight. A delicate crest of feathers flowed back from the smooth, white head. The long, yellow dagger of a beak opened and closed with a faint snapping noise.

'I didn't mean it,' Danny said.

'Did you hit it?' Doug called from the far side. 'What is it? A cormorant?'

'It's a flamin' stork.'

'A heron,' Danny said lamely. He edged forward and picked up his stick. The bird hissed and its bright-yellow eye fixed on him. It made a lunge to protect itself, the beak knifing forward, but its coordination went awry and the lunge took it a foot past Danny's toe. The beak slapped on the short grass like a misthrown knife. An unbidden tear sparked in Danny's eye and he blinked it back.

'I didn't mean it, honest,' he protested. If he could have *un*thrown the stick, if he had simply waited for a second, the bird would have soared into the air, surprised by their approach, alarmed maybe, but it would have risen on those whooping wings and taken to the sky. The eye fixed on him again, bright-yellow with a sparkling, black pupil that widened, then contracted to a pinpoint as the head turned towards the sun.

An awful feeling of wrongdoing settled upon him.

'Bloody brilliant shot,' Billy was saying. 'Got it right in the neck.' He was dancing around excitedly, poking his own stick at the stricken bird. He knocked it on the beak and the heron snapped weakly at the piece of wood. 'Look at the size of the thing. It's like a flamin' turkey. That could keep us going for a week.'

'Can you eat them?'

''Course.'

Danny wasn't listening. All he could see was the bright, glazed eye that seemed to hold him with an accusing glare, and the hissing rasp as the bird hauled for air through its damaged neck.

An ominous sense of foreboding stole over him. He'd thrown the stick and hit the bird. He could see where its neck was broken, down at the base close to the shoulder. It was dying.

A small cloud passed over and dimmed the bright sunlight. It happened all of a sudden and Danny shivered inside himself as a sense of misfortune overtook him. It was as if the deed had been witnessed, the simple casual destruction of a heron, by some force of nature that had darkened the day because of the act. A tear of guilt and regret brimmed over Danny's eyelid and rolled down his cheek. None of the others noticed. Doug had come across the stream and was now crouched down some feet away. Danny knuckled the tear away.

'Bust its neck,' Doug said. 'Spot on. Never knew you were that good.' There was no sense of regret in his voice, merely curiosity and, of course, admiration.

'I didn't mean it,' Danny insisted. The bird was still flopping around, though less frenziedly now. It whirled in a circle and then stopped. The beak opened and it sighed, or at least that's what it sounded like. From that long dagger, it had an oddly unnerving human quality.

'What'll we do?' Billy asked.

'It's dying,' Danny replied. He could hear his own voice, tight and cracking. 'It's hurt.' He took three steps forward, swung his stick in the air and brought it down in a fast arc. It caught the heron on the back of the head. The beating wing went into a spasm of frantic movement, then it slowed to a shivering tremble. The beak opened once and then closed again very slowly. The lifelight faded from the yellow eye and the bird was dead.

It lay there on the short grass beside a clump of ferns. In death it took on a certain dignity, and the twist in its neck, where the fine bones had been dislocated, was not quite so apparent. It could have been sleeping – if herons ever did lie down to sleep – except for the fact that its sightless eye was wide open and fixed, still fixed accusingly on Danny Gillan.

He turned quickly and went across the stream again, this time ignoring the stepping-stones. The small, white cloud passed quickly, taking its shadow with it, and the sunlight flooded back into the valley. But as Danny followed the path back down to where they'd stopped to camp, the strange and uncomfortable sense of foreboding followed him.

Corky had the fire lit and it crackled inside the ring of smooth stones they'd brought up from the stream. He and Tom were peeling potatoes and, in an old dried-milk can, blackened and with a bent wire for a handle, water was bubbling away. Tom stood up when the others approached.

'What's that?'

'A heron,' Doug said. 'Danny hit it in the air. Must have been fifty yards away.' Doug exaggerated. The bird had been much closer. 'Knocked it right out of the sky.'

'Big, isn't it?'

'You should have left it,' Danny said. Corky was looking at the bird admiringly, as Billy spread out the wide, grey wings.

'Never seen one up close before,' he said admiringly.

'I didn't mean it,' Danny said again, and the others looked at him. 'I wish I hadn't hit it. It'll have yunks in the nest waiting for it. They'll starve.'

Billy held the slender neck up in one hand, letting both wings trail. The bird was as tall as Tom when it was stretched out. The blinkless, yellow eye still found Danny.

'This one won't scare all the trout away,' Billy observed. 'We'll get all the fish we want. And we can eat this, too.'

'No,' Danny said. 'Hide it.'

'What's the matter with you?' Corky asked reasonably. 'It's only a bird.'

Danny tried to tell him it was more than that. He'd seen the heron taking off, its neck coiled to rest the head on the shoulders while the great beak pointed at the sky. It had been a magnificent thing, full of wild life and slender beauty, and he'd thrown the stick and broken it. *Killed it*.

He couldn't explain. They wouldn't understand. Billy stood there with the bird dangling from one hand, his dark hair gleaming in the sun and his tanned shoulders making him look more like a young Indian brave triumphantly showing a kill.

He turned and strode up to the gnarled hawthorn tree that spread its twisted branches out in a high arch in the hollow beside a low wall of rock. Before they'd gone off exploring the left side of the stream they'd gathered sticks and branches for firewood and stacked it in the rough natural shelf in case it rained. Billy put the bird down on one log, letting the head dangle over the side. He slipped his old knife from the leather sheath and started to hack away at the neck. It took several hits before the head fell away attached to six inches of white neck that ended in a bloody draggle of feathers.

He held it up, wagging his hand up and down, trying to make the beak open and close.

'Look. I got it to talk,' he called down. Doug laughed. Billy did a little dance that made him look even more like a tribal warrior, slapping his hand against his mouth to give a tribal yell. The ragged end of the neck jangled in his hand and thick drops of blood splashed over his bare shoulders and chest. He looked down at the congealing splotches and pulled a face.

'Oh Jeez,' he bawled.

'Heap Big Warrior, scared of blood,' Corky said.

'It's horrible,' Billy protested. He turned and stuck the head in the cleft between two branches of the hawthorn tree, leaving the beak pointing down towards the camp-fire. He came down towards the others. Out of the shade they could see the large drops of blood, scarlet freckles on his smooth skin.

Doug reached out and speared one with his finger, drawing a line of red down Billy's back. The other boy spun round angrily.

And they marked the lintels with the blood so that the angel of death would pass over. The line from Exodus sprung unbidden into Danny's head, but the feeling of wrongdoing stayed with him, as if he'd broken more than the heron.

'Makes you more like an Apache,' Doug said. He poked out again and smeared the blood on Billy's chest, leaving three thin trails.

'That's really horrible,' Billy said. 'And it stinks as well.' He passed Corky, who reached and smudged the lines, making a criss-cross pattern. Billy jerked away, crossing to the other end of the fire. Through the wavering air over the flames they saw him head down towards the stream. As he passed close to a small wild-hazel bush, a swarm of flies came buzzing out, danced in the air and went following the scent of blood.

Billy did a strange little dance as the flies whirled around him, suddenly taking him by surprise. He flapped them away and then slapped at his own skin. 'Bloody flies. They're eating me alive.'

'Heap Brave Warrior shitting his pants,' Corky said, and he and Doug and Tom cracked up with sudden laughter. Billy got to the stream, waded in without hesitation and then ducked right under the surface. When he came up, snorting for breath, they saw him quickly wipe away the smears of blood. The coil of flies whirled around him momentarily and then flew back into the bush again.

Billy came wading up to the camp-fire, grinning widely.

'What, no warpaint?' Corky asked sarcastically. 'You'll get drummed out of the Cubs.'

'Out of the Brownies, more like,' Tom said.

'Honest to God, those flies are like vampires. See the fangs they've got?' Billy clenched his own teeth in a demonstration and then started to laugh. He came up close to the fire and the water splashing from his soaked jeans hissed on the hot stones.

'So what's for dinner?' he asked.

The heron's head still stared out from the fork in the tree, a trophy to Danny's great skill as a hunter. The staring, filmy eyes snagged him while Billy was wading in the stream, trying to escape the cloud of flies. The feeling of guilt and the underlying sensation of foreboding, of having broken a taboo, still hung around him.

'Come on, Danny Boy,' Billy called over. 'Doug nicked a tin of corned beef. Want some?'

A few large, black flies were hovering around the bloody stump of the dead bird's neck where it flopped across the log. Another one flew up to the head and alighted on the yellow eye, rubbing its forelegs together. Danny turned away, knowing he would have to take the thing down and hide it.

'Will we eat first or fix up the tent?' Corky asked.

'Eat first,' Doug and Billy said simultaneously. Tom voted along with them. Danny came down from the tree and tried to put the feeling of guilt and odd apprehension away from him.

The potatoes were hard from not being boiled long enough and the beans were speckled with ash from the fire, but the boys wolfed the lot and then threw their tin plates in the stream to let the current clean them off. Danny and Corky dragged the tent out on to the flat a few yards away from the fire and untied the stays, to roll the heavy, green canvas out. The bag of tent-pegs rolled to the side and thumped to the ground. Another tightly wound roll of burlap dropped and hit the hard turf with a clatter.

'What's that?' Corky asked. He unravelled the dirty piece of sacking and spilt the contents on to the grass.

'No wonder it was so heavy,' he said. A heavy ballpeen hammer lay on top of the short black curve of a crowbar. Beside it lay a pair of electrician's heavy-duty pliers with insulated handles and a long screwdriver with a crooked blade. Corky flipped the canvas so that all of the contents rolled out. Billy darted forward and grabbed a tightly rolled magazine held in a cylinder with a rubber band. Doug picked up a shiny and expensive-looking Ronson Varaflame cigarette lighter, which was the height of technology of the day. A small box covered in black velvet revealed two gold cuff-links inlaid with black onyx. A smaller canvas bundle showed what Danny thought was a Luger pistol, but turned out to be an old pump-action airgun. Beside it a rattling tin held the lead slugs.

'No wonder he didn't want us to have the tent,' Corky said.

'What do you mean?' Tom asked the obvious question.

'This is where he's been hiding his stash. And his gear.'

'I don't get it,' Tom insisted.

'It's his B&E gear. For getting into places. Like garages and bike sheds. Like people's houses?' He stared meaningfully at Tom, who looked blank.

'Breaking and entering. Like what Mole Hopkirk used to get up to. I never saw that lighter before, or the cuff-links. Or the airgun. He must have swiped them and hid them there.'

'And I never saw tits like that before,' Billy said, spreading out the magazine on the grass. 'Look at the size of them.' He turned the picture around to show the others. 'That's Marilyn Monroe.'

'No, it isn't,' Doug debated. 'But it's like her.' Unconsciously he dropped his hand to his crotch and fumbled himself into a comfortable position.

Corky gave the picture a glance. 'Brenda Fortucci's got bigger ones.'

'She's got bigger everything,' Doug said. 'And a face like the backside of a double-decker bus.'

'We've seen better than that, eh, Dan?' Corky asked, giving Danny a wink. Danny still had that picture of Jane Hartfield branded on his mind, every curve of her as she strode down the path with fire in her eyes and a flush on her face. Doug was about to ask what Corky was talking about when Billy whooped.

'A goddess,' he said appreciatively, lowering his voice to what he thought sounded like a lecherous growl. 'A livin' doll.' He snatched the magazine up and formed his lips into a pout.

'Mmmm,' he kissed the printed breasts, pecked at the red lips of the smiling woman, then dropped his mouth to plant another smacker on the curve of her buttock.

'Wish you could see the front,' Billy said.

'Wish you could see where that's been. Phil's probably had that under the blankets, and now you've kissed it.'

'Argh,' Billy said, drawing his face into a contorted twist of disgust. He spat quickly as if he'd eaten something foul.

'Oh, that's fuckin' awful. You don't think he *came* on it?'

Tom started laughing and even Danny started to giggle, though the two of them were still below the cusp of puberty and, while they'd heard plenty, weren't exactly sure what the description entailed. Something came out and it was white and sticky, but what made that happen wasn't within their scope of experience yet.

'Yeah,' Corky said. 'Every night for a week. All over it, and now you've got it in your mouth.'

'No. Don't say that,' Billy pleaded. He held the magazine up to the light to inspect the pages. 'No, he couldn't have. I can't see anything.'

'That's 'cause it goes invisible,' Doug said, keeping it up. 'Just like germs, but it's worse than germs. If you get somebody's come in your mouth you get VD.'

'What's that?' Tom asked.

'Venial disease,' Doug said. 'And it's fatal every time.'

'No, don't say that,' Billy begged. He stuck his tongue out and began to wipe it with his fingers.

'It rots your skin and it gets into your dick and makes it fall off,' Doug pressed it home, winking at Corky, grinning broadly.

'And the only cure is to get a sharp spike with barbs on it. They put it right down and then rip it back out and it brings all the scabs with it, and all the poison, and it feels like you piss broken bottles for about a year. Maybe more.'

Billy winced, screwing up his face at the very thought. He crossed his legs in an involuntary protective motion against such an event.

'They call it the Wassermatter reaction. Phil told me about it. He knew a guy who had it done, and it left his dick shredded to pieces, and he had to sit down to pee after that.'

'Oh, Jeez,' Billy said, his imagination running riot.

'And if you get it,' Doug said, head turned away from Billy so that his grin couldn't be seen, 'you can never get in the commandos once you've had VD. They do an inspection right down your willy to see if you've had the scabs. And they can tell if you caught it from somebody else's spunk. I read that somewhere. You'd get done for being a queer-boy. Nobody likes them. They can even throw you in jail for that.'

Doug was about to go on when he realized what he'd said. Jail was a taboo subject. He turned quickly to Corky.

'Sorry, man. I didn't mean anything . . .'

Corky slapped him on the shoulder. 'No problem, Doug.' He turned and indicated the pile of tools and goods on the grass. 'If Phil gets caught with this lot, he'll be up in Drumbain himself.' He gave a rueful grin, and Danny thought he was being really big about it. 'See, Billy? Once they catch you, you can have company in the cell. You and Crazy Phil banged up in the Drum.'

'I wouldn't share a cell with that bastard if he was the last man on earth,' Billy said with feeling. He spat again. 'Not after what he's done.'

'Oh, don't worry about it. It might not be VD at all. It might be the *siff*.'

Billy raised his eyebrows hopefully. He might have been the biggest among them and the oldest, but he was the least well informed.

'What's that?'

'Don't you ever read anything except *Commando* comics?' Doug came back in. 'It's even worse than VD. It rots your nose

159

and then your skin; it turns your brain to mush. You end up like a walking skeleton. Like a zombie.'

'That's all right, then,' Tom said. 'Nobody will ever notice.'

Everybody looked at Tom. He looked back, face straight. Then all four of them burst out laughing, all doubled up and howling helplessly, while Billy stood there, scraping his tongue against the edge of his teeth, wondering what they were laughing at, convinced he could already feel the contamination working inside him.

'What's this?' Doug asked. He'd lifted the box with the cuff-links, and the little velvet holder had flipped out, revealing two oblong foil-shapes. He held one up.

'Chewing gum?'

Corky reached for one. 'It's a johnny,' he said.

'What's that?' Tom asked, completely innocent.

'You put it over your dick so you don't get the siff,' Corky said. 'It's got germolene or something inside it. Penicillin maybe.'

'Let's see,' Doug said, snatching it back. He ripped the foil and pulled out the pink shape. The little nipple flopped outwards. 'Couldn't even get Tom's wee willy into that,' he said, and they all hooted, even Tom, who took no offence at all.

'Naw. I've seen used ones down at the sewer pipe,' Billy said. 'They're bigger than that.'

Doug worked at it until the end began to unravel. He held it up, pale and translucent, stretching it between his hands. 'It's a balloon,' he said. 'Who'd stick their dick in a balloon?'

'Daft Phil would,' Billy said, and they all had a laugh at that. Doug brought the rubber up to his lips and blew into the thing. It inflated immediately, even quicker than the bewildered frog had done. He drew breath and blew in again until the rubber was the size of a football.

'That would fit me now,' Tom said, and this time Doug almost choked. The rubber slipped from his hands and flipped away on a bubbling fart of expelled air. It landed in the bush, just out of reach, dangling from the thorns like a thin skin. By this time they were all convulsed with laughter and Billy was actually rolling on the ground, holding his belly. Corky was rubbing tears from his eyes.

Eventually the laughter faded. Doug stuck the other condom

into the pocket of his jeans, and they cleared a space to erect the tent, spreading the guy lines out on either side under Corky's directions and getting the stout centre-pole straight. The original cords had long since frayed, and now the boys used a roll of rough and hairy baling twine that was coiled round a baton of wood. Another length of fine wire that they'd found last summer on a fence post at Cargill Farm stretched from the back pole to one of the trees behind, to keep everything steady. The ballpeen hammer came in handy for getting the tent-pegs hammered into the hard ground. In half an hour, much longer than it would have taken the boys in the scout troop, the old green tent was fixed up, a little swaybacked, and with the side closest to the stream flapping loosely, but it would take them all at a squeeze come nightfall.

Doug brewed some tea in the blackened milk-can and slung in a small sliver of wood, which he said would help draw the fire-ash to the surface. They drank it in their old, chipped mugs and, while they had no milk, they were in the great outdoors, miles away from the town, miles away from the pressures of home, and it tasted just fine.

'Does Phil really break into places?' Tom asked.

Corky shrugged. 'I wouldn't put it past him, but I wouldn't ask him neither, if I was you.' He winked, and then spiralled a finger around his own temple. 'He's not so hot in the brains department, not like his handsome, intelligent kid brother.'

'Ugly and thick brother,' Billy responded automatically.

'Oh, the Big Chief Hunter of Flies has spoken,' Corky said, and gave Billy two fingers. 'Up yours, Harrison. Up to the elbow.' It was all said without rancour, almost like a ritual litany of responses. He turned back to Tom.

'But he'll be mad as a wet hen when he finds out what *we*'ve found out. I'll have to think of something. Like tell him we didn't use the tent.'

'Maybe we should go back and he'll never know we found it,' Danny ventured. It was the first time the thought had entered his mind. It just came up from nowhere and he'd simply uttered it. He didn't feel right about that heron. It had disturbed him, taken the shine off the day, put a shadow on the adventure. This morning Phil Corcoran had thrown a knife at him and his luck had saved him, let him off with a small bruise on the side of his head. Now he felt as if that luck wouldn't hold. He couldn't, if asked, have coherently explained why. Tom looked up at him, blew the steam off the surface of his tea. He nodded. 'Maybe we should go back.'

Corky shook his head. 'Nah, not since we've come this far. That tent weighs a ton, and I'm not carrying it back. Phil can wait until we get home.'

'Can't stop now,' Doug agreed. 'We must be at least halfway there.'

'Yeah, we want to find the dummy village,' Billy backed him up, the threat of disease forgotten and his face now animated. 'We'll be the first. There might be guns left behind. Maybe even machine-guns.' He had dragged the flopped body of the heron away to the side and was pulling the broad flight-feathers from the ends of the wings, each of them coming out reluctantly.

Danny looked at Tom. The feeling of apprehension was still there, but they had come this far. Tom was still unnerved from the gorse fire. He'd had a real scare, and Danny could tell he really did want to go home, but that he didn't want to be the first to back out.

'Come on Danny Boy,' Billy said. 'We can play commandos. It'll be just like in the war.' He held up a bunch of the wide, grey feathers. 'Or even cowboys and injuns.' He took a length of the baling twine and tied it around his head, then jammed some of the feathers through it, making them stand upright. The head-dress made him look even more like a young brave. He grinned proudly, waving the rest of them in his hands and doing a little shuffling dance.

Danny shrugged, and that committed Tom. Corky winked at him and slung an arm around Tom's neck, giving him a quick and friendly headlock. 'The Famous Five ride again, amigos,' he said.

When they finished their tea, Corky loaded the air pistol and they spent half an hour firing at the empty tin of corned beef, which they set up on a stone on the far side. The steep sides of the deep gully spat the pistol-cracks back at them, but only Billy managed to hit the tin and, even then, the spring on the old gun was so weak that it made hardly a dent. Finally, Doug put a stone in his catapult and winged it at the can, hitting it dead centre and sending it tumbling into the air. The sun was high, edging over the far side of the valley to shine directly into the stream. The light spangled up from the ripples below the low falls.

'I vote we go and look for it now,' Billy said. He'd taken off his feathers, which were now looped over the tent-pole, and he was lying on his belly on the short grass, soaking up the sun, while Doug gently touched his skin with a stalk of grass. Every now and again Billy would bat away what he thought was a horsefly. Doug grinned mischievously and kept up the nuisance.

'Too late now,' Danny said. 'If we start early tomorrow we'll have all day.'

'How about exploring the stream?' Corky said. He pointed to the fork ahead where the two canyons met, joining from separate tributaries at a narrow angle. 'I've never been up there.'

'I was up once, catching trout last winter,' Danny said. 'Me and Al Crombie. There's a good bit like a wall, right across the gully, and the water comes out in a big arch. You can get right behind the waterfall.'

'I read that in a book,' Corky said. 'Hawkeye. Him and his pal Chingachgook were hiding under the falls. It was like a cave.' He hauled himself to his feet. 'Let's go see.'

He bent quickly and slapped Billy hard on the reddening skin of his back just where Doug was mischievously trailing the ear of grass. Billy yelped.

'Big horsefly,' Corky said. 'Biggest I ever saw. Had to smack it off before it got you.'

Billy glared at him, unsure of whether Corky was taking the mickey or not.

'Would I lie to you, Billy-O?' Corky asked, knuckling the bigger lad on the shoulder. 'I just saved your life, didn't I?'

CHAPTER SIXTEEN

Interlude

'The trail had gone cold by the time we really started looking,' Angus McNicol explained. 'By God, it was difficult then, and the whole town was in a panic. People were sending their kids away, rather than have them around here, and nobody could blame them.

'What threw us was the fact that the Rankine boy had fallen off the quarry and at first it looked just like an accident. There were always boys coming off the castle ramparts or the Langmuir crags, risking life and limb for the sake of birds' eggs. You'll have done the same, eh?'

His face broke into a knowing smile before he cocked an eye at the spinning reel in the Dictaphone and started talking again.

'We didn't start the search for young Whalen until night, and we got the floodlights set up. It was well after midnight by the time the frogmen came. The dogs had scoured the whole of the quarry and there was no sign of the boy, but that didn't mean he wasn't there. Then there was the business with that boot and the severed foot which gave that frogman a right old scare.

'Anyhow, it was back down to the station in the early hours of the morning. We were coming round to the notion that the other boy hadn't fallen and maybe he'd had such a scare when his friend tumbled that he'd taken off in a panic. So, at that moment, we had a missing boy who had probably made himself missing. He'd be out at some friend's place, or hiding in a gang-hut, and he'd come home when he got hungry and even more scared.

'Then Hector Kelso came in, now that the boy had been gone for well over twelve hours.

'Hector got a brief from the inspector. I remember he listened with a straight face. He asked where the boy's bag was, and said that if young Rankine had been dodging off school, then he'd likely have his bag with him, unless he'd stashed it some place. We did another search of the place and that took us the rest of the day. I could see Hector Kelso was getting worried, for Whalen never turned up on the second night and I spent a bit of time with the boy's mother. That's not a pleasant job, I can tell you. As every minute ticked away, you could see her nerves getting wound up tighter and tighter. There was something in her eyes that I'll never forget, and I swear to you that it was beginning to dawn on her, long before it dawned on anybody else, with the exception maybe of Kelso, that she would never see the boy again. Not alive, that is.

'Then Crawford Rankine came round in the hospital. The boy had a fractured skull and for a while they thought his brains would be like porridge in there, but he was pretty clear about what had happened. He told us about the rail wagon and how he'd been chased and had gone running. He remembered the man all right.

'I recall thinking the boy had a stammer. He was saying "twi-twi-twi" like a sparrow with a stutter. Took me a second to work out he was trying to say "Twitchy Eyes". He'd known who was chasing him.

'We got back to the hill behind the school and down that track between the pigeon shacks, Kelso, myself, Big John Fallon and a couple of others. I remember a big beast of a terrier trying to get at us through the fence, and later Fallon had it put down, for there was a big septic ulcer on its nose where it had been pushing through the wire. We went down to the hut and, inside, we saw the blood handprint and all of us knew then that the killer had taken young Whalen away. The boy was gone and the next week was murder, I can tell you, in more ways than one. By the next morning there was a team of press people camped outside the station and you couldn't move for flash-guns popping in front of your eyes.

'That was in June, fairly close to the beginning of the month. Three dead, including young Whalen, all of them in the space of a couple of months or so. We had a pretty good description, so we had a fair idea of what the bastard looked like. The finger-prints matched those found at the other sites and again there were pages of the bible crumpled about, and not too clean either. Hector Kelso never liked the notion of anybody wiping his arse on the good book.'

Angus raised his eyebrows. 'Some folk seemed to think that made it even worse, but as far as I was concerned it was only paper, and it was a clue. Anything was a clue, but despite that, the trail went cold very soon and Bryce, the criminal psychologist, started talking about *burn-out*, saying that the killer could be so filled with remorse that he'd killed himself. Hector Kelso didn't put much stock in that, and neither did I, as I've said before. He said Bryce was talking through a hole in his backside. But the killings *did* stop. For the next month or so there was nothing, at least as far as we knew, and even Kelso could have been forgiven for relaxing a little at the end of July.

'Then, some time in August, just before the schools went back, Johnson McKay went up to Blackwood Farm to find out why Ian McColl hadn't been picking up his mail from the box and the solids really hit the *punkah*, as the Commander used to say. What a mess.'

Angus stopped talking and rubbed his chin. He dunked a biscuit in his coffee, took a bite, washed it down with a mouthful, and started talking again.

'By this time, of course, we knew what had happened to Whalen and we knew about the girl, and that took us by surprise. It must have been ten days later, less than a fortnight after the boy went missing. Once I've looked out my old papers from up in the loft I'll be able to tell you exactly.

'We knew nothing about the girl until we found her, for she'd never been posted missing. Sandra Walters, her name was. She was nineteen and came from Lochend, as you'll probably remember. By the time we found her, she'd been dead about two weeks, which means she was killed some time in May, near the end of the month, and that figured with the story we got from the family. Some big argument with her father and she walked out. Now I was in on it when we questioned them, in a tenement flat about a hundred yards down from the railway station, I recall. Donald Walters, I remember thinking there was something funny about him. It was only after the body was found that the mother came to us to say she was missing, and it was the dental records that finally confirmed who it was, for the face was pretty much eaten away by the flies and the rats.

'Walters said she'd stormed out, but there was more to it than that. I got to know the look the more I worked on the force. There were three girls, two of them still in the house, about fifteen and thirteen, and the wife, she had the look of a mouse caught in a corner. The girls never looked at anybody, just sat there, heads down, scared to move, it seemed. Walters was cocky enough, a fast-talking, skinny little runt of a fellow, and he was adamant the girl was a whore who'd been putting it about and that he, for one, wasn't having any of that.

'Now when the post-mortem was done, there was plenty of evidence to show that the girl was no virgin. Dr Bell found old scarring on the walls of the uterus which he said was classic evidence of unlubricated sex, or forced entry, as he described it unofficially. We couldn't put anything down to Donald Walters at the time, and it was pretty clear he hadn't killed his daughter, but Hector Kelso was pretty suspicious. The other girls said nothing and the wife, well, she would have backed up everything he said. He hanged himself from the rafters nine months afterwards, and I had a notion Kelso had been leaning on the little bastard, and I can't blame him for that. There was something queer about Walters. After that the family moved away.

'Young Sandra, she'd been hurt bad. Awful. It didn't affect me as much as little Lucy Saunders, broken and torn under the bridge, but this was bad. You'll get the details in the archives, and the pictures too, if you've the stomach for them. She'd been terribly damaged, and she had lasted a long time. Dr Bell showed us the marks around her ankles and wrists and the scarring on her throat where she'd pulled against a ligature. She broke the fuckin' rope. Pardon me for that, but after all this time I still don't like remembering that.'

Angus paused again, his eyes inflamed with the recollection of the dreadful damage. He absently took another swallow of coffee and swirled it around in his mouth as if it would take away the taste.

'Now there was another thing we knew about Twitchy Eyes. He was crazy and he was evil and he liked to cause pain. But he also waited around with the bodies, sitting vigil with them, for at least three days, probably more. By then, they'd be pretty well blown and that didn't seem to bother him. He waited until the maggots had hatched. He stayed until they were covered in flies.'

June

A match flared in the dark, blinding-bright, cut a flaming arc in the blackness, and stopped. Don Whalen watched it waver through a film of tears as his eyes watered. They trickled hot down his cheeks and ran cold on to his neck. The light floated and a candle-flame swelled slowly to life, hardly flickering at all. He blinked away the tears, trying to stay still, wishing his heart would stop thudding against his chest. His shoulder shrieked with every movement he made and his throat was on fire.

He had listened to the sirens, huddled against the wall of the boxcar. The man had been there, a silent presence in the gloom, his breathing low and slow and unhurried. The sound of it carried infinite menace. Don tried to call out, tried to say something, but the pain in his throat burnt in a caustic rasp and all he could manage was a hoarse whisper. It felt as if something was broken in there where the hand had squeezed him. The longer the silence went on, the more frightened Don Whalen became. He couldn't understand any of this. But the deadly silence was somehow even more frightening than the pain.

The sirens had wailed in the distance, howling urgency and emergency. They'd stopped for a while and then they'd started up again, rising in a crescendo as they passed along Lochend Road, before fading as they got to the old bridge. The silence had descended then, broken only by the fluttering of pigeon flocks as they took off from the nearby huts, and by the savage rumbling growl of the pit-bull terrier, like a leopard in a bush. Much later, the bell had rung, and there had been shouts and calls and the sounds of school spilling out. A crowd of boys came down the track, made the terrier snarl and pound the fence, and then they went on their way. The man had gone out, opening the door quickly and rolling it closed. When he came back, some time later, he said nothing at all. He roughly grabbed Don about the waist, dumped him on the flat of the wagon and quickly wrapped him up tight in a roll of something that might have been an old carpet. He felt himself being picked up and slung over a broad back and carried away. The material covered his eyes and he couldn't tell whether it was day or night. Don could hear the twigs crackle underfoot and he knew he was in trees. There was some traffic noise close by and he figured he was being taken along Lochend Road, but through the belt of trees that bordered the winding route to the west side of the town. Out of the trees, he sensed the clamber over rough ground and then the descent down a flight of stairs. A door squealed open and Don Whalen was lowered to the flat surface.

He was still wrapped tight in a rough bundle of thick material, slanted across a flat surface against a wall. Strong hands unrolled it. He felt his clothes ripped away from him until the cool air told him he was naked. The hands pushed him down on to a chair and then very quickly bound his hands behind him and tied his feet to upright posts that felt like chair legs. The smell in the air was dreadful, sickening and thick. The pain in his throat stopped him from retching.

The match flared and a dark shape moved out of the light, and a faint humming sound rose stronger. Black stars floated in front of his eyes and for a moment he thought he was going to pass out, before he realized they were not stars, but flies, hundreds of them, wheeling in the air, disturbed by the light. He turned his head, just a little, trying to see the man, scared to let his eyes light upon him, deadly afraid of him taking him unawares again. His eyes swept round.

The thing on the table screamed silently at him.

For a second his mind refused to accept what it had seen. His eyes continued their sweep and then jerked back at the shape on the table. A catastrophic fright exploded inside him and his heart kicked violently behind his ribs, one solid *thump* that was so powerful his body spasmed sideways.

The head was twisted at the end of a scrawny neck and the mouth was open so wide it looked inhuman. An arm, grey in the dim light and bruise-mottled, was stuck out straight, the fingers clawed.

Absolute terror rocketed through him. He was trembling violently, shuddering as uncontrollable fear rampaged through him, making his head tap against the wall in a rapid staccato. The eyes were crawling with flies. The skin shimmered and rippled with a life of its own.

The dead body's silent scream went on and on, and the flies crawled over the skin. Don bucked against the string binding his wrists as the realization hit him. He had been brought here by the man who had done that. His muscles convulsed in a violent contortion powerful enough to drive the thick twine into the skin of his wrists and open up two abraded lacerations.

He heard himself gibbering uncontrollably, incomprehensibly, though hardly a sound escaped his throat. In his mind he called out for his mother and his father and he prayed to God to get him out of this, and all of the time he knew there was no way out.

The horror on the table gaped and Don Whalen echoed it in his own mind. After a while the overload of terror and dread was too much and he passed out in a dead faint, banging his head against the wall, to leave yet another clue for Superintendent Hector Kelso.

When he came round he was lying on the table and the man was leaning down towards him. The eyes were blinking rapidly and Don Whalen dimly realized this was something he should remember.

He felt rough hands on him and tried fruitlessly to squirm away. His legs were spread-eagled and he knew his ankles were tied to the legs of the table, and he felt a huge cry building up inside him. He twisted his head and saw the other scream, frozen and fly-blown, only a yard away, slanted against the back of the chair. The flies hummed busily and Don Whalen's pain began.

CHAPTER SEVENTEEN

August 1, night
'What was that?'

The pine branches crackled in the fire. The flickering red flames tinged their faces rosy and sent long shadows dancing on the steep side of the gully. The striations of white rock, alternating in thin bands with the dark shale, reflected a pink glow.

'I heard something,' Doug said, turning towards the trees. They had dragged heavy stones up from the stream to use as benches, and Billy had hauled a thick log, its weight ploughing a furrow in the grass, as his own chair. He sat astride it, digging the rusty blade of his knife into the wood.

'Stop that,' he snorted at Doug. 'You've been doing that all day.' He turned to Danny. 'He's just trying to scare us.'

'I saw somebody,' Doug protested. 'Honest.'

'I saw something, too,' Tom chipped in. 'When we were collecting firewood. Swear to God. It was a man, at least I *think* it was a man. I saw his face, but when I looked again, it wasn't there.'

'It was a sheep, dopey-features. No kidding, you're a real bunch of scaredy-cats. If there were other guys up here, they'd have lit a fire. They wouldn't be sitting around in the dark, would they? They'd be barging into everything.'

'It's probably the farmer from Blackwood,' Corky said. 'He'll be checking up on us, to make sure we're not killing the sheep.'

'Not yet,' Billy said. He grinned, and his strong teeth glinted in the light. 'But the night's still young. We could have lamb chops for dinner tomorrow if the snares don't work.' Billy and Corky had used some of the thin fencing wire to set a couple of rabbit snares out close to the bracken but so far nothing had ventured into them despite the plentiful evidence of rabbits there.

'You can go hunting sheep for all I care,' Doug said. 'I'm staying here.' He looked over his shoulder at the gloom downstream, close to the bend where the forest began again, thick and blackly shadowed. A light breeze stirred the topmost branches and made the leaves whisper. Overhead the moon was just a few days away from being full, lending its own silvered light to the wet stones of the stream but, despite its brightness, beyond the range of the fire's glow, it was still very dark.

Something whirred in from the stream side, swooped towards the flames and then out again. Billy jerked back from the motion, throwing his hand up to ward the creature away. Doug laughed scornfully, pointing at Billy.

'Who's the scaredy-cat now?'

'What the *hell* was that?'

'A bat,' Corky said, though he and Danny had seen it was only a large moth attracted to the light. 'Probably a vampire. They get tangled up in your hair and get you in the neck with big, pointy teeth. Kill you stone-dead, no kidding. They find you in the morning and all the blood's sucked out of you. You're just an empty bag of bones.'

Billy looked over the fire at him, disbelief etched on his face.

'Instead of just a big bag of wind,' Doug snorted, and Tom giggled.

'Like the Racine rats,' Corky went on, ignoring the interruption. He turned his head to the side so Billy couldn't see him, and he winked conspiratorially at Doug.

'The what?'

'The Racine rats,' Corky said. 'They're much bigger than the titchy ones you get in farms and old houses. I mean, they're pretty huge. My Uncle Pete told me this, and he would know. He's a great poacher. They live beside canals and rivers, and they burrow under the banks. They come out at night for food, and they'll eat anything or . . .' he lowered his voice to a whisper '. . . any*body*.'

The others leant forward. Tom looked over his shoulder at the darkness beyond the firelight.

'Next time you walk beside the canal, stamp your feet. Or along by the river at the levee path beside the Oxbow Road. You stamp your feet *hard*. That's the way to find out if the Racine rats have burrowed under. You get a hollow sound that's really creepy. It goes *doom-doom-DOOM*.'

Corky paused for effect, his eyes theatrically wide and catching the light of the fire. Billy sat forward, hooked by the image.

'And you know that the rats are there, bigger than anything in the Pied Piper. Big as cocker spaniels, waiting in the dark. Omnivorous. That means they eat meat and blood *and* bones as well. They swim out under the water and wait on the bank for people passing by at night or early in the morning. They don't just have rats' teeth for gnawing things. They've got sharp, pointed ones like vampire bats' for ripping your skin and flesh, and big ones for crunching bones. You hear stories of people who disappeared near canals and the police always say they must have drowned.'

'Like Paulie Degman,' Doug said in a hushed voice, now drawn into Corky's tale despite the wink he'd been thrown. Danny shivered and drew in closer to the warmth of the fire. He didn't want to think about Paulie, not so far up and away from the street-lights. The water burbled hollowly as it tumbled between the white quartz rocks into the dark of the pool, which caught shards of silver reflections on the ripples. Under the surface, it looked black. It could have gone down a million miles. In the dark of night, anything could be down there. Or any*body*.

'Yeah,' Corky agreed. 'Like poor Paulie.' He was now whispering so softly they all had to lean close to hear above the flutter of the low flames. The firelight glinted on his face, wreathing it in shadows. 'They say they've drowned, but that's because they don't want to scare people and make them panic. But they know those folk were caught by the Racine rats and dragged under the water to the burrows and eaten, every scrap of them, even the bones. Even their shoes. That's why they're never found again. Not ever.' He paused and looked around, the light catching the lopsided grin.

'So any time you walk by the canal and you hear that hollow noise, you better run as fast as you can, because that's what they're waiting for. Footsteps up above. Just waiting for a lone walker, waiting to drag him down. That's why you never get me along by the river on my own, not for love nor money. No way, *ho-zay*.'

Doug hunched earnestly over the fire, hanging on every word. He had caught Corky's wink, but the story snared him with a ring of truth. He'd walked by the canal a thousand times, and they went fishing down on the river when the bailiff wasn't around (at least in other summers – not this one), and it really was true. When you walked on the track, you heard that hollow, pounding echo where the bank was undercut, as if there were secret caves just below your feet. Doug could imagine big, sharp, toothed, furred things huddled under there, just listening and slavering.

'Is that true?' Billy asked. Corky looked round at him, keeping his face straight. The fire flickered in his eyes.

'Would I lie to you, Billy-O?'

'*Would I lie to you, Billy-O?*' Corky had asked again in the light of the day, after giving Billy a hard knuckle right on the edge of his shoulder-blade. 'Saved your life, didn't I? That was the biggest horsefly I ever saw. It would have eaten you alive, swear to God.'

They'd taken a turn at the small waterfall where the stream narrowed for the drop into the pool. Billy had taken a handful of heron's flight feathers and stuck them in crevices between the big, pale quartz stones and stood back admiringly.

'Four Feather Falls,' he announced. 'Remember that show? The magic guns that fired by themselves? Pure brilliant.'

They all agreed. It was too warm to argue, and Billy could keep going all day if he was in the mood. They left the feathers there, sticking up like markers, grey and edged with a dark, smoky blue.

They crossed the water on the stones and up the far bank where a narrow sheep-track angled up the slope. Far behind them, well off down the valley, a cock crowed, shrill and challenging, only slightly muffled by the summer's heat haze.

'That's the little red rooster,' Doug said.

'Well, it's slept in,' Billy said.

Doug stuck his skinny elbows out and flapped them a couple of times, pecking his head forward on his thin neck. His red ears stuck out like wattles.

'I am the little red rooster,' he drawled, bobbing forward, long, bony legs strutting. Tom laughed out loud. Danny stuck his elbows out, following the lead. Corky imitated him.

'Too *laaaate* to crow the day,' Doug rasped, and they all went filing up the track, laughing all the while, strutting like cockerels.

They were still laughing when they turned there to follow the smaller brook which fed into the Blackwood stream. This water came tumbling over ledges of hard limestone and through crevices of old smooth-worn basalt. Doug had stripped an ash sapling and was poking under rocks to try to scare trout into the open. Tom and Danny took the lead along the sheep-trail and, only fifty yards up the narrow gully, they came to the natural barrier set at right angles to the flow. They all stopped.

'Where's the waterfall?' Billy wanted to know.

The expected cataract, and the anticipated cave behind it, was nowhere to be seen. Instead, the barrier was much higher than Danny remembered it, and water seeped and sprayed around the edges in a fine mist, catching the sun and forming tight little rainbows of haze.

Doug poked his stick at it. 'It's plugged up. A tree's come down and blocked it off like a log-jam.' The water gurgled down the mass of twigs and branches that had stemmed the main flow. There was no cavern in the rock. They started to turn back when Corky stopped them.

'Wait a minute.' He pointed at the top of the blockage, a dozen feet or more above their heads. The top twigs and branches were white and dry in the sun, but the flow started only a few inches below the topmost edge, trickling through the packed weave.

'How deep is it on the other side?' he asked. Danny pointed at the original lip of the rock cleft which was only head-height to himself, chin-height to Billy.

'Just a couple of feet, I think. Maybe a yard at the most.'

'A lot deeper now,' Corky said, grinning. 'Come on.'

The cleft was blocked, which meant they had to climb the steep side, digging their hands into the shale to get a purchase and finding smooth and unreliable toeholds in the mudstone layers. It took them five minutes of slipping and sliding on the loose gravel to reach the lip of the natural wall. Corky got there first with Tom, who was wiry but agile, close behind. They stood on the hard, stone wall and looked down. The backed-up stream water reflected the blue of the summer sky in a long, zigzagged lake with a surface so calm it threw back a perfect reflection.

'It's a dam,' Corky said, his voice filled with wonder and

satisfaction. Billy and Doug scrambled up behind him, almost knocking Danny off the stone. A small rock rolled and splashed below them with the echoing *plop* of deep water. Ripples spread out to lap at the edges and quickly disappeared.

'It's a damn dam,' Billy said, delighted with his own wit. 'Damnation.' Below them, an old spruce trunk, spiked with broken branches and probably dislodged from further upstream by the snow-melt of previous winters, had jammed itself in the narrow V-shaped crevice which had allowed the water to spill away in a narrow cataract. The spines had trapped heather clumps and divots brought down by erosion, and a weave of reeds and rushes from marshes somewhere up on the moor, compacting them into a thick plug. Behind it, the water backed up beyond the first bend of the stream. Billy stood on his tiptoes, despite the twenty-foot drop behind him.

'It goes back for miles.'

'This wasn't here before,' Danny said. 'Is it deep?'

'About ten feet,' Corky said. He turned to Doug, who still had the slender ash sapling. 'Poke around and see how far it goes.'

Doug got to his knees and reached down. The end of the stick only trailed on the surface. He got up again, reversed the slender branch, hefted it like a javelin and threw it at the water, thick end first. It broke the surface almost silently and went straight down, its seven-foot length disappearing in an instant. They watched, wondering if it had stuck on bottom mud. But a few seconds later, the sapling came back up again, reversing its direction, the thin end rising to three feet out of the water before it toppled slowly to float on the surface.

'At least ten feet,' Doug said. 'Could be fifteen.' He was standing there, string vest tattered and muddied with shale, one knee out of his jeans and a toothy grin wide on his face.

'We must be the first to find it,' Corky said. 'That means it's ours.'

Billy laughed gleefully. 'I hereby name this damn dam . . .' he stopped and looked at them. 'Any ideas?'

'Heron lake,' Tom suggested, but Danny shook his head and shot him a look. He didn't want to be reminded of what he had done to the bird, even though he hadn't meant to kill it. The feeling of foreboding tried to push its way back and he shoved it away.

'The Blue Lagoon,' Doug suggested.

'Lonesome Lake,' Corky said. 'That's just what it's like.'

Billy looked at him askance. 'Was that in *The Dambusters*?' Corky shook his head, almost sadly. Danny thought the name fit somehow. Lonesome Lake, up here beyond the barwoods, miles from the town, in a cleft in the moors. Up here where there was only the occasional moan of wind across the tussock grass and the mournful piping of the curlew. The water dead-still, its surface glass-flat.

Billy turned and clambered off the narrow wall on to the couch grass clinging to the grass of the slope. He heeled off his baseball boots, undid his belt, pushed his still-damp jeans down to his ankles, then stripped them off.

'Last one in's a big jessie,' he called across. Doug hauled his dirty vest off. Billy stripped completely, standing naked and pale. He had a thick clump of black hair on his crotch, in stark contrast to his smooth skin. Tom and Danny stared.

'When did that happen?' Tom asked innocently. Billy looked down. His penis swung from side to side, thick and heavy, more than twice the size of Tom's and Danny's. Billy grinned proudly.

'Huge, innit?'

'Seen bigger,' Doug said.

'On a cart-horse,' Billy shot back. 'I could fill that rubber johnny no bother at all.'

'Too late,' Corky said. 'You've probably got the siff anyway. From kissing Phil's spunk.'

Billy pulled a face, stuck out his tongue and made exaggerated wiping movements with his fingers, flicking his spittle to the side. He spat violently, just for effect, turned quickly and went down to the stone barrier again, braced himself and then dived straight out. Danny called out, too late. The water might have been deep, but there could be other spiky logs down there just under the still surface. He envisaged Billy plunging straight down and impaling himself on a skewer, and immediately the recollection of Paulie Degman came rolling back, stuck under the black water of the river, fighting for breath and clawing for air. Danny shook his head to dismiss the memory.

Billy hit the water cleanly, with hardly a splash despite his weight. He disappeared. Ripples spread out and hit the sides of the narrow lake, washing some of the shale from the valley walls down into the depth. They all watched, waiting, until Billy came up to the surface, spluttering.

'Bloody freezing, but it's terrific. Come on in.'

Doug kicked off his torn and greying underpants. Without his clothes he was even stringier than he normally looked, slat-ribbed and all knuckles and joints. He grinned, scampered on the barrier, then jumped, turning over in the air, holding his nose between finger and thumb. He landed backside foremost, missing Billy by inches and hitting the water with a loud, booming splash which sent a wave crashing to the steep side beyond.

The others got undressed quickly, though with furtive glances at each other to check the comparisons. Corky was showing wispy hairs but little more. Danny and Tom were still boys. Tom scampered out on to the rock, did a little bob, and without hesitation launched himself upwards. He turned, slender and small and graceful, his curly hair pushed back from his forehead. He arched slowly, twisted in a corkscrew and arrowed down. He hit the water so silently that there was barely a ripple. Danny and Corky followed him, more clumsily but just as enthusiastic. The water was cold, colder than any of them would have imagined on a hot late-summer's day, but wonderful to swim in. They splashed and swam for an hour before climbing out to dry in the late sun and, after that, Tom and Corky went exploring up towards the far end of the natural lake. Billy and Doug climbed over the ridge and down to the other tributary, the Blackwood stream proper. Danny went with them, brushing his wet hair back with his fingers to keep it from flopping in his eyes.

'We could bust it,' Billy was saying. 'Just like *The Dambusters*. That would be really brilliant.'

'You can do it,' Doug said. He was about to continue when he stopped abruptly. Billy turned to him. Doug was frozen in mid-step.

'Did you hear something?'

Billy shook his head. Danny turned. Doug's head was cocked to the side in a listening attitude. His eyes were fixed on the gnarled clumps of hawthorn and hazel that dotted the far side of the slope which rose up to the moors beyond Blackwood Farm.

'I saw something,' he said. 'Over there.' He pointed to a hollow where the ferns crowded around some jagged lumps of moraine rock left by ancient glaciers. The other two followed his direction. There was nothing to be seen. Beyond the rock, just a patch of white some distance away, a sheep moved in the ferns.

'Just a sheep,' Billy said.

Doug shook his head. 'No. I saw something. I think it was a man.'

Danny scanned the hollow. He could see nothing. A small shiver of apprehension trickled up his back. They turned back to the brook, heading upstream. Danny couldn't shake the feeling. Since he'd hit the heron and watched it writhe, the weird sense of ill luck had settled uneasily on him.

They got round a tight, meandering bend and began to cross again when Doug let out a sudden, and quite startling howl of disgust. Billy stopped and Danny bumped into his back, shoving the bigger boy forward, off balance. Billy windmilled his arms and then slipped off the stone.

The deer carcass lay half in the stream. Its head was arched back and its mouth was open. The eyes were long gone and the skin and muscle of the cheek had rotted away showing the great, grinding teeth set in a strangely fierce grimace. The thick pelt was worn in places, and they could see the white vertebrae of the neck where the flesh had been stripped. A magnificent spread of antlers reared behind the dead head.

'Christ on a bike,' Billy said. He had stumbled against the foreleg, which was being twisted slowly in the current. The belly and the hind legs, on the dry bank, looked surprisingly untouched but, as Billy moved back, a cloud of flies came droning upwards, thick and whirling. 'What a stench,' Billy said. He turned, and Danny caught a smell of it, sweet and thick, clogging at the back of the throat. He felt his palate click glutinously, ready to trigger a heave.

The ribs were high and curved, poking up against the skin in taut slats. Below them, a gaping hole showed where something had gnawed right into the belly. Billy pivoted on the stone, got upstream of the dead animal and reached a hand out to grab the tine of an antler. He pushed himself back, heaving strongly, and the whole carcass slowly turned over on to its back. He gripped a hand on each horn and twisted hard. There was a dull, thudding sound and then a rip, and the head came free, sending Billy stumbling backwards with the ruined skull dangling between the wide spread of jagged antlers. It thumped to the ground. The heavy body rolled back again, and the skin of the belly ripped. Danny thought he saw something moving in the black, gnawed hole but then his attention was diverted to the mass of wriggling maggots which poured out, white and pulsating, from the gash at the joint of the ribs where the skin had torn. They gushed out in a fleshy dribble, tumbling on to the shingle beside the stream.

The smell now hit him like a blow, and he twisted away, unable to stop himself retching drily. He heard Doug make the same choking sounds.

'A trophy,' Billy said excitedly, his wide face alive and animated. 'Look at those horns. I could tell people I shot it.' He held them up, his arms wide, once again like a young Indian brave. The wide antlers waved in the air, curved and sharp. The dead, cratered sockets stared at the sky.

By the time Corky and Tom came back, Billy had fixed the deer's head up on the gnarled hawthorn tree in at the hollow where the rocks made a natural corner, wedging the antlers in so that the wasted skull with its perpetually gnashing teeth hung downwards. A dribble of foul-smelling liquid oozed out of one hollow nostril on to the moss below. A tornado of small flies whirled in the air when the boys approached and then settled back on the rotting head. The black insects were already clustered all over the sightless eyes of the heron.

August 1, 6 p.m.
He had spent most of the day on the Blackwood slope, in the full glare of the sun. He had been watching from the other side of the valley, staying in the cover of the trees lower down where the gully widened out. From the height of the slope, he could see the narrow crevices where the streams had cut their way through the peat and the stone, forming the branching gorges

that fed the Blackwood stream. From here he could see every-thing. The sun was high and the drone of insects up in the leaves was a sleepy hum on the still air. Down the slope, the stream burbled.

He had watched and listened to their shouts, their calls echo-ing back from the steep sides beyond where they'd put the tent.

A boy had slapped another on the back and there had been a hoarse cry, this one deeper than the rest, and it reminded him of the other one who'd come blundering through the window into the place where he sat in the shadows.

The laughter had come floating up, the laughter of children, ragged on his nerves. There was a faint whiff of woodsmoke on the clear air, not so harsh as it had been on the hillside when the flames had jumped from bracken to gorse and made the air shimmer with the heat. Here the scent was of pine, resinous and sweet. The boys were marching up the defile where the tributary fed down to the main stream. The sun was on their skin, reflecting pale, not dark as one might expect on boys at the end of the summer holiday. These boys had not been out in the sun much this summer.

They disappeared round the first bend; the voices faded away. He sat there, motionless, not in any hurry, not yet. The small one had seen him, turning quickly like a startled animal, and had stared right at him, curly hair flopping with sweat. He had swung his head, about to call to the other boy, who was laden down with dry pine logs, but he'd swivelled back to take another look, and by this time there was nothing to be seen. He had pulled back into the bracken. The small boy had blinked, scratched his head, slapped at a cleg which landed on his shoulder, and looked again, eyes puzzled.

Up the gully the shouts came wavering down again and he saw them traverse the lip of the valley, all walking in single file. In the distance, they seemed to be dancing, and their excited, boyishly jubilant calls came floating down, competing with the flies and the murmur of the stream. When they'd got up the cleft and then on to the high level, the taller one, black-haired and ruddy, had stripped off, and he'd run over the ridge and out of sight. The thin one, with the ragged trousers, he had followed suit, and then the small one had gone. He could hear their cries, high and clear, low and hoarse, a mixture of boy and man, the cracking age of youth. The water below the little falls shimmered as the ripples threw back the glare of the sun and he began to blink. The heat had built up on the top of his head, the deep sun-heat that brought the memories. The light was in his eyes, sharp and stabbing.

She hadn't been able to cry out. There had been no time for the other girl.

He had hit her hard. Two right-handed punches that had thudded like hammer blows, rapid-fire on the side of her face, and she had fallen like a dropped sack. He had caught her before she hit the ground, and her weight had been nothing at all in his arms as he moved through the jumble of derelict buildings and sheet-metal shacks.

The old bomb-shelter was still here, as he remembered from long ago, on the gap site where an even older building had once stood, but it was now an overgrown mess of thorny brambles and jagged rose-creepers. The thorns had snagged at his legs as he waded through them, careful not to push a path that could be followed, but stepping over the clumps so that no one would know anyone had been here. Beyond a tumble of masonry there was a narrow stairway, hardly more than the width of a man, which fell steeply and turned to the left, down a shaft made up of concrete that had been piled in canvas sacks and still retained the imprint of the long-rotted weave. There had been an ancient hasp on the door but it had broken away easily when he had been here before. Beyond the doorway the stairs continued down and turned again before another wooden door that led into the shelter proper where a heavy, woodwormed table was pushed against the concrete wall. The corrugated-iron ceiling curved to a low arch from a dust-strewn floor. The place smelt of old papers and cobwebs, but it was dry and it was hidden. He put the girl down on the table, letting her flop in a series of muffled thuds as elbows and shoulders hit the surface. He lit the candle, letting the light swell and push the darkness back a little.

The girl was silent, but he had seen the tiny flicker in her eye, the reflection of the candle's light, that told him she was awake now, trying to deceive him, hoping vainly for a chance, for an opening.

There were no chances. He spun and clamped a hand over her mouth before she even had time to open it. Her eyes widened, and he could see the fear flare in them, dark eyes, slanted in this light. He had squeezed until the jawbones began to creak. He squeezed some more until she shuddered violently, and her eyes had widened so far they were huge in the candlelight.

Dung-fly. A voice spoke to him, one of the voices from inside his head. He cocked his head, still keeping his hand clamped to the fine features while her body shook and writhed . . .

He was out of this memory and into another.

Conboy was talking to him again, his eyes filled with flies and his mouth grinning widely all the time, showing all of his teeth from stretched-back, ragged lips, while the maggots squirmed under the skin, making it come alive.

'Kill them all, slitty-eyed bastards,' Conboy said, giggling now. 'Shoot them down.'

Conboy had a hole through the side of his forehead, a dark little eye. On the other side, there was a crater the size of an orange and everything had leaked out. Conboy's thoughts had trickled out with his brains, and they could still be heard on the still, stifling air.

Dung-fly. Over and over and over again. It never changed. The children had run away, yammering again, and then the men had come down, creeping with their *parangs* and machete blades held high, edging across the log to where the truck nosed down into the swamp. The sunlight had rippled in the spaces where the water steamed, and the gun had bucked in his hand and he had seen one tumble backwards in a splash of red.

The black eyes had stared at him, and Conboy, half in and half out, had glared accusingly at him through the mass of flies.

The man who crouched in the valley blinked against the sparkle of light from the water, and the memory winked out. Up on the hill the boys were shouting and yelling. Slowly he rose to his feet, cradling the black barrel of the shotgun in his arms, and went silently up the slope and back towards the farm. He would come back later, when it was dark, just to see what was what. There was no rush now. He had all the time in the world.

'Just like *Lord of the Flies*,' Corky said when he saw it.

'Who's that?' Billy asked, predictably. 'Is he in the American comics? Like Lex Luthor, King of Crime?' The way he said it gave all the words capitals for emphasis.

'It's a book, dumbo,' Corky said, irritated at last. 'These kids on an island find a dead body covered in flies and they think it's alive, like a monster. Some kind of voodoo.'

'Has it got super powers?' Billy asked. Corky snorted and turned away, shaking his head.

'Don't you ever read anything that doesn't have pictures?'

'Not if I can help it,' Billy said. 'That's a waste of time.' He poked a stick into the eye socket of the dead stag and left it there, jutting like an arrow. But later, at night, round the fire, with the flames crackling on the resinous pinewood, Billy talked about the flies.

'Must have been what Mole Hopkirk was like, eh? All covered in maggots and flies. Jeff McGuire went loopy after he saw it, right off his head. They had to take him away and lock him up. Old Mole must have stank to high heaven.'

'Would drive anybody loopy,' Doug said. 'His hair growing all over the place, right down his arm and along the floor. That's really creepy. His nails had grown right out like claws. It's true. That's what I heard. If it was me, I'd have died right there on the spot, swear to God.'

They had all heard the stories. Danny and Corky looked at each other across the flames. They had come close to clambering in that back window.

'That wee girl was terrible. The one under the bridge.' Corky had poked a thin twig into the fire and brought it out, jerking his hand to make the glowing tip write on the air. 'He'd left her to die in her own pee. That's how they found her.'

'Don't talk about that,' Tom said sharply. He leant away from the fire and put his hands up to his ears as if to shut out what he was hearing.

'What's up with him?' Billy wanted to know. 'Making skid-marks on his pants again?'

'Just leave it alone, will you?' Tom said tightly. 'It's not funny.'

'But Don Whalen was worse,' Doug said, steering it away.

'Stuck down there in the dark with that body. That must have drove him out of his mind. Sitting there waiting for old Twitchy to come back and do him in. Jeez. That must have been pure murder.'

'He should have fought back,' Billy declared. 'Fought like a man.' He stabbed his knife in the log and left it sticking up on its own. Doug laughed scornfully.

'I suppose you'd take him on.'

'Don't have to,' Billy said. 'They think he's hanged himself, just like Judas, that's what my mum said. But if we had met him, the five of us could beat him no bother. I mean, all of us together.'

A twig cracked sharply in the dark of the forest and they all jumped, whirling to stare at the shadows. The sound did not come again.

'Just a sheep,' Billy said, slowly turning back towards the fire, but his eyes were wide. Doug yawned and said he was going to get some shut-eye. A few minutes later Billy stood up, looked into the shadows of the trees, then followed him in through the tent-flap. A minute later they could hear the muted, pseudo-American accent of the deejay on Radio Christina. There was a pause, and then the Beach Boys were singing, in pretty damn-fine harmony about how they get around.

A while later, they could hear Doug snoring. The Animals were tinnily singing about the rising sun and warning mothers to tell their children. The stolen lighter clicked inside the tent and a flare of light threw a sharp shadow against the canvas. Corky crept to the flap, peered in and then came back, suppressing a giggle.

'He's into the blonde with the big bazookas again. Playing pocket billiards.'

Danny and Tom laughed along with it, almost sure of what Corky was talking about but not wanting to ask. They were still below that cusp and, while some things were hinted at, until they were actually experienced, they had no real meaning.

The fire was waning, and they heaped some thicker logs on it until the flames crackled high and bright. Inside the tent they heard the rustle of the magazine pages and they sniggered again. After a while, Billy started to snore even louder than Doug. The three of them sat in silence for a while until Corky spoke up, turning his fire-reddened face towards Tom.

'When do you go?'

'End of next month,' Tom replied. 'My mum says it'll take a week at least on the boat.'

'But it'll be summer when you get there,' Danny said. 'And it's really hot at Christmas.'

'I won't know anybody,' Tom said, but Corky snorted almost cynically.

'That's a bonus, believe me, Tom. Sooner you get out of this crazy place the better.' He looked up and they could see a sudden, unaccustomed anger tighten on his face. 'Swear to God, if I could leave, the happier I'd be. Really I would.'

'My mum wants away,' Tom said. His voice was thick and sounded as if it might crack. 'She says she can't live here any more, not since Maureen . . .' His words trailed away. The other two nodded, letting it go. Danny remembered back to the day in church just after little Lucy Saunders' torn body had been found under the bridge. Over on the other side of the aisle he had seen Tom sitting beside his parents, head bowed, face tight.

His father's bald head had been raised to the massive crucifix which was suspended over the central aisle, bearing a gory and bloodied Christ, hung, nailed to the tree, each streak of blood lovingly painted on its plaster surface.

Frank Tannahill looked as if he were making an appeal to the bleeding man on the cross. Tom's mother, a thin little woman in a blue coat that had seen plenty of better summers, hadn't sat up to listen while the priest gave his sermon, but stayed kneeling, eyes tight-closed and hands clasped in front of her. If ever there was a picture of desperate misery, that had been it. Jessie Tannahill was surely praying for the repose of the soul of her own daughter whom Christ in His infinite mercy and wisdom had taken away from her when she herself had gone out to the shop for only half an hour.

The boys nodded, letting it go, but Tom wouldn't.

'I hate it when Billy goes on about that wee Saunders girl. He doesn't know. Nobody does.' Across the fire, tears glinted in his eyes. The other two sat silent. Tom started again, opened his mouth, then shut it quickly, as if trapping words unsaid. He slid down off the rock on to the grass and laid his head down on the warm stone. He closed his eyes tight and he looked as if he was holding back more than words. He seemed to be pressing against a tide of anguish that could break through any moment in a torrent.

'Ach, Billy's just a mouth,' Corky said. 'If he had any brains he'd be dangerous. But he doesn't mean anything by it. He just never thinks.'

'Doug'll be in Toronto before Christmas if his old man finds a job,' Danny said. 'Wish I could get away to somewhere different.'

'No chance, Danny Boy. You and me, we're stuck here with the rest of the low-lifers. But your dad's studying, isn't he? He'll get a good job somewhere. Like a teacher. Something in an office. He can wear a collar and tie and carry a briefcase, all posh. Maybe he'll even get a car.'

'Sooner the better,' Danny said. 'We've been flat-stony-broke as long as I can remember. All I want is to get some pocket money once in a while. My old man says it'll be fine when he finishes, but I'll be about twenty by then. Really old.'

'Better than my da,' Corky said. He rarely, if ever, mentioned his father, even though everybody knew it would be another few months before Pat Corcoran was let out and came home again. 'I mean, he's ok when he's sober, but when he's got a drink in him, Jeez, it gets pretty rough, I can tell you. And Phil, he's a few slices short of a plain loaf. He'll end up in the Drum as well, that's for sure. I don't want to be like them.'

'You got plans?'

'Yeah. Plenty of them. Star in films, eh? Be a big star like Sean Connery.' Corky grinned, somewhat ruefully, somewhat sadly, as if no matter what dreams he had, none of them would come true. 'Wouldn't mind making films. Like *Lord of the Flies*. Real adventures. Like what we're having here now.'

'This is just a picnic,' Danny said. He turned to Tom. 'Isn't that right?'

But Tom had fallen asleep, his head on the warm, smooth stone. 'Just you and me, amigo,' Corky said. 'We don' have to show you any *steengking* badges." You ever read that?'

Danny nodded. 'And saw the film. Really dead brilliant.

Especially when the bandits came at the end.' He poked at the fire. 'You think you could really do that? Make movies?'

Corky shrugged. 'Maybe. I think I should be an engineer, though. I can do maths with my eyes shut, but you can never tell what's going to happen, can you? You got to get on an apprentice course, and everybody knows my old man. Mud sticks, you know? And there's no way he'll let me stay on at school. You have to go to college to get anywhere. You have to learn to be like those folk on TV. Wearing suits and talking with a gob-stopper in your mouth. Carrying a briefcase. That's what it's all about. But if I get half a chance, I'm telling you, I'll grab it with both hands.'

'I want to paint,' Danny said. 'And be a naturalist. Maybe go exploring and paint all the animals I see.' Danny poked a twig into the embers and sent sparks floating up to the sky. 'But my dad says I can't take art, because it's not a real subject. He says I have to stick with Latin so I can become a lawyer or a priest. Honest to God, he'd turn cartwheels if I went away to be a priest.'

Corky giggled softly. 'I can just see you as a priest. Father Danny Boy Gillan. I'd have to kiss your ring.'

'The ring in my arse,' Danny said and Corky giggled. 'Anyway that's bishops.'

'You could be the pope. They carry you around in a big chair all day.'

'It's no joke. My old man says it's the biggest honour a man can have, a son who's a priest. Honestly, the only way I'd do that would be if I got to be a missionary down in Africa. I'd get to see the elephants and lions and everything. Explore the jungle.'

'And see all them big native women dancing about with their big bazoombas swingin' as well,' Corky said with a leer.

This time Danny sniggered. 'I'd rather see Janey Hartfield with no clothes on. We nearly did. I thought I was going to faint.'

'Me, too. I'd watch her any day of the week. What a *goddess*.' Corky looked across the fire. 'That's the kind of money I'd want. I mean, they don't even have to think about it, do they? They get everything done for them, and they've got fancy cars and they never have to do a day's work. *Jeez*. See if my old man was rich . . . ?'

'He'd still knock the living shit out of you,' Danny said. His lips were pulled back into a grin, but there was little humour in it. 'Same as mine. Sometimes I reckon Billy's got it made. He's got plenty of uncles and nobody to slap him around.'

'Yeah, but you'd have to be half daft as well, just like he is.' Billy's snoring droned out from the tent. 'He still believes his old man was killed fighting Japs. Hell, I think he still believes in Santa flippin' Claus.' Corky raised his eyes to the dark sky. He yawned widely, stretching his arms wide.

'Time for beddy-byes.' He nudged Tom, who mumbled in his sleep and then woke with a start, his eyes wide and bewildered in his thin face.

'You want to sleep out here?'

Tom mumbled again, getting his bearings. He shook his head, and Corky got a hand under his elbow to help him get to his feet. Tom's neck had gone stiff from the hunched slumber against the stone. They went into the tent, leaving the fire to burn itself down. Billy was snoring loudly and they pushed him until he turned over. Doug muttered unintelligibly, then gave a little high laugh, which made the three of them snigger.

'Little red rooster,' Danny said, and they tittered in the dark, suppressing real laughter.

In the dusty, musty silence of the tent they lay quiet, listening to the snap and crackle of the pine twigs in the fire and the murmuring voice of the stream as it tumbled over the smooth boulders. Some time during the night, Tom cried out. Danny woke up and heard him call out his dead sister's name, a pitiful, plaintive cry that trailed away into a wavering moan that twisted a bleak and forlorn sadness inside Danny's soul.

Some time during the night, footsteps crackled in the thick trees downstream as something heavy clambered over dead logs and dry branches. Corky awoke and listened to the noise, wondering if a cow had come wandering down from Blackwood Farm's high pasture and got stuck in the trees. The noise stopped and for half an hour there was a silence and then, just as he dozed off, the *doom-doom-doom* of heavy footfalls echoed on the hard track beside the stream and startled him awake once more, with images of red-eyed rats snarling in his dream. They faded away into the night. Danny woke up and saw Corky pulling back from the flap.

'Whassamatter?'

'Thought I heard something,' Corky whispered. They listened. Down in the trees a branch snapped with a harsh crack, and the noise reverberated between the trunks. A night bird hooted, low and haunting. Something small shrieked and died.

Upstream, way beyond the first few bends of the meandering gully, Danny heard the harsh and lonely *kaark* call of a heron and the sense of foreboding swelled along with the dragging remorse. He knew it was the female, calling to its dead mate.

August 1, night

The man came out of the shadows and into the moonlight, using the sound of tumbling water to mask his progress. He walked slowly, one footstep at a time, avoiding the dry clumps of bracken that would have crackled and rustled and woken them up.

He had watched them from further up the slope, sitting quietly in the cool hollow as the shadow deepened, watching the red flicker of the fire and listening to their voices, unintelligible in the distance, as they huddled round the fire. After a while he'd gone down to the trees, where the darkness was almost absolute. Once he'd snapped a twig in his hands, just to see their reaction, to watch their heads jerk round warily. They reacted like animals, instinctively on guard in the night.

He'd gone back up the hill to sit in the hollow overlooking their camp, waiting there until the first two had gone inside. He watched the small one fall asleep, then listened to the low mumble of conversation between the two boys. Overhead the moon was almost full, silver-blue in a misty sky. He could see Conboy's face in it, eyes shadowed with dark flies.

The stream mumbled to him, and he could hear a distant voice in that, a low murmur, getting louder, coming closer. He had sat by the dung-heap, watching the clouds of insects eating at the head, and observing the rippling of the maggots under the skin. He had waited for it to speak but it had not said anything to him, not yet. But the voice would come, the way Conboy's would come, getting louder all the time until he could hear all of the words.

The two boys woke the small one and they all went into the tent and, after a while, the man came slowly down the slope to the side of the stream where the grass was short and dry. The zephyr of breeze carried the scent of resin and sap and something else. He sniffed at the air, trying to pinpoint the source, following the smell until he reached the hawthorn tree, thick and gnarled, with low, spreading branches. The deer's skull hung on its own branch of antlers, socketed eyes staring blindly. He had watched the boy set up this totem in the heat of the day, dragging the trophy over the ridge at the bend of the stream. The flies were silent in the darkness.

Dung-fly.

The whisper came from far away or deep inside him. He stopped, cocked his head to listen. Up in the sky, the moon's mouth yawned, and he thought he could hear Conboy urging him on.

They were snoring inside the tent, and he crept past to sit on the rock beside the fire, feeling the waning heat of the dying embers. One of the boys mumbled in his sleep and then cried out. Another muttered, perhaps to himself, perhaps to the one who had cried out, and all the time the snoring, loud and regular and utterly oblivious, continued.

He could go in. He could rip the flap back and swing the opening wide and they'd wake in fright, not knowing where they were or what was happening.

But not yet.

The moon's reflection wavered in the stream and Conboy's fly-eyes shimmered with life. He eased himself up and walked down the bank to where the water ran shallow at the end of the pool, leaving a thick deposit of fine, sandy shale. The man walked along this, leaving his footprints clear in the gravel, and followed the stream down towards the trees. He was almost at the first bend, where the valley jinked to the left in a tight dog-leg. Here the bank was cut away by the action of the water, overhanging a small, but deep pool. He stopped there, standing with his face up to the moon, and then he stamped his feet hard on the firm-packed turf.

Doom-doom-DOOM.

The vibrations seemed to come up from the depth of the water. Up at the tent, one of the boys cried out again. The man faded into the shadows of the trees. In the light of the moon, in the faint glow of the fire, he saw the tent-flap open, and a tousled head poked out, twisting this way and that. A boy's voice whispered. Down among the trees, the man put his foot on a dry twig and leant his weight, making it break with a hard snap. The noise echoed off the tall trunks. Close by, an owl hooted. Up on the moor a bird rasped a night call, hollow and lonely and thin up there in the dark.

CHAPTER EIGHTEEN

July

The stranger came knocking at the door in the early afternoon. Jean McColl didn't hear him at first, engrossed as she was in the delicate task of removing honeycombs from the hives at the back end of the vegetable garden, where the bewildered and angry bees buzzed in clouds. The terriers heard him, as they heard everything, and had set up a racket, insistently barking their high-pitched temper and eventually she had to lay down the smoke funnel and go round through the gate to the front yard to check.

'Looking for work,' the man said. He was tall and angular, though broad-shouldered, and his dark hair hung down over his eyes. In the warmth of the summer afternoon, he was wearing a long coat with a belt hanging loose, the kind they used to wear back in the fifties, and it had seen better days. Over his shoulder, an old army tote bag showed the stains of many miles.

'Saw the sign, did you?' Jean was still wearing her broad straw hat, with the muslin tucked into the neck of a man's chambray shirt. On her hands, a pair of her husband's protective gloves made her look almost comic, like a child dressed in adult's clothes. She unrolled the fine cloth and peered out from under the brim. 'The sign on the gate?'

'I did,' he said, nodding to affirm. He was standing with his feet planted apart. One boot's sole was peeling from the upper.

'Can you dig potatoes?'

'Sure I can. All day, too.' He hadn't shaved in a couple of days and he looked as if he needed a bath. In the angle of the sun, she couldn't see his eyes, but there was no particular need. Maybe the country was changing after the austerity of the years after the war, but there were still plenty of wanderers who couldn't settle, men with no fixed abode and an itch in their feet, looking for seasonal work.

'Well, you look big enough,' Jean said. She was fifty-six years old, ten years younger than her husband Ian and, where he was wide and blocky, she was bird-like and quick. Her hair was pure white and her skin was clear despite a lifetime of helping to run the hill farm, out in all weathers. She squinted up at the big man.

'The labourer is always worthy of his hire,' the man said. His voice was deep and slightly rasped, like he'd been breathing in the cornstalk dust. She couldn't place his accent.

'Amen to that,' she said, picking up the context. He was a religious man. Good. 'Blackwood should be back in a half-hour or so and he'll tell you what's needed. But there's work to be done so he'll no doubt take you on.' She turned and pointed round by the corner of the byre where a half-dozen heavy, red chickens were scratching in the straw, jerking their heads in nervous tics. 'There's a space in the bothy where you can put your kit. Running water's from the tap on the wall.'

'What's he paying?'

'Same as anybody else. A pound a ton and then he'll see how fast you go. You get bed and board and, if he takes a shine to you, well, maybe there's some walling needs done for the winter, but that'll be up to him.'

The big man said nothing for a moment, but remained standing there, almost in silhouette. The sun limned the edge of his hair, making it gleam blue-black, like a Red Indian's hair. He looked as if he'd been sleeping rough for the past few days. Maybe he was hungry.

'I suppose you could have a bite and a cup of tea while you're waiting. Give me ten minutes to finish with the bees and I'll put the kettle on.'

'I'd appreciate that, ma'am,' he said, nodding again. He hadn't said much at all, but that wasn't unusual either. Many of the men on the roads just came out of nowhere and worked a few weeks, sometimes a full harvest season, and disappeared again with hardly a word. It was possible, Jean knew, that one or two of them might have been running from trouble, with the police or the army, but as long as they could work, that was nobody's business but theirs. She came from old farming stock, and farmers in this neck of the woods liked to preserve their own privacy. They respected the need in others.

Round at the home garden, she unshipped the last dripping slab of honeycomb, while a few bees which had been out of the hive when she used the smoker came buzzing angrily around her head. The rich, thick honey dripped into the pan, sending up a luscious, exotically sweet scent that reminded Jean of every summer she'd spent on the farm. She smiled to herself, thinking of all those seasons that made up most of her life.

She was in the kitchen when the man came back, now stripped of his heavy coat. The sleeves of his shirt, faded-blue, workingman's cotton, were rolled up to his elbows, showing a pair of long, muscular arms covered in a mat of black hair. He'd obviously bent to get his head under the hose-pipe tap, for his hair was now slicked back from heavy eyebrows, and beads of water trickled down his cheek like sweat.

'Here, I made you a sandwich,' she said, indicating the table. 'Set yourself down while the tea's brewing.'

Off in the distance, a low rumble told her the tractor was heading back up the rutted track. The stranger sat up straight, head cocked to one side. An odd, indecipherable look flicked across his face. He blinked a couple of times.

'That'll be Blackwood coming back,' she said. It was a tradition in these parts, still is, for farmers to take the name of their spreads. Ian McColl farmed the highest land on the north side of the town, a mix of poor arable and high moorland where the bracken made further creeping inroads every year. They'd some cows, which were pastured down on the edge of the barwoods, and three hundred sheep and a small herd of shaggy highland cattle up on the heath and scrub of Blackwood Hill and beyond. On the south-facing fields below the trees, where he'd spent three back-breaking years stripping out the thick gorse, there was a fair crop of early potatoes and a handy field of swedes, most of which would feed the beasts in the winter. It was a hard life up on the hill, both of them knew that, but for Jean, it was the only life, often rewarded by the late, dropping sun catching the rocks of Langcraig Hill in the distance, or gleaming up from the river estuary in the height of summer. The winters could be bad at this height, but then she'd see a spider's web hoar-frosted and glittering, or a white stoat go scampering across the rocks and, in the depth of January, she'd hear the first bleating sounds of the new life as the sheep dropped their lambs. It was no easy life, but there was a beauty and a symmetry and sometimes a magic in it all, as she would write in her neat hand in her diary.

She brought two big mugs to the table and filled them both. 'The ham's my own. Smoked only last week, and the bread's fresh from the oven this morning.'

Jean never tired of telling folk, even strangers looking for casual labour, about her bacon or her bread. She'd a store out the back with rough cheeses wrapped in muslin, maturing away in wooden rounds, and half a dozen demijohns sealed up with last year's vintage of elderberry wine. All of it, every fermentation, every batch of cheese, was carefully noted in her book. Every new year she'd go down to the town, as long as the snows hadn't blocked the track, and buy a new diary. They were her pride, and her record of thirty years up on Blackwood Farm. On winter nights, when the wind howled around the red-leaded struts of the hay barn, she would bring a book down from the loft and travel back in time to the days when she was young and dark-haired; to when Ian McColl would take time off from the scything of the hay and chase her through the long grass and sometimes catch her.

Outside in the yard the tractor shuddered to a halt. The engine barked twice and Jean knew there would be a plume of blue exhaust smoke trailing away from its rear end. The stranger started back at the sound and his eyes blinked several times, as if grit had got in under his eyelids.

'Och, it's only a backfire,' she told him. 'You'll get used to that soon enough if you're here awhile.'

The man looked at her, still blinking, as if he couldn't really see her, and Jean wondered if he was all right. Just then her husband came in, wide-shouldered and with a day's silver growth of beard ragged on his cheeks. He took off his hat and wiped a handkerchief over the red crown of his head.

'The heat would melt you out there,' he avowed, and slung the hat on to the hook. He turned and saw the other man. 'Looking for work, I suppose?'

The big man nodded again. 'Yes, sir, I am that.'

'Sound like an army man, eh?'

Another nod.

'So you'll not be scared of a bit of hard graft?' McColl said cheerfully. 'Usual start rate's a pound a ton, and maybe a bit more on the up-slope when we reach it. There's a good two weeks' work there on the early crop if you want it.'

Jean McColl brought the tea across and Ian sat down, his scalp fiery and beaded with sweat. He still hadn't set eyes on his wife, but when she laid the cup and a plate of sandwiches down in front of him, he took her fingers in his calloused hand and gave them a gentle squeeze that conveyed a whole sonnet of feeling. 'Good lass. Saved a life.'

The other fellow reached forward for his cup and as he did so his sleeve rose up close to his shoulder, just enough to expose a small tattoo on the outside of his arm below the shoulder.

'That your name? Lesley?' Ian asked, pointing at the blue, scrolled word on the skin. Jean was over at the stove and missed the tattoo. The man had taken a drink of tea and he inclined his head forward. The farmer took it as confirmation.

'Right, Les, if you want the work, then it's yours. You look as if you've got a strong back, and I need the crop in by the end of the month for getting it down to the cooperative. On and after that, I've got some walling up on the moor that I'll need a hand with, so if you work out all right with the tatties, then you'll be welcome to stay.'

'The labourer is worthy of his hire,' the new hand repeated, almost whispering.

Ian eyed him up. 'I'll be the judge of that, you can bet.'

Jean came to the table with her own cup, a delicate, fluted piece of china which looked like a part of a doll's teaset next to her husband's chipped pint mug. The men finished their snack and Ian McColl took the new man through the back to show him the potato field. The stalks were already tall and drying to yellow, bent eastwards by the gentle breeze of the past few days, which had died down now to a sultry summer's day.

'The bothy's fine and dry and the missus is a good cook, so you'll not want for a square meal or a place to sleep. You want anything from the town, though, it's a bit of a hike. More'n five miles by the track. I don't manage down there myself much except for a delivery or for the auctions. You from around these parts?'

'Long time ago,' the fellow said. 'Long time. Before, you know?'

Ian McColl nodded. Some folk didn't give much away and he wasn't the one to push either, though it would have been good if the new hand was more of a talker. It was good to chew the fat across the table when the talk of farming was done and the work was finished for the day. From back in the kitchen, the sound of dishes being washed and stacked came back to them. Jean said something which neither heard clearly enough to make out, but from the tone was unmistakable. The terriers came scrambling out of the kitchen as if devils were chasing them. The door slammed shut.

'Never did like her kitchen getting messed up,' Ian said.

The other man blinked again, as if the sun was in his eyes. McColl moved off towards the tractor and got it started. He beckoned the stranger across and waited until the man hitched himself up behind the seat.

'Might as well get started,' he said brightly, slinging his cap back on his head and shoving the peak up the way farmers do. The tractor coughed bronchially, spat smoke from its stack and lurched round by the byre.

Jean McColl watched from the window, thinking. Help was hard to come by this far up and almost anybody who came through the gate at harvest time got a job for the asking. But there was something about the stranger with the nervous, blinking eyes that didn't settle with her. She tried to think what it was but couldn't get a finger on it. There was something about his face, gaunt and angled, that should have been expressive but wasn't quite, as if everything was being held down inside.

There was something about the man and his deep-set, coal-black eyes and his slicked-back, gypsy hair and the smell of woodsmoke on his clothes. Up around these parts, the tinkers, the travelling folk, were MacFees and MacFettridges, descendants of the refugees kicked off the land in the highland clearances. The new man had a travelling look about him, but he didn't look like a tinker.

Later that night, after the men had come home and eaten a heroic meal, she and Ian had sat at the table while he worked on the model ship he was building out of matchsticks, a labour of love that promised to keep him occupied right through the long, dark nights, until the end of winter when the ground would be soft enough to work. Jean was writing in her book.

New man started today. Big as a Clydesdale plough-horse and with the looks of an Italian or maybe a Polish soldier. Says his name is Leslie, Leslie Joyce. Says he's from around these parts from way back. Looks strong enough for carting the potatoes and that should give Ian a fair hand, and good for his back too. He won't go down to the doctor about it no matter how much I go on about it. Made five pounds of butter today and got six full jars of honey. Best collection yet, and not one sting this time. As ever, I couldn't help licking my fingers for the taste of heather.

She looked over at Ian, swinging her eyes from one black-bound book to the next one, opened beside it. 'You're a week early with the potatoes this year compared to last,' she told her husband, who was gingerly gluing a spar to a curved rib of the old-fashioned ketch. 'And I'm a week ahead with the honey too.'

'It's the heat since the start of summer. It's lasted a while. After the good rains in the late spring. Always gets things off to a fine start. A lucky year for us.'

'Ian says it's a lucky year,' she wrote down. 'We've had our share of them, in between the bad ones.'

She smiled at him, though he never saw it, his red dome bent to the delicate task, thick, gnarled farmer's fingers surprisingly agile, delicately gentle, and Jean knew just how gentle he could be. It was safe enough to write some things down in her diaries. Now and again, she'd read him a piece out loud, an entry from previous years, making him grin with the accounts of young Ian's first tottering steps, or bringing the hint of a lump to his throat when she showed the dried wild-rose she'd pressed between the pages, a small gift brought back from a foray down the valley to the barwoods to round up the strays. But he would never read her diary, never go looking in her private place. That was hers.

Outside in the yard, the terriers barked. The bothy door closed with a dull thud, and the dogs went silent again. Leslie Joyce (if that was his name) must have got up and gone to the outhouse.

The noise interrupted her train of thought. Where had she been?

Back ten years ago to the day she had pressed the rose in the book, a delicate pink with a powerful wild fragrance, a token, plucked in the passing, but a treasure, for he'd brought it home for her. Another lucky year, just like this one. She wrote that thought down, savouring it and the memory it brought back, wondering what she'd think in ten years' time, God sparing.

Out in the bothy, the free-standing stone shelter that served as a bunk-house for the labourers, the man with the tattoos and the black eyes lay stretched out on the bed. The dogs had surprised him when he'd walked silently across the yard and leant in at the corner to peer in the kitchen window, but no one had come to the door. In the house the old woman was writing in a book and the farmer was bending over something on the table. The tall man turned away when the dogs started their yapping, high-pitched chiding and he'd stared down at them. Without a word he moved soundlessly across the dry earth and cobbles of the yard and let the door spring back. It took forty steps from the window to the bothy and he counted them all, just in case he needed to know. Overhead, the moon showed a sliver of silver in a velvet sky. In the shadow of the bunk-house he lay down on the straw mattress and put his hands behind his head, staring into the black.

The dogs stopped barking and settled down at the front door.

The man with the tattoos lay silent but, inside his mind, the thoughts were hot and dark and filled with memories.

After a while, in his thoughts, he heard the high-pitched voice and the steady drone, and he knew it would not be long before . . .

CHAPTER NINETEEN

July, Blackwood Farm

Ian's gone and twisted his back again but he won't go to the doctor while there's a field yet to be cleared.

Jean McColl's script was clean and rounded and she had an artistic swoop on the tails of letters below the feint lines. Thirty years and more had aged the ink from a dark to a faded blue, but they had not diluted the fresh quality of the farmer's wife's account:

He'll come in for his tea with a hand behind his back and his neck all red from bending away from it, just like last year, and he'll say it's just stiff from sitting up on the tractor. God love him. He doesn't want me to worry and yet he'll never take a word of advice. I know where young Ian gets his stubborn streak. The new hand, Joyce, is working well enough though he hardly says a word and doesn't come in for his dinner, but takes it to the shed. They moved nearly ten tons of early Pentlands from the south field, though Ian thinks there's a chance of wireworm in the late crop since it's just been turned this year from old pasture.

Two tinkers have a tent down by the road and they're staying for a day or so while they sharpen the scythes and do a bit of fencing, but Ian says they look a bit shifty for his liking and that's why they're not staying in the outhouse with the new man. Must get the shutter fixed. I thought I saw something moving in the yard and it could have been my imagination, but the labourer's a bit of an odd one, though he can dig potatoes. A letter from young Ian today, saying his barley harvest will keep him busy for the next few weeks, but he says he'll be coming to visit at the end of August. I wish he'd bring me news of a different kind of crop, but I'm supposed to be patient.

The cats have laid out four rats in a row behind the hayrick, as if they expect applause for doing their job. The owl in the barn took a weasel right on the path, and that's one less to be in after the chickens. Morag's been lying in the sun behind the byre. I don't see her making another winter, poor old soul, so we'd better start training another collie soon for next year's rounding.

Picked peas today and shelled them all afternoon. I'll be seeing them in my sleep. There was a Flanders poppy growing in amongst them, a big, scarlet flower standing above the pods. Inside, it was the most delicate purple. Shame to pick it, but they only last a day. I wore a dress that shade of purple to the harvest dance the year I got engaged. Ian Blackwood looked me up and down as if I was royalty. I could have cried when I picked it, but it was lovely just remembering. Better look out the liniment for his back.

The Flanders poppy, each petal wide and veined like a butterfly's wings, was pressed flat between the leaves of the book. The red had turned to a deep brown. Beside it, just below the script, done in pencil, was a small sketch of a barn owl, wings raised, legs outstretched beyond the heart-shaped head, talons spread wide. The weasel was in the act of turning, a slender and sinuous shape on a stony farm track. Both had been drawn by a deft and confident hand, a thumbnail etching of a small death at Blackwood Farm on a summer's day. All of the years since it was drawn had not diminished the action or the finality of the swoop.

He had watched the woman. She had looked at him with her bird-quick eyes, and the pounding had started again in his head.

It had been hard work, trailing behind the rake spines of the tractor, hooking the potatoes out of the ground with the wide-bladed fork, bending and lifting, exposing the white, almost skinless crop like lizard's eggs, to the light of day. It had been hot and sweaty, just him and the farmer out in the field, bending and lifting, then stacking the sacks on the trailer. They'd had a break at mid-morning, just enough time for a cup of tea from the flask, then back to work. Just after noon, they'd stopped again. Blackwood had turned the tractor around and they'd come trundling back to the farm to stack the sacks.

He had been here for three days, and he'd been watching them. The light stayed in the sky until late, darkening it down to a gloaming purple that hid movement. Through the narrow window, she'd be writing in her book, and he would be hunched over his model boat, both of them, hardly saying a word, as if they knew that the shadow of death was upon them.

He could stand still, motionless, so that the dogs stayed quiet and didn't start up their racketing as they had the first night. In the dark, he'd be invisible. The light inside would reflect back from the glass, making it opaque. He could stand here and he could watch and wait.

The shadow was on them. *The shadow of the valley* . . .

When they came back from the field, the woman had left his meal on the barrel out by the door of the outhouse, a tray covered by a white-linen cloth to keep the flies away. She had invited him inside to eat with them, but he wanted to eat alone, so she just left it for him. Strong cheese, light, crusted bread and translucent strips of cured ham. A side dish of lettuce and spring onions and green-tomato chutney. A ploughman's lunch.

He ate in silence, chewing carefully and washing every mouthful down with a drink of thick, warm milk from the jug. The light slanted through the old shutters of the shed where he sat on the low bunk. It formed brilliant chevrons against the wall.

He blinked against the glare, chewing. The light was in his eyes and he felt the pressure build.

She came out of the kitchen and into the yard, lugging a steaming kettle which she placed on the ground beside a tin basin. The farmer followed her, patting his belly and then arching his back as if he wanted to stretch the kinks and knots away. From the shadow in the bunk-house he saw them caught in the light. Their shadows puddled on the cobbles where two cats snoozed. Around them, he could see the dark aura that told him the shadow of death was on them. It was close at hand. He could sense it pressing in. The time was nearing.

The farmer went towards his tractor, heavy boots crunching on the slabs. The woman moved to the chicken coop. He could hear the rattle of the wire-mesh door and the cluck and flutter of the hens as she went among them. The smells of the farm came thick on the air. Beyond the coop, the manure heap, enclosed by walls of stone, angled away from the small byre, empty for now, but crowded with the half-dozen milking cows at four o'clock, when they'd come shambling in from the pasture. Swallows came flicking in and out, red and blue streaks on the summer air. Overhead, squadrons of swifts wheeled and squealed. A mouse, or maybe a rat, rustled and scurried in the next-door tack room where the old bridles and harnesses lay in a heap or hung from rusted nails.

She came back, walking quickly, almost bird-like, holding a white chicken by the feet. It fluttered and flapped in a panic as she crossed the yard to the block. Without any hesitation she laid the chicken across it, pressing down so that its head was over the edge. She jiggled the hand-axe until the blade popped free of the wood, swung it up and then down. The chicken's wings whirred in a sudden spasm as blood spurted from the neck. The head spun away to land close to the door of the outhouse. Its yellow eye stared up into the dark of the doorway.

The smell of hot blood came wafting up.

The sunlight glared from the whitewashed walls of the kitchen. The light was in his eyes and he could see the shadow on the woman. He could hear the approach of the wings. There was a buzzing as flies circled the chicken's severed head. His eyes started to blink.

It was as she expected. Ian had come in with a hand pressed to the small of his back, but it hadn't dented his appetite. He'd left only one slice of the ham and two thick wads of bread, wolfing the rest with relish. She'd had some soup and a cup of tea and little else, not wanting to spoil her own appetite for dinner. Ian had been pleased about the crop, which would be in at the end of the week and down to the co-op store. She'd said she'd kill a chicken for dinner, and he'd nodded cheerfully.

'Make it a big one,' he'd said, giving her a squeeze as she passed him on the way out with the freshly boiled kettle. 'We'll be starving when we get back.'

The chicken's head flew away and, after the flurry of spastic wing-beats, the bird went still but for the slow clenching of the scaly feet into tight talon-fists. Ian was over at the tractor, while she poured the boiling water over the carcass to loosen the feathers and damp them down. As she stood up, she had the strange sensation of being watched, but when she raised her eyes there was no one there. Against the whitewash glare, the outhouse door was a black oval, like a bottomless hole.

Jeannie McColl plucked the chicken with deft, sure twists of her nimble hands, working from tail to neck. The axe lopped off the ends of the wings and within minutes the bird was bare and pimpled, steaming slightly as it gave up its heat. She slung the sodden feathers on the dung-heap and took the chicken back to the kitchen. At the sink, she ran the water and opened the bird, watching the drain darken in a spiral as the blood flowed away.

She bent to the task. Already the leeks and carrots were lined up waiting to be cleaned and chopped and, if she got the bird into the oven early, letting it cook in its own juices for a few hours, she'd manage to get the washing out and dried. It was still soaking in the stone tub in the wash-house, where a trickle of smoke curled out of the boiler chimney.

The man they'd accepted as Les Joyce came walking out through the black hole of the doorway. The movement caught her eye and she looked up. He took two steps out and stopped, with his head cocked to one side. His eyebrows went up as if he was considering something. She saw his lips move and then the eyes blinked, twice, three times, very fast, screwed all the way closed as if he'd bitten into a bitter gooseberry.

Outside, the cockerel crowed again and its rival challenged from the other side of the yard.

The man stopped, and blinked some more, then he bent slowly and picked up the chicken head. He held it up, turning it in his hands as if he'd found something of great interest. A drop of blood fell to the cobble, leaving a stain that looked black on the stone.

Ian called from across the way, but the man seemed not to have heard. He had taken off his shirt and she could see the tattoo high on his arm, dark against smooth, lightly tanned skin. His lower arms were matted with hair. He stood up straight, tall and spare, his hair glistening so black it was almost blue. Ian called out again. The man turned and went back to the doorway. He raised the chicken head up to head-height, holding the door steady with one hand while he scraped the severed neck across the paint-peeled wood.

Jean leant forward, perplexed, leaving her own bloody hand-print on the window-sill.

The man repeated the motion twice and then he daubed the bloodied neck on the doorposts and on the wooden lintel above them. When he had finished, he casually threw the chicken head over his shoulder. It bounced and skittered against an old trough. Immediately a twisting whirl of flies danced over it. The door of the outhouse closed and she saw what he'd done.

A dark-red cross was slashed on the wood. Some of the blood was running in small dribbles, but the cross itself was plain enough. On either side and above it, splashes stained the grey wood.

The man with the tattoos turned slowly and walked in front of the byre. He reached the chopping block and stood there as if listening for something, head twisted, straining to hear. His hand reached out and started to work an axe out of the wood.

A cold sensation twisted in the pit of her stomach. She raised her hand further and pulled back the net curtain, leaving another stain. She leant towards the window, craning to the left. Ian walked into view. He was saying something and wiping at his head with his handkerchief.

The man swayed backwards and his eyes twitched again. Ian leant towards him. The axe came free. Ian turned towards the motion and the sucking sound of metal pulling from wood.

Jean called out, no words, just an inarticulate cry. Fear suddenly pulsed within her.

The man spun quickly, bringing the axe up and then down in a fast arc. Ian jerked away from it. The blade came down and caught him hard on the left shoulder.

'Oh,' he said. He sagged to the left, head following the motion. His handkerchief fluttered to the ground.

The tall man stood blinking, face expressionless. Her husband spun away and went down on one knee. For an instant she thought the blade had missed him, that the man had only hit him with the wooden haft of the kindling-axe. Ian turned, and she saw the look of surprise on his face. His hat rolled from his bib pocket and down on to the cobbles. His arm was twisted at a strange angle and the fingers were twitching with a life of their own.

The big man took a step forward, flattening the white flutter of cloth into the muck. Ian lifted his head up and his mouth formed a perfect circle. The blood seemed to drain away from his red face. Joyce looked at him, bending forward from the waist, like a gardener inspecting a rose.

In the kitchen, Jean tried to call out again, but the words wouldn't come. Over on the far side, against the wall of the byre, the cat sensed violence and slunk away. Ian let out a moan or a groan, loud enough to carry over to the kitchen. It was a dreadful sound of shock and gathering pain.

Joyce straightened up, twisted again, and brought the hatchet down on Ian's other shoulder. Her husband cried out, a horrible animal bellow. Blood did not spurt. It simply washed down the front of his shirt in an instant flood, turning the blue chambray to a silky black.

A wave of sick dizziness engulfed her and she felt herself sag back from the window. The net curtain ripped at the corner under her weight. The dizziness passed over her. Her eyes opened and, without warning, she was sick. It came blurting up, hot and acid, only tea and the crumbs of a scone, some barley soup. It spat on to the surface beside the sink.

Ian was down on the ground. He toppled forward, and one hand went out to stop himself falling, but there was no strength in the arm and it gave way under him. He twisted and fell hard, rolling over on to his back. He groaned, like an animal. His momentum carried him round and he got slowly to one knee, moving as if through treacle. The back of his shirt was soaked right down to where it was tucked into his bib-overalls. His head was angled to the side, and she could see the sun glisten silver on the stubble of his cheek. The left arm was still jittering as if it wanted to fly away, but his shoulder was impossibly slumped, and the stream of blood was right down the length of his sleeve to where it was rolled up at the elbow. Dark drops went splashing off to the ground. Ian got one foot under him, managed to push himself up. Joyce took three steps back and watched him, blinking fast. Ian looked up, his face twisted in agony and shock, eyes wide and unbelieving.

Jean's sick paralysis broke. She turned away from the window, hauling for breath. Outside, the cockerel crowed again. She went round in a complete circle, banged her hip against the heavy table. For a second she did not know what she was doing, and then her eyes lit on the blackened poker leaning against the oven. She bent and grabbed it, got her other hand to the warm, metal handle and ran for the door.

Out in the sunlight the air was thick with the metallic scent of blood, but it smelt different from the thin chicken's blood on the worn stones. This was human blood, her husband's blood.

'No, Jean,' she heard him cry, though the words were hardly intelligible. They came out in a slobber and she saw a bubble of blood froth up. Joyce waded back in again and hit him on the jaw. For some reason the blade twisted and the axe hit flat-on with a hard clank.

This time Ian screamed. There was no other way to describe it. There were no words, just a high bleat of sound, like the pigs in the slaughter pen. His jaw fell to the side and another bubble of blood burst between his wide-open, sagging lips.

The dizziness threatened to come and carry her away, a dreadful, rolling, dark wave that made her knees want to buckle. She staggered forward and raised the poker. Ian's eyes opened wide. She could see the enormous chasms the axe had ploughed on either side of his neck, making both shoulders slump downwards. The blood pulsed up and out at the turned-down collar of his shirt. She went stumbling forward, gathering all of her strength.

A black and white streak flicked in front of her. She had heard it first, although in her horror and fear the sound had not managed to get through to her consciousness.

Morag leapt up, growling in fury. Her jaws opened and snapped shut on the man's upraised arm. Joyce was a big man, and Morag, ten years old that summer, was an old dog, but he was taken by surprise, and the weight of her charge threw him off balance. The collie snarled and sank her teeth in. Joyce grunted, but it was a grunt of effort, not of pain. He dropped the axe.

Jean did not stop, she ran straight in and swung the poker at the man's head. It missed, but it slammed against his shoulder with enough force to send such a jarring vibration up her arm that the metal rod flew out of her hands and landed with a clatter in the yard. Joyce didn't so much as look at her. He turned again, grabbed the collie by the neck and dragged it off his arm.

Morag snarled. He didn't seem to notice. He pivoted on his foot and threw the dog down. Jean bent to pick up the axe, got her fingers around it and spun round. She swung it, even harder than she had swung the poker. Trying to crash the blade right into Joyce's blinking eyes.

The man's hand reached up and stopped the axe in mid-thrust. With a simple twist of his wrist, he snatched it from her.

'The gun, Jeannie,' Ian managed to blurt. 'For pity's sake, get the gun. Save yourself.'

Morag came streaking in again, lips drawn back in a ferocious snarl. Joyce whipped the axe down and split her skull. The old dog dropped like a stone and flopped to the cobbles.

'Oh,' Ian said again, in a sick expulsion of air.

Joyce walked towards him, and Ian's eyes widened. Blood dripped from the hatchet. Jean tried to cry out but no sound came.

'Gun,' her husband muttered, still thinking of her, even in the extremity.

She turned, apron flapping, skittered into the kitchen. She bolted through, feet pattering on the hard, slate floor and into the hallway. The gun-rack stood against the door. She opened it and grabbed the double-barrelled twelve-bore, pulled it away from the wood panel at the back of the rack. She stopped dead.

The chain pulled taut on the trigger guard. The gun was padlocked in the rack beside its neighbour, an ancient Spanish birdgun that Ian had inherited from his father. He'd always kept it locked, since their son had been small, just in case of accidents, just in case young Ian wanted to play with the guns. It had become a habit.

The nausea came looping again. A slimy spittle coughed from her mouth and stained the wood. The chain rattled but it would not come loose.

Find the key. Find the key. It was on Ian's chain. It would be in his pocket!

Jacket or trousers? She scampered back to the kitchen. His jacket was on the back of the chair. She grabbed it, shaking it for the sound of jangling keys. A boiled mint rolled out and on to the floor. The keys were not there.

Must be in his overalls. The realization came in a shiver of cold.

She groped her way to the window again and brushed the curtain back slowly, suddenly absolutely terrified for her own life. She might yet get the keys. She could get them, and get the gun and shoot him, and get Ian on to the tractor and down to the hospital at Lochend. She stood on tiptoe and peered out.

Joyce was walking towards the byre, his whole body leaning forward. If she could get the gun, she'd shoot him in the back. He wouldn't even see her.

Joyce walked further, coming fully into view. He was dragging Ian by the foot. Her husband's shoe had come off and his sock had rolled down. The friction of the ground had pulled his overalls back and several inches of white leg showed. The man was dragging him along, leaving a slick trail of blood on the cobbles. Two of the terriers who had been exploring at the rabbit warren down by the coppice came snuffling into the yard. They reached the trail of blood and bent to sniff it. They whined, confused. Joyce did not stop. He dragged Ian McColl into the byre. Jean watched, listening to the dreadful scrape of wet material against the ground. Her husband's head bumped against the low step and he made a low sound.

He was still alive.

His red head disappeared into the shadow, and that was the last she saw of him.

Jean stood frozen, unable to comprehend what had happened. The dizziness rolled inside her again and her vision faded once more. She held tight to the sink, gasping for breath, and in a moment her lungs were pistoning uncontrollably in a sudden spasm of hyperventilation. She fell over the old sink, feeling the edge press against her chest, and the spasm passed.

The gun. She could get it now. Joyce was in the byre. She forced herself to move, got away from the sink and made it to the door. The axe was lying in the middle of the yard. She darted out into the bright day, bent and snatched it up. Her husband's blood trickled down the handle. Her feet were in a puddle of it, but she couldn't think about that now. She knew he was alive. He'd be in dreadful pain, and he had lost so much blood, but he could still make it. She could still make him live if she could get the gun.

The scraping, dragging sound echoed out from the byre. She squirmed from it and backed into the kitchen, following her route again. She got to the gun-rack and saw the black barrels of the twelve-bore leaning outwards. Without hesitation she chopped at the chain, trying to hit it against the heavy-oak shelf. Wood splintered. Twice the axe bit into the base of the rack and she had to jack it back and forth, making it squeal to release it again. She swung hard, managing to bite down on the chain, but there was no effect. The force of the blow merely pressed the steel links into the wood.

Sobbing sore, she tried again and again, swinging the hatchet down as hard as she could.

Out in the yard, the terriers set up a frenzied yapping. Jean stopped swinging the axe and looked out through the front door. Joyce was walking fast, coming diagonally from the barn to the house, heading straight for her. In his hands he swung the old chopping-axe, the one Ian used for the winter logs. Even at the height of her terror and desperation she realized she would have no chance against it. Instinctively she slammed the door and hit the deadlock snib. Both shotguns were now leaning out from the rack, black and deadly and completely useless. She ran down the hall, went through to the living room, changed her mind and came back again. A shadow loomed at the door, wavering at the other side of the frosted glass, and then the whole pane crashed inwards. The man's hand came through, reaching for the Yale handle, and found it snibbed shut. She didn't wait, but dashed back to the kitchen, right through to the back room and straight up the wooden stairs.

A ferocious crash was followed by the hard slam of the front door against the wall. Jean didn't stop. She got through the bedroom and into her workroom, where her ironing-board and sewing machine were laid out almost side by side, close to the old radio beside the rocking chair where she used to sit and crochet while listening to the evening plays. The door had a heavy, iron latch, which she clicked home. In here, with the shutters closed, it was dark and warm. A chink of bright sunlight knifed through a crack in the old wood and slipped a blade of silver across the room. Dust motes danced in the light.

The muffled thud of the axe came pounding up from the hallway and she shivered. He would kill her. He had axed her husband without a thought, chopped him down like an animal. Her jittering mind screened a picture of Ian trying to get to his feet with both shoulders horribly slumped away from his neck and the sheen of blood silken on his shirt.

Down there, beyond the workroom door, beyond the bedroom and down the stairs, the crashing noise came again. Once, twice, then another two thuds. There was a silence that stretched for a long time. She could hear her heart beating fast against her ribs and both her hands fluttered uncontrollably. She moved unsteadily to the window, trying to slow her breathing, to make it be quiet. On the dresser, sliced by the blade of light, her diary lay angled towards her.

She moved towards it and, right at that moment, a thunderous roar shook the walls. Joyce had the guns. He had got them out of the rack.

In that moment, she knew she was dead. He was going to kill her. She could not get away.

Jean McColl slowly reached for the book and slid it towards her. Out in the byre, Ian let out a loud and shuddering cry, and her heart almost broke in two.

Down in the hallway, she could hear Joyce walking about, his feet crunching on the glass where the window had caved in. He would come looking for her, that she knew. There was no escape for her. Ian groaned again and she tried not to listen to it. She prayed with all her heart for it to be quick and then she sat in the corner and made her hand be steady.

She began to write quickly in her book.

CHAPTER TWENTY

August 2, 11.30 a.m.

'It's like the moon,' Tom whispered. The breeze over the high ridge of the moor snatched his awe-struck words and carried them away. The others stood on the long edge of tussock grass looking down at the wide and barren basin of the heathland that seemed to stretch to the horizon. It was pock-marked and pitted with craters that really did give it a blasted, lunar aspect. The black water in the depressions, each one ringed by a tumulus of heaved-up earth, made the craters seem like bottomless pits.

'Christ on a bike,' Billy said, his voice reduced to a marvelling whisper. He stood up on a thick mound of peat and scanned left and right. 'It goes on for ever.'

It was the eeriest, most spectacular sight any of them had ever seen. The basin of the moor swept down from where they stood on the rim. Fifty yards away, a rusted chain-link fence suspended between concrete posts that angled over, listing like wounded sentries, caught the wind and made it moan, adding to the sense of desolation and old destruction.

Far across the moor, maybe a mile off, but probably more, only the roofs of a clutter of shacks and shanties were visible beyond a lower ridge.

It had been further than they had thought, at least five miles up into the hills from the camp. They'd walked since early morning, after a breakfast of cornflakes and slices of bread toasted black over the flames. Doug had woken first and had disturbed them all in his scramble to get out of the tent, twanging the guy-ropes and almost collapsing the canvas on top of the others.

The fire had still been smouldering and it took only a handful of dry bracken and twigs to get the flames flickering, and in no time at all the pinewood was crackling hot. They huddled around the camp-fire in the cool of the morning, drawing the heat into themselves and watching the magic transformation as the rising sun began to burn a fine valley-mist away.

'We heard something last night,' Corky said. 'Sounded like somebody walking.'

'It was like the sound you get if you walk over a Racine rat's burrow,' Danny confirmed, although he hadn't actually heard that. Billy grinned.

'Oh, I'm really scared. Terrified even. You should have woken me up so I could have trembled all night.'

'You were scared enough in the dark,' Doug derided.

'It's true,' Corky insisted. 'Probably a cow, though. Just as long as it doesn't barge into the tent when we're sleeping. We'd be flat as pancakes in the morning.'

'Maybe it wasn't a cow,' Tom said, still shivering in the cool of the morning. 'I told you I saw a man when we were collecting firewood. I think there was somebody watching us.'

'Bunch of pussies,' Billy said. He went down to the stream with his mug and threw the dregs of his tea out into the stream. He turned and was about to come back up to the camp-fire, when he stopped so suddenly that Doug and Danny noticed immediately. They asked him what was wrong. Billy crouched down, and the others came sauntering over to the stream, expecting some silly joke.

'Was this here last night?' Billy asked. He was hunkered on the gravel, inspecting a wide footprint impressed deep into the surface. They could see the clear zigzag of heavy-duty cleats. Doug bent down beside him.

'I don't think so. I think we would have noticed.'

'Somebody's playing silly baskits,' Billy said. He stood up and then stamped his foot down beside the print. His own baseball boot made only a slight indentation, hardly two-thirds the size of the original print.

'Can't be us,' Corky said. 'You've got the biggest feet. And it's nowhere near that size.'

'Did you draw this?' Billy asked Danny. 'Did you fool around here and make this look like a footprint?'

'Don't be daft. It's the real thing.' Danny came down the bank and got on his knees. 'But it looks old to me. Nobody's been up here in a long time, and it hasn't rained in a while. It's probably been there for weeks. Your boot hardly made a mark and this one's pretty deep. It must have been here before we came.'

Danny wasn't sure of that, but he preferred to believe it, and the shale was hard-packed and fairly dry. The print could have been there a long time, since the last time it rained, some time back in July. He didn't want to think of anybody passing through their camp in the middle of the night. He remembered Corky poking his head out of the flap. There had been a sound, a hollow thud.

And then a branch had snapped.

If it had been somebody, they wouldn't have made so much noise, Danny told himself, rationalizing it. It must have been a cow wandering among the trees.

'Yeah, that's days old,' he said, now near enough convinced. 'Weeks even. There's nobody around here. Nobody daft enough to come all this way up the hill.'

But Tom and Doug seemed less convinced. They were looking round warily, scanning the trees. Nothing moved. Far off in the distance, way down the valley where they knew Blackwood Farm was, a cockerel welcomed the day. Danny flapped his elbows and did a little strut, coaxing a grin from Doug, and they all sat down again. They waited by the fire, toasting more bread on the ends of their sticks while they finished their tea, and then they started off on the trek. They followed the Blackwood stream ever upwards, over narrow falls and through narrower gorges, up on to the high moor, where the water cut its way through deep peat deposits and sometimes disappeared altogether under the thick cover of purple heather. Up at this height, the air was colder and a wind blew in from the west, so that when they stopped walking, it dried their sweat on their backs and, despite the power of the sun in a clear blue sky, it made them shiver.

The stream had become a rivulet, dwindled to a trickle, and then they were beyond it, right at the source, into the damp bog draining the high moor where the clumps of sphagnum moss sank under their feet in soft sponges of marsh. Clusters of papery reed-moths flew up with every step, and marshy gas-bubbles gurgled and burst in stenchy little explosions. It had been slow going here, crossing the boggy land, sometimes sinking up to their knees, and sometimes further than that in the stagnant pools where the mud was oozing and liquid. Corky told them he'd read in *National Geographic* of a man's body found in a bog, preserved by the peat for thousands of years, still with the hair on his head and the leather tunic on his back.

'That's what the smell is,' Billy said. 'It would make you puke.'

'You think there's bodies here?' Doug asked.

Corky nodded.

'Sure. Dozens of them. They used to have battles up here. William Wallace and Rob Roy McGregor. All the clans in their kilts and claymores.'

'Isn't that a land-mine?' Billy wanted to know. 'A claymore?'

'No, it's a sword,' Corky explained patiently. 'Used to hack each other to pieces. We're probably walking over the skeletons right now. They'll be lying down there all rotted and grunged up like something out of *The Twilight Zone*.' He twisted his face into an approximation of a skeleton and curled his fingers into hooks. It looked not unlike Dougie's imitation of the creature from the black lagoon on the day they'd first thought of the expedition to find the dummy village.

Tom hauled himself out of a sinking hole and clambered on to a grassy mound that could take his weight. He had taken off his canvas shoes and had them hanging by the laces round his neck. 'That's horrible,' he said. 'What if we stand on one?'

'It'll probably bite your toe off,' Corky said matter-of-factly. Tom stayed up on the tussock, wobbling for balance, arms outstretched.

'Then spit it out again when it finds out it's your stinky ol' foot,' Doug chipped in, grinning his big-toothed smile, but careful to avoid placing his own feet in the muddy holes. They seemed to go down for ever and, up at this height, they probably sank for thirty feet.

Tom leapt from the mound to another, nimbly landing and swaying for balance as it shuddered under his feet. He jumped to the next, lost his footing and fell to the third one, landing on his belly. Billy dipped, quick as a cat, snatched a wet handful of moss and mud in his hand, then grabbed Tom's ankle. The small boy felt the cold, clammy grip and let out a howl of fright. He kicked backwards, landing his foot in the pit of Billy's belly. Billy gasped and stumbled backwards, stepped into a dip, and his foot went right through the mossy covering into a slick, swampy hole. His foot snagged on a buried root and for a moment he imagined bony fingers clawing on to *his* ankle. Without any hesitation at all, he heaved himself right out again before he fell on his face.

'I'll get you for that,' he bawled hoarsely at Tom, who had rolled over the mound and reached a thin strip of firmer ground.

'You and whose army?' Tom called back. Billy lumbered after him but for once the small boy had the weight advantage. Billy's feet kept sinking below the surface matting and all around him the floating marsh wobbled and shivered in his wake. The legs of his jeans were black with peaty mud.

'The creature from the black lagoon,' Doug jeered. 'Except uglier. And fatter.'

'Piss off, Nicol,' Billy rasped. He clambered awkwardly over a mound of moss. 'I'll get that little shit.' He reached under his T-shirt and pulled the pistol from his waistband.

Tom had made it to the solid ground and was fifty yards away while Billy was still floundering. The rest of them laughed at the blundering pursuit, and that only made Billy angrier. He struggled out of the marsh, breathing heavily, and stopped to get his wind. Tom was halfway up the slope towards the ridge jumping up and down, taunting. His high voice carried down the hill. Billy raised the airgun and cocked the spring. He took aim.

'Christ, Billy, don't . . .' Doug started to protest. Billy fired, but Tom was too far away, and the pellet travelled only forty yards before hitting the ground. Tom jumped up and down, jeering, and the others laughed raucously. By the time they reached the top of the ridge, Billy's quick anger had evaporated and his jeans were almost dry, though now caked with the black mud.

They stopped there and, below them, the heathery lip of the wide depression, the pocked moonscape, stretched out towards the low horizon in a swathe of broken landscape.

'We found it,' Corky said. He pointed across the wide basin. 'The Dummy Village.' The way he said it gave the words capitals. 'I never really believed it was there. I thought it was just a story somebody made up.'

'I *always* knew,' Billy said.

'You always *would*,' Doug observed drily.

The craters dotted the whole of the plain, some of them solitary and isolated, and others so closely packed that their embankments merged and gave them different shapes. The larger ones were deep and dark while those on the slope nearest them seemed shallower, as if the earth itself hadn't been deep enough. These were fringed in dark-green reeds and choked with duckweed and algae. They stretched northward as far as the eye could see.

'The plan must have worked,' Billy said. 'Look at all those bomb-holes. Must have dropped thousands of them up here. Millions. Bet the old Jerries were sick as pigs when they heard they'd all missed their targets.' He put two fingers across his lip and made a mock Nazi salute. '*Schweinhund dirty Brittischers*,' he screeched in a *Commando* comic German accent, making them all laugh.

He held up his stick like a rifle and aimed it at the sky, making hawking sounds at the back of his throat as if he were firing a machine-gun. 'They should have had anti-aircraft guns up here to blast them when they came. That would have been great fun. You couldn't have missed from up here.'

'I wouldn't like to have been here when they were dropping all that,' Doug said. 'You'd have been blown to pieces.'

'I didn't think it really existed,' Corky said, wonderingly. 'Honestly, I didn't. Not *really*. I thought it was just a story.'

Danny nodded in agreement and wonderment. He hadn't truly believed in the dummy village, but he'd *wanted* to believe. It was one of the school-yard legends, like old Miss Dorrian who'd died of a stroke in Castlebank Primary School and now walked the empty corridors at night. It was like the tales of Cairn House, the oldest building in town, where a girl had once seen a white and bloodless face floating outside the window twenty feet above the ground, and where Mole Hopkirk had been found with the nails still growing on his dead fingers. The dummy village had as much substance as the three little girls who'd been playing skipping-ropes and were killed down on Crossburn Street before the war when a cart-horse had bolted and the overturned flatbed had crushed them against the wall. People said that when the mist came off the swampy lowland of the Rough Drain on Hallowe'en night, you could hear them chanting their school-yard rhymes as they skipped on through the night.

The dummy village, the decoy target for the wartime bombers, had not been truly real, though it *should* have been. Now it was indeed real. They had trudged up the length of the Blackwood stream, right up to its marshy source, and clambered through the swamp of the bog, and in the heat of the sun they'd slogged up the hill to a ridge miles from the town where the air was clear and there was no sound but the mewling of lapwings and the warbling song of larks rising into the blue.

It was here. A dilapidated Shangri-La on the far side of the low ridge in a wild moonscape.

'And we're the first,' Danny said. 'Nobody's ever been here before. Maybe not since the war.'

Far overhead, a buzzard wheeled on broad wings, circling on the clear air. Its plaintive cry came down from the height.

And the boys started walking down the hill, towards the craters and the clutter of buildings.

Before the first of the potholes, the chain-link fence, red with rust at the places where the concrete stanchions stood upright, caught the wind and moaned muted protest. At other places, the poles had sunk or listed into the peat and the wire was ripped and jagged, some of it flat on the ground with thick grass stalks growing through. On the periphery, tangles of stinging nettles swayed in the breeze. A square, metal signpost with its sign obliterated by rust hung from a pillar, pock-marked with bullet-holes that Billy claimed were from a soldier's Lee Enfield but which looked just like straight .22 shot to the others. Further along, once they had clambered through the defunct barrier, Tom found another sign, this one angled into the ground. Wind and rain had peeled back the paint on the side that had braved the elements while a triangle of dirty, red corrosion showed where it had been angled under the turf. The red mark eliminated the first letter of the warning.

ANGER! the rest of the word warned. For some reason it seemed apt up here in this forgotten monument to the fury. Danny felt that shiver of foreboding again, although they could all fill in the missing letter.

'What do you think the danger is?' Tom asked.

'It's been up here since the war,' Billy said. 'It was the bombs coming down. It was to let everybody know that if they stayed here they'd get bombed to pieces. Simple.'

'I think it's the craters, telling people to stay away from them,' Doug said. 'Some of them must be pretty deep. If you fell in there they'd never find you again.'

Tom let the ragged sheet of metal drop. It stuck back in the peaty turf again. They went on down, past the first of two shallow craters where dragonflies helicoptered out from the choking reeds. Beyond that, a large, single hole, almost perfectly round, was bare of weeds. The water inside was black and there was a shimmering, dirty iridescence of oil on the surface, close to where the boys passed, giving it a poisonous, somehow evil aspect. They couldn't tell how deep it was.

At the next one, an oval pool caused by the close detonation of two wartime bombs, Doug spotted a boot lying upside-down in a patch of reeds, its sole peeled away from the upper like an opening jaw. Billy stretched with his stick to haul it out of the thick growth.

'What if there's a foot in it?' Doug asked, with a snort of laughter. 'Like the one in the quarry?'

Billy ignored him and brought the old boot to the edge. He up-ended it, and they watched a sludge of water and algae gurgle out. Something black and many-legged wriggled in the flow and made it to the pool before Billy could hit it with his stave.

'If there was a foot in it, you'd have filled your pants,' Doug said. Billy didn't bother to deny it. If there had been a foot in it, they'd all have run, yelling in fear, down the hill and back to camp.

Corky and Danny had moved on together, in a hurry to get to the huddle of buildings. They were halfway down the basin though, for some reason, the shanty town seemed no nearer. The others caught up with them and they trudged over the ridges and heaped earth where the old explosions had thrown up peat and boulders. Billy kept up a running commentary about the kind of planes that would have flown overhead and the bombs that would have rained down, and the noise and the thunder and the excitement of it all.

They skirted another crater, where Doug probed with his ash sapling and got a foetid and oily bubble of marsh gas for his pains. Here, another boot, identical to the first, was jammed against a plank of wood.

'Maybe somebody fell in,' Tom suggested.

'Maybe it was somebody got bombed,' Corky said. 'Like a poacher. Or a shepherd up here all alone at night just minding his own business. Stuck here on his own in bad weather, and he sees the dummy village and thinks "There's a good place to shelter." Maybe he sneaked inside and thought he was safe out of the rain and the snow. Probably a thunderstorm, with lightning all over the place and thunder. He was probably glad of the shelter, and he's sitting there trying to stay warm and then *WHUMP*. . . before he knows it he's been blown right out of his boots.'

'You really think that's what happened?' Billy asked, his face alight. 'You reckon it blew him right out of them?'

'No,' Corky said. 'Look at it. The sole's got a big hole in it. Somebody just threw them away.'

Billy's excited expression collapsed into disappointment.

'But it was a good story,' Corky said, and they all laughed. But as they moved away, Tom looked nervously over his shoulder just in case it *hadn't* been an old boot.

They got over the next small ridge and into the wide depression. There was another perimeter fence here, most of it rusted to pieces, and there were sections where rolls of barbed wire, the kind Billy insisted had been used to snag prisoners of war, had been laid in long, tangled cylinders. They followed it for fifty yards to find an opening, testing the rolls for breaks. In one of the tangles, a dead fox, its fur and most of the flesh rotted away, had been snared by the coils. Its frozen snarl of clenched teeth was still ferocious. Further on they came across the whitened skull of a ram that had suffered the same fate. The rest of the carcass was long gone, picked clean, scattered by scavengers. The skull was pure bone and it bore a massive, ridged pair of curled horns. Billy hooked it out of the wire and tried to set it up on his stick like a trophy. When they found a way through the fence he led them like a standard bearer with the skull held aloft as they finally strode into the dummy village.

A flock of rooks watched them, huddled together like black vultures on a roof down the centre way. The five boys walked warily between the first of the buildings, and the birds sat silent, all their heads turned to watch the approach. There were more than a dozen of them, squat and shiny-black and somehow dangerous. Doug raised his stick and made *ack-ack* noises, and the birds flew off in a clatter of wings and a protest of cawing. They swooped low, close to the tangled moor-grass and then rose over the nearby roof, gaining height until they reached a thick wire that bellied in a curve between two canted poles. They alighted on the wire in a flutter and settled down to observe the intrusion like wary guards in black uniforms.

'That's really creepy,' Doug muttered, keeping his voice low. They had wandered through the gap between two buildings and could see down the centre way. For some reason the dereliction and isolation of the place hushed them to near silence. 'Just like *The Birds*.'

'You're too young to get in to see that,' Billy argued.

'Me and Danny sneaked in at the intermission, didn't we, Dan?'

Danny nodded agreement. He was looking at the line of crows, now even blacker, silhouetted against the sky. He couldn't see their eyes, and that made them seem as if they were blind, but he could sense their gaze. They huddled like judges deliberating on a sentence and he recalled the heron's fall and its broken, graceless ending.

'Scared the bejeesus out of me, I don't mind tellin' you,' Doug said. 'They were all sitting just like that, waiting to come down and peck people's eyes out.'

Danny agreed with that. The film had been disturbing, nature inverted and distorted and out of control. That night, as he lay in the dark, he had wished he hadn't sneaked into the old Regal picture house.

Corky found a rusted bolt in a pile of broken slabs. He lobbed it at the crows and they took off again, winging to the far end of the compound, landed on a roof and sat to wait once more.

The place was eerie. For a moment, when the crows had settled, there was a pause of silence in which nothing seemed to move, and the wind dropped to a sudden stillness. They were in a ghost town. That was the only way to describe it. They stood there, five small gunslingers at the end of the derelict main street where the couch grass and rough reeds poked their way up from a gravel-bed road. The line of wooden shacks, grey with age and sagging under the weight of neglect, angled in a straight line, dwindling in dismal perspective for several hundred yards. The corrugated-iron roofs, intact on only a handful of them, were red with rust and peppered with holes where blasted stones had punched through. Others leant into deep depressions where the ground had subsided, still others were tumbled and crumpled as if a giant hand had smashed them flat.

The place was indeed eerie, a dead and decaying village, broken and picked clean like the ram's skull. It was creepy and shadowed. But it was magnificent in its desolation. They stood there abreast, Danny leaning on his stick, Doug in his string vest, his slingshot loose in his hand, Billy hip-shot in his mud-caked jeans, Corky with a thumb hooked on his belt, a casual arm around Tom's thin shoulders.

'Magic,' Billy said, and for once he was right.

Just at that moment, the wind picked up and moaned through the wire. A metal tin clanked against a post like a tuneless bell, and a piece of twisted, galvanized sheet creaked in protest. The dummy village came alive again. Two swallows came darting in on flickering wings and swooped under a mouldering lintel. The faint twitter of squalling fledglings came from inside. A stream of gold wasps flew busily between two spars to a massive globe of papery nest suspended under a sagging grey eave.

'I never thought it would be so big,' Doug said. 'It's like a dummy flaming *city*.' They started walking down the overgrown street until they reached an intact building with a gaping door-way. They went inside. The place smelt of oil and rust and of age. The floorboards creaked threateningly under their weight and the whole building seemed to shudder as the five of them crept inside. An old, cobwebbed box lay in a corner and immediately Billy bent down to try the lid.

'It's an ammo box. Just like in the war,' he said. The lid hauled up surprisingly easily. Inside, among a tatter of shredded wood, a vole squeaked and darted out through a gaping hole in the bottom. Billy tried to catch it, but it disappeared under the sagging floorboards. Tom and Danny went outside and crossed the road to go into another shack. From the front, it looked almost intact, but once inside they could see that the whole of the back had fallen away into a pile of grey, rotting wood. Even the floorboards had disintegrated. Beyond the walls another row of buildings stood gaunt and crumpled. There was a space where a bomb had blasted a hole in the ground and the neighbouring shacks were smothered under the debris of turf and rocks.

The others joined them.

'Must have been really great,' Billy said. He pulled the airgun out and aimed it at the sky the way he had done with his stick. 'They must have come in low, over the top of the hills. You could have picked them off one by one. My old man was a gunner during the war.' He cocked the gun, fired it, and they watched the pellet climb into the air, hardly faster than a thrown rock. He reloaded.

'Your old man must have been John flippin' Wayne,' Doug snorted. 'He was in everything except the town's brass band.'

'What's that supposed to mean?' Billy demanded, rounding on Doug. 'And what did your dad do? Eh? Tell me that, *Bugs*!'

'Jeez, would you grow up?' Doug said. 'All we ever get is your old man and how he won the flippin' war.' He turned away.

'Just what does that mean?' Billy bawled at Doug's back. 'Come on! Buck-toothed *baskit*.'

Doug spun round. He jabbed his hand up to his temple and tapped hard. 'Think about it.'

'Come on, Doug. Leave it.' Corky tried to defuse them.

'Leave what?' Billy wanted to know. Danny looked at Tom, who looked back, trying to keep his face noncommittal. 'What's Bugs bloody Bunny talking about?'

'Nothing,' Doug said. He turned away again, feigning disinterest, though the others could see the stiffness in his bony shoulders.

'No. It's not *nothing*. You're having a go at me, taking the mick.' Billy's face was reddening. Corky tried again.

'Give it a break, you guys,' he said, cajoling. 'We never came up here to fight. Come on.' He looked from one to the other. 'How about it?'

Doug shrugged. 'Well, tell him not to call me Bugs.'

'Don't call him Bugs,' Corky said to Billy, putting a laugh into his voice. Danny caught it and giggled.

'Or *Lugs*,' Dougie insisted.

'Or Lugs, then,' Billy said. The tension drained away.

'Or Bugsylugs.'

'That as well,' Billy conceded. He grinned, and the tension evaporated. Billy stuck his hand out and Doug shook it, both of them looking sheepish, simple as that, and it was over. Tom and Danny ambled away. They went down the street. Tom went through one of the decrepit shacks and out to the far side where the peat was ridged and grooved in wide black slashes where the land had subsided. Danny found another swallow's nest, just a little cup of hard mud set against a beam. He got up on to an old oil drum to peer in and saw the gaping yellow beaks of the baby birds as they demanded food. Corky was in the hut opposite. He came out with an old beer bottle. He set it up on a piece of angled iron and searched about for stones to pitch at it. Doug leant in through the window of the next shack down, his skinny backside poking out. Corky couldn't resist it. He drew back the elastic and let fly. The small pebble spanged off Doug's buttock. He jerked, let out a yell, and toppled inside with a crash of splintering wood.

They heard him yell some more, while Corky and Billy rolled about, unable to control their laughter, and when he came out he was grey with dust.

'Who did that?' he demanded truculently. 'Put me through the flamin' floor?'

Corky tried to stand up, failed, and sank to his knees in uncontrollable laughter.

'Was that you, Harrison?' Doug wanted to know.

Billy shook his head. 'Honest, I never did a thing. Swear to . . .' His eyes opened wide. Danny and Tom were coming round the side of the building with something big and heavy weighed in their hands. '*Jeeesus kee-flamin'-rist*, where did you get that?'

The two boys grunted as they lifted up the long, brown, rusted thing, straining to get it to waist-height. The four metal flight flanges stuck up like black fins where the end narrowed. A hex nut protruded from the blunt front end.

'It's a bomb,' Tom said proudly. 'We found it. And there's more of them.'

Doug forgot the sting in his backside. Danny and Tom laid

the bomb down gently on the turf. There was no mistake. It really *was* a bomb. It was more than two feet long and heavy enough to indent the ground. The flight blades at the tail were pitted with rust but there was a dark, wet patch close to the nose that still had a skin of paint on it. Some light-coloured letters in stencil were barely visible.

'Is it a Jerry bomb? Or a Jap?' Billy asked, a-jitter with sudden excitement. War and the tools of war were a constant fascination for him. Proximity to a bomb from the war was just about the biggest thing that had happened to him so far. 'Will it still work?'

They all stood around the thing. It was old and rusted at the back but it still looked somehow deadly, like a drowsy adder in the grass that would best be left undisturbed.

'It's probably worth a fortune,' Doug said. 'Maybe we could sell it.'

'There's more of them,' Tom said again. 'They're stuck into the ground out there.' He gestured with his arm. 'The peat must have fallen away.' Corky nudged the thing with his foot, trying to turn it over. It rolled slowly.

'Imagine that. Must have been a dud,' Billy said.

'Might not be,' Doug countered. 'Remember that one up in the reservoir? Broke all the windows at the top end of Corrieside? That just hadn't gone off. It was still *alive*. Blew a rock right through McFarlane's barn roof, so it did.'

'Maybe this one could go off,' Billy said. He kicked the side of the thing and gave a loud yell like an explosion. Everybody jumped as if they'd been stung.

'Hells bells, Billy,' Corky said. 'You scared the life out of me.'

'Smell it? He's standing in it,' Billy said, knuckling Corky on the shoulder. 'You're losing your nerve, pal.' Corky just grinned, not taking offence.

They followed Tom and Danny round the side of the building to where the land sloped away in a profusion of trenches and craters. All of the ground here seemed to be fissured and turned over. A jagged crack a hundred yards long in the peat showed where the summer's lack of rainfall had made it shrink and split, ten feet deep in places and just as wide. It was here that the bombs showed, sticking out from the soft earth of the sides of the small chasm. There were three of them, each maybe forty feet apart, all at the same angle. They had obviously gone into the ground, punching through the soft deposit when the surface had been wet and boggy. Further along, all that remained of another two bombs were their tail-flights. Doug hooked them out of the pit with his stick and tied them to the wood like a trophy. The others hauled the remaining bombs out.

'Can we take them back?' Billy asked. 'A couple of them?'

'Sure. It's a long way,' Danny said, 'but we can strap them to a plank and take shots each at carrying them.'

'Let's do it,' Billy said. 'We can make them work. We could blow half the valley to smithereens.'

They spent the whole afternoon exploring the ruins. Tom found another sign with some lettering that was indecipherable, but might have said that the land was a target area, and that led to another discussion, which led to another argument over whether it was a decoy site or merely a bombing range. They all preferred the decoy version and Tom slung the sign away, ending the argument with stunning logic. They searched every shack for more bombs or bullets. Billy was convinced there might be a gun left behind under floorboards, but all he managed to find was a brass buckle from an old Sam Browne web belt and an ancient Zippo lighter that was clogged with muck and rust.

The sun was beginning to sink towards the west when they decided to head back to the camp. Danny got some wire and managed to secure three of the bombs to a long piece of wooden planking which he and Corky slung on their shoulders. Billy got his stick with the ram skull pinioned on its end and led the way out of the dummy village and up to the ridge. Behind them, the crows watched and waited, and when the boys were far enough away, they flew down one by one to whatever dead thing they had been pecking at in the shallow depression dug out by a wartime bomb.

CHAPTER TWENTY-ONE

Interlude

'We thought he'd gone away.' Angus McNicol's voice, gruff with the years, conveyed the regret that had hung about him since then.

'We all did, even the Commander and Dr Bryce, who was a psychologist from the university. He was a new-fangled kind of expert, trying to get inside the man's head. My boss, Hector Kelso, who was head of CID, he never put too much faith in Bryce and, to tell you the truth, neither did I.

'You see, nothing had happened since the middle of June, a few weeks before the school broke up for the holidays, and Bryce said that gave us two choices. He had either moved on, in which case we would have had more murders somewhere else, or he would have burnt out and killed himself.

'Nobody really considered the truth. The killer just took a break between June and the end of July or he had killed somebody else who hadn't been reported missing. We never found a body, so probably he just took time off. Hell, everybody needs a holiday, don't they? Where he had been, nobody knows and I reckon John Fallon must have been the closest to guessing the truth when he said the man was probably ex-army, and used to living rough.'

The former detective, now silver-haired and only slightly stooped, looked up, and his eyes were filled with remembering.

'Then Johnson McKay the postman got a bit concerned when the mail hadn't been collected from the box at the bottom of McColl's farm road and he took a stroll up there just to check. If it hadn't been for him being curious, then it could have taken another few weeks, maybe a month, before anybody would have found out.

'I'll never forget his face and I'll never forget what we found there and down at the side of the trees alongside Blackwood Stream, not as long as I live. It was a slaughterhouse, a *shambles*.

'I followed Hector Kelso around the whole day, and that man

was damned good. Taught me everything I know. The only detective I ever saw who was any better was John Fallon's boy Jack, and it's a damn shame he's left the force after that trouble a few years back, but that's another story. Anyway, Hector went round the place and gave me a running commentary, like a professor teaching a student. That was exactly how it was.' Angus looked at the little machine on the table. The cassette spindle turned slowly. 'I wrote everything down because we never had tape recorders then, and they'd have been a godsend to us, believe me. The boss was a hell of a lot better than the psychologist, because he could follow a sequence right to its end, and that's how he was able to tell me what had happened. He was a genius.'

Angus closed his eyes, frowning with concentration.

'It was the blood on the curtain. Threw him for a bit, and for a while he thought the wife might have done it, despite the fact that she was a tiny, wee thing. But then he figured it out quickly enough.

' "Gus," he says to me. "Go stand out there on the other side of that patch on the ground." I knew it was blood, we all did, and it had dried there to a crust on the cobbles. I stood there, and the boss bent down, getting himself to about the same height as Jean McColl. He leant forward and took a hold of the curtain, pulling it to the side, then brought his other hand up and laid it on the sill.

'From then on, he just walked his way through it, as if it was some kind of a slow dance. He had that kind of mind. He could choreograph it all in his head.

'The chicken was still in the sink, crawling with flies and maggots, and Hector realized she had been cleaning the bird when it happened. She must have had a ringside view from that window. She'd seen it happening, seen her man die right there in the middle of the yard.'

The policeman had almost total recall of how the CID boss had worked it out, from Jean McColl seeing her husband cut down with the axe. He knew the killer had used the chicken head to mark the bothy doorposts, and he could tell by the slant of the crosses how tall the killer was.

'Hector talked it right through and he walked it right through, never stopping for a moment. He told us where McColl had fallen like a sack and how his wife had fought and how the collie had attacked the stranger. It was all written there in the clues, in the sequence, if you had the experience to look. Hector Kelso had the experience, and the way he told it, never showing any emotion until later, made it unravel like a nightmare.

'I can still remember Hector going through the motions, over six foot tall and built like a wrestler, trying to keep low, the same height as the wee woman. He runs into the farmhouse, through to the kitchen and then to the hall, and he showed how the killer had broken the hasp to get at the shotguns.

'I can tell you straight, we were all pretty damn concerned when we realized he had the guns. He'd shot a couple of holes in the ceiling, maybe just to make sure the gun worked, and then gone looking for Mrs McColl. He'd about two weeks of a start on us, give or take a day or so.

'Dr Bryce, he said he was very close to the edge and it was likely he'd turned the gun around and blown his head off but, while we lived in hope, there was no evidence of that whatsoever. Kelso dismissed it as so much hogwash.

'He asked the psychologist about the chicken's blood smeared on the door. Bryce said the scent of blood had probably enraged him, or maybe it had dredged up some childhood trauma, but he hadn't seen the other places where the man had done his killing. I reckon John Fallon got it right.

'"Read the bible," John suggested to me when we were standing there in the sun, with all the flies buzzing around that crust of blood in the yard. He was never a smart-arse was John but, despite his build, he was pretty clever. "He wants the angel of death to pass over."

'I reckon that was fair comment, from the pages of the bible he left lying around and all the other signs he left, most of them covered in shit. The press, they got the story about the twitchy eyes, and that's how the name stuck but, in the squad, over that summer when we were hunting for him, waiting for him to make his next move, we started calling him the Angel.'

July

She wrote fast, almost tearing the page in her hurry, crabbing the letters together in a slant across the page. Her clear and rounded handwriting changed to a spidery scrawl, almost illegible. The wavering strokes showed how badly her hand was shaking.

'*He's killed Ian. God save me. Cut him down in the yard. Lesley Joyce. He hit him and took him into the byre. Got the guns. He's mad. Killed my man with axe. Cut down. Lesley Joyce.*'

The words began to repeat on the page, just as they were repeating inside her head, ricocheting around almost out of control.

Out beyond the workroom, beyond the bedroom and down the stairs, she could hear the heavy tread of the man's boots. The shotgun had blasted like a thunderclap, and she had felt the whole house shake with the concussion. Her heart had almost stopped dead in her chest. She tried to write more, to put down in words what she had seen, but the fingers of her hand seized up in a tight-clenched fist and the words wouldn't come. All she could see was the picture of Ian going down in the yard, making that awful, deadly sound.

Nausea rolled and surged inside her and a trickle drooled from her open mouth as she tried to gulp it back, tried to clear that image from her head so she could think.

Downstairs, she could hear the man muttering, at least that's what it sounded like in the distance, through the closed doors, but she knew he had to be talking aloud. It sounded like chanting.

Ian's bewildered face swam in front of hers, refusing to vanish. His hat had rolled away on the stones and he had tried to crawl away, his eyes wide and blank, like a bewildered animal in pain. He had tried to crawl away, dripping blood on to the cobbles. He'd crawled away from where she was, even then attempting to draw him away, despite the pain and the shock and the sudden awful fear.

And even then he'd tried to warn her. She jerked, found she could still write.

'*Couldn't get the gun. Ian said to get the gun and shoot but it was locked. He has the guns and he's shooting.*'

Somehow her mind unhitched itself from the crazy ricochet

of images and she managed to scribble more. She had slammed the book open, not pausing to flip the pages to the correct day and date. She'd found a blank page and started writing fast, knowing there was little time. No time at all.

The little window on the thick wall was slightly ajar. In the high summer, it let in the perfumed scent of sweet peas from the garden and the lazy humming of the busy bees, and in the mornings she got a slant of golden sunlight across the old dresser she used as a desk and a workstation. She put the book down and laid the pen on the surface. It rattled from her shaking fingers. Outside, she could hear the whine of the terriers and the lowing of the cows in the far side of the byre. They could smell the blood, and the instinctive fear of the predator had spread among them. The terriers had sniffed at the pool of blood and they were confused and panicky, their tempers now stilled. Downstairs, the man's hob-nailed boots *crumped* on the slate floor.

'*Aaah.*'

Ian's groan came drifting on the pollen-scented air. A bee flew in the window, turning lazily by the latch.

Jean snatched up the pen again.

'*Still alive. He's alive now. Please save him, God.*'

Footsteps came thudding up the narrow stair.

'*Coming now. Gun.*'

The bedroom door kicked open. She could hear the latch spring and the wood splinter and the slam of the heavy panel against the wall. It sounded loud as gunfire. Almost.

She dropped the book on the bed. The workroom, on the east gable of the house, was a low, square space with slanted walls that followed the pitch of the roof. Just above the dresser, a small trapdoor, barely two foot square, led to a crawl-space under the rafters.

She could hear the man's breathing. He had kicked the bedroom door open and he was standing there. She could visualize his dark and blinking, mad eyes.

Jean McColl clambered silently on the dresser, pushed the hatch upwards and, despite her age and her freezing terror, she managed to haul herself up into the dusty space. She lowered the door closed again as silently as she could and began to crawl over the beams, careful not to slip and fall through the plaster of the ceiling until she got out of the narrow roof-space above the workroom and into the loft proper. She crabbed her way through the narrow gap in the stone, on to the bare planks. Ahead of her something squeaked in the dark and she couldn't tell whether it was a rat or a mouse. Underneath her the workroom door blasted open and crashed against the wall, just as the bedroom door had done.

Footsteps, even louder now, thudded on the boards where the rug didn't cover. The tinkling of glass. A vase? The window? She couldn't wait. In her mind she kept seeing Ian trying to crawl away, mortally hurt, with the shadow of death reflected in his wide, stunned eyes. She heard again the dreadful animal groan.

Below her, the man called out, and whether there were any words or whether it was simply a bellowing cry of rage or anger or madness, she couldn't tell. She crawled further into the roof-space until there was enough room to let her gingerly get to her feet.

Thunder roared.

In the confines of the loft, that's what it seemed like. It was as if the world had exploded under her feet in one enormous blast.

Splinters of lath-wood and pellets of dry plaster erupted upwards from the floor just behind her. She tripped, rolled on the boards and the thunder crashed again, even closer. Instantly, a hole, maybe six inches wide, appeared in the floor just beyond the limit of the planking. Dust and splinters blew out in a fountain and rapped against the slanted sarking-planks under the slates. Jean reeled back and hit her head on a jagged nail showing through the wood. It caught her behind the ear and an instant trickle of blood flowed. She spun round and saw the column of light, like a blazing pillar, reaching from the hole in the floor to the slant of the roof.

He could hear her moving. He could hear her moving and he was trying to follow the sound and blast her to death with the shotgun.

His footsteps clumped almost directly underneath her and sudden terror unfroze her legs. She whirled, using the light coming through the gaping blast-hole, and ran for the corner, pushed through the second hatch to the space over the main part of the farmhouse and clambered over the trunks and boxes that had been stored there since before she was married. Beyond the clutter a dusty skylight showed a dull rectangle of light. Behind her the shotgun roared again, a vast and deafening sound in the close confines of the loft, but for the moment there was no danger of the blast coming through the old boxes of crockery and pre-war clothing. Dust billowed chokingly, making her fast breath rasp in her throat. At the far end of the attic there was a narrow wooden stairway that would lead down to the storeroom where Ian stacked the potatoes and turnips and the clumps of carrots. She thought about reaching the stairs and following them down, but that would put her out into the closed yard where he could shoot her from almost any position.

She had to get away, get help. Against a man with a gun, against the crazy, blinking man who had smashed Ian to the ground, there would be little chance, hardly a chance at all, but she had to try. If she could make it to the far wall without being seen, she could use the hedge as cover and get down the track, escape to the Lochside road only three miles down, heading west. If she could get to the road, then she could make it, and call the police and an ambulance.

Through the blast-hole, she heard the man's voice, rough and ragged and dreadfully angry. The shotgun's metallic clash came up to her over the growling rumble, a deadly and cold sound in itself. He was reloading.

It snapped closed again and she knew there were two more shells in the chambers.

Jean got past the collection of boxes and reached the skylight. The glass was festooned with cobwebs that had gathered so much dust they made the window almost opaque. She twisted the catch, got it free in a couple of seconds, and swung the heavy frame upwards. It squeaked alarmingly and then stopped when it was almost upright. Thankful that it hadn't crashed down on the slates, she crawled out on to the slope. The shotgun boomed again, dreadfully loud, but not so deafening now that she was out. A puff of dust rolled out of the skylight like flour in the kitchen when she baked her bread. It smelt of lime and burning.

She managed to get a grip on the iron lip and swung herself up, moving gingerly lest she slip on the moss-covered shingles, reached the ridge of the roof and got to the down-slope. From here she was hidden from the yard. The roof fell away to the pasture side, a long slide of black slate warmed by the sun. She negotiated it, trying to keep her feet flat on the surface to give her as much friction grip as possible, reached the far end where the farmhouse proper merged with the old barn. Here there was an old door at the corner, set high in the wall where Ian used to mount a block and tackle for hauling sacks of feed and bales of straw up to the high store. She got there and pushed at the door, but it was locked.

Inside the house, the man was talking to himself. From where she perched it was just a low rumble. Ian had fallen silent, and in a way that was better than the awful groaning. She wondered if he was dead and a part of her prayed, despite the devastation of that loss, that he was not suffering any more. Footsteps sounded below her and she turned away from the door, climbed back over the ridge to the end of the barn and let herself slide down to the level of the gutter. She managed to grab a hold of it and lower herself down to the window-ledge and let herself in through the old shutters. Here, in the old sway-backed store-room, old tack lay in heaps, mouldering bridles from the days they'd kept Clydesdale horses for pulling the plough, giant horse-shoes dusted with rust, a set of twisted and cracked traces hanging from nails. Rats scuttled and scurried in the shadows, alarmed at her passing, while down in the yard, the terriers had set up a strange, frightened howling. The tack balcony led to the space above the byre. She had to push aside a pile of old sacks, sending a family of mice squealing and running for cover, and then she was through to the ledge overlooking the tiled butchering shed that was tacked on to the byre.

A shape moved close to the far door. Her heart lurched, thinking the man had discovered her, and then it kicked hard in her chest and seemed to stop beating altogether.

It was Ian. He was hanging down from the hooks, head close to the ground. A spreading scarlet puddle caught the light beneath him. A sluggardly ripple showed that fresh blood was still dripping.

There was no sign of life. Jean leant on the metal railing, breath locked in her throat. One of Ian's shoes was down there in the trough along with his blood, and she could see where the butcher's hook had spiked through his heel. He'd been hung up like a carcass, spiked by the Achilles tendon, the way farmers hung pigs to let them bleed.

She started for the steps, knowing they would take her down to the yard when, outside, right then, the shotgun thundered again. She flinched, expecting the blast to knock her off her feet, but immediately a screaming sound, like a stone-saw cutting into granite, cut through the air. The dogs started up a frenzied yapping, and the gun fired again and they went silent. A moment later, a shadow appeared at the butchery door and the man came backing through, dragging a heavy weight just as he'd pulled her bleeding husband over the step at the door. The cause of the sound was clear enough. He'd shot one of the yearling pigs. It was still alive, still screeching, but there was a gaping hole in its side. He pulled it past Ian, put the gun down, hoisted the pink, shivering animal up to a hook and let it twist there. He picked up the gun and reached behind him for the knife he'd stuck down his belt. She watched as he leant forward and slit the pig's throat. It kicked into a spasm, sending blood spurting all over the floor and all over her husband. She groaned aloud, an involuntary blurt of shock and fear.

The man whirled round. His eyes had stopped blinking. He looked up and those eyes were like pits, black and mad. She pulled away, went back the way she had come, heart bucking inside her. His feet clattered on the stone stairs. She got back through the window, tried to climb on the gutter, slipped back, and her blouse snagged a rusted bracket which caught right through the material. Her feet scrabbled for purchase, slid off the stone wall and she slipped forward before being brought up sharp by the hook of metal. She was left hanging there.

The man reached out a massive hand and gripped her arm. Without ceremony and with no hesitation at all, he pulled her back in over the window-sill, ripping her blouse from collar to waist and leaving a white rag flapping on the bracket. He dragged her across the tackroom and down the steps to the byre. She tried to pull away but he clamped his hand on her neck, fingers and thumb almost touching, and walked her past her dangling husband. Her feet splashed in Ian's blood. She tried to look to see if he was still breathing, but the hand held her tight, made her face straight in front. She felt as light as a feather as he propelled her across the yard, past the bodies of the three dogs and the dark patch where her husband had fallen, through the front door and into the farmhouse.

She awoke when it was dark, and when she tried to walk she could not move. Dull and heavy pain throbbed inside her and stayed with her until the sun came up in the early morning. The light flickered in the sky, just visible through the open shutter, and the bantam cocks were the first to greet the dawn. It seemed to take for ever for the early light to creep round the corner of the byre and brighten the wall of the little slaughtering pen where Ian was dead.

She knew now that he was gone. There had been no sound, except for the grunts made by the insane man when he had finally left her alone and had gone out to the byre, swinging the big blade of the knife. He muttered to himself constantly and it seemed as if he was talking to someone standing beside him. She couldn't make out the words, but the tone of it sounded like conversation. The man would ask a question, cock his head as if awaiting a reply, and then he'd nod, or he'd shake his head in answer. He had gone out to the byre, swinging the knife, and she'd heard him grunt with effort. There had been a dull crack, like the sound of a stone dropping on another, and then the man had gone walking away, muttering to himself.

Now she was huddled on the floor, something angled and hard pressed against her ribs, but unable to do anything about that. A dark tide of despair welled up in her heart. Way off in the distance, the blast of the quarry rumbled like an approaching storm. It reminded her of the sound of the shotgun.

She closed her eyes, squeezing away a tear that was mingled with blood from a burst vessel at the edge of her eye.

And she prayed that he would come with the gun and stop the pain.

In the night he had taken the head and put it on the top of the manure heap, waiting for the sun to come up. Every now and again he would hear the voice whisper to him, faint for the moment, and he would try to catch the words.

The smell of blood was still hot and thick, and he remembered how the woman had stared at him, paralysed with fear, her whole body trembling uncontrollably. The owl hooted back in the barn and he waited under the moon, not cold and not hungry. The sun began to rise and when there was enough light in the sky he could see the flies crawling over the pale, round face.

Dung-fly . . .

Like Conboy. The eyes crawled with flies. Like the boy in the back room of the old house. Like the girl under the bridge. Like the boy who had come in through the door of the old wagon he'd taken over as his bivouac.

The flies buzzed and danced and, as the day lightened and the morning mist trailed away, there were more of them, flying in from the trees, round the coppice at the far end of the pasture. Already the pool of blood in the yard was a crawling mass of them, coming to feed and coming to breed. He cocked his head to the side, listening to the small voice, one of the many that tugged for his attention, whispering softly by the light of day. At night they'd maybe talk louder. After a while, he slowly got to his feet and went back into the house, leaving the farmer's crawling eyes staring at the sunrise.

The woman did not move. Her eyes followed him, devoid of all expression. He considered lifting her back up on to the table but, after another while, eyes blinking hard, he turned and went back outside. He picked up the gun and crossed the yard, climbed the fence and into the pasture.

Three of the cows were moaning, and two of the others were down on the grass twitching. Their udders were swollen like the bellies of starved children. He considered putting them out of their misery, but then he blinked some more and went striding sunwards along by the wall and down towards the trees. A half a mile down he could still hear the crowing cock. The land sloped towards the stream, a densely wooded valley here, downsteam from the high moorland pasture, thick with oak and beech trees. He'd been here before, in the lush valley that reminded him of that other gorge, long before . . .

Up at the farm, the old man had glared at him, just as Conboy had done, through the crawl of flies that festered in his mouth and under his brows. The tongue protruded between grey lips, blackened and torn where the blow with the flat of the axe had sent the teeth snapping together, biting right through the flesh. There were thousands of them now, all laying their eggs, breeding fast on the glut. The head stared at him, and he waited for it to speak, but it stayed silent for the moment. He could wait. He sat there, in the sun, contemplating the thing on the dung-heap, listening to the drone of flies, and then he went back to the house, to the kitchen. Here the smell was thick and heavy and the buzzing was loud in the confines. The woman was crumpled on the floor, her arms twisted awry, and her thighs stained black in streaks and dribbles. There were biscuits in the barrel and a joint of smoked ham up in the cold-store. He cut a slice, not at all put off by the cloy, familiar scent of rotting flesh. He ate slowly, sitting on the table, then drank some tepid water from the tap.

He finished eating and laid the chewed ham-bone down on the table, then went back out to sit by the side of the dung-heap to wait for a while. He could sit as still as stone.

Chapter Twenty-two

August 2, 4 p.m.

Billy raised the air pistol from seven yards away, sighted down the barrel. He squeezed the trigger and the gun coughed a sound like a thin branch breaking. The slug smacked Doug in the left buttock and he let out a howl, more of surprise than pain.

'Great shot from Dead-Eye Harrison,' Billy bragged. 'Runs in the family.' They'd been firing at the can again, trying to knock it off the rock, taking shots each while the potatoes and carrots boiled in the blackened pot. Billy and Doug had been niggling each other as usual and, when the can tumbled from the stone, moved by a chance eddy of wind and not by any sharpshooting, Doug bent to reset it. Billy had aimed and fired at his skinny buttocks, then laughed like a donkey while Doug did a skittery little dance.

'Christ sake,' Doug said angrily. 'Would you get a grip of yourself, you crazy fucker.' He was rubbing the patched seat of his old jeans. 'Swear to God, you should be in special school for *retardos*, you loony.'

'First kill to the Commandos,' Billy crowed. Corky looked at him sideways. Billy was jumping up and down, the airgun heavy, black and sharp-edged, like a German Luger clenched in his hand. Even with the spring slack and useless, he should never have fired the gun at anybody, they all knew that. It was one of the rules.

'That's enough,' Corky said. 'Give me that before you put somebody's eye out.' He held out his hand towards Billy.

'It's not yours.'

'No, it's my brother's, and that makes it mine for now.'

'And he stole it from somebody, didn't he?' Billy's voice was rising. 'So it's not his.'

Doug picked up a stone and lobbed it at Billy with a quick overarm flick. It hit him on the knee with a resounding crack. Billy dropped the gun and started hopping around on one foot, holding his knee with both hands and howling loudly. Corky snatched the pistol up from the ground and jammed the barrel into his pocket.

'Serves you right, fatso,' Doug jeered. 'That's the brave commando wounded. *Hopping* wounded, and crying like a baby.'

'I'll get you for that,' Billy bellowed, trying gingerly to put his foot down.

'You and your old man, eh? The big *war* hero?'

'You leave him out of it, *Bugsylugs*,' Billy said through clenched teeth, and the pair of them were off again. 'He did more than your old man, that's for sure. Fought the Japs *and* Jerries.'

'So how come mine's got medals?' Doug demanded, grinning toothily. 'Real medals.' His ears had gone bright red again, which was a sure indicator of his excitement and anger.

'My dad won dozens of them,' Billy retorted, still rubbing his knee, his face now as red as Doug's ears. 'That's what my mam says and you better not be calling her a liar if you know what's good for you. My dad was a hero in the war.'

'That's where you're wrong,' Doug countered, his lip curling now into a sneer. 'A hundred per cent dead wrong on that.'

Danny came wandering up from the stream, only half listening to the bickering voices. Doug and Billy were always at it, rubbing each other's fur up the wrong way. Next minute they'd usually have their arms round each other's shoulders, just like last time, digging each other in the ribs. They both had short fuses, but generally, as compensation, they had even shorter spans of concentration.

'What are they on about now?' he asked innocently.

'Just telling this fat bastard his old man couldn't have died in the war,' Doug snorted.

Everybody froze.

'Come on, Doug . . .' Corky broke in. His voice trailed away.

'What do you mean?' Billy finally asked. His voice had gone cold.

'Think about it, stupid-features. Can't you count?'

' 'Course I can count. And multiply and subtract. Better than you any day of the week, *Bugs*.'

'That should make it easy for you, then.' Doug's face was red and his lips were drawn back from his big rabbit-teeth in an angry snarl. Danny had never seen him look so much out of control and suddenly he knew with absolute certainty that Doug was going to let it slip, say what everybody except Billy himself knew as a fact.

'Ok. Try this one,' Doug's voice was all tight and grating. 'See if you can do it in that thick skull of yours. Mental arithmetic, if you *can* that is.' Doug stopped. Corky took a step forward, trying to get in between them. Both Billy and Doug each held up a forestalling hand, telling him to keep out of it, that this was between the two of them, something they could sort out without interference. Corky looked at Danny, eyebrows raised in question, but there was nothing Danny could say. Everybody teetered on the sharp edge of the moment.

'When were you born?' Doug demanded. 'What year?'

'Nineteen fifty-two. Same as you, why? You forget?'

'And when did the war end?' Doug kept it going.

'Nineteen forty-five. Everybody knows that.'

'And your old man died in the war! Seven years before you were born? Has nobody told you the facts of life?'

'Stone the crows,' Corky whispered, shaking his head.

Billy stood there, fists clenched, lips just forming around his reply. His mouth tried to work, but no sound came out. Danny and Corky held their breath. Doug stood stock-still, eyes wide, hands trembling. They could see Billy's mind, not especially fast at the best of times, but he wasn't stupid either, seizing the problem and working it over.

The silence stretched a few seconds longer. Finally Billy spoke.

'That doesn't mean . . .' He floundered to a stop, tried again. 'Just because he . . .' The three of them on the sidelines could see that Billy had never really considered this glaring anomaly, or if he had, he had slung it to the back of his mind. Everybody in Corrieside knew that Maggie Harrison had got pregnant to a big American sailor from the NATO base at Dunoon, from whom Billy had inherited his thick blue-black hair and his height. The Yank had finished his tour of duty and gone back to Arkansas and never written once.

Billy backed away from them and almost knocked Tom over.

'That's pure *shite*. It's all a load of crap.' Real distress twisted his face. 'I mean he was in the Commandos . . .' His voice sounded as if it was cracking. 'And he fought the Japs and all.'

Doug stood facing him, anger still suffusing his face. 'Did he, hell.'

'That's enough, Doug,' Corky said quietly. 'Quit it *now*.'

'Well, he shouldn't have called me that. He's always going on and on, and he shouldn't have shot me either. It's about time he wisened up. Somebody should wring his bloody neck. He's always bumming and bragging, as if he's better than the rest of us. He thinks he's a big shot.'

'Bigger than you are, you ragged bag of bones. And better.' Billy was obviously still trying to digest the enormous truth of it, but his temper was still up and fighting. 'At least my mother feeds me. Not like yours.'

'Stop them, Corky,' Danny said, almost pleading. 'This isn't any good.' He could see it coming, rushing towards them like the Great Truth Express, nobody at the brake. There were no real secrets in the street in Corrieside where they all lived.

'And at least my mother buys me decent clothes,' Billy snarled. 'Not rags like you get to wear all the time. You're like a tinker. She dresses me proper.'

'From the money your *uncles* give her? Some uncles. Uncles, my *arse*!'

'Jeez, Doug, quit it,' Danny begged in a futile attempt to prevent the head-on crash.

'Don't you start on my mother, Doug Nicol. Don't you bloody dare.' Billy took two steps forward and raised his fist. Doug flinched back. The anger and fear was evident in his eyes and in the tightness of his voice and the taut hunch of his shoulders.

'Well, it's true,' he insisted. 'You've got more uncles than I've had hot dinners.'

'And what about your mother? Eh? Tell me that?'

Danny put his head in his hands. Corky stood transfixed. He held both of his hands up, like a referee in a boxing ring trying to keep the protagonists apart. But they were like fighting cocks now, angry roosters. They didn't even seem to notice his presence.

'Why is your old man in Toronto? And how come your wee brother's got ginger hair and freckles? Everybody else knows why.'

'What are you trying to say?'

'Because he isn't your brother at all. Everybody knows about your mam and that tallyman from the Housemarket Company, the one that used to come round for the money on a Friday. That's why your da's gone to Canada. He's too ashamed to show his face in the town.'

Billy's words hit like blows, worse than blows. Doug reeled back. The others could see his mind working the way Billy's had done. His big teeth were clenched together hard enough to crack. A spittle dribbled from his lip.

'That's not true,' he finally gabbled, spitting the words out like bullets. 'You're a fuckin' liar. You're just a big fuckin' *bastard*.'

But they could all see the dawning realization on his face. The signs that he'd missed. His father's withdrawn silence, the raised voices in the living room late at night. The sounds of crying in the dark. And little Terry, red-haired and freckled, a dozen years his junior.

His mouth opened and closed, much as Billy's had done.

Corky moved right between them.

'That's enough,' he said flatly.

'Piss off, Corcoran,' Billy snarled. He tried to shove past him. 'I'm not finished with that *Bugsy* bastard.'

'Yes, you are,' Corky told him in a soft voice that had suddenly gone very cold. He was a head shorter than Billy, but he stood with his feet planted apart and his back straight, body all set. Danny could sense that Corky knew he should have stepped in before, but hadn't known how. The moment had gone too quickly. Now Corky looked Billy straight in the eye, his own green eyes bright and unblinking.

'It's finished.' Danny could sense the quiet threat there. Billy was too far gone to hear it. He pushed at Corky's shoulder and the other boy simply held himself tight, not letting himself be moved. Doug's skinny chest was heaving with anger.

'It's over,' Corky said. 'I mean it.' He took a hold of Billy's hand and dragged it down from his shoulder. He stared into the bigger boy's eyes for a long moment, forcing him to back down. Corky had that ability. He held the gaze until Billy dropped his and, for a while, before Billy conceded, Danny thought he might even try to have a go at Corky. Finally, he took a step backwards, and Corky then turned to Doug.

'What are we trying to do? Kill ourselves? Haven't we all got enough problems?'

The man watched them coming back to the camp. The boys stopped up on the narrow gully side, where a rivulet had cut the ground into a deep and narrow chasm. They were out of sight, round a dog-leg bend, but he could hear them yelling gleefully, the way they had when they had swum in the backed-up pool. Every now and again one of them would yell 'Bombs away' and the rest of them would whoop and cheer. He could hear the heavy thuds of something falling on to the shale. After a while, they came on down the shoulder of the hill where the two streams met, carefully negotiating the narrow rocky point to descend into the valley. The biggest boy was in the lead, holding his long stick over his head. The bones of the ram's skull were stark-white against the grey of the rock. He sat quietly, stock-still, in the shadow of the hollow where the setting sun could not pick him out. One of the boys stopped dead and looked across the valley, seeming to look right into his eyes. He held the pose for ten seconds, maybe more, raised his hand over his brow to cut out the light. The man leant further back into the shadows. The boy shook his head and continued down the ridge.

They arrived at the tent, and the dark-haired boy clambered into the natural amphitheatre below the steep face and spent several minutes fixing the ram's skull into the hawthorn branches beside the deer's head and the pointed heron's beak. This done, he did a little Indian dance, and his whooping shouts echoed from the valley sides. The man watched, interest quickened. The flies erupted from the stag's face in a visible cloud, disturbed by the death dance.

The others lit the fire, and the thin one balanced the blackened milk-can pot on the stones surrounding the flames. The sky was clear except for some long, pink clouds way out to the west, far beyond Blackwood Farm. The moon would be full tonight, pale and yawning. He watched them for a while more, until he was satisfied that they would be here for the night and then, very slowly, he eased back into the bracken and silently followed the sheep-track back up the hill.

At Blackwood Farm he ate some more of the dry meat and

finished the hard bread. There were some jars in the pantry with fruit in syrup, and there were eggs in the coop. He ate them in silence, listening to the buzzing of the flies as they whirled around the woman. The smell was thick and choking, but he was used to that. He had *got* used to that. When he finished eating, he went out to the manure heap and talked to the head. It buzzed back at him incomprehensibly. After a while, the moon rose and Conboy whispered to him from a velvet sky.

It had been a magical day right up until the fight, and then the magic had snuffed right out.

They had borne the bombs back to the camp on the plank litter, carrying three of them, taking turns as pall bearers, and Billy trying to avoid his share of the work by claiming to be standard bearer. It took them two hours to get back, though the going, downstream when they got past the smelly and stagnant bog, was much easier than the trip up to the dummy village. They had been elated and excited with their find, their own discovery of the fabled place. The fact that it was dilapidated and derelict had done nothing to diminish their sense of discovery and achievement, or detract from its legendary status. On the way back to the camp, they had agreed to start out as early as they could the next morning so they could explore the whole of it, right to the far end of the blasted moorland. Tom had said he'd rather go home, but again he was outvoted and he went along with it. It was a long walk back home, and he didn't want to travel over the hill and down the other valley on his own and, besides, if he arrived without them, his mother would know he hadn't been with the scouts and he'd have hell to pay. Tom's mother was living on the edge of her own grief. She could not use any more. Apart from that consideration for his mother, and it was a real one in Tom's mind, the trees were thick and crowded and anybody could get lost on their own if they didn't know the place so well.

They followed the lip of the valley, where sheep had worn a beaten track through the turf, staying up on the far side until they came level with the camp on the ridge which separated the stream from the tributary. Doug and Corky let down the plank with the three bombs and rubbed the stiffness out of their hands.

Billy stuck his stave in the turf, letting the ram's skull gaze out over the gully.

'Let's try them now,' he said.

'They won't work,' Doug said. 'If they'd have worked, they'd have gone off when they fell.'

'You don't know that,' Billy countered. 'We could at least try one and, if it works, we could sell the others for a fortune.'

'Who'd buy bombs?' Danny asked.

'The army, for one,' Billy avowed. 'Their bomb-disposal squad takes them away and defuses them. And gangsters. They could use them to blow up bank safes.'

Doug laughed derisively at the notion, but Billy ignored him. He bent down and unwound the rusty wire which had strapped the nearest bomb to the plank. He worked at it, twisting the thin metal back and forth until it weakened and broke. The bomb slid free and began to roll down into the chasm. Billy lunged and stopped it with his foot. He grabbed the tail-fin and hauled it back up, managed to lift it from the ground and raised it above his head. For a moment he looked as if he was making an offering to an unseen god on high.

'What if it does go off?' Danny asked.

'It'll go bang,' Doug said. Danny looked at him. There was a moment's silence while Billy still stood with the bomb held over his head, and then everybody just fell about laughing.

'Of course it'll go bang,' Danny said, when he got his breath back. Billy was trying to keep the heavy weight up, but the laughter had taken all the strength from his arms. He was giggling uncontrollably.

'But won't it be dangerous?'

They had all seen bombs explode in films. They went off like enormous firecrackers. People threw their hands up and somersaulted into the air. There was always a flash and a lot of dust thrown up in a black cloud. In Billy's *Commando* comics, the bombed Nazis cried '*Himmel*' and '*Donner und Blitz*'. They put their hands up in the air and were marched off as prisoners of war.

'No,' Doug assured him. 'It'll be great.'

'I think we should move back a bit.'

'What for?'

By now Billy's arms were sagging. He tried to hold the weight, but failed. The bomb tumbled out. Doug tried to grab it but only succeeded in pushing it to the left. It thudded against Billy's thigh. Billy howled like a banshee. The bomb tumbled, hit the ground right at the edge of the ridge, landing tail first. For a second it seemed to balance on its own, like a miniature space rocket, teetering on the edge, and then it slipped over. Billy was still bawling and cursing Doug, who was trying to explain that it was an accident. The others watched the bomb roll down the steep few feet of shale where the edge had eroded away. Below that, there was a ledge of mudstone that stuck out two or three feet and overhung the much steeper drop to the trickling rivulet meandering through the tumble of water-smoothed boulders below. It skidded down the shale, rolled on the ledge and paused again as if considering the next move.

'I'll get you for that,' Billy was promising Doug.

'It's going,' Corky said, voice rising.

'I think we better get back up,' Tom advised, now apprehensive. The bomb flipped over and then it dropped. Billy caught the motion out of the corner of his eye and his cursing stopped. Everybody turned to watch. The black shape fell. It rolled several feet and then seemed to flip up and out. The tail-fins wobbled and then the thing just dropped straight down.

'I'm getting out of here,' Tom yelled. He turned and headed up the slope of the ridge, but his eyes were still glued to the bomb. His heels treaded at the slope, digging the shale away in small grooves, going nowhere.

Nobody else moved or said a word. They watched as the bomb went plummeting. Its fall took only a few seconds and, for an instant, from up on the edge, it looked as if it would slam straight on to the rocks below. It missed by a good twenty feet and thumped on to the soft gravel with an almost silent thud. A cloud of dry dust and sand spewed up, leaving a small, shallow crater from which the bomb's tail stuck up straight in the centre.

'Damn and blast,' Doug said.

'Damn and no blast,' Billy corrected. 'It didn't even go off. Must be a dud.'

Tom breathed out slowly, relief written all over his thin, freckled face.

★

'There's somebody here,' Danny said later, when they were heating the can of soup on the fire. 'I'm sure of it. I thought I saw somebody in the bushes from up on the side when we were coming back from the village.'

'Me, too,' Tom agreed. 'Honest. When we were collecting wood.'

'That's just your imagination,' Billy said dismissively. His face was still tight with emotion.

'What if it's a guard?' Doug said. 'Somebody from the dummy village. Maybe he saw us taking the bombs. We could get into big trouble.'

'If there had been a guard he'd have kicked our arses and chased us,' Corky said. 'But there was nobody up there, unless there was a tinker sleeping rough. Can't see anybody staying up here, though, can you?'

'I still think there's somebody here,' Danny said. 'It gives me the creeps.'

They had all calmed down to an uneasy truce after Billy and Doug's dreadful confrontation. That had been hours ago and still neither of them would look each other in the eye. The whole camp-site was tense with the undercurrent of conflict. It had not gone away. It pulled and tugged at them with its own gravity. Billy and Doug needed to get away from each other, to get away from everybody. They had momentous things to consider. But it had been too late. Corky had used the force of his personality to cap it all, but it had been too late. The sizzling, almost palpable tension sparked from one to another.

They were all round the fire and Tom had stoked it up with pine logs so that it burnt bright enough to force them all to sit on one side. Corky had used a long stick to get the soup on to the heat and then he'd poured it out on to the tin plates. The bread was hard and stale but, dipped in the thick broth, it tasted just fine. Even Billy ate hungrily. Doug stayed at the far side, looking down into his plate and eating steadily.

'We can explode them tomorrow,' Danny ventured, trying to do something to remove the pressure. If they could get back to where they'd been in the morning, that would be fine with him. Nothing was perfect. Billy was changing and Danny did not know that this was a normal thing. Billy had hair on his balls and the beginnings of bum-fluff turning dark on his top lip, and he was becoming increasingly aggressive. He'd grown a head or more taller than everybody, except Doug, who had always been lanky and thin, and he was pretty powerful now, even if much of it was spare baggage. Danny did not know how long it would be before Billy put out a real challenge to Corky. He hoped that would not happen, though if Corky was aware of it, he didn't show it and seemed not to be concerned. It wasn't as if he'd put up a case for being the natural leader. That was just the way of it. He had nothing to prove.

'Yeah, we could maybe rig up a catapult up there on one of the trees, just like the Vikings,' Tom came in, speaking fast, as if he too had the same notion.

'That was the Romans. The Vikings used a battering ram.'

'Was that Kirk Douglas?'

'Who cares,' Doug said from the edge. His head was still down. Above them, the moon was just peering over the top of the hill, as close to full as possible. It reflected on the burbling stream and gave everything a magical limning that only Danny and Corky noticed. The rest of them were wrapped up in their own thoughts. 'Who gives a damn? Eh? It was just a film. Just make-up.'

'It was a good movie,' Tom said. 'I liked it. Especially at the end, when him and Tony Curtis had the big fight.'

'And remember them skipping along on the oars?' Danny came in. 'That was a hoot.'

Doug sniffed and slung his plate down to the grass. 'Want some more?' Corky offered. Doug sniffed again and shook his head. Billy sat on the other edge, half turned away. He was looking at the ram's skull in the corner where the bush butted against the rock. The moonlight and firelight combined to light it up, making it seem to float ghostly in the dark, eye sockets staring out at them. The flies were humming still.

'I wouldn't waste it on the likes of him,' Billy said sneeringly, and Corky finally exploded.

'Bloody hell,' he spat, and even Danny jumped. 'Look at the pair of you? would you? Just a couple of bloody morons, a couple of selfish, bloody *bastards*.'

Tom and Danny looked at each other. Corky was tough as

old boots but, despite his background, he hardly ever swore. When he did, it was a real serious matter. Danny recalled him saying that to get on, you had to speak with a gob-stopper in your mouth. Corky made an effort not to sound like his crazy brother Phil, who would end up in Drumbain Jail for sure, or like Paddy Corcoran, who was pretty guttural at the best of times. When Corky said 'bastard' he was up and running, firing on all four.

He suddenly jumped to his feet and slammed his plate down on the stone at the edge of the fire. The thick soup gouted out and sizzled on the hot rock with a vicious cat-hiss. Everybody jerked back. Billy spun round, startled, and Doug twisted in alarm.

'You keep your mouth shut, just for once,' Corky said, his finger right up against Billy's face. Billy's mouth snapped closed. '*And you.*' Corky rounded on Doug. His back was to the fire and they could all see the red in his face, made ruddier by the heat and the reflection of the flames.

'Don't you ever think?' he said, almost snarling, finger tapping his temple for emphasis. Danny heard the catch in his voice.

'Don't any of you ever think? *Jeez.*' He reached out both hands and held them up, palms open almost in supplication, and exasperation too. Danny put his plate down on the grass. Right at that moment, the air in the valley seemed suddenly even more charged than before. Corky took two steps forward, away from the fire, up on to the small, grassy lip, and walked out beyond them all before he turned. The flames danced on his face.

When he started speaking, his voice could hardly be heard over the cackle and hiss of the pinewood fire, but they never missed a word.

'Look at us,' he said, and in that moment he sounded achingly desolate. 'Just look at us.

'You'd think it was tough enough, but no. Somebody's got to go and rip it all up and tear it all, and spoil it.'

'But I didn't . . .' Billy spluttered. Corky turned his eyes on him, blazing in the red flame-light, and Billy shut up. Doug thought better of whatever he was about to interject.

'It's not just you. Or Doug neither,' Corky said. '*Listen!* This is the first time we've been out for months. Really out. The whole summer, we've been stuck in, while they all shit themselves. Sometimes I think I'm going to get bored crazy. The whole summer! So we come up here for some fun and find the village, and it should be great. But what happens? We start ripping it apart.'

He held his hands up again. 'This is all we've got. It's the only adventure some of us are going to get, *ever*.'

He turned to Billy. 'You think you've got it bad? Maybe. Tough. Same as me and Danny and Doug and Tom. We're all screwed. All of us. We've got damn-all, we've got nothin'. If we all chipped together we couldn't buy a packet of smokes, and Billy's the only one without a patch on the arse of his pants.

'We're jiggered.'

They could hear the crack in his voice, ready to break. Corky's chest hitched and the fire blazed in his eyes as if he was burning up inside. He came walking slowly back towards the fire so they were all turned to face him.

'We're all up the same creek, aren't we? So there's no need to go picking each other off. That crazy shit's done enough of that with Mole Hopkirk and Don Whalen and that wee kid. If we can't back each other up, what the hell's the point?' He paused just enough for a breath, and ploughed on.

'So who's got it bad?' He turned quickly, swinging to face Billy. 'You Billy-O? Doug? Look at Tom. Shit, if I'd a wee sister and she died, I'd be half crazy, that's for sure. I'd be pure mental.'

Tom flinched back as if stung. Corky had reached down into the taboo, Tom's private thing, and touched it. It was as if he'd scraped on raw flesh, and Corky realized that immediately. He looked over at Tom, and gave him a look of such compassion, such fierce and honest sorrow, that Danny felt a dry lump swell hard in his own throat.

'Sorry, Tommy, just trying to say, Ok?'

Tom had no words, not then. Corky turned away. 'I know he must be all screwed up about it, really ripped open. So us, we got to give him a hand, give him back-up, because he's our pal, isn't he? Our mate. So we got to back him up. Us.'

He stopped, and then added for emphasis: '*All* of us.'

Billy nodded guiltily, remembering how he'd chased Tom across the bog.

'And you, Billy. So what? Your engine's all seized because your old man wasn't a great hero, or whatever he was, who the hell knows? I'm sorry. We're all sorry, even Doug with his big mouth, he's sorry too. Sure you are, Doug?'

Doug looked up, opened his big mouth, then thought better of it. He did look sorry. He looked wretched, blinking shiny eyes.

'You'll get over it. Believe me, fathers aren't all they're cracked up to be. We know that, don't we, Dan? Look at me. My old man's up for swiping the pigeon-club money. I've got to live with that, and so's my ma. You can have a da like mine if you really want. When he gets out he'll knock me arse for tit. You got worries? Shite on a bike, we've *all* got worries! Every one of us.'

Corky was up now, going hell for leather, unable to pull back on the reins.

'You want to be like Tom, or me? How about Danny Boy? Jesus, he can't even open his mouth in his own house. Prayers all the time.'

Danny cringed, feeling the other faces on him. He was suddenly exposed.

'You ever think about what that's like? Jesus *bloody*-H. Every time Dan farts they've got the priest round to him, that creep, Father Fingers. Dan hardly ever gets out and, when he's in, his old man's got him doing school work all the time, non-stop.'

Corky's voice was tight with the pressure now and there was no stopping him. 'We're all jiggered. Ok, Doug, it's rough on you, but wee Terry's still your brother, you've got nothing to be ashamed of. You'll be away in Toronto. At least you're getting to go someplace new where nobody knows you or where you're from. And Tom going to Australia. That's a chance. That's a real big chance.'

He paused once more, and his voice went quiet, as if he was suddenly scared it would catch and stumble and throw him; as if he had come galloping along the edge to where it fell in a long, sheer drop and he had to pull back hard.

'We won't get that chance, me and Dan and Billy, so we got to stay here and get on with it. But that's just it.' His hands were right out in front of him, balled into fists. He looked as if he wanted to punch. 'It's bad enough as it is without giving ourselves a bad time. So why should we be fighting over what we can't help?'

He paused and looked at them all, his eyes fixing each in turn.

'But up here, we're away from it all, just for a couple of days. It could be the last time. Probably is, and I don't want to remember it because we all blew apart. That's going to happen anyway, no matter what we do, so at least, just for now, we can stick together. It's us against the flamin' world, know what I mean? We're all in the shit.'

He turned towards the fire, head down, shoulders shaking.

'After this summer, it's all going to break up. I want to remember this time. We came up here for a last chance and we found the dummy village, and that's special. It's what I want to remember, because we don't have enough good things to remember. None of us.'

He stopped talking and his shoulders slackened as if the tendons had been cut. The four of them sat there in silence, looking at Corky, stunned by the force of what he had said. He had touched them all, right inside of them. He'd been aware of everything, known all the dark secrets, and until now he'd never said anything, not a word.

Danny looked from Billy to Doug to Tom. They were all sitting there on the short grass while the flames sent colour flickering on their faces. All of them were looking at John Corcoran, as if waiting for him to say something else. None of them seemed capable of speech. He had stunned them all.

Corky's shoulders heaved and his head went down into his hands, and Danny felt a powerful ripple of shock. Corky was crying, standing in front of them all, and he was crying, and that was something that had never happened before. He wanted to reach out and touch him.

Yet it was Tom Tannahill who stood up and walked forward, closer to the fire.

'Don't,' he said. He reached up and put a hand on Corky's shoulder. 'Please, Corky.'

Chapter Twenty-three

Interlude

'Hector Kelso agreed with John Fallon,' Angus McNicol said. 'Our man had put the blood on the doorposts to ward off the angel of death, and that made him some kind of psycho. We knew that already, but Kelso disagreed with the shrink, who still thought he'd put the gun barrel in his mouth. Hector said the killer thought he was possessed, and none of us on the investigation disagreed with that. He'd a devil in him.

'Old Jean McColl, she'd been a gutsy old lady. Kelso showed how she clambered through the attic and where he'd tried to shoot her through the lath and plaster of the ceiling. That must have been a nightmare chase, and it took guts to stop and write in her diary. It wasn't until the next day that we found what she'd written, and that gave us a better description of him, and maybe a name.'

Angus McNicol's eyes were focused far back in the past, and the tape turned slowly, picking up his gruff voice and not missing the crackling emotion behind the words as he recalled the savage butchery at Blackwood Farm.

'Remember that song? "A nice wee lass, a fine wee lass, is bonny wee Jeannie McColl"? I saw the photographs on the mantelpiece and it could have been written for her. She'd been a looker in her day, fine bones, a lovely smile. When we found her against the wall she hardly even looked human.

'We found the back of her blouse on a piece of metal up there. He dragged her inside and down the stairs again, put her on the table and put it into her. He broke her arms, high up, close to the shoulder, and he tore all the ligaments and cartilage on her elbows. Doctor Bell and Hector Kelso agreed that he'd just spread-eagled her and put his weight down. But that didn't kill her. Looking at the bruising and the internal damage, Bell thought she probably didn't die until at least the next day. Can you imagine it? The team called him the Angel, but he was the devil incarnate, believe you me.

'He raped her, and then he used the logging axe to cut off Ian McColl's head, and he stuck it on the dung-heap. Whatever Bryce thought, this wasn't a man with any remorse. He waited for the flies to come.

'We checked every lead, but the name we had never meant a thing. We must have pulled out the files on everybody called Leslie Joyce. Birth, army lists, even church congregations, hospital patients; and there were quite a few Les Joyces who got a visit. We even tried the Joyce Lesleys too, just to try to get a hook on this nutcase but, after Blackwood Farm, the man just disappeared, and Bryce was crowing that he'd been right all along.

'But I never thought that bastard committed suicide. Not then and not *ever*. Maybe whatever was frying inside his brains finally burst and he fell down dead and, if that's what happened, then it was too damned easy for him. But it was better for me and for all of us to think of him dead than to believe he would turn up again and that we'd see it start all over.

'We waited a long time, right through until the following year, past the next summer. The Angel, the one you lot called Twitchy Eyes, he simply vanished. Really I hoped he'd gone up on the moor and got stuck in a bog, and taken days to die while the crows picked out his eyes.

'No matter what, the killer disappeared and the killings stopped. Nobody ever knew why.'

Interruption

I could tell that Angus McNicol had spent a lot of time thinking about the killer. A lot of it had come back to me since I saw those eyes on the street, those flat and empty eyes that showed no spark and no recognition. There was a lot I'd buried down in the depths, along with plenty more unwanted baggage from way back then. They say if you remember the sixties you weren't there, and that's the biggest crock of crap anybody ever made up. We were there. We were kids, but we knew, like Mick Jagger told us, this could be the last time, and it was, of course, because the world was changing and everything was blasting apart.

Up in a valley barely four miles from Blackwood Farm where a twitchy-eyed killer mutilated the farmer and his wife and sat until the flies ate their eyes out, a boy several months short of fourteen told his friends a truth about themselves.

Everything was changing, some of it for the better and a lot for the worse.

When the Who were the wild men of rock 'n' roll, Roger Daltry sang that he hoped he died before he got old and, of course, he didn't follow through. He just got rich. There were a few that summer who had the life taken from them and they weren't singing about it. It was a summer like none other. It would be another year at least before Jimi Hendrix made the hairs on the back of my neck stand up when he played 'Purple Haze', and my mother had looked at him as if he were old Twitchy himself, acting the way mothers do when it comes to music, as if it could steal their children away and bury them in a cellar and damn their souls for ever. Clapton and Bruce and Baker were about to put sounds together the way we'd never heard them before, but the flower power hadn't touched this little pocket of the world. We did not have a love-in, it was not groovy.

There were five boys just on the wrong side of innocence up there in the valley that day when . . .

August 3, morning
The man stepped out from the bushes and cast a shadow across the water of the stream.

It had been a fitful night in the aftermath of John Corcoran's soliloquy. The long silence after he finished speaking and stood with his head down and his shoulders jerking stretched on and on while the flames of the fire Dopplered down in a slow diminish from yellow to red and then to glowing embers that pulsed with a life of their own in the merest breath of warm night air. Corky stood there, staring into the flicker of light, and Tom hovered beside him, a hand still to the shoulder, just a couple of silhouettes from Danny Gillan's viewpoint. Over to the side, Doug sniffed again a couple of times, and Danny couldn't tell whether he was crying or not. Billy had his head in his hands, eyes fixed on the fire, like a big Apache, for once silent.

After a while, after what seemed a long time, Corky turned round and went into the tent. He came out with that old army blanket his old man had swiped from the Territorials hall when he and Deek Galt, Campbell's old man, had heisted a box of grenades for poaching the salmon up at the Witches' Pots on the Corrie river where a generation later some folk would go hunting something else and burn the whole forest down to charred stumps.

'I'm going to sleep out here,' he said, wrapping the blanket around his shoulders and lowering himself to the grass about six feet away from the fire. Everybody stood there, shaken, with the red of the fire on their faces, making them look wild and bleak and somehow feral, like young warriors, like young braves.

'Me, too,' Billy finally said in a soft voice that was unlike him. He and Tom crossed to the tent and got their own blankets. After a while, Danny and Doug did the same. The tent stood dark and empty while they all hunkered around the fire, huddled around their thoughts while the flames faded and slowed and turned the logs to mere glowing embers. Up on the moor a poor curlew bleated soulfully and the dented moon rose over the high sides to shine down into the open valley.

Some time in the night, Billy cried out and then subsided into a snuffled sob. The noise woke them all, but none of them could tell whether Billy was awake or asleep. Some time in the night, Danny Gillan thought he heard footsteps downstream and woke up with a start, breathing quickly, nerves suddenly tight and alert. The fire had sunk down now to barely a glimmer, which gave off some heat but not much. As he fetched some thick pine logs from the pile he and Tom had collected, he scanned the darkness down in the valley where the trees crowded blackly, holding their inky shadows. He could sense eyes upon him and he shivered in the cold night air. A trickle of apprehension rippled down his spine and he hurried back to the circle of the camp-fire where the others were dark, huddled shapes on the ground. The logs quickly caught fire and sent the heat blazing out, but the cold trickle inside Danny took a long time to diminish.

In the morning, when he awoke, he was still tense and his hands were clenched into fists. His fingernails had dug red crescents into the skin of his palms.

Tom and Doug cooked the last of the sausages in the old pan, frying them up in their own sparking fat while the tin of beans with its saw-blade top, angling up in a jagged halo, sat at the edge of the fire, bubbling away in the heat. Billy took a while to rouse but, as soon as the sausages, burnt almost black, were on the plate, the smell brought him round as if he'd been slapped. Tom handed him his breakfast. Billy nodded his thanks, keeping his eyes down. Normally, he'd be full of talk and blether in the mornings while everybody else was yawning and scratching and just trying to find their bearings, but now he was silent, and for the moment there wasn't much to say.

They ate quickly and licked the plates clean. Danny said they'd have to set some more snares for rabbits and catch some trout in the stream if they planned to stay much longer. Doug had the notion he could find a pheasant's nest down in the trees and get some eggs, but at this late stage in the summer that idea was voted down with some derision. Most of the eggs would be hatched and the others would be addled with half-formed chicks. Doug then remembered Mole Hopkirk clambering down from the railway arches with the pigeon's egg burst in his mouth, and the rousing derision when he'd puked it all up. It got a laugh, feeble in the light of what had happened to ol' Mole, and in the aftershock of the fight. They were all talking now, all except Billy, who seemed still cocooned inside the happenings of the night before. When Dan went down to the stream to use the fine sand to wash the plates clean, Corky followed.

'You stick with Billy, right?' he said. 'He'll be ok in a while.'

'You reckon? He was pretty cheesed off last night. We all were.'

'Yeah,' Corky conceded, somehow sadly. 'It had to be said though, Dan. They'd have been at each other's throats in a minute and then we'd all have been hooking and jabbing. That's the way it goes. Billy's a bit crazy these days. You know that. Not bad, just cracked.'

Danny nodded down at the water where the rippling water broke his reflection into wavering patches of shadow. Up by the fire, Billy was trying to pick up some music on his radio, but all he got now was static. Tom and Doug were already halfway up the side of the valley, heading for the heights where they'd left the bombs from the dummy village.

'He's always been a bit flaky, but now he can be pretty mean with it. I don't think he can help it, and what Doug said didn't help, did it? Jeez. It's like it's been building up, though, and I had to say it last night because if Billy explodes . . .'

'We'll all be covered in blood and guts and shite,' Danny finished for him, wanting to keep it light now after the dismay of the night before. What Corky had said had got under his own skin, making him realize even more strongly than before the limits of his own world and the constraints upon himself. The bad fire, his own nightmare. *Hell and damnation in the fire.* Corky had known without saying until last night, when it all came out. Corky had Crazy Phil on his back all of the time and would have his old man back out of Drumbain Jail soon, and Corky would have to handle the regular knock on the head or the belt buckle. But was that really worse than the constant and inexorable weight of pressure and the never-ending litany of prayer and piety? Danny Gillan wanted out from under just as much as Corky needed to escape.

'Too true. And guts and hot air,' Corky said, and he laughed aloud, jerking Danny back to the moment. 'Blood, guts and gallons of lard. The size of him, he'd cover the whole camp-site.'

They used the thick fishing-line to make more snares, which Danny set in the runs he'd found by the bushes further up the valley where they'd already seen some rabbits when they arrived. The line, Danny assured him, was better than the fencing wire because the rabbits wouldn't see it. When they'd finished, Corky went up the track to join Doug and Tom. The sun was rising fast and the heat was gaining on the day, bringing out the bees and damselflies and the big dragonflies whirring in squadrons over the pools. Down in the trees, pigeons murmured sleepily and the slow water muttered, like conversations almost fathomed.

Billy and Danny went upstream to catch trout in the shallow pools and under the rocks where the water tumbled. Up on the plateau, close to where the natural dam had backed up the stream to form the long twist of Lonesome Lake, the others were whooping excitedly, the cares of the night forgotten, or at least banished, under the heat of the sun.

'Bombs awaaaay.' Tom's high voice came wavering down.

There was silence, then more whoops and gales of laughter. Danny couldn't help but smile.

'You think they'll explode?'

'Hope so,' Billy said. He'd his head down, hair trailing the burbling surface of the clear water, both hands jammed under a flat stone, eyes fixed with concentration. 'Big one in here.' He twisted, pushed further. Danny could see his shoulders working as he tried to get a hold of the trout. Finally, he slowly withdrew his hand from under the rock, keeping his balance, brought out a thick, spotted fish that twisted and torqued powerfully in his big hands.

'Beauty,' he said through gritted teeth. 'Bet that's nearly a pound.' He held it tight in his left hand and hooked a forefinger into the trout's mouth while it bucked for freedom, pulled on the upper jaw until the mouth gaped and the head drew right back. There was a watery squelch and then a small crack. The fish shivered and then flopped to limp stillness, its neck broken. Danny watched dispassionately. They'd been catching trout since they were no size at all. It was different with fish. It was *normal*.

Behind and above them, in the narrow chasm leading off the main valley, Doug and Corky were balancing the bombs on the branches of a twisted hawthorn tree that leant out over the side of the drop. They were using some of the hay-baling twine from the roll that served as guy-ropes for the old tent and, despite the straining effort, they'd managed to pull one branch right back until it touched the ground. Tom had snagged the twine around the tree's own root and he plucked it, making it sing like a deep guitar string.

'Try it now,' Doug said. Tom got his old army knife with the spike for taking things out of horses' hooves, opened the sharp blade. Gingerly he hacked at the hairy string, covering his eyes in case it whipped back and blinded him. The blade bit through before he expected it to and the branch uncoiled with a whiplash crack. The bomb went straight up in the air, maybe ten feet or more. Tom went sprawling back.

'Bombs away,' he yelled, scrabbling for balance before he tumbled over the edge.

'Watch out,' Corky bawled. Doug shrieked with laughter. The

bomb went straight up and came straight back down again, tail first, but already beginning its turn. It hit the very spot where Tom had been only a second before, landing with an earth-shuddering thump on its side, and then it toppled over the edge as the one had done the previous night to slide down the shale slope and come grinding to a silent halt.

They all burst out laughing together.

Danny and Billy, stripped to the waist and with their sloppy-joe shirts tied by the arms around their waists, had taken six fish in the first hundred yards, none of the rest as big as the one Billy had tickled from under the stone, and now they were threading twine through the gills to carry them back to the camp.

'Did *you* know?' Billy had asked, and Danny hadn't bothered, hadn't needed to ask what he was talking about. He'd been waiting for the question, uncomfortable in its proximity and unsure of what he would say when it came.

'Yeah,' he finally said. 'I knew. Stood to reason, didn't it? Doesn't matter though. None of us is bothered about it. We don't care.'

'I never thought about it. Honest to God.'

'We knew that, Billy.'

'But my ma's been lying to me all these years.'

'Everybody's mother lies. She just wants you to feel good.'

'But I *don't* feel good. She said he was a hero.'

'And he could have been. Might have been. Who the hell knows? Look at Corky's old man, he's no hero, that's for sure. Nor mine. Corky was right. It's not worth fighting about. We've all got troubles.'

'Yeah, but *Jeez*, I never thought. How stupid can you get? I could have belted Doug last night. I could have really gubbed him. I still could, you know? Because of what he said.'

Danny saw Billy's shoulders twitch again, this time with the internal pressure of a held-back punch, and he was immediately reminded of Corky's words. He did look as if he could explode. The twitch was like a small seismic shiver, but the body language so eloquent. In his mind, Billy was lashing out to land a fist on Doug's nose. Danny was glad it was still held in tight, glad it hadn't come to it. What Corky had done, what he had said, had touched them all. He'd stopped it.

Billy bent to threading the string through the gills. Up on the hill, another cheer went up into the still air, followed by yet another gaggle of laughter. Danny thought it would be a good idea if they dumped the fish down at the camp and went up the hill to join in. Once they got Billy laughing again, it would be ok (*until the next time*). He was just about to turn and suggest this to Billy when across the stream, where the hazel bushes crowded together, a trickle of gravel went hissing down the slope. Danny looked up.

And the man stepped out from the bushes.

Danny jerked back in surprise, his breath drawn in quickly in a hiss. Billy hadn't noticed. He was still crouched down, concentrating on the task of inserting the thick, fibrous twine inside the gill and out through the gaping, bloodied mouth.

The man stood there silently on the far side of the stream. He was tall, very tall, and his hair was black as Billy's, though uncut and greasy. His eyebrows shadowed his eyes and he stood stock-still, in a long, shabby coat that came down below his knees and looked too warm for the summer's day. He was wearing a pair of scuffed, black boots laced up to the top with pieces of twine. One of the soles was peeling away from the upper.

'Billy,' Danny whispered.

'Shouldn't have said it anyway,' Billy muttered tightly, still replaying the scene. 'He was just having a go at me.'

Danny nudged him and for a moment Billy just continued his self-bound conversation. Finally, Danny reached and clamped his hand round the other boy's meaty wrist.

'What?' Billy said, turning his head. He saw Danny's eyes, fixed and unblinking, staring across the tumbling water. He slowly turned, caught a glimpse of the figure standing on the far bank. His head jerked up and his own eyes widened. His whole body started back in surprise.

The man stood there for a long moment, still as rock. Behind him, the little shiver of shale still trickled down the steep slope, possibly where his coat had brushed the dry surface. It sounded like a slow breath. In Danny's hand, one of the fish bucked, even though he'd been sure the blow on the head had killed it dead. It shuddered and then went limp. The man stared at them, though they couldn't see his eyes under the beetling brows. His face was craggy and angular, and his hair, thick and dark, hung down lank and turned up at his collar. It was spiked near the crown, as if he'd cut it himself, and on either side of his mouth, deep furrows formed black, angry brackets.

The moment of contact stretched on. Neither of the boys knew what to do. Up on the hill they could hear the excited yelling of the others, but they couldn't call out to them while the man was staring at them. Was he a farmer? A gamekeeper?

Both of them knew he was neither. He was ragged and dirty and unwashed and unshaven. His work trousers were torn at the knee and covered in dark stains. His mouth was curved downwards. Danny touched Billy's arm again and moved backwards, still crouched on the grass by the bank. The fish on his string slithered towards him with the movement, its eyes blinkless and dead, mouth agape. Billy scrambled back with him.

'Who is he?' he whispered out of the corner of his mouth.

'Don't know.'

The sunlight on the moving water sent spangled reflections on to the steep slope behind the silent figure and dappled shimmering light on his threadbare coat. It flashed into his eyes, and he blinked several times, very rapidly. He turned away from the light, quite slowly, as if it hurt his eyes, until his face was in profile, then he jerked once and seemed to galvanize into motion. He took a heavy step forward, crunching on the gravel and small stones by the side of the stream, took another step, which put his foot right into the water with a loud splash. There were enough stones to allow him to step across and stay dry at this time of the year when it hadn't rained for more than three weeks and the water was low, but he ignored them. The dark brows had come down again to shutter the eyes, but they knew he was staring right at them, so intently he did not even seem to notice his boots were under water.

Danny and Billy cringed backwards. They got to their feet, hearts suddenly thumping. Behind and above, Tom and the others were hooting with laughter again.

'Mister, we . . .' Billy started '. . . we're just catching some fish for our dinner. Honest.'

Neither of them knew who the man was, or what power, civil

or official, he might wield, but Billy was already working on mitigation.

'Fish.'

The word came out in a soft hiss of breath, almost dreamily. 'Fishes.'

The man crossed the stream and came up the bank, mounting to the flat in two or three big strides. When he reached the turf where they'd been threading the trout he stood up straight, towering over them.

'I will make you fishers of men,' he whispered, his voice slightly hoarse, as if he'd been shouting. The boys drew back a step, standing closer together now. The whispering voice made no sense, though Danny had heard the words before. The man was still staring at them, his face completely impassive, as if there was no emotion in him, as if he was looking both at them and right through them.

'What do you want?' Danny asked, and both he and Billy heard the apprehensive little tremble in his voice. The man was just standing there and that was scary enough. They'd been chased by gamekeepers and bawled at by irate farmers and that was the way of things with boys. But this big scarecrow of a man had just whispered, not raised his voice, and that was somehow very unnerving.

'They said, "*Lord, here is a boy with a few fishes.*" ' The whispering became a grating rumble, coming up from deep inside the stranger. 'A *few* fishes.'

He took several steps forward, alarmingly quickly. Danny and Billy flinched yet again. The man reached and picked up the biggest of the fish, the one Billy had been trying to loop on to the string. He held it up to them. The still-wet scales threw back the light in iridescent sparkles. Without hesitation the man brought the limp trout up to his face, opened his mouth and bit down on its head.

Danny's heart seemed to drop like a stone.

'Jeez,' Billy gasped, backing into the smaller boy and almost knocking him sideways. Danny had to grab his arm, to keep from falling.

The teeth came down on the head and they both heard it crunch wetly, almost with the sound of a boiled egg being cut open with a blunt knife. The fish flapped twice, the way the other trout had done, showing it was still, even if barely, alive. Danny could not believe his eyes. His throat clenched and he felt as if he was going to vomit. Close by, he heard the sound of Billy gulping for air.

The teeth clenched tight and they stood fascinated, mesmerized, unable to draw their eyes away. The head crunched and the man's head pulled back. A piece of flesh flipped out from between the teeth and then the rest of the trout pulled away. They could see that the wide, grey head had been bitten clean through to just behind the eye. Black blood welled from the small braincase. Dark blood trickled down on the man's clenched teeth. He swung his head, in an animal motion, the way a dog does, and chewed hard. The sound of the fish head crunching, an innocuous little sound in itself, was suddenly appalling in the still air of the day. It was nothing and yet it was immense, of great importance, of earth-shuddering consequence. Of a sudden, both of them, standing elbow to elbow, with the sun hot on their shoulders, felt completely and terrifyingly defenceless.

The man stared into them from the shadows under his brows and he chewed slowly and deliberately, letting them hear every disgusting, sickening sound. Then he swallowed and the lot went down his throat with not a shiver or a tremor.

Danny tried to turn to run, but for some reason he was frozen to the spot. Billy was jammed up against him and he could smell his sweat, feel the peculiar shiver in the face of this craziness.

The man stepped forward and held the torn trout out. 'Take this and eat it,' he said to Billy, pinioning him with black eyes, now visible this close. He cocked his head to the side, a strangely dog-like gesture. 'He took it and gave it to his disciples.' Danny had also heard those words before, heard them many a time, read out in the nightly family prayers around the empty grate of the fire. Words from the bible, from the new testament. *This is the word of the Lord.*

For a crazy moment he heard his own father's voice transposed on the raggedy man's low rumble.

Billy was backing away. The man stepped forward, jabbing the bloodied end of the fish at the taller boy. 'Take this and eat it,' he repeated. The eyes were completely devoid of colour, like holes under the shelves of the brows. Billy whimpered.

'I don't like . . .' he started to say.

'Eat. Eat.' The voice rumbled. The torn end, showing the curve where the eye had been ripped from the socket, rubbed against Billy's lips. He gagged, shaking his head in disgust.

'Come on, Billy,' Danny said, voice rising. He grabbed his friend by the arm and pulled him backwards. 'Let's go.'

Danny hauled hard enough to spin Billy round. The big boy turned, eyes wide in fright. A slick of blood and fish slime coated his mouth like a smeared, viscid lipstick, and his normally sallow skin had turned fish-belly pale. Danny felt his heart flip helplessly like the jerking twitch of the dying fish. The sense of danger simply inflated inside him. He pulled again. Billy blinked once, twice.

'Come on!' Danny urged, pulling him. Billy seemed to lurch out of a dream. His muscles seemed to unlock. He jerked, and then he was moving. Danny leapt down the slope to the next downstream level with Billy in front of him. All the while he could sense the man reaching for him, a big, gnarled hand with fingers outspread to grab him by the skin of the neck. He could imagine the man's breath. He thought he could hear his big boots pounding after them.

Billy was moving, only a couple of feet ahead, his red T-shirt flapping like an Apache breechcloth. His big, meaty arms were swinging, and Danny could hear the panicked tremble in his breathing. His own breath was coming fast – short, gasped pants for air – and it felt as if his heart had raised itself up about six inches to block his windpipe. The track beside the stream narrowed between two large boulders at the turn where Billy had caught the big one and they both went through the gap like startled rabbits. Off in the bushes a blackbird went clattering away in a scold of alarm. They smashed through, where before they had gingerly angled, avoiding scratches from thistles, now crunching and crushing the hogweed and wild rhubarb. Billy was like a tank, heedless of any obstruction.

They came out of the shadow at the bend and into the sunlight. The other boys were high up on the edge, further up the gully of the tributary, oblivious for the moment to the drama down below. Billy ran as fast as he could, tasting the blood and raw slime from the fish, suddenly more afraid than ever before. It had happened so fast and it was so inexplicable it was truly terrifying. The fact that the man had bitten into the living head of the fish had been scary enough, *wrong* enough to be dreadfully shocking, but then he had forced the thing at Billy's mouth and, if a man would do that, he had to be crazy for sure. He had just stared at them and then spoken in a harsh, creepy whisper. His eyes had blinked under the brows and Billy had thought . . .

Billy had thought there was something . . .

Billy thought . . .

Twitchy Eyes.

He had never been quick on the uptake, but as soon as the fish had jammed into his mouth and he had caught the reflection of the light on the man's black eyes, seen the rapid-fire blink, like some flickering Morse, the image had come smacking into his head and his knees had almost given way.

'*Oh holy Jesus, please us,*' a childish voice had yelled inside his head, and Billy had instantly felt very small and dreadfully vulnerable. Danny had been pulling at him and he'd frozen just for the moment, not able to make his feet work, while the smell of fish was thick in his nose and the back of his throat. And then he and Danny were running, him first, down the track, and he knew if they could get to the next corner and down to the camp they'd get away, because the man would see the others and he'd know he couldn't get away with anything if there were witnesses, and everything would be . . .

They came scuttering round the corner, angling their bodies to take the bend. They made it past the clump of stinging nettles, past the cluster of dockens waving in no breeze the way dockens do in the summer. A hunting swallow flew right in front of them, jinking at the last moment in a flare of gun-metal blue-black.

Then Billy's foot stepped into a cow-pat that wasn't old enough to be caked and dry. The top surface slid across the wet and greasy inside and his foot slipped with it.

It all went wrong just as quickly as that.

He put his foot down, still running at an angle, reaching with his left hand towards the stand of hazel saplings to get enough purchase to swing his weight around, and next thing he was up in the air. His foot skidded out from under him and the other foot couldn't come back down quickly enough to regain his balance. He hit the ground with such a thud that his teeth gnashed together with a jar of sudden pain. Another pain jolted up from his backside to the top of his head as all his weight compressed the bones in his back. His breath came out in one loud, whooping expulsion.

Danny was only three feet behind. He saw Billy go down, tumble and bounce, and then he was flying over Billy's head. Both knees hit against the other boy's shoulder and his own momentum flipped him up and over. He landed with a numbing crash right at the edge of the track where the bank dropped about six feet to a shallow pool. It was only the fact that his torn jeans snagged a protruding hazel root that prevented him from plunging forward head first on to the rocks below.

Up above, on the rim, startled voices came rolling down.

'Hey, what's up? You ok?' Danny vaguely heard the drumming of feet as Corky and the rest came haring down the hard-back sheep-track. Billy groaned, grunted, turned himself over, got to his knees. Danny eased himself to his feet, aware that he should be doing something, but momentarily dazed by the shock of the fall.

'Hey, Dan!' Doug bawled.

The man came round the corner just as Danny got to his feet. Billy was still on his knees, facing downstream. He saw Danny's face go slack and his eyes raise themselves upwards, higher than Billy's own. Behind him, something brushed against fabric, and then a cold, hard edge pressed against the curve of his jaw-line.

'Oh, Billy,' Danny said, but there was no need for explanation. Billy knew it was a gun.

'And again a little while and you *shall* see me,' the man said, and there was a hint of shivery laughter, a kind of cold glee in his rumbling voice.

Doug and the others came hurtling round the bottom bend. From up on the rim they had seen both boys tumble, but the track had curved down behind one shoulder of the slope and they had not seen the stranger pushing through the foliage.

They all skidded to a halt when they rounded the crumbling

corner of the dog-leg of the valley, Doug first, Corky hard on his heels and Tom only a few feet behind.

Everything stopped dead-still.

A lone cuckoo sang out downstream, where the forest crowded down to the water, a lazy, somnolent summer sound, almost smoky in the warm air. Two black and gold dragonflies chased each other between the two frozen groups, for a long, extruded space the only movement in that part of the valley. Three boys stood there in attitudes of sudden stop, hands out, bodies twisted, as if they'd been photographed at the beginning, or the end, of a race. All of them were open-mouthed, wide-eyed.

Danny Gillan was further up the track, half turned, eyes fixed on Billy, who was still down on his knees, his black hair in awful contrast to the now pure white of his skin. His own dark eyes looked like pits. The long, shining barrels of the shotgun had him just behind his ear, their gaping mouths a dark and infinite figure of eight laid on its side.

Billy's eyes were blinking fast, blinking almost in time to the tic in the gaunt man's own eyes. Everything was frozen in a tableau except for the eyes and the dragonflies whirring past about their own business, oblivious to the drama.

For that stretched moment of time there was no sound at all except the murmuring of the stream and the robber bird down in the trees.

'And so he came amongst them,' the ragged man finally said, 'and they got down upon their knees.'

This time he laughed. It was the first time the other three had seen him, the first time they had heard his voice. John Corcoran felt a deadly-cold chill trickle upwards on his spine and he knew instantly they were in the most appalling danger. For what seemed minutes, he was frozen, yet on many levels he was aware of everything, even the far-off cuckoo and the mindless chattering of the stream. He gauged the distance back to the curve around the little knoll of rock on the shoulder, out of the line of fire of those long black barrels. Would the man shoot Billy? For a second he considered running, turning on his heel, thinking the same thought Danny had already considered, that the man would not dare shoot if there were witnesses free to point the finger.

In the man's other hand, he saw the dead trout, saw a trickle ooze down to the ground, wondered where it had come from. Billy's eyes were wide and pleading, not fixed on anything, but jittering left, right, up and down, beseeching the very air. He looked as if he expected his own brains to come blasting out on to the grass. Danny was standing, hands shaking now, his whole body a-quiver with tension, his back to the rest of them. He looked slight and fragile against the tall stranger whose shadow blocked the path.

'Oh shit, Corky,' Doug said in a tremulous whisper. 'He'll kill him.'

The man stood stock-still, the way he had on the far side of the stream when he'd come across Danny and Billy. Everything was frozen, a moment of exquisite tension. Corky took in the whole scene, the gun close to Billy's neck, the look of absolute fear on his face, the shadows under the craggy brows on that gaunt face. In that split second he knew he could not run. They had come scampering down the hill and into madness on a summer's day. All the odds, all the distances, all the estimates of speed and flight evaporated. The man with the gun stood there, blinking in the bright light of the sun. There was no flight now, Corky knew with complete and instinctive certainty. The gun would simply blow Billy Harrison's head from his shoulders, and then it would talk to Danny and then . . .

The man leant forward and put the dead, ungutted fish against Billy's mouth. The entrails were squeezing out of the hole where the mouth should be, little, slithery, green strings. The stranger leant over and whispered something that none of them heard. Billy's belly muscles seemed to shiver. His head moved from side to side, but his mouth opened and his teeth came down on the trout and he bit into the gill covers. Purple blood splashed on to his cheeks.

CHAPTER TWENTY-FOUR

Billy was sick.

He had taken two mouthfuls of the trout – skin, gills, bones, and slick, cold entrails. They all heard the slush-crackle as he chewed, jaws working in a crazy stammer. He swallowed, eyes closing tight, mouth twisted in utter revulsion. The gulping sound he made turned Danny's stomach and for an instant he thought he would vomit the sausages he'd eaten for breakfast.

Billy beat him to it. He swallowed a second time, and then his mouth opened and all of it came back up again in a projectile gush which propelled the glutinous mass out on to the grass.

The man laughed again, this time a fast, almost girlish giggle of sound, as if he found the whole display completely hilarious, and that laugh was just as chilling to Danny as the very fact that he had made Billy eat the slimy fish or jammed the gun against his friend's head. The whole day had flipped, in the space of a few seconds, into a surreal and terrifying kind of nightmare.

The man's next move surprised them all. He reached forward and took Billy by the hair and hauled him to his feet. Billy yelled in pain and fright. Danny took an instinctive step forward and the man speared him with a fathomless look, froze him to the spot.

'Don't, mister,' Billy yelped. 'Ah, that's sore. Please. Let me g . . .'

He was up on his toes now, head back and eyes screwed up, both hands raised above his head, wanting to take the fingers out of his hair, afraid to touch them. He arched upwards, trying to slacken the grip and take the dragging pain out of his scalp.

'Leave him alone,' Corky bawled, body bent forward, needing to do something. 'Get off him.'

The man ignored him. Instead, he let Billy get both feet flat on the turf, and pushed him, still gripping his hair in his left hand, making his head nod rapidly with the force of the sudden shove. Billy almost fell forward, got his balance, and the man walked him along the track. He raised the gun and pointed it straight at Danny's belly. The hollow black figure of infinity, the horizontal ebony eight at the gaping ends of the barrels loomed suddenly vicious. Danny's sphincter puckered into a tight little nub and he still felt everything might just let go. One squeeze on either trigger and that black mouth would roar and it would blow a plate-sized hole from front to back and kill him in a flash of light and noise.

'Come on, boy,' the man said, very gently, almost sadly. 'Let's all go down together.'

Danny turned, his legs almost unable to bear his weight, and led the way, all the time aware of the gun. The skin on his back puckered too, in dreadful expectation. His heart thudded with such sudden pressure that twin pains pulsed in his temples and his vision swam.

'You three,' the man said, his voice louder, raising his face to Corky and the others on the higher track. 'At the double.'

Danny thought of Billy. That's what he had said after he'd crushed the dragonfly larva and thrown the bloated frog back into the crater.

Come on, you lot. At the double.

That now seemed like a long time ago. Now Billy was on his tiptoes, face contorted in pain. The tableau on the slope froze for an instant of dreadful indecision, then began to move again. Corky said nothing more.

They came down the hill, just ahead of Danny, and they all went down together.

There was no sound but the burbling water and the thud of their footfalls on the short turf where the highland cattle and the black-faced sheep had cropped the grass to a short mat. But for that half-wild hill cow, and its half-baked cow-pat, they could have been downstream and gone.

Behind him, Danny heard Billy grunt in pain or exertion, but he was too numbed to look round. He had seen the madness in the man's eyes. The fervour had reached out and touched him. The eyes were as black as the barrels of the twelve-bore shotgun, but their black was deeper, like holes in the world, as if there was a space behind them that went on for ever and never stopped. It was only the rapid-fire blinking, as if they were burning with their own black intensity, that briefly cut off the pull of their awesome gravity.

Twitchy . . .

It had come to Danny as it had come to Billy, that epiphany, the sudden and apocalyptic recognition.

'*We know he's a tall man,*' big John Fallon had said as he stood in front of the class, with Sister Julia standing beside him, each in different versions of black and white uniform. She had looked up at him, half his size, a third his weight. They had all looked at him. '*Maybe as tall as me,*' the big sergeant had told them, and they'd listened. '*He's got black hair and he blinks as if he's got something wrong with his eyes.*'

John Fallon had been right. This man was big. God he was *huge*.

Twitchy Eyes.

Billy Harrison had looked up from where he was threading the thong through the fish gills and the man had filled his entire vision. Now he filled his whole consciousness, his entire world. The hand gripping his hair held tighter, keeping his head pulled back, and the pain screwed into his scalp, making his eyes water.

Danny Gillan felt the skin on his back squeeze and ripple all the way down his spine. His whole attention was taken with the knowledge of the barrels upon him. One slip. One small tug of the finger, a squeeze, a stroke, and the gun would cut him in half. He could feel a whimper, a little animal sound that was born of pure fear, try to bubble up from his throat and push its way out of his mouth and he was afraid that if he made a sound the man – *Twitchy Eyes* – would react just the way a cat does, jerk at the least sound and then . . . *oh, then* . . .

Behind him, Billy grunted.

No, Billy! Danny silently pleaded.

Billy made a deeper sound. The man still had him by the hair. Without turning, Danny knew Billy's head was still hauled back in that merciless grip, his face white and open and slack. Ahead of him he could see Corky's shoulders, all tensed up, the way they got when he was angry. Danny could not remember Corky ever being really scared. He wasn't big, but he was strong enough, and he had a profound depth of resources within him. He'd taken his licks, taken his beatings. He'd been turned over right royally on occasion by a couple of real experts and come bouncing back when the wounds healed and the bruises faded, or so he let everybody know. Now he knew Corky was scared and angry both at the same time. He could read that in his tight posture.

Don't do anything stupid . . . please. Danny heard the small and whimpering voice inside his head and he was too stunned and afraid to feel ashamed at the tremor in it.

Ahead of Corky, Doug was walking fast, head slowly swinging from side to side although he was trying to hide the motion.

Don't do it.

They were just coming to the edge of the bend where the stream took a dog-leg to the left beside the small cascade into the gravel pool. Here, another small tributary fed in through a narrow defile. Tom approached first, walking with his head down and his arms not swinging as they normally would. His shoulders were moving up and down and he might have been crying. Danny was more worried about Doug. He was thin and rangy, with long, stick-like legs, but he was also fast. Whenever they ran from trouble – from big John Fallon, whenever a lucky (or unlucky) slingshot cracked the bowl of a street-light; from the big boys down on the Rough Drain when they decided it was their territory – when Doug ran from trouble there was never a chance of him getting caught. He could cover the ground like a startled deer. He was all limbs and angles, knuckles and knees when he walked, but when he ran, all of those angles smoothed and merged into a fluid grace, an effortless glide that was as sure-footed as it was fleet. Danny saw his head swing slowly as he reached the corner. Up that runnel, he could be hidden from view for four, maybe five seconds. That might be enough to get him most of the way up, even on the slope, to get to the rocks at the far end and the trees beyond. It was just a small and narrow gully and there would be some cover.

'*Don't.*'

Danny clearly heard Corky's urgent whisper, over the sound of their footsteps and Billy's panicked grunts. Doug's head pulled back, just a fraction. Behind Billy, the man with the gun made a sound, maybe as if he was clearing his throat. Tom went past the mouth of the gully.

Corky had read the signs in Doug, as clearly as Danny had done. Doug's head swung again. His eyes glanced up the runnel, gauging the distance, knowing his own speed.

No! Danny's mental plea came at exactly the same time as Corky's urgent hiss.

Doug might have been fast, but it was uphill all the way, over boulders and rocks and a slick patch where the water flowed over a flat, smooth ledge of rock strata that was covered in slick algae. He might have been fast, but he only had seconds, and fast wasn't fast enough. He could run, but he couldn't outrun a gunshot. Danny knew that, with good reason. Down at the Whale's Back, the big spit of tidal sand at low tide on the firth, out from the gunbarrel sewer pipe beside Ardmhor Rock at Arden, Danny had seen what shotguns could do. His Uncle Mick had taken him down there on cold winter mornings to get the duck as they hit in, flying in rapid wedges, wings pumping hard, flickering on the surface. Uncle Mick would wait until they were level and then he'd haul up on his feet. The chevrons of duck would see the motion and then veer away, croaking alarm. They were fast, wings whistling as they scooped air, necks outstretched. Mick always took them on the back, once they were past, doing maybe fifty, maybe sixty. He said it was best to take them under the feathers rather than head-on, which might just wound the birds. The gun would roar like a thunderclap and the report would go reverberating in a harsh and strangely hollow ripple of noise across the flat of the tidal sand, and up there in the sky the feathers would fly and the birds would tumble through the air, over and over and over until they hit the ground in hard thumps, ripped through by the lead shot.

Doug was fast, but not as fast as a fleeting widgeon, or a big sheldrake. He couldn't do fifty or sixty on the flat, never mind uphill, over rocks, over slick stones, over the moss at the top. The gully was a funnel. Anybody firing up there, with the spread pattern a twelve-bore had, would hit anything. For forty yards there was no cover at all.

No! Corky hissed. *No!* Danny's mind bleated, already seeing Doug getting halfway to the trees before the twin barrels and their black infinity swung up the runnel (*and a small and shameful part of him wanted Doug to suddenly swivel and take off like a*

276

mountain hare because that would take the glare of those barrels off his back) and the trigger pull back and the barrels spit thunder.

Corky reached and touched Doug. Danny's heart nearly stopped dead. Something like a giant hand gripped all the muscles in his belly and squeezed hard. Corky reached and touched Doug, and Doug jerked as if he'd been stung. Any moment Danny expected to hear the apocalyptic roar.

Nothing happened. Doug's high, tight shoulders sagged to slackness and defeat. He continued walking, on past the mouth of the gully, following Tom's short, fearful steps, splashing across the inch-deep trickle of tributary water. In five strides he was past the chance of escape, and away from the certainty of retribution. Corky nodded, an involuntary motion that spoke eloquently of his relief, and in that motion Danny read that Corky could not try anything either. His friend's back was still rigid with anger and tension and fear, but Corky was not going to dive into the bushes, or pick up a smooth rock and try to take this stranger's eye out. He had gauged all the chances and come up with a zero. At least for now.

In that glassy moment, the exquisite conjunction of reality and unreality, each of them was wholly and completely alive as they had never been before. A powerful survival instinct had kicked into them all, raising them up to heights of perception where every motion, every sound, was imbued with amazing clarity.

Corky had read Doug's posture too. Everything seemed to go in slow motion. The somnolent murmur of the water deepened to a low rumble. The lone cuckoo way down there in the trees hummed its diphthong, stretched out and hollow, the sound trailing on and on as it faded to eventual silence. The dragonflies, a twin pair, striking in black and gold, came gliding over the water. On the side of the valley, a small stone, dislodged from the steep gravel, rolled down to a ledge and then fell off, tumbling in the air to land with a bass thud of sound in the pile of soft shale close to the bank.

Corky's thoughts were flicker-fast, sharp as glass, clear as ice. *Not now.* He thought hard. *Not now.* As if he could beam the words at Doug.

'You three, at the double.' He had sounded like a soldier, like the sergeant down at the drill hall where his da had hiked the grenades. The gun was now jammed against Billy's neck, just under the jaw-line where his blue-black Indian hair curled thick, and they had seen the man's stance and the sunlight had frozen on a summer's day.

Crazy, Corky thought. Anybody who would put a shotgun up against a boy's neck had to be loony-tunes. Anybody who would force him to eat a dead trout, straight out of the stream, with the blood and guts hanging out, they had to be non-*compost-mentis*, as Billy would say. It stood to reason. A farmer might rant and rave a little, convinced you were worrying the sheep or stealing eggs. He might put the toe of his boot up your backside, the way Big John Fallon might do if he caught you swiping stuff out of Woolworth's down on River Street. That was an accepted level of violence, the *quid pro quo*. A boy could take that, come and go, roll with it and blink back smarting tears before anybody noticed.

This was different. The whole texture of the day had cracked and splintered and then frozen over. The man had laughed that odd sound and his eyes had blinked in the sunlight, and Corky had known. Anybody who stuck the barrels under Billy's chin would be crazy enough to shoot, because the very fact of it could get you thrown in Drumbain for a stretch.

Not now.

Corky had done his own calculation, his brain suddenly up there in the high levels of clarity where cold, clear winds blow. He could see the big picture, the lines of contact, interconnecting them all in a lacy weave: Tom to Danny, Doug to Billy, to the crazy man with the blinking eyes – *Twitchy Eyes* – and to Corky himself. If there was a time to move, it was not now. The wrong move would get that gun talking, sure as hell it would. There might be another chance.

And then again there might not, a nasty little voice whispered. He shied away from it, though it seemed to echo persistently . . . *then again . . . then again . . .*

There might be another chance, once they'd all gone down together to the camp. Maybe they would go further, down into the trees.

Make it the camp, Corky prayed. *Stop there.* Up here in the valley, they were still in the open, with only scrubby hawthorns and hazels clustered in the rocks and some thick ferns that came up to shoulder-height or even higher further up the slopes, but here it was mostly open to the sun. It was far up from the town, but there was something about it being open that, instead of making him feel more vulnerable, seemed to convey a thin coating of protective cover.

Out in the open, you could be seen.

Down beyond the camp, where the trees began, there was dark and shadow under the spreading pines and the broad beech and oak trees. Nobody could see what was done down there. If he – *Twitchy Eyes* – took them down there beyond the line of the trees where even the water of the stream was deep and dark at the spate-carved potholes, then he would do whatever he wanted.

They would die.

A shiver ran up and down Corky's back, hard enough to make him feel as if his shirt was visibly rippling, and he tried to force the feeling away. He could not let them, Billy and Danny, see he was scared. He could not let them know how scared, because if they knew, they'd panic and that would make him panic and if he did that he'd have no say at all, no choice and no chance.

The big man with the gun was an all-out, shrieking screwball. Corky had seen it in the stuttering blink and the odd, head-cocked posture and the way he'd said, quite softly, that they'd all go down together. Corky did not want that man to see the ripple he felt must be visibly writhing under the fabric, for he'd know how scared he was and that would be a bad thing. You never let a dog see the fear. Not a *mad dog*.

Because then it would react. Then it would attack.

Say a prayer, Danny Boy, an oddly cool third voice said, almost languidly, over the cold sparkle of his thoughts. *Now's the time to collect on the 'Hail Mary's and 'Glory Be's round the fireplace.*

A mental image came unbidden, of Danny going up with a slip to the window in the confessional like a punter collecting on a line from Harvey Bracknell's betting shop, trading it in for some saving grace. A little shivery giggle tried to bubble up inside him, like a pocket of poisonous gas in the bog. He swallowed it down hard, in case it rolled up to the surface and burst out. He didn't want to hear the sound he might make. It might be a little high and shaky. A little hysterical and maybe mad.

Billy could see Corky only when his head happened to chance in that direction. The pain in his scalp, where the man had his hair in a vicious grasp, felt like fire, like a bad Chinese-rope burn that went from one ear to the other. Tears had already sparked, then spilt, and were cold on his cheek, and his thoughts too were high and sparking. He was floating in a bubble of fright and pain and he could hear the blood pound in his ears with the same double-beat rhythm as an old Zodiac engine with its big-ends gone.

The man was muttering something under his breath, but Billy couldn't make out the words. The taste of fish slime and blood, the texture of the fresh skin and hard gill-case, that had been awful, but not as shudderingly awful as the plummet of pure fear when the gun barrel had nudged cold under his chin. He had wanted to be a hero, all his life, as far as he could remember, knowing he had the stuff, had the guts to brave the worst. In the films, in all the war movies, he'd seen men shot and killed. They died like they did in the Westerns, bravely, with honour, no fuss and with very little blood.

Now he knew. In an instant of clarity when his mind had come suddenly fully awake from the day-dream that was his normal state of mentation, and now when it was as clear as glass, he realized it had all been a lie.

No hero no hero no hero.

His father had been *nobody*, and in another ice-sparkle of clarity Billy Harrison knew that he had known that all the time. It had been an unwanted knowledge, lurking out there in the shadows, to be kept at arm's length. He had wanted a father maybe, needed one perhaps, and the one he wanted was not like Corky's da, rolling drunk on Friday nights, blagging the pigeon-club money for booze. Not like Danny's dad either, ram-rod straight behind the family in their Sunday best and with a look of disdain for the boys smoking stolen cigarettes at the corner of the street. His father would have been a hero, *should* have been, like his mother said he was.

It was a lie. All of it. The films lied. Men didn't smile bravely when they were shot, fall into comfortable positions and look tragically valiant. He had felt the barrels under his jaw line and suddenly the real truth fell upon him like an enormous weight. The gun could blow his head clean off his shoulders in a splatter of blood and slime. It would leave him like the fish, shivering and headless and dead for ever.

Behind him the man spoke again, a muted, almost breathless mutter that was incomprehensible. The voice was low and rumbling, not the high and scary titter of a laugh.

'*Dumb fry*' it sounded like.

Up ahead, Tom Tannahill was walking, head down on the track, keeping his body curved in, as if by making himself even smaller, he could become invisible. He felt suddenly exhausted, as if the fright had drained everything out of him. His legs were shaking so badly there was a real danger that they'd give way or that he'd lose his step and the man with the gun would think he was trying to run away and . . . He did not want to think of that.

It was enough just to concentrate on putting one foot in front of the other and keep walking. He felt light-headed and trickles of sweat were beading just under his hairline to spill down his temples. Every couple of seconds, a flush of heat swept through him, as if he were blushing madly, but it was worse than that because when that happened, there was a roaring noise in his head and the sounds of their footsteps faded away, while little white sparkles appeared to dance in the corner of his vision.

Tom took a breath and heard it flutter as his chest hitched, the way it did after he'd been crying for a long time, and that sensation made him think of Maureen and how he'd cried then, for days at a time, trying to get to grips with that appalling, incomprehensible loss.

Billy whimpered, just a shiver of inarticulate sound, and Tom felt his lungs hitch again. His bladder wanted to let go. The pressure built up suddenly, fierce and urgent, and he clamped his hand down on his crotch, pressing hard until the feeling subsided from a burning pain to a warm pulse. A deadly weight of hopelessness dragged down on him and he wished Corky would do something, anything, to get them out of this.

The man with the gun said something, a mutter of sound, barely audible, and Tom almost stopped, fearing an order had been issued and he'd missed it but, even more fearful right at that moment to make any mistake at all. Some instinct made him keep moving and he walked, legs boneless and trembling, sweat dripping down the sides of his face, and the nagging pressure to piss rising to a twisting burn. He screwed up his eyes, the way Billy had done when the man grabbed his hair, and forced himself to concentrate. He did not want to piss himself.

The thought of that, of the damp, hot stain spreading on his jeans, was unendurable.

'Convoy.'

The sudden sound startled Tom so badly he almost slipped off the track and down the shallowing bank. Doug reached to help and the motion twisted him over on his ankle with a wrenching snap of pain that flared like a match and made him gasp through gritted teeth. The pain flashed high and then faded. Doug bit back tears and limped after Tom. There was no sound at all from the others, not even a whimper from Billy. Their senses were wound up to a pitch of tension. All of them listening for what would come next.

The man did not repeat himself. Not then.

Convoy? It had sounded like that even to Danny, who was nearest to him, except for Billy, held captive at arm's length. Did he mean we were all in line?

They all went down together in their convoy, past the slope of the turn at the white quartz rocks framing the head of the pool where Billy had first jumped into the water to clean the red silt off his jeans and stained the water in streaks of blood-red. The water was cool and dark and clear now, the surface dimpled with the small swirls of turbulence. A brilliant-blue damselfly wove silently over the moving surface, a silent line of coruscating light. They filed past the turn to where the canyon of the valley widened to the swathe of green where the tent stood, a little lop-sided, close to the shade of the rowan trees. A thin, blue line of smoke rose perpendicular from the embers of the morning's fire where the thick pine log was still smouldering lazily. Further down, a highland cow, russet and hairy but with a spread of horns like cattle on any Western ranch, turned slowly and watched with impassive black eyes while its calf nosed in at the udders. Eventually the animals moved off into the high ferns at the edge of a clearing, barging through the undergrowth with a crackling sound that reminded Danny of the noise down in the dark of the trees when they'd sat round the camp-fire talking about old Mole Hopkirk and the flies. Had that been a cow? In the dark, he had sensed eyes watching them, but that could have been imagination. Could have been.

But the doom-doom-*DOOM* sound that had woken him out of sleep, that had been no cow. He knew that for certain now. The man with the gun had been watching them from the cover and the shade while they had laughed and fought. He'd probably heard Corky's tale about the rats under the bank, the Racine rats that came out and ate lonesome travellers beside the water. In the hypernatural clarity of the moment, Danny understood now about the footprint in the shingle and the booming sound coming up from the hollow bank downstream. The man had been announcing his presence, trying to scare them. He had been telling them he was here.

And now he *was* here.

They walked into the clearing and the man's footsteps thudded suddenly loud behind them, and Danny knew that was his imagination. Everything about the moment was magnified, from the crackling blunder of the cow and calf to the shimmering streak of the damselfly and the smell of the pine smoke.

'Yea, tho' I walk through the valley of the shadow of death.'

The voice spoke out, clear and boomingly succinct, a deep contrast to the snicker of the laugh up at the high pool.

'I will fear no evil.'

Billy's foot slipped on a dried ball of sheep dung and he almost fell forward. The stranger's hand pulled him back with a strong twist and another yelp escaped the boy. Pain flared in his scalp and tears sparked again in his eyes. If the man had let him go just at that moment he would have fallen forward right on to his face.

'Nearly there, convoy.' This time the voice was almost a growl. Corky assumed he was talking to them. 'Can you hear me?'

Corky nodded, risking a turn towards the man, letting him know he had heard and understood, but the stranger was turned away, his head cocked to the side, as if in conversation with someone else.

'You listening, Conboy?'

Not 'convoy'. Corky heard it clearly. *Conboy*.

'He makes me lie down in green pastures. He leads me beside quiet waters. He restores my soul.'

Danny heard the words and recognized them, too, from long repetition. For some reason his heart sank even further; it felt as if it shrivelled inside him.

CHAPTER TWENTY-FIVE

Billy fell headlong when the man released the tight grip on his hair. He went sprawling past Danny, arms pin-wheeling in a fruitless attempt to regain his balance. He made a little croaking noise and the fingers of his left hand caught at Doug's vest, almost managed to grab it, but only skimmed the fabric. He fell with a thump that knocked his breath out in a whoosh, rolled and fetched up face down on the turf next to the stones around the fire. Another foot and he'd have caved his skull in on the smooth rock. Another two and he'd be face down in the hot embers of the fire. Doug instinctively moved to help him and then froze, half bent, with his arms outreached. Very slowly he drew them back to his sides again and pulled himself back. He turned round even more slowly. Danny did not move.

'Ahah,' the man said, and none of them knew whether he was just clearing his throat, though it sounded like the confirmation of preconceived suspicion.

Corky broke the stillness. He walked past Doug and bent to get a hand under Billy's armpit. Tom took two steps back and helped him. Billy gasped for breath as he got to his feet, both hands clamped to his belly and his face slack with the effort and hurt. A streak of ash had glued itself to the tears on his cheek and smudged there, making him look as if he'd a black eye. On the other side, two straight lines of soot had striped the skin, like Indian-brave warpaint. But at that moment, he looked less Indian and less brave than ever.

'Well, well,' the stranger said. Danny looked up at him and quickly looked away. Corky completely ignored the sound.

'You ok, Billy-O?' he asked quickly, voice hushed. He had one hand on Billy's shoulder, an unconscious and eloquent gesture of solidarity and support. His other was under Billy's elbow, steadying him. Billy swayed a little.

'Yeah,' he finally said in between gasps. '*Jeez*. That hurts.'

Tom, on the other side, equally unconsciously and quite unceremoniously brushed some dried bracken off Billy's shirt.

'Thought you were diving into the fire there,' Corky told him. 'You were nearly a goner.'

Danny could only stand amazed at how calm Corky sounded. It was as if they'd just been wrestling on the short grass and somebody had got winded. Danny could sense the man's eyes taking in the whole scene.

Yea, tho' I walk through the valley . . .

Psalm twenty-three, verse four. Danny knew it off by heart. He'd heard it a thousand times, one of his father's favourites, one of the many engraved on Danny's brain through endless repetition, like the 'Hail Mary's and 'Glory Be's of the tedious rosaries. And acts of contrition.

I will fear no evil.

They had stopped in the valley. The sun was shining and the lark was rising on a pillar of song in the warm air, but there was a shadow now, here beside the stream.

Shadow of death . . .

Danny felt it clearly. He had looked up at the man and seen his eyes, not twitching, not then, but taking in the scene, flat and soulless as the eyes of a dead trout, as if they stared into infinity. All down the path, he had felt the bore of the gun aimed on his spine, all the time expecting it to blast out and break him. It hadn't happened, but Danny could sense the proximity of death and the casual mindlessness of the violence inside the man.

I will fear no evil.

He feared evil. Oh, sweet Jesus! He very much feared it. An evil indifference radiated from the man who stood there, his shadow between Danny and the sun, long and black, the gun now held in folded arms, cradled as if it were a baby. He was indifferent for now, but how long that would last before he switched back his attention, Danny could not guess. But it would change and then he'd focus on them.

He maketh me to lie down in green pastures.

He had made Billy lie down on the green, thrown him flat with a move of his hand. Billy stood there waiting for the next move. They all did.

The man slowly swept his eyes round the clearing beside the stream.

Dumb fry.

It came out as a murmur, half strangled. They all heard it. It meant nothing, made no sense. He jerked his head to the side, cocked it again as if listening for something. Corky watched, keeping his expression flat, giving no cause for action or retribution. He'd taken a risk going to help Billy, but that had happened almost instinctively. A friend was down and hurt. He had moved without thinking. It was only now, afterwards, that he realized the man could have acted just as reflexively.

The intruder was talking to himself. A bad sign. Billy was breathing heavily, as if he couldn't control it, and, beside him, Tom looked tiny and fragile, one hand pressed against his crotch.

'What do you want?' Corky finally said, hardly able to contain his own surprise that he'd found the nerve to speak.

The man seemed not to have heard at all.

'Mister?' Corky risked another venture.

The man turned, not towards Corky, but towards the stream. The sun was shining over the lip of the valley, up high where the mudstone strata poked out under the line of the high moorland turf. The light beamed from the water in coruscating flashes.

'*Dumb fry*. That right, Conboy? *Only words they understand*. No souls. No damned souls.'

He stared at the water and they all stared at him, wondering what would come next. Doug's narrow chest was rising up and down and his ears were redly translucent in the sunlight. Danny watched the man and the gun, fearful that he'd simply turn from the stream and shoot. There was a tension in the air, a sense of unbalanced and brittle craziness. The man blinked and muttered to himself as if he'd completely forgotten them.

Tom could wait no longer. The pressure was spreading over the top of his thighs and he thought again he'd piss his pants and that was enough for him. He unzipped with a quick rasp, turned half around and let flow a stream. They all heard his instant sigh of sudden relief and then, just as instantly, the hiss of steam as the arc of bright water struck the hot rock. The stone steamed and a bubbling spot of urine sizzled on the stone sending up a sour, hot billow. Tom stepped back, head jerking around to see if the noise had attracted the man's attention. In doing so, his body half swivelled and he was still emptying his bladder. The motion caused him to spray a line right across Billy's scuffed shoe and, under any other circumstances, such a lapse of judgement or aim would have merited him a rough knuckle on the scalp, or a headlock or even a dead leg. Billy did not notice. His eyes were fixed on the man who stood with the gun cradled in his arms and his gaze looking down at the flashes on the surface of the water.

Twitchy Eyes.

Billy's mouth formed the words, though he made no sound, but they all heard him as if he'd shouted them at the top of his voice; all except Tom, who was desperately trying to finish quickly to take any possible attention away from himself, yet found he had huge liquid reserves that kept coming and coming. The grass turned dark green with damp and then a puddle formed. For such a small person, he seemed to have a limitless supply. Everybody waited and finally Tom finished. He sighed audibly once again, zipped himself up and raised his eyes to look at the man.

The stranger blinked rapidly, and as he did so his whole face contorted. Deep lines formed round his eyes and Danny could see it wasn't so much a blink. It was more like a jittery tic. A twitch.

'What's he going to do?'

Doug's whisper could barely be heard above the burbling of the stream but all of them caught it. Danny shrugged, hardly a movement at all, just the merest hitch of his shoulders.

None of them knew what the man was going to do, but all of them knew they were in trouble.

Twitchy Eyes, Billy mouthed once more, and this time Tom read the message. Billy was not telling them, merely talking to himself, snagged on his awful comprehension. He had one hand on his scalp, gingerly rubbing at the tender place where it still felt as if his hair was being pulled out. His face was slack and dreadfully scared. His eyes were not fixed on the man at all, but focused somewhere in the distance. Corky nodded and so did Danny. Tom's eyebrows went up in question and then the recognition dawned in his eyes too.

Beside the flashing water, the man's head was still twisted to the side. His coat was long and heavy, despite the heat of the day, and torn under the armpit and at the pocket, as if too much weight had been put there. The hem hung right down to his calf, caked with dirt or mud, and his boots were old and worn. One of them had a shark-mouth split where the sole was peeling away from the upper and looked just like the boot they'd found up at the crater on the day they'd walked over the ridge and seen the devastation on the moor surrounding the ghost-shacks of the dummy village.

'What if there's a foot in it?' Doug had asked, giggling. He wasn't giggling now. He remembered telling Billy if there was a foot in it he'd have shit himself. Billy hadn't denied it then. He looked now as if he couldn't force the air out hard enough to make a sound. There was an association here that had sparked yet another. The divers had found a boot in the pool down by the quarry and there had been a foot inside it. That had been when Crawford Rankine had been thrown off the quarry and cracked his skull on the rock.

Twitchy Eyes . . .

This man had done it. Doug felt a sudden swoop of panic shudder through him and his breath back up in his skinny chest until his lungs couldn't hold any more.

He'd done it. Thrown Craw Rankine down from the ledge on to the flat rock and then he'd gone back and got Don Whalen and taken him away . . . *Oh, Jeez* . . . suddenly Doug's lungs did want to work, tried to draw in more air, and there was no more room. Everybody had heard what he did to Craw. He could feel his chest moving up and down while a heat of cramping pain started swelling under his armpits and he was making a sound like a distressed dog on a sweltering day.

The man turned round, away from the water, but his eyes were still blinking hard, still *twitching*, though they were looking well over their heads and not directly at the five boys. Doug tried to stop panting, but his muscles would not obey. His chest heaved even faster, small, shallow and violent breaths that shook his body, made his shoulders jerk up and down. His face was deathly pale, the way Billy's had been, and even his ears had lost their red glow. Corky heard the noise get louder and stared at him, shaking his head very slightly, but firmly, keeping his eyes locked on Doug's. He did not have to say it, the way he had spoken on the way down the valley. If anything was going to happen, it could be now. They all sensed it. But the more Doug tried, the faster the panting got. The lines of rock striations on the valley sides began to waver as a loop of dizziness brought on by the hyperventilation swept through him. A dry heat built up in his arid throat. In the corner of his eye, shadows flickered, and he felt as if he was going to faint.

To his great surprise, Tom Tannahill stepped up beside him and grabbed him through his old vest, his small hand surprisingly strong. Tom gripped the fabric and a handful of skin and clutched so tight he felt something would rip. He just wanted Doug to stop panting.

A stab of pain lanced across Doug's ribs, sore enough to momentarily divert his attention. A cry built up way down inside him and he clamped his gaping mouth shut to keep it in. He grunted softly.

The man kept his eyes firmly on the distance, maybe on the sky or on the high valley sides where the scrub alder and hazel mixed with the thick ferns. The gun gleamed, blue-black and shiny clean, a complete contrast to the raggedy stranger with his greasy hair and his gaping boot and the thick, sour smell from his coat. The real difference was that the gun could be put down on its butt end and it would hurt nobody by itself. This crazy man had a depth of hurt inside him, bursting to get out.

Should have run, Doug thought, *while I had the chance*. His lungs still hurt but the panic panting was over and the dark shadows had faded away from his peripheral vision. His ankle pulsed painfully yet and he knew he could not run now if he wanted to. Billy was still mouthing the same two words over and over again as if the sudden comprehension had engraved them on his consciousness. Corky looked like a cat, all tensed up, ready to jump one way or another. Tom had his hand still gripped to Doug's vest, but not clenched into his skin, when the man finally lifted his hand and pointed at Billy.

'You, boy,' he said, not yet looking down, 'come over here to me.'

Billy looked as if he would faint on the spot. His mouth opened, closed, opened again. Everybody heard the dry click of his throat.

'Mister . . .' Corky started in. The man turned his head

towards him, eyes still fixed on the far distance, as if watching something happening elsewhere, maybe as if seeing visions. His hand was still raised up, fist tight and showing white knuckles. One long, thick finger was pointed straight at Billy's face.

'I said, come here.' The voice was low and rumbling, with a slight accent, maybe from the east coast, but it could have easily been from the north. It was not a local accent, no glottal stop, no truncation of the endings.

Billy's mouth kept opening and closing as if he had strength enough to clench his teeth but not enough to hold his jaw tight. Doug started panting again and Tom gripped his skin once more until he subsided. Corky looked as if he might speak again, but the man's face was still towards him and he dared not risk it. Billy's feet moved him closer and Danny thought he looked like a rabbit faced with a stoat. He and Corky had seen that happening up on the moorland to Langcraig Hill, a stoat in autumn colours, dark and long with a jet-black tip to its tail and eyes like beads of coal, weaving sinuous in front of a mesmerized rabbit that looked as if it had stopped breathing. The deadly predator swayed, up on its hind legs, body like a cobra, while the rabbit simply waited for the bite on the back of its skull, unable to escape. Billy was unable to escape. He took one slow step and the man's head turned and the black eyes fixed on him and in that moment Danny saw the stoat inside the man. His eyes had the same depths, and the same animal intensity. They bored into Billy and there was nothing the boy could do. He took another step, then another, walked across the turf from the edge of the fire to the edge of the stream. He got to within arm's reach and the man's arm simply dropped down and clapped on his shoulder with a soft thud. Billy did not faint, though Doug felt the strange, nauseous wavering inside himself.

Billy stood rigid, face up.

They were fixed for maybe a minute in silence, joined by the man's reach.

'You hear it, boy?'

'Hear . . . hear?'

'You hear it, don't you?'

'I don't know mister. I don't hear . . .'

'Oh, you will then,' the man said. He stared straight into

Billy's eyes for another long moment and then turned his head, ignoring the others, until he faced the hollow by the gnarled hawthorn.

'You'll see it too,' he said, raising his hand off Billy's shoulder and holding it above his head before dropping it slowly, almost gently, to the dark hair. He patted first and then stroked down.

'Hurt you, boy?'

Billy couldn't help but nod.

'Part of the process. All part of it. No need to fret.' His voice dropped almost to a whisper, but they could all hear it.

'You see it, boy. I know you do.' He indicated the hollow where the dead-deer skull gnashed its teeth in a fixed and silent grin. The eye sockets were crawling with flies, masses of them, like a moving mat. The wasted nostrils, pulled back in flaps, showed a sliver of bone and a hollow dark space alongside the flaccid skin which moved with the abundance of maggots under the surface. The clogged eyes seemed to stare out of the shaded place. Above it, the imperious, white skull of the ram on the pole was a stark, ivory sculpture, white against the dark of the green, its eyes gaping and haunted and bracketed by the heavy-ridged double curve of horns. Below them, the heron's severed head stared out, the delicate spear of the beak now shut, a useless and blunted weapon. Below it, the ragged neck had attracted its own swarm, but the yellow eye gazed blinklessly.

The eye caught Danny's own and a feeling of guilt swamped him. He hadn't meant to kill the thing but it had died anyway, neck broken, graceless and flapping before the final shiver of severed nerves.

It did bring bad luck, he thought, aghast. Billy had cut off the head, and the yellow eye had fixed itself accusingly on Danny, bright and glittering while the droplets of blood had sprinkled out on to the grass and on to Billy's skin. Danny had killed it and a cloud had shadowed the valley right then, and it had felt completely wrong. Now the eye still stared, flat and lifeless, and it felt worse now. The shadow was back in the valley in broad daylight, in the sultry burn of the noonday sun. They had fought last night, Billy and Doug telling each other terrible truths that had been better left unsaid and Corky telling truths that they all had to hear. More bad luck.

And now the man had started to move and was walking Billy out beyond the camp to the hollow where he'd set up his trophies. The gun was casually slung over his free shoulder, barrels pointing at the sky. He ignored the other four, as if they did not exist. They stood frozen while the man and boy moved out along the second trail made by Billy's feet trampling down the short ferns there at the edge of the clearing. The flies were faintly audible, a soft murmur of sound, like someone moaning softly in the hollow. It was no more than thirty yards away, far enough for the smell not to carry down to the camp-site.

The man led Billy ahead of him, the hand still laid on his head, but not twisting the hair now. He looked like a priest with an acolyte, with an altar boy. They got halfway to the hollow when Corky slowly turned to Danny and whispered.

'We've got to get out of here.'

'How?' Doug asked. 'I've hurt my foot. Twisted my ankle.'

'What about Billy?' Tom wanted to know. 'What's he going to do to him?'

'It's that crazy guy, isn't it?' Danny said. He felt his own breath back up, as if his body didn't want to respond, to say those words. He compromised. 'Him.'

'Twitchy Eyes,' Doug hissed. Corky nodded.

'Has to be him. That's why we've got to get out. Get help.'

'But he's got a gun.'

'Yeah, but he's not going to do anything right away, is he now?' Corky said. He waited until they had all digested that. 'Not to all of us.'

Danny was astonished at Corky's grasp of this situation. Like he'd done the night before, he had cut to the heart of it, through the gristle and connective tissue, and laid it all bare. What was worse? Reality brought its own added terrors. They had all heard the stories that had run around the playground, brushfires of truth and surmise, but mostly truth. A town like Levenford could hold no secret for long. Every detail of what the man with the twitchy eyes had done had been gone over and been picked at, by men in the bars; by women over tea cups; by boys braving it down on the edges of the Rough Drain warily listening for the passage of strangers; by little kids scaring each other in school. The starkness of what Corky said, spoken in just a whisper that would not have carried for four yards, had the impact of a scream.

Mole Hopkirk had lain for a long time before he'd died, hurt and bleeding and alone and unable to call for help. Don Whalen had been carried away to the old bomb-shelter in the scrubland where the old glue works had once stood down near the Highcross road. The shelter had not been a place of refuge for him. The man had taken him down there and hurt him until he died beside the open-mouthed corpse of that girl from Lochend. And the killer had taken his time with Sandra Walters, too.

Corky was right. He would not do anything to them right away, not to all of them, not *right now*. But he would do something terrible if they didn't get away from here. The knowledge of who he was and what he had done was laid right on them by the bleak simplicity of Corky's statement.

Tom thought of the little kid under the bridge and was reminded of the story he'd read to his sister in the last days, 'Billy Goat Gruff', with the nightmare hiding in ambush under the dark arch. He felt his bladder complain again and he concentrated until the protest faded. This man had killed the little girl under the bridge.

There was no doubt in any of their minds. They had seen the twitch. The man was big and – *oh Jesus please us, hug and squeeze us* – it was him all right and he was here. Tom felt a ripple of intense fear shudder through him and he thought about death, not for the first time. He did not want to die like that girl under the bridge. He didn't want to die in his own piss.

My fault, Danny thought, with the image of the heron crashing to the ground, broken and twisted, one wing carrying it round in stupid circles. He'd brought the bad luck. Everything had started to go wrong for them after that.

And Billy had hung the head up.

Now Billy was paying the price. He had stained himself with the blood which had splashed from the ragged neck.

And they marked the lintels with the blood so that the angel of death would pass over. The line from the bible came back to him, unbidden. He'd thought of that when Billy had cut the head off the bird, a *biblical* quotation. And the angel had not passed over. He'd come as if summoned and he was quoting the bible, a grotesque parody of Danny's own father. Danny shied away from the connection. His head was buzzing under the pressure of sudden overload. Corky's voice pulled him away and back to the here and now.

'What's he doing?'

'Talking to Billy,' Doug said. He was up on tiptoes, using Tom as a leaning post. The stranger was half hidden behind the first low clump of scrub. He leant and put the gun against a flat face of rock, butt down on the grass. For the first time, hope swelled.

Over by the hollow, the man was talking, not very loud at first, but the words were amplified by the hollow curve of the stone face. They could just make out what he was saying. Billy could feel himself shaking all through, as if he'd become a tuning fork. For some reason his stomach kept twisting all on its own, and that made him belch constantly, little pockets of air bursting at the back of his dry throat.

'Hear them, eh?'

'What?' Billy managed to blurt.

'The flies, boy. Children of Beelzebub, purifiers of the dead. In the midst of death, they are life. You hear them? They talk to us all, those voices. You just need ears to hear.'

The man brought his head down until his cheek was against Billy's ear. He could smell his breath, flat and cloying and rotten; he could smell his sour sweat. The man's beard bristles rasped against the side of his face and Billy had no strength to pull away.

'Got to go down into the valley and out the other side. Come through trials and tribulations to reach the great truth. You want to make that journey, boy? You want to listen to the voice of the dead?'

'Crazy,' Doug whispered. 'He's off his flamin' head.' Tom nodded slowly.

'We have to get out of here first chance,' Corky said. 'Soon as we can.'

'Can you get help?' Doug wanted to know. 'I can't run. I twisted my ankle.' The bitter disappointment was etched on his face. If anybody could have gone for help, gone quickly, it would always have been him. That little stumble as he reached out to help Tom had cost him his speed. Cost them all.

'I *have* to get help,' Corky said. His eyes were fixed on the enactment in the hollow by the old hawthorn. The man was leaning over Billy now and, for a moment, they could have been father and son, both of them tall, though the stranger towered over the boy, and both dark-haired and sallow of skin. Not the father Billy would have wanted, not the hero.

'Watched you set this up, boy.' The voice came, chilling in its casual, matter-of-fact flatness. Billy couldn't speak. The stranger took the hand off his head and reached towards the deer's skull. Immediately a cloud of black flies peeled off and into the air in an angry little tornado. One of them landed on Billy's cheek, a big, fat, blue thing. It edged down towards his mouth and he got a whiff of the dead meat it had fed on.

'*Dung-fly*,' the man said. This time they all heard it. 'Conboy knew. He knew what they meant, godless heathens. Am I right?'

Billy nodded in quick response, though he hadn't a clue. None of them had. Corky looked straight at Danny, his mouth set in a grim line. They had both climbed up on the roof behind the old surgery at Cairn House and had seen the flies patter like rain against the window. They hadn't known then. They knew now.

'When?' Danny asked. Corky was about to say something when a high-pitched squeal pierced the air, startling them all. The stranger's head snapped up and he seemed to come out of that dreamy, far-off state.

'What's that?' he asked sharply. Billy looked up at him, face blank and open, a picture of miserable bewilderment.

'I dunno,' he finally managed.

Down at the bottom end of the clearing, where the low hazels crowded together with some tangled blackthorns, the cry came again, a squeal of pain or panic. The man moved backwards from the hollow, leaving Billy on his own. He turned and walked, not towards the waiting group, but cut round the edge of the flat ground, head cocked, the way it had been before, but this time obviously listening for the noise. He reached the tent and skirted behind it. The sound came again and this time Corky recognized it.

'It's a rabbit,' he said. 'Maybe one of the snares worked.'

The man seemed to have forgotten about them for the moment. He moved into the clump of blackthorn, then beyond a thick hazel, and disappeared from sight. They all stood stock-still. The gun was up there at the rock, only yards from where Billy stood.

'Get it,' Corky said between his teeth. He wanted to shout but couldn't risk it. The man had gone into the scrub about thirty yards away, but he was still closer to the gun than they were, or so it seemed. Billy was only a few feet from it. He had half turned towards them, but his whole attention was fixed on where the stranger had gone.

'Billy!' Corky hissed. Doug turned round and did the same, waving his hands for emphasis. None of them had the nerve to run to the hollow, just in case that's what the man was waiting for. Down in the cover the rabbit squeaked again, weaker now. They knew the noose would be caught on its cheeks and it would be trying to force itself free, drawing the fishing-line snare tighter with every move. If it had been round its neck, the pressure would have strangled the sound.

'Billy.' Danny gesticulated too. 'Get it. Get the gun!' His Uncle Mick had let him fire a few shots down on the Whale's Back sandbank on the estuary. They didn't even have to fire it at all, just threaten. Twitchy Eyes might be crazy, but he couldn't be so crazy he would ignore a gun threat.

But too crazy for Billy to risk going for the gun . . .

Danny's legs twitched, as if they wanted to get started, get moving, as if he was already running for it. Something inside of him wanted to see the barrel pressed up against the man's throat, to get revenge for the dreadful sensation of fear that had swamped him when he had felt it aimed at his spine, ready to cut him in half.

The noise cut off. For a moment there was silence.

'Billy!' Tom hissed. Billy's attention was still fixed on the spot where the man had gone into the rough. Once again he looked like the rabbit mesmerized by the stoat. Off in the cover, the other trapped rabbit had stopped crying.

Corky took two steps back. His head swung left and right, gauging the distance to the gun, to the stream. His hands balled into thick, tense fists and of a sudden his eyes glinted like emeralds.

'Wha . . .' Doug started to ask. Corky forestalled him.

'I got a chance,' was all he said. He swivelled round to estimate the climb to the top of the rim, shook his head, crouched like a runner waiting for the gun, hands spread for balance. It was a high, steep slope and the loose, shifting gravel would slow him. Both Danny and Doug could see that. The agony of indecision stretched out for what seemed like a long time, but must have been only seconds. He shook his head again, making the decision.

'I'll come back,' he said. 'Honest. Try to . . .' He did not finish. Out in the scrub beyond the camp-site, a low, thudding sound punched out. Because of the dense foliage of fern and alder, none of them could say from what direction it came. It was enough, however, to galvanize Corky. He gambled on a downstream run. Despite his previous misgivings about being taken down into the trees – and they had been real fears – he worked out the best option. It was a downhill sprint, following the sheep-track beside the stream – that would give him the advantage of speed. It was on the other side of the camp-site to where the gun was, so even if the man came blundering back and reached for it, he could easily be two turns of the stream ahead and out of the line of fire. If he reached the trees, they would give extra cover. He could hide in the shadow, use the shade and cover to get up to the edge of the valley and get down to the town. It was a *chance*. There was a good chance that the man would come after him and that would give the others the opportunity to scatter, and the more of them that got away, that would give anybody else more hope. Corky was only thirteen years old, but he had a bright instinct for odds and chances, honed, possibly, by the years of sliding between his violent father and his loony brother.

He spun, leapt over the smouldering fire and hit the ground on the other side. He went down the slope like a hare, arms flashing, feet thrumming, racing along the bank.

Doom-doom-*doom*. Corky passed the overhang where the stream had dug under the edge and the noise of his passing echoed back to them. Hope leapt in Danny's chest. His heart did the same, beating so fast he could actually feel its pressure high up under his throat.

'Run for it, Corky,' Doug muttered to himself, to the three of them. '*Go on, man.*'

Corky made it down to the next pool. He skittered across the stones where the stream narrowed at the tight bend and then ran back across the shallows beyond, sending up a fine spray that caught the sun and made a series of brilliant rainbows. He reached the turn, grabbed on to the upright trunk of a slender sapling to propel himself round the corner.

The man came right out of the bushes at the side of the clearing.

For an instant Danny thought the big, charging shape was a highland cow that had been startled by the sudden motion, until he recognized the man's size and shape. He came streaking out, almost silent but for a couple of twigs that crackled underfoot.

'Oh, fuck,' Doug said emptily.

The man had been further downstream than they had realized. They could have got to the gun if they'd known.

Corky caught the motion out of the corner of his eye. They all saw that. The black figure came streaking out of the bushes. Corky's face turned and one hand went up in a reflex protective action. He swerved to the side, too late, for he was hemmed in now by the steep valley side and had no room for manoeuvre. He tried to run faster, reached the flat turf at the edge of the stream, got one foot on the shingle at the bottom end of the pool, and the man lashed out with his foot and caught him a savage blow right on the hip.

They all heard the dreadful smacking sound as the toe of the boot connected. It sounded exactly like the noise they'd made when they swung the thick logs on the stones to break them into firewood. Corky made a noise that did not sound exactly human. The force of the blow knocked him right up into the air, legs twisting from under him. He flew in a low arc and landed on the shingle with another loud thud, scattering small stones as he ploughed into them.

'Jesus,' Doug said.

Down by the pool Corky tried to get to his feet. They could see his left leg dig in at the shingle in a desperate attempt to raise himself up again and propel himself further down the valley, but his right leg was not moving at the same speed. A cry of pain or desperation or bitter defeat escaped him and came echoing up to where they stood. He got to the edge of the water, his left hand scattering shingle into the pool. The man took a step forward and kicked his backside. The blow wasn't as violent as the first one had been, and obviously wasn't even intended to be.

Corky lurched forward, off balance. His hand skidded out from under, making his body flop at the edge of the shallows. The stranger took another step and put his boot in the small of Corky's back.

'Jesus,' Doug mouthed again. They had all moved forward, all except Billy, unable to stop themselves, getting to the lip at the edge of the slope, unable to draw their eyes away from what was happening further down the valley. The man leant forward and Corky's arms thrashed in the water.

'He'll drown,' Tom said in a shivery little bleat of panic.

Corky's head went under the water. It wasn't deep, maybe three or four inches, but with the weight of the man himself pressing down on him, driving him into the shale, it was deep enough. He raised his head up from the water, hands splashing furiously, waving to get some purchase and once again sending up coruscating prism colours. He tried to pull himself from under but there was nothing to hold on to. His head flopped down and they all heard him gasp and splutter under the water.

'He's killing him,' Tom said, almost in a whimper.

Corky yelled frantically as he exhaled, managing to lift his mouth and nose clear for an instant, just enough to haul in a breath. It was an inarticulate sound of no words but the desperation in it was clear and stabbed them all.

Danny was moving. He did not remember starting to move, or even deciding to do it. The animal sound Corky had made simply released something in him, and before he knew it he was down the slope and belting along the track. Somebody shouted behind him and the sound seemed to draw itself out like warm toffee. It might have been Doug or Tom, for Billy was probably still paralysed up by the altar of the skulls. Danny ran over the stones, travelling in a straight line the way Corky had done, then across the shallows at the first pool, before he even realized what was happening and, by that time, everything was moving too fast, including himself. Corky's head was down again and all of his limbs were thrashing about. The stranger was laughing or saying something. Unbelievably, he had a rabbit in his hand, about half grown, still alive and kicking, trying to squirm away much as Corky was doing. Danny was too far committed now, moving too quickly to turn round and tell Doug to get the gun. He would have cursed to himself if there had been time, because he should have got the gun and come down and shot the man, but all he'd heard was that animal sound, a deadly noise of a drowning boy, and inside Danny something had clicked like a thrown switch; like a pulled trigger. He'd got a vision of Paulie Degman rolling over in the water and the sick feeling of proximity to death came welling up in him and, all of a sudden, he'd had no choice at all.

He splashed across the shallows of the upper pool, down the slope to the second, across the narrow part of the falls, and landed with a thump on the shingle, scattering an arc of stones much as Corky had done when he fell. His momentum carried him forward, feet pattering through the few inches of water. Behind him somebody was screaming and he couldn't tell who it was. He skidded forward, barked against the man's right leg and almost fell. Despite the speed of the collision, the man hadn't even moved. Danny felt as if he'd run smack into a tree. He bounced, body twisting, feet skidding, but did not stop. He simply grabbed Corky's ankle, got his other hand to it, felt the powerful and desperate kick as his friend fought for air, fought for life, and dragged backwards. For a fraction of a second, nothing happened, and then Corky jerked back, only a few inches, but enough to get his head clear of the water. His face scraped across the shingles, still pressed down on the ground. He hauled for breath, a great whoop of suction, coughed violently, retched, then whooped again. The man took his foot off his back and Danny's weight pulled Corky even further back from the water.

Danny fell on his backside, suddenly numbed by the enormity of what had happened. A loop of nausea bubbled up inside him, burning the back of his throat, then subsided without any conscious assistance. He started to get to his feet when the man's shadow fell on him.

'The earth trembled and it quaked,' he said, very slowly and clearly, almost dreamily. 'They trembled because he was angry.'

A hand reached down and took Danny by the neck, lifting

him to his feet in one swift, smooth motion. He felt something creak in under the grip and a twist of pain shot from one side to the other at the back of his skull. His feet came almost clear of the ground, the way Billy's had done when the man grabbed his hair. The fingers squeezed, not monstrously, but enough to get the impression of great and irresistible strength. Danny remembered thinking he should shout to Doug or Tom to get the gun, but he was too scared to even open his mouth.

'Suffer little children to come unto me,' the man said. He twisted Danny around and forced his head back so that he could look right into his eyes. He bent forward, blotting out the blue of the sky, and locked on to Danny. The obsidian eyes in that dark and seamed face seemed to expand by some alchemy. They fixed on Danny, black as night, and held him tight. They were so dark that no pupil could be seen, only the depth, like empty holes. He leant in close, and the sour, unwashed smell enveloped Danny. The man was dirty and he was mad. The eyes held him, completely expressionless, not angry, not even mad-looking, and that was creepiest of all. Danny was up on his tiptoes, while this man stared right into his soul with those black searchlights, leaning forward like a hungry animal.

He's going to eat me . . . A panicked and jittery thought bubbled up. *He bites people. Oh, man, he eats people* . . .

'Don't hurt him,' Corky pleaded. He'd been coughing the water out of his throat when the man had turned and grabbed Danny. He lurched to his feet, biting down on the auger of pain that drilled right up high on his hip where the blow had almost dislocated the joint. His leg was numb and stiff, like the worst dead leg he'd ever had, and everything from mid-thigh down was jittering and jiving of its own volition. He hauled himself upright, and now he could see his friend caught by the neck, and the raggedy man was bending over him. Corky pushed in, trying to get himself between Danny and the intruder. He was scared, dreadfully scared, but he knew Danny had come for him and he had to go for Danny.

'Let him go, mister,' he bawled, reaching up to grab the arm that had Danny by the neck. Danny was making little croaking sounds while the black, and for once blinkless eyes seared into him. Corky dragged downwards, trying at least to get Danny's feet flat on the ground, just in case the man shook him and broke his neck. For some reason, the motion broke the connection. The man blinked once, as if coming awake, swivelled his head to look at Corky.

'What?'

'I said, let him go,' Corky said.

Without a word the man held up the rabbit by its hind legs. It jiggled there, trapped in his grip, making little reflexive running motions. Its brown eyes rolled in the sockets. A tiny pink tongue, like that of a newborn baby, lolled sofly.

Without warning the man jerked his hand. The animal swung in a brief arc and came down with whipping force. Its head connected with Corky's cow's-lick hairline at the top of his brow. There was a wet crunch. A metallic smell misted the air. A red stain pulped across Corky's head. He fell to the ground, landing on his backside with such a force that his teeth snapped together hard enough for Danny to hear. The man had lowered Danny's feet to the grass, and the grip on his neck eased considerably. He twisted just enough to see what was happening. Corky was slipping backwards, eyes open, but with a wide, bloodied mark right across his head. He grunted, and it was the most deadly sound Danny had ever heard. It was an animal sound, mindless and helpless. It was the kind of sound the Aberdeen Angus bullocks made down in the slaughterhouse pens when the malletmen fired the bolt into their brains and they dropped, stumbling to the tiles with a grunt of expelled air, dead before they fell.

Corky made that awful animal noise.

Both his hands were on the ground. He rolled slowly and lay flat.

He's killed him. Oh!

Horror and shock wheeled right through Danny.

It had happened with such brutal force, such unexpected speed. A whip and a crack, and Corky was down. The enormity of it was still trying to impinge itself on Danny's mind when Corky suddenly moved. He jerked, much as the man had done, as if coming awake. Both hands flew up to his head and dabbed gingerly. He blinked several times and then he moaned, not loud, but the way someone does when they've bumped their head or barked their shin. He winced as he did so. His hands came away bloodied and Danny expected him to find bits of skull and bone there too, at that part where his skull had been caved in.

Corky's face twisted into an expression of disgust and he rubbed gingerly again at his scalp. Danny turned back, completely bewildered, and saw the rabbit swinging in the man's hand. Its head was a red ruin. The little animal's skull was flattened and pulped and a trail of blood dribbled from the nose that had been twitching only seconds before. It was stone-dead.

CHAPTER TWENTY-SIX

August 3, night

The moon rose over the high edge on the east side of the valley, a slow, bright dome, just a shave short of full. Doug had watched it from where he sat, up against the pole of the tent close to the open flap, seeing the coarse grass fringe limned in silver, then silhouetted against the light. The others, Danny, Tom and Corky, who were at the back, could only see the effect on the valley and the water of the stream over by the falls where Billy had stuck the feathers.

The upstream curve of the valley gradually lightened as the moon rose higher, sending ink-blot shadows contracting slowly on the westward sides of the rocks and trees. The water at the falls was a flow of rippling quicksilver and even the small cascade itself seemed to be imbued with a kind of magic, softening its sound down to barely a whisper. The four feathers of the dead heron were narrow, curved blades sticking up from the rocks. Danny turned his head from the silver stream, drawing his eyes down the bend to the edge of the camp-site. The change in the light was perceptible over the distance, graduating from an ethereal moondew out in the basin of the valley to a baleful red glow by the fire, where the pine sticks crackled and spat and sparks rose up into the blackness above. The stranger sat hunched on the far side, close enough to the flames for them to reflect on the smooth gun barrel. If he had not been there, the light would not have looked so hellish, merely warm. His presence changed everything and took the magic out of the moonlight.

Billy's face was a pale blur close to the man, flickering in the dance of the flames. He was huddled on the log he'd hauled himself as his camp bench. His old, rusty, Sheffield-steel knife was still embedded into the grain at the end furthest from the fire. It wouldn't have done him any good even if he'd been able to reach it.

The man was silent for now.

He was only a yard or so from Billy, but he looked as if he was completely alone within himself. He sat still, solid as the rocks at the falls. Four Feather Falls, Billy had called it, and they'd all recalled the little puppet show with the hero whose magic guns would swivel in their holsters and fire at the bad guys, mainly the Indians. The idea of a gun going off by itself was now a nightmare.

Billy huddled motionless. They could all see the red glint on the fire-side edge of the long barrel and the silver streak at the top where the moonlight reflected. Those parallel lines of flickering red and silver followed up from the stock to the far end which was jammed under Billy's jaw-line.

'We will all sit vigil,' the man had said. 'Pray that you will not fall into temptation.'

Danny knew, from long experience, what he was talking about. The image of the agony in the Garden of Gethsemane came to him. *Pray!* Corky hadn't had the same indoctrination, but he instinctively picked up the sense of it. Billy's eyes were red in the firelight, wide and scared. The man had sat him down and taken some of the baling twine, which he wrapped quickly round the ends of the barrels and then looped around Billy's neck to tie it back on the gun-metal again. The noose was not tight enough to strangle, or even cause serious physical discomfort, but the agony of anticipation should have been enough to make Billy sweat blood.

The business end was right under his chin and the butt dragged on the ground. The trailing edge of the baling twine went under Billy's knees and the man quickly bound his hands there, once again, not savagely, just enough to make it difficult for Billy to move much. With the gun jammed against his neck, pointing straight up under his chin, Billy was too scared to move at all.

'Therefore keep watch, because you do not know the day or the hour,' the man told them, and the crazy emptiness was back in his eyes once more. They all shrank back from it.

He had made them build up the fire until it was a hot roar of heat. Doug and Corky had broken the logs which Danny and Tom had dragged down from the fallen spruce tree close to where Corky had struggled for breath in the shallows of the pool.

There was no escaping now, not while Billy's head was wired to the gun. The man knew it. He had them in his grip now and there was nothing they could do.

Corky wondered when he would start hurting them. He did not even consider that they had been hurt yet, despite what they'd been through. The rabbit's dried blood was smudged on his forehead and the bruise there throbbed warmly but not very painfully. The side of his face was swollen and angry and his shoulder and thigh hurt like all hell. It was possible that the shock had anaesthetized him. He leant back, drawing his eyes from the outside to the dark of the tent. Danny's gaze was fixed on the man, half of his face pinked by the reflection of the fire, the other half in moonshadow. Tom was just a pale blur. Dougie's breathing was light, but shallow. They were still alive.

For a bad moment after his escape attempt, Corky had thought the man would kill them all. With the natural insight of one who had lived cheek to jowl with a natural level of violence, he knew it had been close.

'What's he waiting for?' he wondered, not realizing that he had whispered the words aloud.

'I dunno,' Danny said. His stomach was rumbling emptily, although he did not feel hungry. He was thinking about Billy sweating blood and he wondered about the gun, whether it would go off if Billy slumped forward during the night. He wished the man would untie it. Danny's Uncle Mick, who was his mother's brother and the black sheep of the family, his gun had a filed-down trigger lever that made it fire, so he said, if anybody looked at it the wrong way. If Billy fell, or even jerked to the side, would the gun go off? No wonder he was sitting there like a carved Indian statue. He looked as if he was scared even to breathe. The safety catch was off. *Now* it was off. Too late.

The man had hit Corky with the rabbit and Corky had dropped like a sack. The move had been so unexpected, so unnatural, that it had taken them all by surprise, and Danny had thought Corky was dead. The enormity of that sudden loss was matched only by the fear that he himself would be next. For a moment everything went completely and utterly still. Then Corky had jerked as if coming awake, and had rubbed at the red splash, and they had both realized at the same time that it was only rabbit blood.

Corky had got to his feet, very slowly, as if he too was still surprised to be alive. The man had stepped forward and grabbed him by the neck the way he had seized Danny only seconds before. Without hesitation he propelled Corky back up the slope and across the stream, ignoring the stepping stones. His boots splashed in the water and Corky's splashed beside him, more dragged than stepping. He made no sound. Danny followed on, unable to do anything else. The man ignored him, as if he had forgotten all about him, but Danny knew that was not so. If he ran, the man would turn and catch him and this time he might not use the pulped rabbit to fell him. He might pick up one of the smooth stones by the river and smash him down with it and keep on smashing.

They got to the edge of the camp. Dougie was standing to the side of the fire, shoulders dropped in defeat, his ears red and translucent, his vest torn and sagging. Billy was over by the hollow, down on his hands and knees as if he had suddenly gone blind. His face was upturned and his eyes were open, but they looked as if they were fixed, the way the stranger's had been, on the far distance. Tom was moving forward from the low rock wall. Danny hadn't noticed him at first. For a second he thought he might have run upstream and got away, gone for help before it was too late, but then he saw him moving forward and his heart lurched.

Tom had the big gun in his hands.

He had raised it up to his shoulder and the end of the barrel was waving around as if he was conducting a slow piece of music. The muzzle ends, the black infinity shape, swung round to Danny, who winced in fright until it moved back to point at the man who was pushing Corky in front of him.

'Stop!' Tom's voice was high and thin, almost a bleat.

The weight of the gun looked too much for Tom's small frame. The end dropped slowly, rose, sagged again. His hands were shaking. Danny saw his finger on the front trigger. The muzzle wavered down again.

'*No, Tom,*' Danny tried to say, but the words wouldn't come.

His mental shout was just a clamour inside his head. If Tom fired, he'd surely hit Corky, who was now being shoved up the incline to the camp-site.

The man did not hesitate. He pushed Corky ahead, walking quickly, his boots thudding the turf, and then, without warning, flung the boy ahead of him with a violent push. Tom's eyes followed his friend's progress, pulling his attention away from the real threat. The man strode forward and took the end of the gun in his hand with almost casual swiftness. Danny saw Tom's finger tighten reflexively on the trigger, but nothing happened. The end of the barrel was pointing straight at the man's head, *but nothing happened*. The gun did not roar, did not spit fire and lead shot. The big, dirty hand clamped on the end and drew it away from Tom. The man's other hand reached out and took the small boy by the face, thumb on one side, fingers on the other. The fingers flexed, squeezed hard until the ingrained knuckles showed white.

Tom made a small *oomph* sound as his face contorted, lips forming a vertical, squashed-violin-shaped slash. A flick of spittle whirled out. The man squeezed harder and Tom's eyes bulged. He moaned in pain, face drawn upwards by the grip. Both his hands were shaking furiously and his feet did a jittery little dance. Over by the hollow, Billy was turning his head as if he'd just realized they were there.

Corky got to his feet, shook his head to clear it, saw what was happening and said something. It was just one word.

'Don't . . .'

That was as far as he got, but it was enough to save Tom's face from being crushed and broken.

The man let go, simple as that. Tom fell to the ground, both shivering hands immediately flying to his face which bore the full imprint of thumb on the left cheek and four fingers on the right. There was a vivid red mark just under the curve of the jaw where the man's smallest finger had dug into the skin, the dirty nail slicing through the surface. Tom let out a long-drawn cry of pain, and his eyes were closed tight, concentrating on the hurt the way boys do, so he did not see what happened next. Corky said his one word and the man dropped Tom, as if he'd just flicked something off his hand. He spun, and to Danny it seemed as if it happened quite slowly, but he was riding high on that ridge of fear and dread in which everything seemed to happen at a different speed from normal. Corky was suffering no such time distortion. Despite his wealth of experience in such matters, he didn't see the blow coming at first. The man spun and his hand swung with him, splayed open, palm first. It was the hand that had gripped Tom's cheek to the point of crushing his jaw, which was fortunate enough. The other hand was gripping the barrel of the gun and, if he'd swung that, it would have taken Corky's head off at the neck.

Corky saw it coming just in time, like Pony's roundhouse punch, and he instinctively went with it, so that it sounded loud enough, but caused no damage. He did a little somersault and landed on his hands and feet and scuttled off out of reach. The man did not pursue him further. Danny heard Doug's breath catch. The man swept his eyes across them.

'Again a little time and you *shall* see me.'

Corky looked up warily. They all held their breath, thinking now that this was it. The gun was up now in the crook of the man's arm, pointing at the sky.

'Could you not watch one hour with me?'

Danny heard the reference to the garden. None of it made sense. He waited for the barrels to dip once again, but again nothing happened. The man stared down at Corky, who gazed up, unblinking, as if caught in headlights. His eyes focused, locked on the man's own almost in challenge. Danny and Doug watched the exchange and later they thought it was the bravest thing they had ever seen but, at that moment, both of them were silently begging Corky to look away, to deflect the heat. The pair of them, man and boy, stayed like that for several seconds, Corky's chest heaving up and down in rapid hitches, the man still as stone, looking as if he did not need anything as banal as air to exist. Finally he turned his head to the side, like a teacher who has decided to be lenient this time.

'Don't run again, boy,' he said. 'We have things to do. Wonders to perform.' He turned away, and Corky's eyes closed slowly as if he was suddenly exhausted. The side of his head was red and angry and swelling fast.

The man moved towards the fire and picked up the body of

the rabbit, and it was only then that Danny noticed the safety catch of the shotgun was pushed forward. Tom hadn't known about that. His fingers had definitely tensed on the trigger and nothing had happened because it had been locked. But Tom had pulled, whether by accident or design. He had a chance to get them out of it and the chance was gone. Yet deep inside Danny there was a sneaking suspicion that even if the gun had roared, the big ragged stranger – *Twitchy Eyes* – would still be standing there by the fire, holding the rabbit up by the ankles. There was something so depthlessly evil about him that he seemed to be indestructible. Corky had been right.

'He's not going to do anything right away, is he now?' he'd said. 'Not to all of us.'

But it was starting now and they were caught here, miles from the town. Beyond the man, the four feathers on the falls fluttered in a waft of breeze and Danny's stomach clenched.

Bad luck! He'd brought this on them, hadn't he? He'd killed it and the shadow had come across the valley. *The valley of the shadow of death!* The luck had blown and flown. Tom had pulled the trigger and nothing had happened. Corky had run and the man had anticipated it. He'd stepped on his back while he sprawled in the water and Corky could have died.

Now it was night and the moon was over the edge and beaming down into the valley, and the sparks from the spruce and pine were flying up on the up draught. Beyond the flames, they had heard the man gnaw hungrily at the rabbit, making animal feeding sounds. He'd made them gather the wood and break the logs on the stones, each smash sounding just like the sound of the rabbit's skull on Corky's forehead. *Twitchy Eyes*, there was now no doubt in any of their minds that this was the man who had done the dreadful things to the little girl under the bridge and to Don Whalen and the others.

Twitchy Eyes. He had gutted the rabbit and thrown the entrails on to the fire, watching them sizzle and shrink like some crazed warlock casting an augury. The intestines and lungs shrivelled to charred lumps while he very quickly stripped off the skin, peeling it like a tight coat. He severed the head with one quick, frightening twist of his hands and put it to the side, looking over at the corner where the three other skulls hung in the hawthorn.

Doug saw the look and knew the rabbit's head would end up there.

And who else's?

He shivered visibly. *Oh Jesus please us, chill and freeze us.* His lips moved in the gloom, but no sound came out. On the other side of the fire, limned by the flames, the man held up the skinned rabbit. Its limbs dangled and it looked like a newborn baby. The stranger looked like a red-eyed devil, hunched on the edge of the pit. He took one of the branches and skewered the little annual, stabbing it through the rectum and up to the gaping hole at the throat. Very expertly and without fuss, he fixed up two other branches on either side of the fire and put the meat across the edge beside the flames and above a hot section of glowing embers. In a matter of minutes the smell of cooking meat billowed out. Doug's mouth watered, but he was not at all hungry.

'What's he waiting for?' Corky had whispered a long time later and Danny hadn't known the answer. The moon had risen, only a couple of nights short of full, lighting the canvas of the tent enough for their night vision to let them see each other, however dimly. Corky's face was swollen on the right side as if he'd the mumps.

'We'll have to get out of here,' Doug said.

'I tried, really I did. If you hadn't hurt your leg, maybe you'd have made it, but *Jeez*, he was dead fast.' Corky swivelled and tried to get his hands to the edge of his hip where the man's boot had caught him and knocked him flying. The baling twine whipped around his hands made any motion difficult. The bonds, roughly pulled tight, were connected to another loop around their necks. If they tried to squirm free, it choked them. It was very effective.

'I thought my leg was broken.'

Despite what he'd been through, he sounded remarkably composed. Danny could see the dim light reflect in his eyes, could make out the concentration there. The sparking crackle of the fire was enough to cover their whispering.

'I thought he'd killed you,' Danny said flatly.

'*You* thought? I never expected him to banjo me with a rabbit. Swear to God it was hard as a rock.'

'Not as hard as your head, though,' Tom said, and for some

reason, Corky started to giggle, not out loud, but in a whispery, suddenly uncontrollable heaving of his shoulders. The motion caused him to fall slightly to the left, against Danny, and that in turn tightened the twine which was looped around his neck and then fixed to the tent-pole. The laugh cut off in a strangled gulp which they all heard. Corky raised himself back, tears running down his cheeks and a shadowed smile still stretched across his face.

'What are you laughing at?' Doug wanted to know, and Danny felt the hysteria bubble up inside himself. He bit that down because he did not know if he could keep it quiet and he did not know that if it started, he'd be able to stop, or if it would be laughter for long. It might change into blubbering, snivelling tears. He felt close enough to them already.

'Not as hard as my head,' Corky said, still grinning, and in the light coming through the flap, he looked just a little mad. 'No kidding. I heard that poor wee thing crack like a nut, and I thought it was my head caving in. Next thing all I could see were sparkly stars right in front of my eyes.'

'I saw the blood,' Danny finally said. 'I thought it was . . .'

'But it wasn't,' Corky interjected, forestalling him. The look on his face had changed, the crazy grin gone in a wink. 'It was just a slap. It was nothing. I've had worse from my old man. I'll look like old Quasimodo in the morning.'

'But he nearly drowned you,' Tom hissed, his voice as tremulous as Danny felt.

'But he didn't, did he?' Corky said sharply, and Doug's eyes flicked to the figure beyond the flames to see if he'd heard. Danny's memory brought him back a picture of his friend helpless, wriggling and fighting for breath. The hysteria tried to bubble upwards in a sudden release.

'He didn't. 'Cause Danny came and gave me a hand,' Corky said, and now they could all see the faint glint in his eyes. Doug looked down, all ears and teeth, not moving, but a picture of shame and embarrassment. Corky inclined his head as far as it could go without cutting off his breath again. Even in the dimness they could read his posture.

'Doug,' he said, 'I never meant you should have done anything. You'd have run if you could, but you couldn't, so don't worry about it. Sure, it was me that stopped you on the way down, wasn't it? You were going to go up the side like a ferret up a drainpipe. Even with him and his gun at your back. That took guts. Plenty of them.'

He nodded his head again. 'Wee Tom here. *Jeez-o!* I thought he was going to shoot me. Bad enough Old Twitch knocking the feet from me, but Tom? Our pal?'

Corky grinned again, this time a quick flash, and Danny understood, with a flash of desolate sadness, what he was doing. He was thirteen years old and he'd told them all great and terrible truths about themselves to hold them together, and now he was doing the same thing. Holding them together with his own special power.

Old Twitch.

The man out there beyond the flicker of the fire, hunched only a yard away from where Billy sat motionless, the man who'd stalked their town and done his killing.

Old Twitch.

'I couldn't get it to fire,' Tom said.

'Safety catch was on,' Danny explained.

'Just as well for me,' Corky said, almost speaking aloud but checking himself quickly. 'The way that gun was jiggling about, I'd have been a goner for sure. Try explaining that when you get home. Sorry, Mrs Corcoran. I never knew the safety catch was on. That's as bad as "I never knew the gun was loaded."'

Beyond the fire, perched on his log, Billy sat still as stone while the man devoured the rabbit. He had thought he was going to die when the gun had been tied tight to his neck, either from the blast when it went off, or from the pounding of his heart, which was so powerful, and so stuttering, that it felt like an engine firing on three cylinders. It felt as if it could burst inside of him and, for a long moment, he was so scared to breathe that his peripheral vision took on the hue of the splash of dried blood still smeared on Corky's forehead.

He hadn't been able to move. Not then, not before even, when the man had put his head down close to his cheek and spoken directly to him.

They talk to us all, those voices. You just need ears to hear.

The man brought his head down until his chin was against

Billy's ear. He could smell his breath, flat and cloying and rotten; he could smell his sour sweat. The man's beard bristles rasped against the side of his face and Billy had no strength to pull away, no strength at all.

Got to go down into the valley and out the other side. You want to make that journey, boy? You want to listen to the voice of the dead?

And he'd bent further and taken the soft skin at Billy's neck between his teeth, gently enough, but Billy had been waiting for the dreadful pain of the bite.

Oh, Jeez! Oh, mammy! He'll eat me.

Like he'd eaten the fish, heedless of the head and eye and raw guts. Like he'd bitten the kid from school, bitten pieces out of him. Billy had felt his legs begin to buckle when the small screech had startled the man back. After that, everything had been a blur. One of them – had it been Danny? Corky? – had run off, but Billy couldn't get his eyes to focus. Somebody had called his name, as if from a long distance, something about a gun, but by now his legs had given way and the world was just a haze in the pounding of his heart and the shudder of absolute fear. It had happened so fast and he was moving so slow and it was all jumbled up.

Parts of it came back to him, jerky little pictures, little flashes, blurred and fast, almost like half-remembered dreams; Tom raising the gun; Danny yelling something down by the stream; Corky falling sideways and making a long, low sound that seemed to go on and on.

Now he was beside the fire, eyes fixed on the flames. He could think now, but it was a slow process, as if his brain had become fogged with the same numbness that had slowed him during the day when the man had bent to his neck and promised him . . .

Over in the tent the others were together and he was alone, singled out again, the way he had been singled out when the man had stepped over the stream and forced the fish into his mouth, and when he'd led him to the hollow to watch the flies crawling over the dead skulls. Every now and again he imagined he could hear the others talking, over the whispering hiss of resin bubbling from the end of the spruce logs and the flutter of the flames. He imagined he could hear them whisper but he hoped they were all asleep.

Talk was dangerous. He knew that, even in his dull state of shock. If they were talking, they could be planning to escape and, if they tried that, there was a gun at his neck, and even Billy knew that was a warning to them all. One wrong move, and the man would – *bite!* – reach for the gun and squeeze the trigger. He would make Billy come through trials and tribulations to reach that great truth.

You want to make that journey, boy? You want to listen to the voice of the dead? In his mind he could hear those words, played over and over again, the way his mother used to play those Western tunes on the old Dansette, like the song from *High Noon*. Do not forsake me. Oh my.

He'd been singled out, kept apart from the others. *Forsaken.* And that meant the raggedy man planned something for him, something different. He had wanted to plead and cry and beg for mercy and fall on his knees, but that hadn't happened, not until the man had followed the rabbit's squeal and walked away, and then he'd been left on his own, forsaken again, with nothing to cling to. He'd been singled out and the man had told him what would happen. Not how, but what.

Want to hear the voice of the dead? They had all heard the stories of Don Whalen in the bomb-shelter, stories told in graphic detail, because nothing stayed secret for long, even the secrets of policemen. They'd found him dead and stiff and fly-blown, with his head twisted to the side, facing the screaming mouth of the girl.

When the man had asked him the question, that was the image that had flashed into his mind: Don Whalen listening to the dead scream of the dead girl. *The voice of the dead.* And Don had made the journey, down in that squirming shelter, tied to an old table. Hadn't he?

On the fire, one of the logs rolled over and crashed into the ashes, startling him enough to make him jerk, but only for an inch. The weight of the gun stopped him, along with the sudden freezing that came with the knowledge of those barrels pressed against his flesh. A shower of sparks shimmered upwards on the hot draught of air.

Billy hauled for a difficult breath, wondering when it would happen. Beside him, the man gnawed at the rabbit, making little snuffling and gobbling noises as he did so, sounding like a pig in a sty. Every now and again he'd flick a bone into the red embers and listen to it crack and warp. The rabbit's head was off to the side, but too close to the heat to have attracted any flies.

After a while, the fire died a little and Billy's numbness slid into a kind of exhausted torpor. His eyes closed and his head drooped just a little, finally coming to rest against the muzzle of the shotgun.

'Slitty-eyed vermin!'

The man's sudden utterance woke Billy with such a start that he almost fell backwards off the log. Over in the tent, Danny and Corky, sitting side by side and both connected to the upright pole as well as to each other, banged heads.

'Wassamatter?' Tom asked dopily. Danny, just coming awake, hazily remembered Corky winding Billy up about the disease he could have caught from Phil's stash of pictures.

'Whassermatter Reaction,' he mumbled, beginning to smile, then he came fully awake as the loop of twine rasped against his neck and brought him right back to reality.

'Hush it,' Corky hissed.

'Am I right, Conboy?' The voice was low, but jerky, like a sleepwalker's disjointed diction. 'You can see them. See everything you do. Got a third eye now, eh? See all!'

'What's he saying?' Tom asked, a disembodied whisper in the dark corner furthest from the flap. The fire was still glowing, but not aflame now. The moon was almost directly overhead, sending its wan light through the thin, stretched canvas of the old tent, and forming almost solid shafts of silver through the few puncture holes in the slant roof where it caught the motes of old dust.

'Dunno,' Corky said. 'Listen.' He had not been quite asleep, but he'd been dozing fitfully, as had the other three, tired and drained from the events of the day but still in a state of fearful apprehension that precluded the possibility of deep sleep. The very fact that the man had started talking, after such a long silence, worried him badly. Was it the start? He couldn't guess, despite the guessing he'd tried ever since the man had marched them all down together. Good or bad? He did not know. Bad probably, though the fact that Billy was still tied to the gun was good, depending on the standpoint. Corky had figured that as long as Billy was tied, he was a hostage for their good behaviour. The warning was clear. It was in all the best and worst of Western movies.

One wrong move and the boy gets it.

Good for them. Bad for Billy. But the man was talking now and he was a crazy lunatic and the normal rules, if there could be any normal rules in this tortured craziness, would not apply. Would it start now?

Danny was aware of Corky's tension. He could feel it through the twine that coupled them and he hoped Corky was all right. If Corky caved in, then that was it. None of them would make it. Danny held his breath tight and tried to figure out, the way Corky had done, whether it was all going to start now.

'Not talking now, Conboy? Eh?' The voice rumbled over the murmur of the stream. 'What's the matter? Flies got your tongue?'

The man laughed, not high this time, but almost as low as the voice itself, a kind of derisory, guttural sound.

'I know you can hear me. I know. Not long now, Conboy. They'll come back soon, slitty-eyed, yellow scum. *Dung-fly!* We'll wait for them. Just you and me, and we'll finish them all. Wipe them all out! Dung-fly. Only word they know.'

There was a moment's silence, then the voice was back, a little louder, a little more jerky. 'Only word. Hear what I'm telling you, Conboy? You have to stay awake. Keep an eye out. Ha. An eye.'

In the tent, Corky and Danny, side by side, shared the same posture, sitting with their heads back, cocked and listening. Over on the other side, Doug sniffed.

'Who's he talking to?'

'Who knows?'

'Is Billy ok?' Tom wanted to know, typical of him. Danny remembered him from the night before, even after Corky had reached and touched a finger in the jagged wound of Tom's loss, how Tom had reached to touch Corky and offer his support.

Doug leant back, squinting through the flap. He moved slowly, held his position for some time, then turned back. 'Still there. Can't see if he's asleep or not. The gun's still there.'

'What about *him*?'

'Same place. He's finished the rabbit. Still sitting. Can't see his face. Maybe he's turned round.'

'What do you think he'll do?'

Corky shrugged. So did Danny. Neither of them wanted to say what they thought.

Outside, the man's voice lowered a little and maybe he had turned round, for the words were hard to make out, and they'd a double-toned quality to them, as if they were echoing back from the steep sides across the stream. The tone had changed too, not quite so vehement. Danny strained to listen. It sounded as if a conversation was going on, almost furtively. It continued for some time, rising a little, falling some more and, finally, after a long time, it slowed and stopped. The fire continued to glow.

Down in the forest, an owl screeched like a banshee moorland ghost and its cry tapered away to a hollow moan. Later on, with the moon now crossing to the far side of the valley, something small squealed and died. The glow of the fire lessened.

It was much later, with the embers now a pink circle of light in the boundary of hot stones, that Danny woke up with a start. Corky had moved, perhaps, shifted enough to wake Danny.

He came swimming up, panicking, out of a fitful dream where he was alone in the valley and the night was coming down dark and heavy and all of the scrub alders and hazels had turned into gnarled thorn bushes with black spikes, all twisted into circlets, into crowns of thorns dripping blood. The sides of the valley soared up into the sky, steep and gravelly and seeming to curve in threateningly at the top, as if the edges would cave in and bury him under their weight.

An unseen voice was asking if he could not wait up an hour to pray and he did not know if it was his father talking to him or God or someone else, some other awful presence who was now striding like a giant down the valley of the shadow of death with a doom-doom-*doom* tread and a terrible blank and crazy look in his black eyes.

'Whatever you do to the least of these, you do also to me,' the voice rolled out, echoing from the walls, and the heron flew past him on ponderous wings and, though he now tried to haul back, the staff in his hand whirled through the air and hit it in the neck. It floated to the ground, broken, its yellow eyes speared on him accusingly. The beak opened and instead of the harsh *kaark* call, it spoke to him in a voice he recognized.

'Done it now, Danny Boy. You killed one of God's creatures and it's the bad fire for you. You're going to burn, boy. Burn *for ever.*'

He turned away from the searing eye and found himself clambering through the boiling liquid on the old linoleum floor, scrabbling for purchase and finding none, while the heat ravened all the way down his back and he could feel his skin blister and sizzle, while behind him Father Dowran, smiling that wide, toothy grin of his, was reaching to touch him and instead of hauling him out of the dreadful, scalding fire, he just rubbed his hands slowly over Danny's bare skin and chuckled softly.

Danny came out of sleep hauling for air as if he were drowning. Corky nudged him with an elbow, keeping it pressed in hard against his ribs, enough of a contact to let Danny know where he was.

'You ok?' he asked. Danny was still shivering as if he was cold, although, despite the night, it was warm inside the tent. He blinked rapidly, almost the way the man had done, shaking away the remnants of the dream until he was just about free of it. The odd and hungry grin hovered in the near distance before it fragmented.

'Yeah. Suppose so,' Danny whispered back. On the other side of the tent, Doug and Tom were leaning against each other, both asleep, their breathing shallow. Doug muttered something unintelligible and Tom stirred, but not enough to wake completely.

'We have to get out of here.'

Danny nodded in agreement. 'You nearly made it. If that rabbit had got caught in the top snare you'd have had a good start and you'd have made it. It was just rotten bad luck.'

'Yeah. Bad luck. It's always bad luck.' Danny could hear the bitterness underlying Corky's whisper.

'It was my fault.'

'Don't be daft. It's nobody's fault. Just that crazy nutcase out there. It's his fault.'

'No,' Danny insisted. 'I knew when I killed the bird. The heron? Remember?'

''Course I do. Great shot.'

'I knew right then I shouldn't have done it. I knew something bad was going to happen, and it did. We all started fighting and then he . . . *him* . . . he turned up.'

'Aye, and if you believe that, you believe in Santa Claus,' Corky said. His head was only inches away from Danny's and the sarcasm was thick in the sound of his voice. 'No kidding, Dan, you should listen to yourself. Ol' Loony-tunes didn't need you to magic him up here. This must be where he's been hiding all this time. The bird was nothing to do with it. *Jeez.* I've lost count of the number of street-scrag pigeon chicks I've had to wring. And trout. And remember that time we got a half-dollar for wringing the chickens at Boghead Farm? It was just a bird.'

'But it was . . .' Danny paused, tried to think, remembering the slow whoosh of wings. The image of the dream came back, that yellow eye spearing him. 'I dunno. It was special.'

'Special, my arse,' Corky said. 'No kidding, Danny. It's got nothing to do with you.'

'What do you think he'll do?'

'Christ knows. We can't hang around for it anyway. He's waiting for something.'

'You think there might be two of them?'

Corky shrugged. 'Up here there could be a whole army of them. Maybe he's been up here since the war. Shell-shocked or something. You know, with the bombs and stuff. Whatever it is, he's as mad as a wet hen. Honest to God, I thought I was a goner today when he stepped on me. I thought I was drowned for sure.'

Danny recalled that Corky had veered off that subject when Tom had said the same thing earlier, when the man was eating by the fire. He recognized that this was for him only.

'One of us will have to get out. You reckon you can make it?'

'I'm not as fast as Doug.'

'Nobody's as fast as him. He's built like a starved greyhound. I don't know what he'll be like in the morning. Maybe his ankle will have stiffened up.'

'Maybe it'll have loosened off,' Danny said, more in hope that it wouldn't have to be himself who took the risk.

'Aye. Maybe. But I don't know if this time he'll just freeze. He would have run this morning and if he'd done that . . .' Corky left it hanging for half a second, then changed tack. 'Just in case. You think you can take off if we get the chance? Tom hasn't a hope, and my leg's going to be black and blue in the morning.'

'Is it sore?'

'Only when I laugh, arseface,' Corky said and turned to grin again. Danny knew he'd ask again and forestalled him.

'If I get the chance, I'll run. Maybe I could get into the bushes and up to the ferns. If I could get that far he'll have a job finding me. So long as he doesn't keep firing, 'cause that gun could fire through bushes no bother at all.'

'He's not got enough cartridges, I don't think. I had a look at him. He's got no bag with him and his pockets don't seem that full. I think he's just got a few. If you get to the edge of the woods, you could be up and away. That's where I was heading for.'

'It'd be quicker to go up the top and down the moor. Quicker to get home.'

'Sure, as long as you weren't out in the open for too long. If I had the chance, that's the way I'd go, so long as he didn't have the gun, and as long as he leaves us alone for a while. He'll have to take a piss some time, or go for a shit. I was hoping that fish would give him food poisoning.'

'I'm just glad he didn't make us eat the rabbit. Raw trout-guts would be bad enough.' Danny felt Corky twitch with spontaneous laughter, and a bubble of hysteria swelled in his belly. He swallowed down on it.

There was a silence for a moment, then Corky whispered, 'Dan, I don't think we'll get a lot of chances. I don't know what's going to happen tomorrow. I think we're all right for the night, or he wouldn't have tied Billy up like that. He's got to sleep some time too. But whatever he's waiting for, he's not going to wait long. If one of us gets home, he'll run, because he'll know they're after him.'

'He'll kill us,' Danny said flatly, and he was amazed when the words came out just like that. The enormity of it. The end of his life, contemplated and made concrete in three small words.

'Don't think that way,' Corky hissed urgently, digging hard enough to hurt with his elbow. 'Danny. Listen. He's crazy, for sure. It's the guy they've been looking for.' Danny noticed he didn't spell it out, but he didn't have to. They all knew the list of names. Corky's voice had gone very cold and earnest and of a sudden he sounded all grown up. 'We can't think about what might happen. If I did that all my life I'd be a nervous wreck by now. Billy's no use. You can see it in his face. He's thinking ahead and that's why he can't move. You see that in the fights at the back of the school when somebody doesn't want to. He's all seized up.'

Corky dropped his voice even lower, so that there was no chance anybody but Danny could hear it. 'I think maybe Tom and Doug might freeze as well. Honest, if my leg's ok I'll do it, but it might not be. I think that nutter nearly broke it.'

He twisted round as far as he could, so he could just get a look at Danny.

'If we get a chance, Danny Boy, we have to take it.'

CHAPTER TWENTY-SEVEN

August 4, 7 a.m.

Danny came awake again, swimming up to the surface, this time pursued by no dreams that he could remember. It felt as if he hadn't slept at all. The tent was cold and his mouth was gummy and bitter. Corky was sitting upright, eyes closed and, in the thin light, Danny couldn't tell whether he was awake or not. On the other side, Doug and Tom were huddled together.

The tent-flap was still open on the left side. Danny squirmed, pulling against the loose loop of baling twine as it rasped against the skin of his throat, until he could see outside. For a moment he thought he was looking through a white veil, all colour leached from the early morning.

The world was dead-still.

A ground mist, thick and pearlescent, had crept up from the stream to the camp-site, dense enough to make the striations on the far side of the valley blurred and indistinct. Danny could see, through the small, triangular space, the edge of the bank and the thick end of the log Billy had dragged up from the trees. The knife was still stabbed into the grain and the tendrils of mist grasped around it like ghostly fingers, creeping almost imperceptibly. The fire had almost completely burnt itself out. In the circle of stones, the ash was grey and light, showing that the heat had lasted all night. The smooth boulders themselves would still be blistering hot, warm enough to cook on, but the embers had died down and there was now no smoke.

The valley, what he could see of it, had taken on an eerie and insubstantial quality, as if seen in a dream. Danny knew he was awake. The tent smelt of sweat, old and new, and mildew from long, unaired days, rolled up, hiding Phil's stash of tools and stolen gear. Tom twitched; Doug's nasal breathing snuffled near the entrance. Corky was completely still.

There was no wind. The day was light, but it was early, in the shallows of the morning, and the sun had not yet risen. It would be hours yet before it soared, the way the moon had done, over the eastern lip of the valley. For the moment, viewed through that triangle flap, the section of the valley looked like something from a fairy scene. Danny could not see the man and, from where he sat, Billy too was hidden from view. For all he knew, the man could have gone, vanished into the shadows of the night. Even as he thought it he knew that was not true. The crazy stranger would still be there.

But for the moment, in the strange solitude of the early morning, the mist smoothed the outlines and harsh edges, making it a soft and peaceful morning. It brought to mind the story he'd read in the book they'd swiped from the treasure chest at Overbuck House. Corky had shown him it on the first day they'd arrived here (and that seemed a million years ago), the passage about the legendary battle of the hero Cuchulain at the ford in the stream.

'Give me a song for a soft morning,' he'd told his friends on the night before he bravely went down to single combat, a real hero, heedless of personal danger. Danny wished he could be the same, but the fear that had settled on them all had stayed with him, even during the fitful and uncomfortable sleep, and it clung to him now.

This stolen minute, however, gave a semblance of tranquillity. The mist smothered the burbling tumble of the stream, fading it down to a distant murmur. No birds sang, not even the far-off cockerel, the little red rooster down at Blackwood Farm, whose early morning call sometimes drifted up to this height on the westerly breeze. Now there was no breeze, hardly a stirring of the air, and for the moment, Danny Gillan was alone. The day seemed to hold its breath before wakening.

He wished the world would stay asleep. He did not want to think of the whispered, urgent conversation in the dark.

You reckon you can make it?

I don't know. I don't know.

I don't want to . . .

He didn't want to think about it. The man had come streaking out of the bushes and kicked Corky and nearly broken his leg. That had been without the gun. Danny stretched to see if Billy was still tethered to the barrels, but the string dug into his windpipe and he had to lean back under the tension before he choked and woke everybody.

If we get a chance, Danny Boy . . .

He knew that. He tried not to think about his muscles freezing, like some kid who didn't want to fight in the yard. In his mind's eye, in the fitful pictures that had unreeled in his mind last night, despite how he'd tried to shake them away, he saw himself in the dreamscape sequences where his limbs locked in a strange and terrified paralysis, or where no matter how he ran and jinked, every path, every sheep-track through the ferns, somehow led him back to the camp and that black infinity at the end of the shotgun's muzzle. In the slow light of the morning, he shucked those images away and tried to breathe easy.

All the could-have-beens and might-have-dones. If. *If.* Billy Harrison was fond of the phrase: 'If' is a very small word with a very big meaning.

Big consequences.

If they hadn't been gathered on the fallen elm tree that day. If Paulie Degman hadn't fallen into the river in the spring while the silver sparkle of light flashed from the back of Cairn House into Danny Gillan's eyes. If they hadn't been talking about the explosion in the quarry bringing the body to the surface. If they hadn't argued about the bomb the waterworks men found in the reservoir up on the Overbuck estate, they wouldn't have talked about the dummy village, and if they hadn't conjured up that old legend they wouldn't be here.

If. Might-have-beens and should-have-dones.

'I bet you wouldn't come down here at night,' Billy had said, and Tom had agreed with that.

'Not when the mist comes off the river,' he'd said vehemently, because Tom was living with his own ghost. 'You never know what's in there. It creeps like it's alive.'

'*Gives* you the creeps,' Billy had said, laughing. Now he was out there with the man with the gun and he was not laughing. The mist was crawling like it did down at the river, the one Corky said hid the ghost of lonesome Paulie Degman.

Danny closed his eyes, half hoping that when he opened them again he'd wake up from a dream and find that he'd imagined it all. When he opened them again, the triangle of grey pearly light was still there at the front of the tent, and thin tendrils of mist were inching around the wooden pole. He was still here.

And *he* was still *there*.

The brooding presence of the man with the black and twitching eyes, unseen, but somehow sensed, was still there on the other side of the circle of stones. All was silent until Doug snorted softly. Danny turned his head towards the sound, slowly swung back to look through the entrance.

A red squirrel stood four-square on the short grass. Its stubby little legs were planted far apart on its four corners and its tail curled right over its back like a rich feather plume. Its head was up, nose sniffing the air in little twitches. At his movement in the shadow of the tent, its coal eye fastened on Danny's. It moved in rapid little jerks, halting to sniff, then twisting in a flick of russet to examine something on the grass. It picked up something that looked like a baked bean, tested it quickly, then sat up on its hunkers, tail still curled in a cloak against the cool of the morning, and quickly ate it in a series of tiny, gnawing bites. Danny watched the whole process, unable to move in case he scared it. For a brief heartbeat, his fear was forgotten. The little squirrel, half the size of the big greys which ruled in the beeches and oaks further down the valley, searched around for more morsels, constantly on edge, alert for danger. It froze, spun in a blur at some motion beyond the camp and then disappeared in a silent, red-russet streak.

Danny's heart kicked. Had the man moved? Was he awake now and coming for them?

He stretched against the loop, heedless of the pressure on his throat, trying to see what was happening out there. The mist was just beginning to lessen, thinning a little as the dawn slowly changed into a still day.

Something moved and his heart lurched again, and that was when he saw it. He'd been staring right at it, unaware because it had been still as a statue, but when it moved, just at the edge of vision, stalking through the mist, which was thicker down there at the water, he recognized the heron. It took one step, slow and graceful and silent, the head motionless at first and then slowly getting into position, its eye a piercing bright-yellow, the only colour for the moment in the grey and white of the morning. It stepped again on its long, elegant leg, dipping the toes into the water with not a splash of sound. It stopped still and, for an instant, Danny thought the eye was looking straight at him, the way the squirrel had done, the way the dead eye up at Billy's altar of skulls had done before the flies settled upon it. The eye was round and almost fierce, full of life. The head came forward, very slowly. The tall, grey bird froze. The beak pointed at the water, then lanced down, quick as a blink, still with no sound, and came rising back up with a small trout flapping uselessly. The bird jerked, opening its beak so the fish was head on, swallowed it with a second twitch and the beak closed with a soft *snick*.

'Move on,' Danny urged silently. The bird would be the female whose lonely call had echoed down the valley from the dark in the night. It was the mate of the one he'd brought down. Now it crept upstream, hunting alone, only yards from the man with the shotgun. 'Go,' he mouthed. 'Get out of here.'

He wanted to see it gone, to get some of the luck back. No matter what Corky said, he could still feel the weight of prescience. The motion, no matter how stealthy, could catch the man's attention. He'd blast it out of the air in a puff of feathers and there would be no more herons on the stream. They only hunted in pairs in the summer and it would be a long time before a new pair of the fishing birds would come hunting on the Blackwood Burn.

'Go on,' he whispered. 'Skedaddle.'

'What's that?' Doug said, not quite aloud, not quite awake. The bird turned round, cocking its head to the side, the eye now fixed on the tent. Danny nudged Doug with his foot. The bird watched for a drawn-out moment, then satisfied itself there was no danger. It took two more elegant and silent steps, a grey ghost in a white mist, and then was gone from view. Doug had come fully awake and watched it from where he sat, closer to the flap and with more of a view.

'It's the other one,' he mouthed. Danny nodded slowly. He jerked his head, raising his eyebrows in question, and Doug leant as far as he could, eyes wide. Danny saw the recognition and sudden defeat in his posture. The man was still there. Doug's nod was redundant.

'Billy?' Danny asked. The other boy nodded.

'Still tied,' he whispered. Tom stirred, blearily opened his eyes and looked around timidly, then closed them again as if he would rather not stay.

'Is he sleeping?' Corky asked softly, surprising Danny, who'd been completely unaware he had been awake all this time. '*Him*.'

Doug leant again, pulling on the twine that connected him to Tom. He inclined his head. 'I think so. I can't see his eyes. Looks like it. Wait a minute.'

Very slowly, big teeth clenched on his bottom lip for concentration, he reached with his foot and raised the flap up further, letting more light into the tent, widening the opening. The swirl of air that came in was damp and morning-cold. Both Danny and Corky stretched as far as they could. Tom huddled closer to Doug, his head twisted to see.

The man was still hunched on the little ridge of turf close to the fire. He was like a black scarecrow against the white of the haar mist and the light grey of the tall gravel bank on the far side. He'd draped a blanket around his shoulders, Tom's old red tartan one, which had been left out since the previous night when they'd all slept around the fire after the big fight. For a moment, despite what Doug had said, Tom thought Billy had gone, escaped. He was no longer sitting on the pine log. His heart flipped in hope, a flutter against his ribs, and then dropped like a stone into the pit of his belly when he saw Billy huddled against the man's bulk. The gun was still looped against his neck, but it had loosened somehow, so that the barrels were pointing not under the chin, but past it. Billy's dark hair was tousled and his face pressed up against the man's chest. His eyes were closed. The stranger's arm was clamped around his shoulder, holding him close. In any other scene, they could have been taken for father and son. The heavy blanket was draped around them both.

Danny remembered the biblical quotations of the day before and shuddered. He'd made Billy sit vigil with him, holding him close, like an affectionate parent protecting a child, like a shepherd with his sheep. Like Abraham with his son before the sacrifice of the morning.

Therefore keep watch, because you do not know the day or the hour.

Dougie brought him back to the here and now with a tap of his foot. His other long leg was still holding the flap up and he motioned outside. They all leant as far as they could again. Nothing had changed. The heron was gone and Danny hadn't heard the whoop of its wings in the air, so it must have stalked off upstream and around the corner.

'What is it?' Corky wanted to know.

'The gun,' Doug whispered. His eyes were wide and suddenly bright. 'Look at it.'

They looked. Corky started to ask again, then Danny stopped him with a dig of his elbow. He had seen it, and his heart leapt in a surge of sudden and fearful excitement. The gun was broken open. He could see the dark curves at the stock end of the barrels where it hadn't been closed properly. He strained to see, wishing now there was more light. He focused as hard as he could, trying to see if the shells had been taken out of the chambers. Some time during the night the man, *Twitchy Eyes*, had moved Billy closer to him, taken him under his arm. He must have moved the gun, opened it to make sure it didn't go off accidentally and blow his hostage to kingdom come. Even with the safety on, that could be knocked out by a nudge.

Were the shells still in there? Could he simply snap the gun closed and fire the thing? Danny's heart was pounding furiously, somewhere up near his throat. He was now completely awake, and he could feel himself, his consciousness, begin to drift higher into those slow-motion chilly heights of the adrenaline surge.

If we get a chance, Danny Boy, we have to take it.

A chance. A possibility. He turned to Corky, eyebrows raised, and Corky misread the question. He shrugged, leaving it up to him. What Danny wanted to know, to his shame, in his fear, was whether Corky's leg was good enough this morning. He was about to ask, bit it back in a dry gulp.

'Look,' Doug hissed again. He nodded once more and they all looked, the motion of the four of them making the tent-poles quiver. The hunched figure was completely motionless. The gun was laid across the man's knee, with a big, horny hand resting on the stock. In at his side, Billy's face was pale and bloodless. 'On the rock,' Doug said insistently. Danny's eyes trailed away from the gun to the flat stone close to the ridge where the man sat. One shotgun cartridge sat in a small dip in its surface. The other one had rolled to the grass below and lay there, bright red against the grey-green of the dew-damp grass.

Danny recognized it immediately. It was twelve-bore birdshot, going by the colour. Even from here he could read the lettering on the side. 'Hy-max'. He couldn't make out the number, but he didn't have to. The colour was enough. His Uncle Mick, whom his father disliked because he cursed now and again and drank whisky, he used them all, and the bright-red ones were ideal for pigeons or woodcock. It was packed with light shot with a good spread for fast moving birds, not the heavy-grain for shelduck on the firth tidal banks or the ball-shot which could knock a Greylag goose out of the air, or put a hole through a mountain hare or even a roebuck. Birdshot would scatter wide, useless for big animals, great for fast birds. Up close though, you couldn't miss with that kind of filling. Up close it could easily cut a grown man in half.

Danny's heart was up there, bobbing and hopping, filling his throat and making it hard to breathe.

Corky swivelled to look at him and Danny knew Corky's leg was still hurting pretty bad. He gulped, made a little clicking noise that sounded like the heron's beak closing, managed to nod, and saw the acceptance and maybe even a glint of admiration in Corky's eye.

'Can you get loose?'

Danny shook his head. 'Who's got a knife?'

'What are you going to . . .' Tom started to say, but stopped when Danny nudged him.

'Where's your knife?'

'In my pocket.'

'Can you reach?' All of this in dry, little, shivery whispers. Tom shook his head. Corky looked at Doug.

Doug nodded that he'd try. He dropped his foot and let the flap fall, suddenly making the inside of the tent much darker despite the lightening of the sky over the valley. Somewhere beyond them, close to the place where Billy had hung the skulls, something rustled, and Danny hoped it was the squirrel and not one of the big hill cattle lumbering down to drink from the stream. He wished it to silence, wished it away from here in case the sound woke up the gaunt man.

Doug was squirming to the left and Tom was stretching to the right, both of their hands wound round with the hairy baling twine. Tom lifted his skinny backside off the flattened grass and Doug's fingers found the lip of his front pocket, groped inside. Tom grunted with the effort of holding the position while the string tightened on his neck. They could see his arms quivering with the strain. Doug's eyes were closed and he was biting down on his lip again, his head across Tom's thin shoulder. He fumbled in the tight pocket, twisting his wrists hard enough to make the binding dig into the skin, then tensed. He torqued back and the knife came flipping right out, a black, whirling shape. It landed with a dull little thump close to the door-flap.

Everybody froze.

Doug's mouth was open, lips curled back from his big teeth, a picture of tension and dismay. Tom was still leaning back, holding his balance. The knife lay there by the edge while they all listened, wondering if the noise had woken the man. From out there, no sound came except the muted burbling of the stream. After a moment, Tom eased himself back up to a sitting position. Doug stretched his foot outwards, his old, black and scuffed baseball boot missing one of its rubber ankle-guards. He tried to hook the army knife back towards him, almost got purchase by pressing it down into the ground to get his boot beyond it, but succeeded only in pushing it further away.

Danny's heart flipped again, in hope and in dismay, each tugging from a different direction.

'Careful,' Corky snapped, more loudly than he meant. Doug shot him a look, tried for the heavy knife again, sent it another inch closer to the flap. Tom's breath let out in a long sigh. The knife sat there, almost out of reach.

'Anybody got another knife?' Corky demanded, eyes blazing. Billy's blade was still stuck in the grain of the log. Doug had lost his some time between the day at the river and now.

'Hold it,' he said, managing a quick grin. He drew his foot back, pulled his other up and shoved the heel with his toe. The tattered baseball boot squeaked and the old laces groaned as he stretched them. He pushed harder and they all watched the boot loosen off, pulling down past his heel. Doug applied more pressure, shoving really hard now, and suddenly his boot came flipping off with a hollow, sucking sound. Triumphantly he held his foot up again. His grey sock had a wide hole at the end, through which poked three skinny white toes.

'Watch this,' he told them, stretched forward to his fullest extent, twisted to the side, and his two largest toes spread like fingers. He dipped them down on to the knife, curled them tightly and gripped it. Danny felt the bubble of hysteria ripple up again and he swallowed it down. A part of him was hoping Doug might drop it out of reach and that would mean he'd have no burden to bear. Corky was unconsciously easing his leg up and down, as if trying to loosen a cramp in his thigh. It was clear his injured leg had stiffened badly in the night.

Doug's prehensile toes gripped the knife, like a miniature grab-crane, swung it over and flipped it, with surprising expertise, towards the other two. It landed at Danny's side, only inches from his fingers. He found it and worked it closer until he could grip it tight with one hand while his fingers worked on the awkwardly tight blade until he eased it open, almost splitting his thumbnail in the process. The big blade next to the spike for taking things out of horses' hooves snapped back with a metallic click that was muffled between them. He managed to twist it upwards, felt the sharp edge against the skin of his wrist, manoeuvred it back and sawed it against the binding twine.

'Got it?' Corky wanted to know. Danny concentrated. Everybody waited.

The string snapped with the sound of a bowshot, not loud, but definite. Doug heaved a long sigh and managed a grin. Tom just looked worried. The blade cut quickly through the rest of the twine, each one parting with the same little tug and, in less than a minute, Danny's hands were free. His wrists looked as if he wore scarlet bangles and the little ridges where the bonds had bit immediately started to itch. He rubbed them briskly, chafing the blood back, trying to loosen the stiff numbness from his wrists.

'Good man,' Corky said under his breath. He motioned to Doug, using head and eyebrows. Doug lifted the flap just a little, leant to peer out, came back and winked an affirmative.

Ok.

Danny's heart was now tripping fast. He brought his hands forward and changed position, crawled ahead just a bit, only to be brought up by the loop at his neck. With an almost vicious swipe, more in panic than in anger, he raised the knife and sliced the noose. Without hesitation he turned and cut Corky free, quick as he was able. Corky took the knife and started to move towards Tom and Doug, wincing hard as he did so. Danny read it. Corky looked at him, and his expression did not change.

You reckon you can make it?

Danny felt a sweat trickle down his back, remembered the new testament quotation from the Garden of Gethsemane. He could have used an extract of his own, from the many that had been diligently and religiously drummed in.

Let this chalice pass.

The knife cut the others free. Danny moved to the front, peering out from the shadow. The man was motionless, his eyes closed. The gun hadn't moved, but some of the mist had thinned. The cartridge on the stone was still there, and the other one a few inches away on the grass. The air was now clearer and he could see the empty chambers of the barrels. The gun was not loaded. He breathed out slowly.

'What's happening?' Tom asked. Corky put a finger up to his lips. Danny moved to the back of the tent, into the shadows where their old haversacks were stored in a pile. At the far side, opposite to where they'd set the fire, opposite the man who held Billy close, he gripped the bottom edge of the tent with both hands and pulled hard. Nothing happened. He tried again, but the base stayed pegged and he remembered how they'd used the ballpeen hammer to set the old wooden pegs. They were driven down a foot into hardpack. It would take more than a few tugs to pull them out.

'Cut it,' Doug whispered, realizing what the problem was. He leant out to make sure the man was still asleep or, at least, not rousing. He held his hand up, thumb perpendicular. *Ok.*

The canvas slit straight down, parting with a soft, scraping buzz, leaving a gash two feet long and dead straight. The tension of the fabric pulled the edges apart, letting in more daylight. An earwig fell through the hole and scuttled for shelter.

Doug's thumb was still up. Danny couldn't speak. His heart now felt as if it was kicking somewhere up around his ears, drowning out all other sound. He was convinced the whole valley must be able to hear it. He imagined flocks of woodpigeons clattering from the trees in alarm, crows rising in accusing squadrons, attracting attention, disturbed by the sudden noise. He swallowed hard, was distantly surprised that he was able to.

'Go,' Corky whispered, feather soft. 'Best of . . .'

Danny's head was outside, through the gap, and he did not hear Corky's blessing. Immediately the green, clean smell of morning suffused him. In the open, the sound of the stream was louder than it had seemed from inside the tent. There was still some mist, quite a lot of it pooled in the hollows and runnels further downstream. For a moment he was almost frozen with fear and apprehension. He turned back, eyes searching them all, and they were all fixed on him, none of them seeming to breathe. The moment stretched out, brittle as glass. A nerve in the back of his leg started to twitch and the sinews on his arms felt as tense as bowstrings. Corky's green eyes, now grey in this dim light, were on him, sharp and hard, and full of anger and full of life. Danny locked with them and it did not make his fear go away, but it gave him enough impetus to swivel round without a word.

He crawled out, carefully lifting one knee then the other over the splintered tent-peg, making sure he didn't catch his feet on the shredded canvas. He turned his head, just able to make out the edge of the forest way downstream. There the mist was still thick and opaque, an almost solid wall, rising halfway up the tall trunks. Down there would be shelter, but that was where the man was facing. There was little or no cover down to the second bend where Corky had been felled. Danny sat still, telling himself to calm down, forcing his brain to function.

It'd be quicker to go up the top and down the moor. Quicker to get home.

He felt that slow-motion, treacle-time sensation began to overtake him again, the almost dreamy clarity of unbearably high tension. Corky had put his finger on it. Over the top and down the hill, if he could get to the canyon lip without being seen. Danny knew he could walk quietly when he had to. Now he really had to. He swallowed down again on the pounding of his heart, found it was going slower than he thought, found he could make his legs move. He went round the back of the tent, keeping low, crawling silently on all fours, making sure he missed all the guy-ropes, which would have thrummed like bass strings if he'd tripped over any of them. Beyond the farthest peg, still out of view from the ridge at the fire, there were some low ferns close to a small clump of cow-parsley. He reached that, staying low now, until he got close to the natural wall where Billy had hung his skulls. The flies were slow and lethargic, waiting for the heat of the day, but they still clustered thickly and, this close to the deer's head, the smell was pretty fierce. Danny did not look up to see if the dead heron's eye was still fixed on him. He had seen its mate, fishing alone, its eye gleaming with bright life. He imagined he could feel the black, twitching eyes of the mad stranger on his back, told himself he *was* imagining it before a tide of panic swamped him. Just beyond the edge of the hollow, where there was a narrow cleft between two boulders that led up slope to the next level of the stream, he stood on a dead twig that snapped underfoot, loud in his ears as a cannon shot. He froze, turned round slowly, every hair standing to attention on the back of his neck.

The stranger did not move. Danny could just make him out, hunched beside the ring of stones, like some Indian shaman, like a scarecrow waiting for the day. Billy was hugged in tight, both of his legs flopped lifelessly, jutting out in front of him. Danny got a sudden, chill suspicion that Billy might be dead, that the man with the twitchy eyes had strangled him in the night. A sick feeling of nausea welled up and he choked it down, for he couldn't afford the noise of retching. After a moment, he unfroze, managed to get his limbs moving, and made it through the crevice.

For the next three or four yards, he was hidden from view, but to his left, another stone face, maybe a dozen feet high, stretched on towards a clump of moraine boulders that had been rolled down here by some distant spring flood. He couldn't scale it quietly, even though there were a few scraggly rowan roots hanging downwards to offer handholds. He kept low, still scuttering like a spider, trying to avoid the dried twigs and hollow saxifrage stems closer to the stream. He got to the end of the slope cover, came to the edge of the water, held his breath and raised his head slowly as he was able. Finally his eyes were above the low stone ridge. Down there, back where he'd come from, he could see the slit in the side of the tent. None of the others had followed, which was as well, because that would only increase the risk of attracting attention. He slowly swivelled his eyes until he could see the man sitting there, still as a rock. He looked ghostly and ghastly, and even his motionless posture radiated awesome threat. Billy's arm hung down to the short grass, as if he were caught in a killer headlock. From where he peered, Danny could not see the gun.

At this part of the stream, just up from the four feathers on the low falls which dropped down deep into the pool at the camp, there was a shallower pool, which was maybe ten feet wide. It had some large quartz rocks in its centre, white as the morning mist, but no fish. Danny crawled down to the edge, to a margin of small, flat stones, and began to cross, taking one step at a time, breathing shallowly as possible, mouth wide open so he couldn't snuffle and cough. There was some summer algae on the smooth bottom where a lip of mudstone protruded, and it was slick as spilt oil. Danny stayed on all fours, even when the water came up to his chin, to prevent himself from falling, and made it to the other side. He got to the bank and made his way upstream for about twenty yards before he realized that there was no cover for the next hundred. From where he sat, the man could see down to the second bend, and upstream, along a relatively straight section of the valley to the runnel where Doug had almost made the decision to run. There was no cover, and Danny was not sure he'd be able to get as far as that along the shingle and shale without making some sort of sound.

Corky's words came back. It would be quicker to go up the top.

Danny paused, feet squelching quietly. His jeans were wringing wet. For a few breaths he waited, unable to take his eyes off the figure sitting by the ring of stones. Up to his left, a shoulder of the ridge that separated the two narrow tributaries, shaped like the upside-down prow of a ship, came down at a steep angle. The upstream tributary was the larger of the two and led to the natural dam which had plugged the basalt crevice at Lonesome Lake. The right side was shallower, but got steep a hundred feet back. Between them, on the ridge of the shoulder, there was another worn path where sheep had come down to drink at the stream. They'd used this before when they'd found the backed-up lake, and again when they'd gone to find the dummy village. There was no choice now. Danny's legs locked for a panicked moment and then he started to climb. When he reached the top, he'd be out of sight, and then he'd have a run down the moor, just a few miles to the barwoods, down past the pylons, through the blackened gorse and down to the town and help from Sergeant Fallon.

And I'm never coming back here again, he swore to himself.

He went up the path, hand over hand, moving as quickly as possible, as silently as he could, and the more he climbed, the more muted came the sound of the stream below. The daylight was brightening fast and the mist seemed to be sneaking away from the light, oozing into the shadows of the edge of the trees which crowded further down the valley. Danny moved upwards, trying not to pant, but it was hard going, twenty feet, forty, fifty. The hill seemed to go on for ever, up a compacted shale incline, over a ledge of mudstone, round to the bare face to miss out a steeper climb where he could slip. A couple of times he did slide backwards, losing two yards, but he gained them back fast as he could.

He got to the first level of the shoulder. From here it got steeper, maybe seventy feet up from the floor, no more than that. He risked a glance down and it looked further. The tent was a dark-green oblong against the lighter green. The circle of smooth stones was as clear as a clock face, with the dark shadow of the man sitting at eight o'clock. Danny's breath started to thump. He was getting there, getting close to the high edge. Once over he had one feeder valley to traverse, a slide down and a scramble up, and then he'd be away, well out of sight, running hell for leather down to safety.

He was getting there, only forty feet or so from the top. He eased round the corner away from a thin layer of white mudstone, edging into the second tributary, when something moved, caught in peripheral vision. Danny's head whipped round in a panicked jerk, just in time to see the grey heron take off, as the first one had done, in a powerful sweep of wings. The sudden motion itself had made him take a step back.

Kaark! The bird called out loudly, and its cry was funnelled by the tight confines of the narrow chasm and amplified in a hollow and accusing double echo.

'Oh, no,' Danny said aloud, still moving, trying foolishly to get the bird to hush. Its head was drawn back, beak pointed to the sky, its left wing close enough to the gully side to sweep off some fine grains of shale. Danny's foot slid on a piece of stone, lifted, shuffled for balance, and found a ledge. He reached to grab a firmer handhold, but the flat ledge he'd stepped on crumbled under his foot. There was a muffled click, like wet wood breaking, and the piece of mudstone simply sprung away, a piece about a foot square. Danny quickly grabbed for it, got half a grip, but the fine dust on the smooth surface slipped through his fingers and the rock rolled out, slid down the soft shale slope for five feet or so and hit the other line of rock with a harsh clunk.

'Hell!' Danny hissed. His foot was still slipping from lack of purchase and for a moment he had to ignore the fallen stone. The heron was a blur to his right now, pinioning its way into the sky. Danny got a grip, pushed himself upwards on to the steeper part of the slope, moving round the spur to the gravelly slant they'd slid down when they first came over the rise and down into the valley. Below him the tumbling rock hit another, bounced out into the air. He turned, saw that it had dislodged the other stone. The two of them bounded, whirling together out from the slope, landed one after the other on the soft shale like dull footsteps, digging twin furrows, rebounded again over a ledge and fell twenty feet in tandem. Danny watched them go, unable to move. His whole attention was focused on the tumbling rocks as they hurtled down the side. Way down at the bottom, in the curve of the stream, there was a mound of soft sediment which had trickled down the steep side of the valley and piled up in a hollow. If the stones landed there, they might stop with hardly a sound. Danny knew he should keep going, but the stones held his attention and would not let him go.

Some distance up from the valley floor, the mudstone boulders flipped out over the shale, now spinning in the air. They seemed to fall in slow motion. For a moment Danny thought they were dropping straight for the soft gravel pile, but from where he clung to the spur, the angle was deceptive. The rocks plunged down and smashed on to a hard, stone ledge with two harsh cracks. The sound was like gunfire in the valley.

The hammer blows ricocheted from one side to the other, so loud that Danny almost lost his grip. He twisted to look down at the camp. For a brief moment there was complete stillness.

Then the man moved. His head turned towards where the rocks had smashed on the ledge, while the echoes of the impact were still reverberating along the curves of the canyon. The rocks had smashed on the harder stone and scattered like shrapnel on the smooth surface of the shallow pool he'd crawled across. For a second, no more, he looked at the water, then his head angled up. Danny saw the pale oval of the man's face as it turned towards him.

They stared at each other across the distance, one looking up, the other staring down.

Then the man was moving. Danny turned, panicking, started scrambling up the scree. He reached the next level, feet slipping and sliding on the crumbly surface, whimpering in fear and desperation, and clawed for the top up the almost vertical incline. He got to the nearest level of strata, managed to get over it, feeling as if his whole body was shivering violently enough to throw him backwards, but miraculously keeping his grip.

Down below somebody screamed and somebody else shouted. The man's hoarse voice bawled out and Danny could not prevent his head from turning, even as his feet tried to find purchase on the crumbling shale.

Down at the camp, the man was on his feet, standing dead-still. Beside him, on the short cropped grass beside the ring of stones, Billy was on his knees, body arched back. Somebody else was sprawled and motionless on the grass. Close by, two of the others were waving their hands and yelling frantically. Danny turned back, managed to get another two feet higher, stopped, swung back again as his brain registered what his eyes had seen.

The man had the gun in his hands. It was swinging round towards the slope.

Hot panic exploded inside him. Danny scrabbled at the slope, nails digging into the surface. He had only a dozen feet to go before he reached the top edge and safety. Only a dozen feet. It could have been so many miles. He sobbed in sudden fury and fear and bitter disappointment, eyes fixed on the skyline above.

Up and over. *Up and over.* His internal voice was bleating it out, a jittery litany. Behind him, other voices were screaming, high and urgent and fearful.

'Go Danny! *Go!*'

He sensed the gun swinging upwards, his back completely exposed. A dreadful cold shudder rippled down his spine. And he forced himself another step, another.

Up and over. Oh, please.

Ahead of him, in the morning sky, the heron was just a distant shadow.

Doug and Corky had been watching for him from the dark inside the tent, knowing that he would not try a downstream run this time. Danny had slipped out through the slit and although he'd moved as silently as he could, they could hear the occasional rustle and scuffle as he made his way towards the hollow and the cleft between the stones that would take him up to the next level. Doug was holding his breath, listening for more sound, but once Danny had gone through the cleft, there was nothing more to be heard, except for the muttering of the water. They slowly crawled to the front of the tent again, while Tom held back in the shadows, trying to calm his breathing. The day was already lightening perceptibly, though it was still early and the smell of the dew was thick and damp. The mist was thinning quickly.

Doug caught the motion first, on the far side, just up from the low falls. Danny was on the sheep-track, heading up the spur. He seemed very small against the grey mass of the jutting ridge. Doug pointed and Corky peered out.

'I see him,' he whispered. 'Go man, go.'

Tom came up alongside them but did not look out. He just hoped Danny would make it out. That left only four of them, and there was no guarantee that when the stranger discovered one of them had escaped he would not go into a frenzy and hurt them all.

Or worse.

But there was nothing else to do. If they all tried to make a run for it now, they couldn't stay silent, and that would wake the man up and then all hell would erupt.

The other two followed Danny's progress, higher and higher. Doug's eyes kept flicking to the dark, hunched shape by the fireside, watching for signs of stirring. If Danny moved fast, he could be down in the town in an hour, and have help up here before the sun had really risen. There was a chance that he'd be back before the crazy man woke up. A chance.

Then the heron had sent out its shrill cry and Danny had dislodged the rock. The pair of them had stared up, unable to believe the bad luck of it. The stone had knocked the other out and they'd both come bounding downwards, and the double crack of thunder when they hit was deafening in the morning silence.

'Oh, fuck,' Doug said, stupidly.

By the fire, the man jerked awake. Twisting left then right, trying to get a bearing on the sound which echoed back now from all the sides and curves of the slopes. He spun to the pool, where the shards of broken stone were falling like hailstones, and then he looked up.

Danny was pinioned to the steep slope, hands spread wide for purchase, his head almost turned round completely. He seemed only a short distance from the valley edge.

Go, man, go! Corky silently urged.

The man roared wordlessly. He jerked to his feet, snatching the gun up as he did so. Billy squawked, only half awake. The noose tightened around his neck as the stranger hauled at the gun, forgetting how he'd tied it the night before. Billy was hauled to his feet, flipped like a rat caught by an angry terrier, but hands up at his neck. A strangled sound blurted out.

'He'll kill him,' Corky bawled, aghast. Without thinking about it, he pushed his way out of the tent. Doug was right behind him. Over on the short grass, Billy had stumbled to the ground, his hands still trying to force themselves between the twine and the skin of his neck where the loop had tightened ferociously.

He had fallen over the log where he'd sat for some of the night, his backside landing with an audible thump.

The stranger growled savagely, jerking at the gun. Billy flopped, hauled this way and that, and the man seemed not to be aware of his presence except as a weight hindering his use of the gun. The boy gagged, making a strange and somehow deadly rattling sound in the back of his throat, but the man ignored that. Without any hesitation he brought his foot down on to Billy's shoulder, pressed hard, while he tried to drag the gun away.

'Leave him alone,' Corky bawled, trying to overcome the stiffness in his thigh and get to his feet. He tripped over a guy-rope, rolled and crawled for two yards. Doug was jabbering incoherently just behind him.

Billy's breath was cut off completely and his face suddenly went purple. The man pulled again and, for a moment, Corky was convinced the twine would cut right through his neck like a cheese wire. In his mind's eye he saw Billy's head come tumbling off his shoulders to roll on the grass.

Then the man saw the old knife jammed into the grain of the log. He dropped Billy to the ground, reached for the sheath knife and pulled it from the wood with one quick wrench. He twisted it and swung the blade in against Billy's neck. The string parted and Billy went rolling away, still making those deathly sounds in his throat. Corky was bawling at the stranger but Doug was crawling past him, trying to get to his feet, stumbling towards the flat stone. The man was just turning away from where Billy writhed. He raised the gun up the slope. Doug reached the stone and grabbed the red cartridge which sat in the little hollow on its surface. He swung round and threw it, hard as he could, away from them. It whirled in the air, like a miniature red stick of dynamite and plopped into the pool below the feathers on the falls. He was turning for the other one, which had fallen on to the grass when the man spun, realizing the gun was unloaded, saw what the boy had done and crossed the flat in a few strides. He lifted the shotgun and in a smooth and brutal jabbing motion, smashed the butt end against Doug's head. It made a sound like wood on stone.

Doug stumbled away. Corky was crossing the flat towards

him. Tom veered across to where Billy was rolling about, face purple, hands scrabbling at the string still twisted around his throat. Doug took two faltering steps to the left, as if he'd lost all sense of direction. He fell down on his backside, got a hand to the ground, raised himself up, head turning. The man had hit and walked past him, now slotting the one cartridge into the chamber. The barrels snapped closed with metallic finality. He was raising the gun.

At the edge of the camp-site Doug got halfway to his feet, tried to say something, then pitched forward heavily on to his face. Tom snatched up the knife and was straddling Billy, trying to get him to stay still while Billy, almost twice his weight, bucked in blind and desperate panic, almost throwing the small boy off. Tom got the blade under the twine and worked it back and forth. The sharp tip scored two small punctures in Billy's neck, not deep, but bleeding freely. The string parted with a twang and Billy's breath instantly howled inward. Corky was running towards the man, yelling frantically. He hadn't even thought about it. All he saw was the gun swinging up towards Danny, who was pinioned on the steep slope, completely exposed. He was moving past Doug, who lay spread-eagled on the grass, beyond Tom and Billy, running to try to snatch the gun, to give Danny one chance.

The gun thundered.

CHAPTER TWENTY-EIGHT

August 4, 9 a.m.
White-hot fire seared across Danny Gillan's back.

The excruciating pain was like a splash of molten metal, an incandescent surge of agony. He was slammed by a giant hand against the steep shale slope only yards from the top and freedom. His face drove in against the soft surface with stunning force before he could even scream.

He had just been reaching for the next handhold when all the world turned to flame.

Somewhere in the distance, a clap of dreadful thunder shook the valley in a cannonade of shattering sound, following on the searing pain that ripped across Danny's shoulders and his spine. His nose slammed into the gravel, burst with a wet sound like a tomato, but he was soaring so high on the fire of the other unbelievable hurt that he felt nothing of that.

His whole body jerked, even as his hands tried to dig into the surface. The noise went on and on and on, rolling up and down the valley, reverberating from the chasm walls and Danny was surrounded by noise and pain, completely encased in it for what seemed like an eternity.

He was burning. He was on fire.

Oh God, don't let me . . .

It had all happened in the blink of an eye. The man had turned, raising the gun. Corky had been screaming something unintelligible but utterly clear in its meaning. He had been bawling at Danny to move, to climb, to get up and over. And the gun was swinging upwards and the hot, sour panic had erupted, and the shudder of anticipation had shaken him from the bottom of his spine to the top of his head. He'd scrambled desperately for that top ridge, feet sending out avalanches of shale, fingers clawing at the incline, knowing the black barrels were swinging up on him.

The pain had hit before the sound had swallowed him, and

he had been batted against the slope by an enormous force and he was on *fire*.

That first instant seemed to stretch on and on, trapping him inside a vast and implacable bubble of pain. His vision went black and he knew he was dead. Dead and gone. There was just the pain and the noise, and he was burning. Dead and judged.

The fire consumed him. He was being burnt away, cauterized, scorched, scalded. All down his back a molten river was eating into him, corroding the skin and muscle. Inside the cocoon of time and pain, he was catapulted back ten years, crawling on that slick linoleum, and the boiling liquid ate into his hands and the tender surface of his knees, while on his back the skin was peeling and bubbling like tar. Around him, through the thunder, he could hear again his sister's scream mingling with his own and his limbs jerked.

He was dead and this was the bad fire. This was the burning. He was searing and shrivelling, skin warped and contorting. Still the noise went on and on and on and somebody was screaming and it wasn't his sister Agnes who was making the noise. It was John Corcoran, somewhere far below, screeching like a banshee while Danny was burning up.

And he was falling.

The pain did not diminish, but the strange, timeless bubble that had encapsulated him suddenly burst and he was not dead at all. Fire raced across his back, huge gouts of it, but he was not dead. He coughed and gravel and blood spat out. His hands were clawing away, working on their own, trying to get a grip, but he was falling. He felt himself peel away from the slope while his hands clawed at the air and the thick taste of metal was clogged in the back of his throat. He dropped, almost in slow motion, to the gravelly surface, ploughed a boy-wide furrow, tumbling head over heels. He landed on his feet, twisted, came down on his shoulder, still somersaulting as he dropped from the high ridge.

All the time, despite the dizzy spinning of the world, the enormous burning consumed him and the noise reverberated. His shoulder hit a spur of mudstone and he flipped on and out into the air, arms wheeling, legs kicking. There was sky and then green, grey of the slope and then blue sky again. Everything whirled as he spun out above the drop. No sound escaped him. There was no time. His hands were still trying to grab at the shale slant way above him. He fell the way the stones had fallen, bouncing, tumbling and then out from the slope, and he realized that the pain would end.

He was falling to the rocks below and it would all end here and there would be no more fear.

Corky was screaming his name and he wanted to close the pain off for a moment to tell him not to worry, but there was no time for anything at all. The ground leapt up at him, the canyon walls whipping by in flickering striations of grey and white, like candy stripes. He fell.

The bellyflop into the deep pool knocked all the breath from him. The force of the flat impact was like hitting a wall. His nose took another blow and both his knees drove right into the sediment at the bottom of the pool.

Danny was so stunned he did not even know he'd landed in the water. Everything went black and for a wonderful moment all pain was snuffed out. For the second time he believed he was dead but now he simply welcomed the cessation of hurt.

And he fell for forty days and forty nights. His father's voice came to him from a long distance. *Forty days and forty nights without stopping, cast out to the exterior darkness.*

He'd been falling, burning up in the fire, and he'd hit and it had been easy. He'd hit and the pain had gone and he floated in the dark, slowly turning. Paulie Degman's face floated beside him.

'All right, Dan?'

He tried to answer but he couldn't say anything because he had no mouth. Paulie opened his own mouth and a bubble, silvered and wavering, rolled up to the far surface.

'Are you in a state of grace, Danny Boy?' Paulie wanted to know, all white and bloodless and twisting in the current. His voice sounded like the noise water made when it tumbled down under the heather runnels, cold and hollow. There was a buzzing behind the words, and Danny knew it was the flies, sent by Beelzebub, the Lord of the Flies, one of those who had fallen forty days and forty nights with the searing incandescence of Lucifer falling with them.

And there will be weeping and gnashing of teeth, Paulie was saying, in Danny's father's voice, and the buzzing got louder. He did not want the flies to come and lay their eggs in him when he was dead and he did not want his hair and nails to grow, the way Mole Hopkirk's nails and hair had grown in that room at the back of Cairn House.

Danny!

Paulie was calling to him, calling him down into the mud. The pain was starting up again in his back and there was a new pain in his face and the taste of blood in his mouth and that was funny because, except for the fire, you weren't supposed to feel pain at all when you were dead.

Danny! The voice called him and he tried to turn away from it, and the buzzing had changed into a hissing sound, like millions of bubbles bursting on a shingle beach, then a muffled roar that sounded just like water cascading, and his hand was snagged on something. He couldn't do anything about it. He tried to breathe and an awful cold flooded his throat and he suddenly choked. In that instant his consciousness surged back to him and his slack muscles instantly galvanized. Somebody was pulling him by the arm while the pain rippled and burnt across his back, now heating back up again after a brief, cool respite.

Danny! Not dead Paulie, but John Corcoran. Corky was bawling his name at the top of his voice, dragging him up from where Paulie's face was wavering into the dark.

The gun had roared. A sudden punch of sound that slammed into Corky's head. He was only feet away, reaching for the barrels that were raised up towards the far wall. Everything had suddenly gone mad. The butt had taken Doug on the side of the head, a swift and vicious jab, and he had stumbled away, got up, then drifted sideways before falling down to the ground, and Tom was over with Billy, who was writhing and choking, and the man was raising the gun. Corky had watched amazed as the first cartridge had gone flickering through the air to land with a quick plop in the pool, amazed at Doug's sudden comprehension and his dash to get them away from the crazy man.

He had almost made it. Danny, high up on the side where the slope got steeper before the fringe of couch grass at the edge of the moor, he had almost made it. He only had yards to go.

But then Doug was down and out and Billy was rolling on the ground and the barrels went up and Corky tried to get them down again. He was diving, hands outstretched, bawling at Danny to get a move on, to get up and over the top and out of the way, and then the gun had roared and a noise like thunder hit him so hard he heard only the first explosion followed by a repeated clapping sound and a high-pitched ringing inside his head. Even in the brightening morning he saw the flash of fire at the end of the muzzle and then the sudden belch of smoke, just a shade darker than the fading mist. His head had swung upwards and Danny's arms had suddenly shot out just as a hundred small eruptions of gravel for two yards on either side of him where the spread of lead peppered the steep slope. Danny seemed to shove himself forward, right on to the shale face with both arms out on either side as if he'd been kicked hard right between his shoulder-blades. The hands were scrabbling at the face, trying to catch a grip as he slid for thirty feet down the steep shale, then he simply peeled away and began to tumble backwards. It all happened in the space of a split second.

There was no sound but the strange internal cracking inside his head and the reverberating thump that could have been his heartbeat or his mind's echo of the devastating blast. He was trying to shout Danny's name, over and over, but he could not hear his own voice. He moved past the man, head up, oblivious to the danger.

Danny fell away from the high side of the spur, flipping right over in a complete somersault. He landed twenty feet down, on his feet but now facing outwards, much like a ski-jumper. His momentum drove a wide furrow in the soft gritty marl, sending up a bow wave of powdery rock, and then he tumbled over again, arms pin-wheeling, face just a white blur. His shoulder glanced off the ledge twenty feet up and then he was falling straight down. Corky froze. His friend was coming down, twisting in the air, heading straight for the quartz rocks at the head of the pool where the four feathers still stood. Despite the silence, he knew there would be a deafening, deadly thud; then Danny hit and then nothing – no cry, no moan. Nothing.

Danny missed the rocks by scant inches and hit the water with a smack that sent up a wide, curving splash.

He disappeared under the foaming surface, right in at the deep basin where Billy had jumped in on the first day to clean the mud from his jeans. Corky's legs got him to the edge. The wave of Danny's entry had splashed right up on to the stones on either side and sent a little roller curving up over the shingle at the shallow end. Danny's shirt was a red blur down in the depths, his hands pale fish. For a second Corky thought the dye was coming out of the shirt in a thin cloud, the way the red grime had come washing off Billy. He reached the edge, jumped in across the shingle, up to his knees, kept moving, up to his waist. The basin sloped away and he was under the water, bawling Danny's name, now hearing the words, but as if they were far off. He ducked down, got a hand to one of Danny's and started hauling him up to the surface. The hand was slack and lifeless. Under the water Danny's head turned and in the blur Corky could see the red smoke billowing out from the front of his face and knew it was blood.

Had he been shot in the head?

Oh my God, Danny, oh my God.

For an instant he panicked, thinking that Danny's head must have hit the rocks, must have caved in on the sharp quartz edges, or maybe the shot had blasted through from front to back. He felt his heart buck wildly and very quickly, out of control. Everything seemed to shrivel in the pit of his belly. He pulled, got a foot to the shallows and a hand to one of the edging rocks, dragged his lifeless friend upwards, away from the dark at the bottom of the pool, while the blood trailed out and faded in the moving current. He made it to the near side, knowing it didn't matter which side, got Danny's head out of the water. For a long count Danny was completely still. Blood was pouring quite freely from mouth and nostrils as he hung, slumped over the stones close to the shallows, and then, by a miracle, his shoulders hitched violently. A gout of water came sneezing out, coloured by blood and snot. He coughed, tried to turn, raise himself up, much as Doug had tried to do, managed to get to his knees.

He raised his hand towards Corky, his streaming eyes wide open and blind, mouth gaping. He gasped, coughed, gasped again, and then he let out the most pitiful whimper of pain Corky had ever heard. Danny started to fall forward and Corky waded back behind him to get a hand round his shoulder and help him up. But as soon as he touched his back, high up close to the neck, Danny squealed like an animal and sank to his knees. The blood, what was left of it, drained out of his face, and he looked as if he would faint. Corky ducked, managed to get his own shoulder under Danny's belly, grabbed him behind the knees and, with a monstrous effort, got to his own feet, carrying his friend on his shoulder. He waded backwards out of the pool, gasping now for a breath of his own, oblivious of the man who stood there watching the whole thing, motionless and silent.

The noise was still reverberating in Corky's ears. Water sloshed in his boots. Over by the ring of stones Billy was sitting, legs spread, hands at his throat, coughing uncontrollably. Tom was now tending to Doug, gently raising his head up. Doug was grinning or grimacing, his big front teeth pressed against his bottom lip. His hands were shaking like fluttering birds trying to take flight.

Corky put Danny down, gently as he could despite the weight, in the lee of the slope at the cleft he'd crawled through on his failed escape attempt. Danny's eyes were dazed, focused far off, not quite aware of what was happening. Corky was amazed that he was still alive.

'The heron,' Danny mumbled dreamily. 'I saw the heron.'

'Very good, Dan,' Corky said. He sat him down. Twin trickles of blood were running down from each nostril and dropping on to the shirt, making hardly a stain against the deep red of the fabric. Danny sat back, but as soon as his shoulder touched the soft moss he yelled aloud and twisted violently to the side.

'He shot me, Corky,' he managed to squeeze out. 'Bloody shot me.'

Over by the side of the stream the man still stood motionless, watching them all curiously. After a while he turned and slowly walked back to the ridge where he'd been sitting and eased himself down again, in exactly the same spot, holding the gun the same way, across his knees. It was somehow animal, somehow mindless, the way he moved back to the same place, as if nothing much had happened. He hunched there, seemingly oblivious to them all now, waiting.

The stillness of him was somehow even more scary.

August 4, 10 a.m.

Danny was crying. Tears were streaming down his face and he twitched violently while Tom held his hand tightly. Billy watched with strange, glazed eyes, while Doug held his own head in his hands and sat quite still, as if any movement would bring pain. This was true. The back of his head felt as if it was coming apart. There was no blood, but the thumping pain was almost enough to bring tears to his eyes, and his neck ached abominably. The only thing he could do for the moment was sit still and keep his eyes closed until it faded. He'd felt sick for a while, but that had passed. The pain was lessening beat by beat, but still each beat was a pounder.

Danny had lain for a long time, trying not to move, lying more on his front than on his side, head twisted to the right to keep his aching nose off the soft moss. It was tender and bloody, but that was the least of his concerns. The pain was burning into his back, a sheet of relentless heat like a blowtorch flame on his skin. He imagined he could smell himself burning. Corky risked crossing the stream to fill the can with water and give first him and then Doug a cool drink.

'Shot me,' Danny bleated again. His shirt was already drying in the sun. It was plastered to his back; Corky could see no bullet wounds and he wondered where the damage was.

'I'll have to have a look,' he said. 'Where does it hurt?' He was speaking in a muffled murmur again, not wishing to attract the attention of the gaunt man who sat like a crow beside the dead fire.

'My back. Oh, *shit*, Corky. It's really bloody sore.'

'Hold still and I'll have a look,' Corky whispered, hushing him as best he could.

Tom held Danny's hand, clasping his fingers with surprising strength. Corky started to raise the shirt, peeling it away until he had exposed the middle of Danny's back. That's where the bruise started. There were a few puckered little dents in the fabric up between Danny's shoulder-blades, and three smaller holes. He eased the cloth upwards, and heard Tom's sharp intake of breath at the dreadful discoloration of the puffy skin which had swollen under the tight cloth. Further up he peeled it away, with Danny wincing and sobbing all the while. Finally, up high on the back, he had to pull gently but firmly where the weave formed the small, pitted dents. It was only then that he realized what had happened.

The birdshot, tiny lead pellets, had slammed into Danny's sweat-laced shirt, hard enough to drive him against the face, but from far enough away not to kill him. The spread-out pattern had reduced the force and his damp shirt had acted as a buffer. Even so, some of the shot had driven the fabric right into the skin, causing those small dents in the swollen flesh. Corky had to ease each of the slugs out one by one, pulling gently but firmly and, as each of them came out of their embedding craters in the unbroken skin, Danny howled in agony and the tears ran freely down his face.

'Easy, Dan,' Corky tried to say, but by this time, he was crying too, and Tom's face was a picture of silent misery. Tears were trickling in the dust down his cheeks and dripping slowly from his chin. He held Danny's hand tight as he could, for both their sakes. When it was finished, Corky managed to ease the whole shirt off and he rolled it up to jam it under Danny's face as a pillow. They let him lie there until the sobbing stopped. The bruises on his back were violet and risen, like bursts of thunder on the white of his skin. Between the shoulder-blades were three small dark spots which did not bleed. They looked like ink-marks. Corky realized that some of the little pellets had driven through the skin. There was nothing he could do about that.

Tom filled the canteen again and brought it over, again braving the attention, but ignored by the man, who sat still as stone, as if waiting for something to happen. He gently poured it on to Danny's back while Corky held his quivering wrists.

The cold was at first a terrible explosion of pain, and Danny stiffened as if a bolt of high-tension power had arced through him, but then it settled into a gentle, soothing coolness which helped take the burn out of his back. Tom kept it up, letting the cool stream water trickle over the hurt to help the swelling go down, and after a while the heat began to fade a little.

CHAPTER TWENTY-NINE

Interlude

Angus McNicol eased himself back, put the bottle down on the table and unscrewed the top.

'Put some of this in it,' he said. 'The sun's well past the yard-arm now. Coffee'll keep me up all night unless I take it with my medicine.' The big old policeman grinned, just a burst of white before it was closed off again in his remembering. He poured two hefty shots of whisky into the half-cups of coffee, put the bottle down, raised a cup and clunked it against the other. He took a manful swallow, savoured it, swallowed, then let out the gruff sigh of someone who's appreciated a drop of scotch for half a century.

'Takes the bad taste out of the mouth as well.' Another quick flash of teeth and then his eyes changed and it was obvious he was looking a long way back into the past once more. Once he'd started, he'd been able to talk for a long time.

'I thought it was all dead and buried and gone, you know. Should be, too. Oh, I still recall it sometimes, even now, but I have to tell you now, son, it's not the kind of thing I like to dredge up.'

He looked over the table, over the rim of the cup, and drew his brows together.

'Why the interest now? There's better stories to tell about this town. Not many worse, except that business with John Fallon's boy a few years back. He got himself hurt pretty sore when he went after that fellow O'Day. That was the year I quit the force, on doctor's orders. To tell you the truth, I was glad in a way. You don't know you've had enough until it's over, and then you realize you never ever want to see another mother's face when you tell her a child's dead and gone.'

Dead and gone. Angus McNicol had used that phrase twice, each in a different context. It should have been all dead and gone. Should have been, but the world's full of what should have been and never was. It should have been gone, but it kept on coming back, like the bad penny; certainly, in the bad dreams. I had managed to bury most of it, deliberately so, because it was something I never wanted to remember and dwell on, not as long as I lived, and then once I had kids of my own, it was something I wanted to keep down there under lock and key. You just can't begin to think that history might repeat itself and that one of your own might ever be touched by a madman. Can you?

I'd managed pretty well until I saw those dulled eyes swivel in my direction down on River Street and then pass on with hardly a flicker or blink, and some of it all came back in such a rush I felt my belly drop a hundred feet, or so it seemed, and there was the smell of raw fish in the air and the scent of pine smoke and dead meat and a crazy man's sour sweat; in my ears I heard the old, lazy buzzing of busy flies and the murmuring of slow water in a stream and I was instantly back *then*.

It doesn't take much to trigger those switches. Some things don't stay buried; some things don't stay dead.

Yet I *had* managed to bury it all for a while, shoved it down there in the depths, where it was kept bound and gagged to stop it clawing its way up and eating at me. Then, on the sunny morning on River Street, with the light reflecting from the sky-lights on the roof of the old boat-yard down at Keelyard Road, where a bunch of boys had talked of a drowned boy in the river and had first planned to take a trip to the mythical dummy village, I looked into the empty depths of a pair of eyes and it all broke free, like some beast in a cellar.

No matter what I did, I could not put this old thing back in a box. It was out and growling and it was pawing and clawing, and the only thing for it was to meet it face to face, to go right back to the start and take it from there.

I had to know.

Crazy? Possibly, but I'd *seen* crazy. I'd looked into its blinking, twitching eyes. I had to know.

I had no real answer for Angus McNicol. I said I was researching a book, and there was a sliver of truth in that. He looked at me over the top of the cup and he took another sip, swallowed, and began to talk again. Who knows, maybe the old policeman had his own ghosts to bury.

'Dead and gone. Too many people over the years, I can tell

you,' he said. The tape was running again. 'But not dead and gone in here.' He raised his free hand and tapped the side of his head.

'The one thing Hector Kelso drilled into me when I had transferred over to plain clothes, was to remember everything. Remember everything and keep your own records for ever, he always said. He used to stand there and never move a muscle except in his eyes. He never wanted anybody to touch anything, not a thing, until he'd been there and seen the lie of the land. If you did that, you got a picture in your head that had everything in it, even the sounds and the smells. I can still close my eyes and conjure up old Ian McColl's head on that dung-heap and I can remember that it was mostly cow dung, but there was a dead chicken there as well. It's got a different smell. I can still taste the dust in the tack room where old Jean McColl was dragged down the stairs.

'I remember thinking that the man, your Twitchy Eyes, was probably ex-army. We found a place down at the east end of the Rough Drain, the place that's still all overgrown. It was a bivouac. We knew it was him from the pages of the bible. He'd used them to wipe his backside.'

Angus drained his cup and put it down, eyes still focused back.

'We worked round the clock, going through every army record, but at that time there were thousands of boys and men just out of national service. There were thousands more who'd been in the war and trained to kill and were still young enough to have been this beast. It was a broad field we were ploughing up. We turned up Scots soldiers who'd been to Aden and done some terrible things themselves. There were a few people who'd survived the Jap death railway and a few of them were as crazy as all get out, but there was no way we could pin down this devil.

'We really wanted to nail him. We went through parish records, but we still drew blanks. I was beginning to think he had just come out of nowhere. Maybe he did. Maybe he just did. Maybe he was a devil. Remember the Whalen boy? He was snatched on June 6, '66. All the sixes. Some of us thought that was some kind of ritual thing. Who knows? Maybe it was.

'There was claim and counter claim over what drove him on, but I thought it was just sheer and utter badness. He was evil. I think it was just depravity. The man had a taste for killing and hurting. If Charlie Saunders had caught him, he'd have ripped him apart with his two hands for what he did to that wee girl of his. Big John Fallon, he was just as worried as anybody about his boy and girl and, if he came on this Twitchy Eyes first, there was a good chance it would never get to the High Court.

'But we never did get him. We rounded up a few ex-soldiers and anybody with any record at all for flashing or peeping through bedroom windows or stealing underwear off the washing lines. We had a couple of identity parades and all for nothing. The man came out of nowhere. He always seemed to be one jump ahead. We sweated out the whole summer wondering where it would happen next. It was a while before Johnson McKay came careening down that farm track in his old post van.

'All we had to go on then was a description from the girls he'd tried to pick up the first time and a name from Jean McColl's diary. She said his name was Leslie Joyce, though the spelling changed to the female version, but that was when he was stalking her. There was every chance he'd just made it up, but we had to check that too. We turned up half a dozen of them, spelt whichever way, and four of them had been in the army. One was a woman who'd been a sergeant in the WRACs. Two were old men and one was in a wheelchair. The fifth was a Free Kirk minister from up by Creggan, and I can tell you he got the fright of his life when me and a couple of the CID boys grabbed him in his greenhouse when he was watering his tomatoes. He'd been an army chaplain in the war. He was five foot tall and he'd a withered arm from childhood polio. He couldn't have punched his way out of a wet paper-bag. The sixth one had been banged up in Drumbain for five years for a smash and grab. That was the way of it.

'Our killer, he could have been anybody. Anybody at all. But he wasn't any of the people we found called Leslie Joyce. We never got close, though we even did a trawl in the local parish year books to see if anyone of that name had been baptized, but still we got no closer.'

August 4, 7 p.m.

'Unless a man be born again, and cleansed of sin.' The man's voice was clear and rumbling. He was standing at the edge of the stream, both feet in the water. The gun was five yards away. Billy was standing beside him, his skin pale in the dimming light. Danny wondered if he could reach the gun. Corky wondered the same thing. Tom and Doug watched the scene at the water, each of them unsure of what would happen.

It had been a long day since the gun had spoken, since their talk in the shade of the line of low hawthorns that led to the hollow.

'You ok, Dan?' Corky had asked.

He spoke low, but not in a whisper. Danny twisted, and that cost him a wrench of pain between his shoulder-blades, but if he moved slowly it wasn't too bad. Occasionally the light breeze would feather across his skin and trail a sensation like pins and needles but, for the most part, the bruises, swollen and risen though they were, stayed numb. The fire had damped well down, but Danny could still remember the awesome burn of it.

'He *shot* me!' The enormity of that hovered over him and weighed him down. Over and over he saw the world spin and saw the white quartz of the rocks rushing up towards him. His nose ached for the moment, where he had driven it into the shale. It pulsed more fiercely than did the bruises on his back. Another throb of pain beat out from his shoulder, where it had hit the outcropping of mudstone that had probably saved his life by twisting him just a little downstream so that he fell straight into the deepest part of the pool and missed the rocks where the heron feathers stood.

'Thought you were a goner,' Corky said again. Beside him, Tom silently agreed. His face still bore the faint imprint of the man's fingers and he had a dark bruise on his jaw-line. Every now and again he opened his mouth and moved the jaw to the side, as if testing for fractures. It helped take the stiffness out of it.

'Thought *I* was a goner,' Doug said. He drew his fingers down the side of his head, just behind his right ear, rubbing slowly. 'I think I still am.'

'But you got the cartridge away. Honest to God, Doug, that was brilliant. And it really took a lot of guts an' all.'

'Thought I was going to *puke* my guts,' Doug said, and he gave a strangely fearful grin. His big, protruding teeth made him look gawky. His string vest was torn now under his armpit and hung on him like a tattered net.

'But if you hadn't pitched it in the pool, Danny would have got both barrels for sure. You should have seen him, Danny Boy.'

Billy said nothing. He was sitting just to the side, closer to the hollow where he'd hung the stag's head on the thorn branches. He was absently massaging the skin of his throat. It was raw and inflamed. He had that far-away, lost look in his eyes that Danny found somehow scary. It reminded him again of the rabbit and the stoat, as if Billy had somehow accepted all of this, as if he knew what would happen and was just dumbly waiting for the inevitable. Tom glanced over at him. He'd panicked for an instant, suddenly more frightened than he'd ever been in his life, even more so than when the man had grabbed his face and squeezed.

Billy had been down on the ground, making gagging, hissing sounds in his throat, the kind of sound the heron had made when its neck had been broken and, for that instant, Tom had thought he was dead, even though his heels were drumming into the turf. Doug had been down too.

Danny was falling in the air towards the rocks. Corky was running towards the man, and Tom was certain the stranger would turn and swing the gun on him. At that range he'd cut him in half and Tom would be left alone. It had all happened so unbelievably fast.

In his mind's eye they were all dead, all except him, up here in the valley with the man with the twitchy eyes. The knowledge froze his insides to slush and for an instant his vision wavered.

Then reality, even colder than the fear, had cut through the fear like a shard of ice. Billy had both hands up at his neck and he was breathing raggedly. Tom found his hand reaching for the knife and in a few seconds of bewildering violence as Billy blindly fought him, he had cut the noose and Billy was hauling for breath. All of this unreeled again as they whispered together.

'And Tom,' Corky said, recalling it at the same instant. 'He cut Billy free. He would have strangled otherwise. Did good there, Tom-Tom.'

Danny was amazed at how calm Corky sounded. Even Doug, with his big, stupid grin, sounded close to normal. Just a few hours ago, they'd been crying, and dying. Danny knew that Corky was trying to keep them all calm, waiting for the next chance, if they could *get* a chance. If it came, Danny did not know if he'd be able to move, and that frightened him badly, as much as Billy's scary far-distance stare. Doug might have made it downstream if he hadn't twisted his ankle. Corky might have made it up the slope if he hadn't been hurt making his first run. Danny could have got to the top but for the heron flying out of the gully. Tom wasn't fast enough and Billy just couldn't move.

If the chance came, what chance would they have?

Danny shook his head, sending a wave of dull pain across his back, over his shoulder, and another wet pulse into his tender nose. He couldn't think like that, no matter how hopeless it seemed. He didn't want to be like Billy, sunk so deep in the swamp of his own fear that he couldn't move. If he worked at it, he could keep the fear battened down, and try to keep at a distance the recollection of the gun barrels raising up towards him.

'Where's the knife?' Corky was asking, this time in a whisper. Tom used his eyes to indicate the curve of root just beside him. The bone handle was barely visible. Very surreptitiously, Corky eased his way towards it, reached even more slowly, and then drew the knife towards him.

'I don't think that'll do any good,' Tom said. Corky shrugged. His eyes had that thoughtful look again. No matter what happened, Corky wasn't going to wait for it. Standing straight, he barely came up to the man's chest, but he was still thinking of how to get them out of this.

The man had opened one of the corned-beef tin cans, the last they'd swiped from the self-service shop round on Braeside. Corky's stomach was twisting savagely and he could smell the meat on the air. They'd only drunk some water Tom had brought up from the stream in the canteen. None of them wanted to risk attracting attention yet by trying to get some food.

Over by the little ridge, the man sat still. He'd eaten the block of beef, gnawing into it just the way he'd eaten the rabbit, making little snuffling noises. Corky's mouth had watered and he'd actually dribbled. The stranger had ignored them. Occasionally he'd cock his head and then mutter something, always speaking over his left shoulder, to whoever he saw there.

'Unless a man be born again, of water,' the man said, now that it was late and the sky was beginning to darken. The moon was not yet up and Corky had an idea that it might be full tonight, and he thought maybe that was what the man was waiting for.

He had surprised them all when he'd stood up and taken his coat off, letting it slip, almost theatrically, to the grass. He'd turned then, just as dramatically, and they all looked in his direction, suddenly scared again. He stood looking at them for some time, as if pondering his next move. Danny felt his heart beat faster. Billy stayed frozen. Finally, the man came walking towards them.

'You hear them?' he asked, quite softly. He was standing with his back to the fading light and his eyes looked like holes in his head. He inclined his head towards the hollow. The flies were humming busily. He angled his head and stared down at Billy.

'Listen to them, boy. They're talking to you and me.' He crossed to the fire and picked up the rabbit's head by one flopped ear. A trail of flies whirled upwards and headed for the hollow. 'Another trophy? You know what to do with it, don't you?' Billy took it without a word, crossed to the hollow where the heron's eye was now a seething mass of insects, and put the head in the nearest fork. They could see him look around, left and right, as if seeking a way of escaping, but he did not seem to have the wherewithal to risk it. He came back to the tent and sat down again. The man reached down and took him by the edge of his shirt. Billy whimpered, a little animal sound, but when the man pulled him upwards, he went with the motion without a word and got to his feet.

'Those voices. You just need ears to hear.' Billy gave a little shiver.

The man bent down as he had done before, when he'd walked Billy towards the gaunt skull suspended in the branches.

'Must go down into the valley and through to the other side. There will be weeping and gnashing of teeth and then the great truth. You know it, boy. You want to walk down the valley with me? Conboy knows the truth, he sees it with his magic eye. Wait

361

till you see all the things he can show you. Beelzebub's millions; the Lord's minions.'

Billy stood completely motionless, but his whole body seemed to be vibrating with tension. His mouth was open and for a moment his breathing stopped completely. The man held him with his eyes. Billy's breath caught and then he was hauling in fast, panting like a panicked animal.

'In the midst of death, they are life. I saw you build the altar. Watched you. I choose you now.'

He bent down and put the gun butt-first on the turf with the barrels resting on the ridge by the stream bank. He clapped Billy's shoulder. 'So now prepare ye the way. Make straight the path.'

Very gently he reached and took the bottom edge of Billy's shirt and raised it up. It was like a parent with a child. Billy dumbly raised his hands and the man slid the shirt up then let it fall silently to the grass. He unbuckled his Indian-bead belt, pulled his jeans down. It all had the slow quality of a ritual. Billy stepped out of his baggy underpants, leaving them white on the grass. The man put his hand on the boy's back, then slid it over his shoulder, almost tenderly, drawing him close beside him.

Danny felt Tom shiver beside him. His own heart was clattering away inside him, almost out of control. Corky's teeth were grinding, quite audibly. Doug was totally silent.

Billy was led down to the water.

'Unless a man be born again, of water, he may not pass through.' The man's deep voice echoed from the far side. Danny recognized the mix of quotations. It was a distortion of all that he had learned from the countless Sundays. The man dropped his hand from Billy's shoulder and took his shirt off and unlaced his own boots. They all watched, fascinated, wondering what would happen next. Only Danny had any idea.

Billy's skin was pale in the dimming light. Beside him the man was almost completely naked. He had a line of dark hair running down between his shoulder-blades, and a pair of black tattoos up on the tops of his arms, one on each arm. From where they sat, Corky and Danny could read one name: Lesley. The evening was far from dark, but the sun was down beyond the western rim of the valley and the long shadows of the trees downstream had crept up to the edge of their camp. The quartz rocks at the falls seemed to glow against the grey shade of the far bank.

The man waded into the shallows. He held Billy by the arm and forced him ahead. The ripples spread out to the far-side shingle. Up on the moor the poor curlew bleated again and some slight breeze drifting between the hawthorn spikes sent a cloud of flies buzzing upwards in a furious little whirlwind. The strange pair in the stream were further out, into deeper water. It was up to Billy's waist, then up to his navel, up to his chest, just in so many steps. The man guided him further.

They heard Billy gasp for breath as the cold of the stream curled around his ribs. They saw him shiver, not in the high-tension way that Tom's body was vibrating, but in a deep shudder of cold and fear. His breath was coming in harsh spikes and the man was mumbling something, speaking into his ear. None of the others could hear what was said, not then. Billy stumbled, and the water lapped his chin. He got to his feet again, gasping harder, a jittery, panicked sound.

'What's he doing?' Doug asked, out loud. They were all still sitting, almost paralysed with apprehension over beside the wall of rocks where the scrubby roots looped and twisted into the small crevices. They hadn't moved.

In the stream the man waded forward, and now the water really was up to Billy's chin, rippling around the stranger's broad back at chest level. He looked like some old water god, something out of the adventures Danny and Corky had read in the book they'd found at Overbuck stables.

'Prepare ye the way,' the man said, now speaking aloud. He raised his head and looked up at the darkening sky. Billy's head was just a dark shape on the surface, at the centre of the ring of ripples, the man had his hand on the crown. He leant forward and pushed Billy's head under the water. Billy panicked. His hands flew upwards and thrashed wildly as he tried to lever himself up for air.

'He's killing him,' Tom cried. Corky scrambled to his feet. Both his hands were balled into fists. Danny felt a great urge to jump up and run down to the stream and grab the man's arm, but an even greater urge to keep himself away from the crazy stranger overwhelmed it completely. Doug was jabbering something unintelligible. Down at the stream, Billy was struggling frantically.

'Unless a man be born again, of water,' Twitchy Eyes was bellowing, 'he shall not cross over.'

Billy lunged upwards, spluttering and gasping, his mouth a wide, dark circle. Water sprayed out from his nose. The man simply forced him down again. The four of them were on their feet now, Corky closest to the water. They could see Billy's pale shape under the surface, arms flailing, body heaving, but the man was too strong. He held him there. A big bubble of air rose up and burst on the surface, carrying with it the hollow bleat of Billy's terrified cry.

'Leave him alone . . . you loony *bastard*!'

Corky's yell echoed back and forth from the sides, repeating his last word over and over in a diminishing sequence.

'He's killing him,' Doug wailed.

Corky turned to face them all, eyes blazing. 'We have to do something,' he raged.

'What?' Doug asked. The gun was over by the downward edge of the pool, beside the ridge. They would have to circle the pool to reach it. The man was only five steps away from it.

Danny's hands were trembling with the need to act. He turned away from the stream, just at the same time as Corky did, both of them heading in opposite directions. Danny picked up a smooth stone, turned and threw it with all his strength, right at the man's head. The motion sent a searing, white-hot pain across his back as his skin stretched under the torsion of his muscles. The white stone, a piece of stream-rounded quartz, flashed across the distance and, like the stick that had killed the heron, would have connected with the back of the man's head if the stranger had not bent down to force Billy further under the water. The stone whirred past, missing him by a mere inch. The man twitched, as if buzzed by a wasp. The stone carried on, smacked against the boulders at the head of the pool where the falls tumbled, smashed into half a dozen fragments with a loud crack. A splinter knocked the nearest heron feather out of its crevice and into the air. The man began to turn. Both of Billy's hands came out of the water, waving desperately.

'Let him go, you big, dirty, crazy *bastard*!'

Corky had crossed almost to the edge of the stream, yelling at the top of his voice, even louder than before. When the stranger had stopped, Danny's heart felt as if it had stopped as well. He had thrown the stone on impulse, on instinct, the way he had thrown the stick at the bird, and with his usual accuracy. But when the man froze and then began to turn, he realized that he had made himself the next target for punishment. Then Corky had butted in, diverting attention once again, and Danny felt a shameful surge of relief once more.

'Come on, then,' Corky bawled, his voice cracking with the effort. Danny swivelled and saw he had Billy's knife in his hand. The old, rusty blade was held out in front of him, knife-fighter style. Corky's legs were spread, and despite the fact he was half the man's size, he looked suddenly ferocious. He looked like a young warrior.

The man finished turning and stopped dead. His eyes swept across Danny, past Doug and Tom, lighted on Corky. The eyes started to blink rapidly. Billy came spluttering up to the surface, coughing and gagging, unaware of what was happening.

'Yeah, you big fuckin' creep.' Corky was screaming now. 'Come on. Let's see what you've got.' His left hand made a come-on gesture, a man-to-man invitation.

The man smiled slowly. He took a step forward, then another, pushing a bow wave in front of him. Danny could see the name on the other tattoo now. For some reason it held his eyes. He did not want to see the feral grin on the man's face. Just below the blue lettering, a series of rips had been chewed into the skin, like saw-teeth cuts, the scars still dark and fresh. Tom and Doug shrank back. Billy was stumbling to the other side of the pool, towards the shallows, sending out great splashes of water to the shale bank. The eyes were blinking like dark strobes now.

'What's this, Sergeant Conboy? See this?' He cocked his head, still grinning, still twitching.

Corky held his ground and the man came up the bank. His shorts had slipped, dragged by the weight of water. His penis, unshrivelled by the cold water, pushed out to the side, like a dark, thick, club. Coarse hairs ran up to his belly and down his thighs. He looked like a savage giant. He came out of the water, went straight towards Corky, who stood his ground until the man was a yard away, then backed off, still holding the knife up. There was no contest. The man reached. Corky swiped with the knife in a low arc and the man's left hand came up and hit him on the side of the head. Corky reeled to the side and the man simply reached again, grabbed his wrist, bent his hand downwards with a violent jab and the knife went tumbling out, spinning in the air, towards the clump of roots where Corky had picked it up in the first place.

He did not hit Corky again. Instead, he turned, still dripping, towards the ridge. Corky was breathing fast and the others on this side of the stream swung their gaze from him to the stranger.

Twitchy Eyes picked up the gun.

Nobody moved. He picked it up, turned, quite purposefully and with none of the dramatic, ritual slowness he'd displayed as he led Billy down to the water. He walked back over the gravel from the low turf ridge, swinging the butt upwards, one hand to the barrel. His fingers locked on the stock. Corky stood there, breathing hard, chin up defiantly. The rest of them were scared speechless.

'And again he defied him,' Twitchy Eyes growled. 'For a second time.'

Denied him, Danny mentally corrected. He was back up in those realms of icy clarity brought on by yet another burst of extreme fear. *Not* 'defied' *it's 'denied'*! He almost expected the cockerel down at Blackwood Farm to crow again, in some parody of punctuation for the biblical quotation, and if it did, Doug might burst into his red rooster strut just to complete the picture of unearthly craziness.

'Don't,' Doug breathed. He was not strutting now. Tom's spastic dry swallow was just a series of throaty clicks. Even Billy was silent now. The man turned his head towards Danny and speared him with those black, jittering eyes.

'Let he who is without sin throw the first stone,' he rumbled. 'Are you without sin, boy?'

Danny couldn't speak. It was as if his own throat were bunged full of dry paper.

'Are you in a state to meet eternity?'

He stared on for a long, drawn-out moment, the eyes screwed up, hardly twitching at all now, then he turned away from them.

Tom groaned like someone in pain. The eyes swung back to Corky and transfixed him.

'And again he defied him.' The voice was rising now, getting back up to that creepy, dreamy level. 'For the second time.'

He bent closer. 'You afraid, boy? You scared?'

Corky said nothing. His teeth were still clenched and his lips drawn back as if he was holding himself all together with a tremendous effort. His chin was still up.

'You will cross over, boy. You will know what waits on the other side. Prepare ye the way.'

The gun came up, barrel pointing at the sky, then swung down. The man was less than six feet from where Corky stood with his arms held out to the side, like a miniature wrestler who didn't know yet which way to swivel. The man slowly stepped forward and brought the muzzle right up against Corky's cheek.

There was no movement. They all watched that barrel maw as if it was a poisonous snake, completely mesmerized. It rose up, a centimetre, an inch. It was directly over Corky's eye. Danny could see the other eye, looking up, unblinking, still somehow defiant. He could not quite believe what was happening.

The man's finger tightened on the trigger. 'If thine eye offends me.'

NO!

The scream rang inside his head, high and desperate and echoing on and on, but his mouth could not form the word. His lungs couldn't force the air out. He was caught in the ice of freezing terror.

The fingers squeezed. The voice almost wheedled now. 'Pluck it out.'

Silence fell. The trigger pulled back. The silence stretched out.

A loud metallic snap cracked the silence. The shotgun's hammer pin slammed down on to an empty chamber with a sound that was suddenly deafening.

John Corcoran swayed backwards. Very slowly his legs buckled under him. He slumped to the ground and his eyes rolled up so far only the whites were visible.

CHAPTER THIRTY

August 4, night

The moon rose high in a cloudless sky, now almost completely full.

The night was full of noises. Far down in the dark of the valley, a pheasant hawked in alarm, sounding like a tin-can scrape on rough stone. Far up on the heathery moor a grouse croaked. Up on the slope-side, some small thing, maybe a weasel, dislodged a stone and sent a trickle of gravel down in a whispery hiss. The stream murmured. The fire, now hot and red, crackled and sparked.

Billy Harrison sobbed. The pitiful sound of it, hardly muffled at all by the canvas of the tent, tore at them. It was the sound of utter despair and dejection and it was the sound of pain.

Corky sat silent, staring at the flames of the fire, his eyes glinting and reflecting the flickering red. He had not said a word for hours. He had the same far-away look that Billy had had in his own eyes earlier that day, the mesmerized, glazed stare of someone who has recognized the closeness of his own end. They had all seen Corky's end when their captor had squeezed on the trigger, but the gun hadn't roared and bucked. The gun's firing pin had slammed down on the empty chamber with a solid crack. Corky had fallen to the ground as if all the nerves in his body had failed, as if all his sinews had been cut.

Now it was night and the moon was up and the sounds of the valley were overlaid with the sound of a boy's crying.

The knife was over in the gloom beside the boulders where it had landed. It would do them no good now anyway.

Corky had lain there, still as death, arms spread-eagled for nearly a minute, and they had all stood there immobile, just looking at him. None of them had been brave enough to move to help him.

'It's empty,' Doug was thinking. Despite the fact that Corky was down on the ground, he knew he wasn't dead. All he could think about was the fact that the gun had been empty all this time. Since the morning, when Danny had gone clambering up the slope and he himself had managed to get a hand to the second cartridge and send it flipping into the pool, he could not remember the man reloading. He'd assumed the lunatic had jammed another two shells into the breech, but he must have forgotten. If he'd done that, then Corky would still be lying there, but the rocks behind them would be painted red with the insides of his head. Sudden relief made his legs feel boneless.

The man had slowly lowered the gun and looked down at Corky, almost curiously, as if surprised that the gun hadn't fired, as if only mildly astonished that the boy's head hadn't been blown right off his shoulders. The mad anger that had been in his eyes was now replaced by a mad incredulity. He had stood there, possibly contemplating his next move, and the three of them had stood around him, all of them wanting to run, none of them daring to, even though they knew the gun wasn't loaded. Water dripped down the man's legs. The word 'Joyce' stood out clearly on the side of his brawny biceps. Finally he turned his head and gave a little shrug, as if that was this scene over and his interest in it was done. He crossed to the stream, went down to the shallow part where Billy was crouched on low, flat stone, pale and shivering, and took him by the hand.

Corky's eyelids fluttered and his eyes rolled down so that the white crescents disappeared. He gave a little start, like somebody just coming awake, and raised his head dopily, as if unaware of his surroundings. He shook himself, making his eyes focus, remembered where he was and jerked up, spinning as he did, to get to his knees.

'Take it easy,' Danny hissed at him, getting a hand to his arm. Tom stepped forward to help him to his feet. Corky's face was slack and pale. He turned to Tom, as if he didn't recognize him either, swung round to Danny, but he didn't look at him, he looked *through* him, his gaze fixed on something in the far-away distance.

'Corky?' Danny asked. Tom was slapping his friend's knuckles, the way people were supposed to do with folk who'd fainted. Corky didn't seem to notice.

'You ok? Hey?'

Very slowly, Corky nodded, but it was almost automatic. Billy came up, led by the hand, his height and robust build still slight by comparison to the man's. He was shivering visibly and droplets of water dripped from his elbows and from his chin. His hair was sleek and plastered to his head, and goosebumps had risen all over his skin. He seemed entirely unaware that he was completely naked. The man pointed at Doug and Danny, then flicked his hand to include the other two.

'Fire,' he said. 'Get it going.' He pulled Billy over to where his clothes were lying and told him to get dressed. Billy did so without a word. He did not look at any of them, not then. It was as if he had become isolated, by the depths of his fear, by the fact that somehow the man had singled him out, specially, no matter what he'd done to the others. The man pulled on his shirt and denims, jammed his feet in the old boots and then slung his coat around Billy and made him sit down.

The others had backed off, Tom pulling Corky as they went, down to the pile of logs they'd dragged up the previous day, and began hauling them up to the circle of stones. Corky moved slowly, as if he'd not come entirely awake. The embers had cooled to grey ash, but Phil Corcoran's stolen Ronson lighter was still in the burlap bag and they used that to light the bundles of dry bracken to get the fire started. The twigs caught quickly and soon the flames had spread to the thicker branches, wavering bright, casting a glow around the clearing and once again sending trails of sparks into the sky. They dragged more logs up from the pile while the man heated the last tin of oxtail soup.

By this time, Doug was faint with hunger, and it may have been that which made him go to his own rucksack and take out the bag of potatoes they'd swiped from the field. There were still a few left. He risked close proximity to the crazy man, edging close to the fire, holding one arm across his face to shield it from the heat of the blaze, while he stuffed the big, early potatoes into the ashes by the side of the stones. The man finished his soup in silence, dipping the now-stale bread into it and wolfing it down like an animal. He offered some to Billy, but got no response at all. The others sat down, closer to the tent, waiting for what would happen next, and the valley got darker as night began to fall. After a while, half an hour, maybe a bit more, the stranger stood up and used one of the branches to scrape the potatoes from the fire. He rolled the largest one clear of the others and trundled it closer to where he sat. Doug didn't wait. He took that as tacit permission and used a twig to get the rest free, leaving little trails of ash as he manoeuvred them back from the heat. They had to wait a while until they were cold enough to handle. They were black and carbonized on the outside. They were still a bit solid and uncooked in the centres, but to Dougie and Danny and Tom, those three baked potatoes were the best food they could remember. Corky ate his slowly and in complete silence. He was still distant, his mind far away, or so it seemed. Danny wondered if maybe he'd cracked, and he knew that if the crazy stranger had pointed the gun up to his eye and pulled the trigger, he'd have shit himself, pissed his pants and *then* cracked. The pain of the birdshot at more than a hundred yards had been bad enough.

They ate and, despite everything, they felt better for it. There were three potatoes left in the trail of ashes and the man took two of them. He thrust one at Billy, told him to eat, and finally Billy took it. The others watched him slowly consume it, black skin and all, until it was done.

Another half-hour of silence stretched on while the shadows lengthened up towards them and finally darkened everything except for the circle around the fire. Eventually the man stood up and stretched, yawned loudly and looked up at the sky. The moon was still unrisen. Over by the corner of the tent was the roll of fencing wire and the twine that had been used to loop them together the previous night. Now the man took the thin wire and began to unravel it.

'You're welcome to stay the night,' he said to Doug, and his voice sounded so normal, so ordinary, that it startled them.

Danny almost blurted out the instant reply that sprung to his lips: '*No, it's ok. We'd better be going now.*'

He said nothing because the man simply took a hold of Doug's shoulder and pushed him backwards, herding them all across to the wall where they'd sat in the heat of the day after Danny's failed escape attempt. He made them sit down again, then fastened a loop of wire around a thick root that coiled from a crevice in the rock. Very quickly and expertly he slipped another around Doug's neck, quickly twisting it until it was tight, then braided it before he repeated the motion with Tom, then Danny and finally a silent and slow-moving Corky. The loose end he whipped around the trunk of another gnarled hawthorn stump, leaving them hobbled together, separated only by braided strands of wire. The nooses were tight enough to prevent real movement, but not biting like the garrotte that had almost taken Billy's head off earlier in the day. The knife was well out of reach and even if they could have got to it, the old blade couldn't have cut through the metal wire. They were caught, like rabbits in a snare. If they moved, they'd choke and strangle.

After more of a while, the moon finally rose over the high edge. The man with the twitchy eyes was facing it this time, sitting on the tent-side of the fire, on one of the flat stones. Billy was close by, like a pet, but unleashed. There was no need of a tether when the man had some sort of mental noose that had already roped him and bound him.

'Almost there, Conboy,' he said. 'Down in the valley again.'

They all listened, because there was nothing else to do.

'What's that? Oh yes. You can sit there smiling if you like, but they'll be back again. Yellow, godless vermin. Not long now, but we'll be waiting. Nowhere else to go.'

He laughed again and Doug shuddered because the laugh just sounded mad. 'Flies got you Conboy, but you still smile on through, because you know, don't you? You can see through.'

He giggled and Danny felt a cough tickle in his throat, and he tried to breathe with his mouth wide open to prevent it. The stranger was gone again, gone to wherever Conboy was, and he did not want to attract attention. The moonlight glinted off the gun barrels again.

'Dung-fly. *Dung-fly!* Conboy. I hear them again.' He raised the gun up in an expectant, protective way, peering into the gloom on the far side of the stream. The conversation went on like that for a long time while the moon crossed the stretch of sky that hung over the valley. Every now and again, they'd hear the strange cry: '*Dung-fly.*' None of them knew what it meant. Danny expected the man to fire into the shadows, because he knew he couldn't have many shells left and if they had any chance at all, they'd have to take it. It was just the second day since the man had stepped across the stream while he and Billy were fishing, but he knew now, with a desperate certainty, that there would not be a third night. He was not sure they'd even survive this one, though, despite everything, the wire holding nooses around their necks was actually a good sign, but they'd be dead by the time the full moon climbed into the sky.

The man's rumbling voice tailed off into a guttural, incomprehensible jabber, which became a muttering and then a silence for a while. Doug had dozed off and Tom snuggled against Danny for warmth. Corky's eyes were open. Danny could see them if he squirmed round to look. They reflected the firelight and hardly blinked at all and Danny quailed at the thought that Corky might have lost his marbles and be unable to think, unable to act when they had to. Corky was the one who could think on his feet and the one who could lead them when they needed to be led.

'You ok?' he asked very quietly, nudging his friend. Corky never blinked, but he did nod slowly. Finally, after what seemed like a long time, he turned round, taking his eyes off the man.

'Don't you worry about me, Danny Boy. Get some sleep if you can.' Relief surged. Corky hadn't gone crazy. He'd looked death straight in the eye, the bravest thing any of them had ever seen, and by rights he should be dead. He'd maybe just taken a while to come to grips with that idea.

A half an hour passed and the flames were beginning to die down a little. Doug was snoring very softly, his big buck-teeth catching the light. Tom was still jammed against Danny's side, when the man got up and, without ceremony, lifted Billy by the collar. Billy, who was almost asleep, whimpered in sudden fright, but the man ignored it. He hefted the gun in his other hand and crossed over to the tent, dragging Billy behind him through the ashes beside the stones. With not a word, he bent and went into the tent, pulled the boy behind him. The flap slipped down and closed.

'What's he doing?' Tom asked. He had woken with a start, digging an elbow into Danny's back, and the sudden flare of pain had almost brought a blurting yell that was only just swallowed back.

Billy whimpered again. The tent was just a long, dark oblong against the deeper dark of the hollow. Only the front was visible. There was a knock and a vibration as something jarred against the upright pole. The man said something low, and Billy wailed. It was just a soft sound, but it was a wail. None of them had heard him make that sound before.

'What is it?' Tom wanted to know. He was pulling against the wire and it gave his voice a strange, tight quality that would otherwise have been funny and now just sounded strangled.

'Just take it off,' the man said, now quite clear.

'Dirty bastard,' Doug hissed. 'He's touching him.'

They couldn't know that for sure. Billy made that little child-like noise again, the way a kid will when it's forced to do something it doesn't want to do. It reminded Tom of his little sister Maureen. She hadn't liked the taste of the medicine and she'd shaken her head, moaning like that, trying to let it dribble out of her mouth. He jerked against the wire, suddenly tense and shaking.

'He's touching him,' Doug repeated. 'He's a dirty *bastard*!' In the light of the fire his face was twisted into a snarl that managed to convey disgust, anger and horror. They all knew that anyway, from what had happened to Mole Hopkirk, from the awful damage to him whispered in the classrooms and on street corners, not quite fully understood by boys just on the cusp of comprehension.

The man said something else, almost in a whisper, almost wheedling, and Billy began to cry. It was soft enough, but it was a desolate sound. Doug made a little growling sound in the back of his throat, probably unaware that he made any noise at all. There was nothing any of them could do. The wire held them by their necks, like tethered animals.

'What for?' Danny asked stupidly. He knew, albeit vaguely, about queers, the kind of people who wanted to touch boys and stick their dicks in their backsides, although he didn't quite understand why they would want to do so.

'Because he's a fuckin' dirty, homeo *bastard*,' Doug grated.

Over in the tent the sounds stopped and Doug froze. Corky had his head cocked to the side, just listening, sitting completely motionless. Tom was trembling quite violently now, though the night wasn't cold. Danny's back was throbbing again and the skin felt tight and strained, as if it might suddenly split into cracks and fissures.

'No,' Billy said in a small, pleading voice, not at all like his robust, bragging cockiness, which aggravated all of them most of the time.

'It's all right.' Soothing, strangely more frightening than ever.

'No, but . . .' Billy's voice rising in panic.

'Shut up, boy.' There was a thud which could have been a fist on a face, or a head hitting turf. Billy grunted, much the same way Doug had done when he'd been knocked to the ground by the gun butt. He cried out and the man snarled something incomprehensible. Fabric ripped. At first Danny thought it was the scrape of a zip unfastened violently, then he saw the pale hand gripping the fabric of the tent at the ragged edge where he'd cut the canvas to crawl through. The canvas ripped further and the opening yawned blackly before the hand was suddenly whipped away and the two edges sprung back together again.

Billy screamed. Corky jerked forward and was pulled back, gasping, hands up to protect his neck.

'Jesus,' he gasped.

The man grunted, a sound like a beast in the dark, and Billy screamed again, high and girlish and sharp as glass, a dreadful sound that cut into the still air. The man grunted again, deep and hoarse, a guttural wordless groan of effort.

'He's killing him,' Tom cried, voice on the verge of cracking into tears.

'Bastard,' Doug said. He was quivering like a bowstring, his long arms out in front of him, hands curled into impotent, bony fists.

Billy could cry all he wanted. He could scream for help and screech and howl, but nobody would hear him. Up here, this far from town, nothing could be heard. Here in the cleft of the valley so far up beyond the barwoods, the clatter of the trains, or the clanking of the steam hammer down at Castlebank shipyard, or the screech of hot metal in the old forge, none of the noises of town penetrated this far. The screams of a hurt boy wouldn't carry much into the dark of the trees before it was smothered by the shadows and the leaves. From a few hundred yards down in the forest, it would just sound like an injured fox.

The sounds he made were dreadful, harsh and frantic, cutting right into the others, punctuated only by the mindless sounds of the man in the shadow of the tent.

'Stop it!' Tom whinnied. 'Stop it stop it *stop it*!' He had his eyes tight closed and his hands up at his ears, knuckled right into them to cut out the awful sounds. Gentle Tom, who hadn't wanted this adventure, who had wanted to stay at home and try to get by, and find some accommodation with his aching loss. He'd stood and put his hand on Corky's shoulder on the night everything was blowing apart and had somehow managed to keep the bonds from breaking, but he could not cope with any more of this. Tears were squeezing out between screwed-up lids and catching the red of the fire and the white of the moon. For that moment, he had lost his fear for himself. He just wanted Billy to stop crying and to stop hurting.

The grunting sound was coming faster and Danny could visualize the old boar at McFall's farm, a great heavy brute with mean eyes and slanted teeth that could cut through an ash sapling in one snap. Other farmers would put it to their sows and half the time it would try to hook them with its tusks, gouging thin slashes up their flanks. Then it would mount them quickly and it would grunt and snort, dribbling snot from its snout and saliva from its oddly grinning jaws. Danny had seen it get ready, with its long spiral dick punching in and out, twisting like a vicious corkscrew. In his mind's eye, he imagined the crazy man on top of Billy, just like the pig, and despite having seen the crazy stranger's penis swing like a club, he imagined the corkscrew boring in to flesh and blood, ripping and rending. He shivered and his own sphincter puckered and tightened of its own volition.

Billy screamed again, and the grunts and porcine snorts were coming faster. The noise was getting louder too. Danny wanted to shut it out and began to raise his own hands up when he felt a tug on the wire, hard enough to pull it firmly against the skin of his neck. He twisted round, wincing against the sudden flare between his shoulder-blades, and stopped dead.

Corky had arched his neck out of the loop, pushing so far forward that the fencing wire was biting into the skin just inside the collar of his shirt. Danny could see the white line where the wire was dug right in. Corky's body was twisted and his hands were pulling at the wire to let him get his jaw down to the braided piece that connected him to Danny. His face was screwed up into a grimace of concentration that looked like pain and *was* pain as far as Danny could tell. His teeth were flashing in the moonlight.

The tug came again, a metallic thrumming sound that sent a vibration across the wire to Danny's own neck. Danny had to twist almost as uncomfortably to see what was going on, and even then it took several seconds for it to dawn on him.

Corky was trying to gnaw through the wire.

Danny could hear the grind of teeth on metal, a dreadful scraping sound that was like fingernails on a blackboard, chalk on glass. It made the hairs on the back of his neck stand up in unison. Corky's eyes were closed and his teeth were gritted on the wire and he was working the metal back and forth, desperately trying to chew his way through the tough steel. The sight of it made Danny quail. It was as much animal as the grunting pig sounds from inside the tent, and the awful, mindless screech of pain from Billy.

It was like a rabbit caught in a snare, or a fox caught in a gin trap. They could gnaw their way through their own foot, biting through fur and skin and gristle and bone to get free, no matter the cost. Danny could hear the thrumming of the wire every time Corky's teeth slipped off the thin braid and the jarring clash of his teeth as they ground together.

If Corky was desperate enough to try to gnaw his way through the wire, then he must be really frantic, Danny realized. The thought of such desperation brought a sudden surge of black fear that swamped him to numbed stillness.

Tom was shuddering now, making little jerky movements while he cried silently. Doug was snuffling and rocking back and forth to the extent that the wire noose would let him. Danny sat still and thought about what Corky was doing and what the man was doing and he wished he could close his eyes and make it all go away. A deadly, lethargic tiredness was dragging over him, brought on by the brutal attack of freezing terror. For a moment the sounds faded down to hardly anything and the light of the fire diminished. All he could feel, for a while, was the thrumming of the wire as Corky tried to bite his way free.

After a while all the sounds stopped. Corky slumped back, exhausted with the effort. His neck audibly creaked and he moved his shoulders up and down to get the cramp out of them.

Billy started to sob. The loud and frenzied pain-scream had faded now to a shuddering, liquid moan inside the tent, a desolate, lost sob of profound despair and hurt that was as bad as the shrill cry of pain. The man spoke, now soothing again, that creepy, oily sound they'd heard before the dreadful grunting. Doug was still rocking, like an animal in a cage, needing to move.

The tent rustled. Some scuffling sounds followed and the man came out again and went towards the fire. He was naked from the waist up. His skin glowed red in the firelight and he looked up, like some primitive savage, at the moon now halfway across the black sky. Danny expected him to howl at it, but he said nothing at all. He looked at the moon for a long while, then ambled across to the lower rocks, opened his trousers and sent out a crescent of piss that glittered in the moonlight. After a while he came back towards the tent. He stopped close by and looked over at them.

'Peaceful night,' he said, quite solemnly, with no hint of a grin or a mad smile. He bent down and went back into the tent.

Billy was sobbing softly. The night noises, silenced by his screams, had started up again in the trees and on the moor where the curlew piped its lonely notes. The night wore on and the fire began to fade as Billy's snuffling tapered to silence. The moon crossed further and the fire-glare died to a warm glow, Dopplering down through the levels of red while the logs settled as they turned to ash.

After a while Tom snuggled back into Danny's side again and Doug crouched with his head rested in his hands, dozing lightly. Corky arched his neck again, pulling at the wire, and started to gnaw once more.

'You'll never get through it,' Danny whispered.

'No such thing as never.' Corky pulled back from the wire, breathing heavily with the effort. He opened and closed his mouth several times, easing the straining muscles.

'Not in one night,' Danny said. 'You'll need a week. Can't you reach the knife?'

Corky shook his head. 'No. It's too far. And we don't have a week. We've got to get out of here. He's hurt us all, but I think he'll get worse. He's waiting for something.'

'What?'

'Christ knows,' Corky said. 'Full moon or something. He's a bloody vampire or a werewolf. He's off his head.'

'But you'll never get through that tonight,' Danny said, unhelpfully.

'You got a better idea?' Corky's hiss sounded hard and angry.

Danny shook his head. Corky's eyes gleamed, almost ferociously. 'Me neither. Wish I had. I should have stabbed him today. I could have. I could maybe have hit him with it. Stuck it in his throat if I'd thrown it.'

'You can't throw for peanuts,' Danny said, and a strange, panicky little laugh tried to bubble up inside him. 'You're as bad as Phil.'

'Thought you were a goner today, Dan, honest to God.' Corky changed the subject, giving Danny a quick and almost desperate grin. 'Scared me to death when you came off that slope. Thought you were dead for sure. I couldn't believe it when you hit the water, and then I couldn't believe it even more when you weren't plugged full of lead.'

'Me, too,' Danny agreed. In his mind the world still whirled as he fell. On his back, the pain pulsed, not hot, but steady and warm.

'And I thought *I* was dead today. Jesus, I really did.'

'Me, too,' Danny repeated. 'Scared the shite out of me.'

'I never knew it wasn't loaded. It was all happening. He was drowning Billy and I just got angry and I couldn't stop myself and then when he pointed the gun at me, I don't know what happened. I just stayed angry and I wasn't going to let him know I was scared.'

'Weren't you? I was really shitting myself.'

'Honest to God, Danny, I don't remember. I was looking him in the eye and staring right up the end of that gun barrel, and I heard it go off. Like *boom*. It hit my eye-bone and I thought it had fired and that was it. I just fell down dead. I couldn't believe it when I opened my eyes and saw Doug over there. The sun was shining through his ears and it was kind of funny-looking. I must have fainted, I suppose. I never fainted before. It's not all that bad.'

He paused for a moment, looked up at the moon, then turned to Danny.

'It was Doug that saved me. If it wasn't for him, I'd be a goner, or you would be. If he hadn't got that other cartridge and slung it in the water, you'd have had both barrels, or I'd have had it in the head. That took guts, real guts.'

Danny was picturing Corky snatching up the knife to challenge the crazy man, sweeping it in front of him as he approached, not flinching at all. He was thinking about the look in his eye as the gun barrel trailed up to the other one, unblinking, not giving an inch.

'Not as much as you,' he said vehemently. 'I hope I never see anything like that as long as I live. I couldn't even speak, I was so scared. Weren't you frightened?'

''Course I was, but it was really weird. I thought that was it for me. I really did, and I went all sort of cold, like numb, you know? Everything was really slow. His eyes were twitching away, and I thought, "This is it, Corky" and you'll never believe it, but you know Cuchulain. The hero? I thought about him and what he'd do, and I thought, "I'm not going to let him see I'm feart." '

'You really thought that?'

'I think so. But maybe I dreamt it when I fell down. I just remember looking into his eye and everything was frozen cold. But I know something now.'

'What's that?'

'If I get out of here, I'm never going to be scared of anything again in my life. Not Phil, not my old man. Nobody and nothing. If I can beat him, I can beat *anything*.'

'Hells flaming bells, Corky,' Danny said, feeling the mad ripple of laughter trying to erupt again, 'I never thought you were scared of anybody anyway.'

'Shows you what a good actor I am, doesn't it?'

He smiled quickly, suddenly boyish for that one moment, then he arched his neck to get his teeth to the wire. He started to gnaw again, making that awful grinding sound. After a while he had to lean back and take a break from the exertion.

'Dan,' he said, easing his jaw once more, and panting heavily. 'I didn't mean just me. Getting out of here, that is. We'll make it, honest we will. Bet you any money. You and me, we got a miracle, so we did. We're still alive when the both of us should be dead, so I know for sure we'll get another chance.'

He looked over again, and any boyish grin was gone. 'But it has to be tonight, because he won't give us another chance after this.'

CHAPTER THIRTY-ONE

Interlude

'We called him Gideon,' the old soldier said.

The name gave me a shiver. It somehow fit. He was remembering and so was I. It had taken me a while to track him down, an old trooper from one of the old Highland regiments. I had an advantage now over Angus McNicol, for by this time I'd listened over and over to his gruff voice on the tapes, and I'd looked through a bunch of papers I'd managed to turn up along with the ones he gave me. Old Jean McColl's wild-poppy petal was still pressed between the pages of her diary, a distant memory captured. The pages of Doc Bell's pathology reports on Jean and Little Lucy Saunders and the others, those pages were yellow now with age. The words on them, however, were still stark and somehow still deadly. The catalogue of ruin carried out at the hands of a true madman was appalling. Forgive me if I don't list it here. You don't want to know.

I spent some time taking notes and asking questions, because I had to know. I was driven along. There were clues I knew, clues I hadn't thought about in a long time, but now, in hindsight, they stood out like beacons. Those tattoos, for instance. *Lesley Joyce*. Old man McColl had read them wrong first time. Jean had seen them on the day she died and that's why she'd underlined them in her frantic message. Poor, doomed woman had been trying to tell them.

Lesley and Joyce. Probably old girlfriends from way before the madness.

And Sergeant Conboy, the name the man kept muttering, twitching his head every time he called it out. Another clue. McNicol had thought the man was army and I put two and two together. A newspaperman can talk to anybody. For the price of a few beers, most folk will talk their heads off. I knew it had to be a soldier, somebody who had served abroad. It took a while to find the old army lists and some time longer to search them all. There were four Sergeant Conboys way back in the fifties, and I travelled a bit to find some of the men who had served with them.

Finally I found the man I wanted to talk to.

'Gideon. He always had his nose stuck in the bible and he was always quoting tracts. The name just stuck. I'm telling you, he was one scary nutter. He thought the locals were animals, less than beasts. We were with the Gordons, but most of us were on national service, just two-year men. It was two years I could have done without.'

Albert McAulay was a barrel of a man with a full head of iron-grey hair cut in an old-fashioned crew cut, the kind you see on German colonels in old war movies. He drank pints of Guinness slowly and steadily, sitting in the corner of the Horseshoe Bar up in the city. At first he was a bit hazy, saying he couldn't remember that much, but it was clear he just hadn't thought about it for a long time, or maybe didn't want to. When he did start talking, once he got into gear, he couldn't stop.

'A real lunatic. I remember that Vietnam stuff, you know, that My Lai carry-on where the Yanks shot up a village? When that happened I thought it must be more common than you'd think. A lot of bad things happen in wars.

'Gideon, he went really crazy some time in the second year, when we were jungle-bashing in Malaya. We were somewhere in south Selangor, on patrol, hunting the CTs, what we called the communist terrorists, and you never knew who was who. They all looked the same and they all spoke the same. Some of our boys called them the Dung-Fly People, because that's what they said all the time. It meant something like "We're friends" or "Don't shoot." Nobody knew what. Or cared. It was hot and sticky and we were scared shitless most of the time. You couldn't see a yard in front of your face until you got to a clearing, and then you had to watch for grenades or crossfire. It was murder.'

Albert wiped his florid face and took a deep pull on his beer.

'"*Non tare roger.*" That's what the signals man said on the radio. Nothing to report. And sometimes there *was* something to report. We were to deny food and comfort to the enemy. We rounded up villagers and put them in trucks and took them fifty miles down the road. That was to drive the bandits deep into the jungle, but that was bad for us, who had to go in and get them, us and the Iban scouts who could scent a trail like dogs. They were nothing much more than animals.

'So one time we came across this place, deep in at *Ipoh*, a village at the bottom of a steep valley. Me and Sergeant Conboy and crazy old Gideon, we took the right flank and, all of a sudden, there was gunfire and the shit was hitting the fan and everybody was yelling. Smoke from a couple of flares, and a lot of confusion. The village was pretty big – pigs and kids running about, screaming like banshees. Gideon, he came out from the side and let rip. Me and Conboy saw him. He just raked a whole group of kids and I remember the grin on his face. Conboy pulled him back, trying to shout over all the noise and, despite that, yon mental bastard turns round and grins.

'"Heathens," he says, and I heard it clear as day. "Worse than animals."

'He just turned back with his gun. Two women were running for cover and he shot them both, laughing all the while. Just then, two of the locals came out with *parangs*, big machetes, and came running for us. There were shots behind them and we thought it had to be bandits, so we opened fire and put the men down. By this time the bible-thumper had vanished and we were in the middle of it. It wasn't until later that we found him round the back of a burning hut with a girl. He'd been giving her one, just a little kid of ten or eleven, and he had cut her. Swear on a stack of bibles, he had cut her little tits off and slit her mouth from ear to ear. She was still moving.'

Albert drank deep, remembering now.

'I'm telling you, it gave me the shivers. I was still fired up, still all going from the excitement, and it didn't shock me the way it normally would, but I still had the shivers. Conboy pulled him away. God, he nearly hit him with his rifle, and the big fellow, he just turned round, grinning, as if he'd just told a good joke.

'After that, we had to keep an eye on him, until we got back to the platoon base. Nobody said anything, but Conboy had been called back to operations and Major Cantley told him to take Gideon with him, just to get him out. In those days, out in the jungle, what happened was left there. Things didn't leak out the way they would now. Official secrets and all that. Anyway,

Conboy's in the truck and they head off, and that's the last anybody hears of them for three weeks. They sent search parties out, but it was needle-in-a-haystack stuff over there. We heard the RAF lost a flight of five transports just forty miles from HQ, and none of them were ever seen again. That jungle was thick, man.

'The Suffolks in the south, they got word. Some tribesmen came out and said two or three of their boys had been killed by a soldier. They checked it out and, sure enough, they found your man and Conboy in the truck. It had gone off the road and rolled down to the edge of a river, and Conboy, he was as dead as a dodo. He'd been shot in the head and his brains were all gone. The Suffolks told us there was nothing left of him. The flies and the ants there are pretty fierce and they keep themselves busy. Gideon, if he was crazy before, he was really gone now. He'd kept himself alive by catching the little fish and eels in the water that came right up to his waist in the rains and he'd blown a couple of the natives to kingdom come when they came to investigate. I remember the brass were pretty suspicious, because Conboy's head injury looked like a close-up shot, but by that time an investigation would have been a waste of time. Gideon was round the twist. Completely barmy.

'After that he was shipped home, mad as a fuckin' hatter. Last I heard, he was in Chessington, where they take all the army head injuries. After that, I dunno. Maybe it was Broadmoor or some other loony bin.'

August 4, midnight

'None of your damned business, Conboy. You just sit there watching, that's all you have to do. Flies in your eyes.'

The voice boomed out from the hollow. The stranger was just a black shadow, hunkered down now in front of the stag's head. The flies were silent in the dark. A breeze of wind in the cooling night air carried the scent of carrion past the man and over to the line of boys looped together beside the low wall of rock. It was greasy and foul, the stench of corruption.

'They crossed over too, dirty heathens. Dirty. *Dung-fly!* You can see them. Shouldn't have tried to stop me neither, should you? *Non tare roger.* Got another eye to see with now.'

He had been talking for a while now, over in the dark where his shape was just a shadow in the rest of the shadows. His voice rose and fell. One minute he would quote a passage from the bible, and the next he'd be talking to his imaginary listener. None of it made any sense.

None of the tethered boys risked talking. Over in the tent, Billy's whimpering had slowed down and stopped. Corky's efforts on the wire had ceased for the moment. He was leaning back as far as the noose would let him, with the side of his head against a tussock. Doug was still sitting with his head resting in his hands. He was breathing shallowly.

After a while the man's hoarse babbling died away and there was silence for some time, broken only by the night noises and the tumbling water of the stream at the falls, where now only three heron feathers stood. After more of a while, the man's shape appeared quite suddenly, his face caught by the moonlight as he walked silently from the hollow. He was quite naked, like a primitive warrior, his broad frame glistening with sweat despite the cool of the night. He stood looking at them for a moment, as if considering what to do, or maybe just checking that they were still there and that the wire would hold them until morning, then went back inside the tent. The moon slipped down beyond the west side of the valley, casting their glade into a deep darkness that was alleviated only by the silver light in the sky and the dying embers of the fire.

Danny dreamt.

He was falling. He was tumbling over and over with the fire searing and burning across his back while his skin shrivelled and melted.

'Defied me thrice. *Thrice!*' It was the voice of the twitchy-eyed stranger, yet at the same time, impossibly, it was his father's voice, echoing down from on high, forbidding and reproving. 'Forty days and forty nights did they fall to the exterior darkness where there was weeping and gnashing of teeth.'

Up where the moonlight rippled on the surface, he could hear the boom of the cannons on the ramparts of the old castle, fired to bring the bodies to the surface. Dead Paulie Degman's face swam in front of him.

'*Yea*, we are in the valley of death, Danny, and *yea*, we fear evil. Prepare ye the way. Make good the path, for He comes when you do not expect Him and He will cut . . .'

No! Danny tried to scream. It was all wrong. In his ears, the beat of his heart was like a drum, and he struggled for breath, panicked, flailed to get away from Paulie. The dead boy's eyes were pale in the dark, pale and blind, and the lips were flapping in the flow of the river water.

'Defied me thrice, defied me thrice,' another voice was rasping out and Danny closed his ears to it, because if he defied thrice something would happen and that would mean it was . . .

He woke with a start and a scream half blurted on dried lips. The wire was pulling right into his neck and he gasped aloud, hauling for a painful breath. He had slipped down and his back was scraping on the old twigs and thorns that had fallen from the hawthorn tree, setting his swollen bruises aflame.

'You ok, Danny?' Tom asked softly.

For a moment Danny was unfocused, disoriented. The moon was gone and the fire nearly dead. He realized he was still alive and not drowning and not falling and that ghostly Paulie had only been in his dream. He turned round quickly, rasping his neck and back in the process, to check Corky, still able to see his wasted face floating in front of him, grinning sadly.

'I think so,' he whispered back, very shakily.

'He took Billy out. I saw him. Billy needed the bathroom and he let him out. They went down to the stream and he washed him down with water.' Tom's voice was thin and shivery. The night had gone cold. 'What's he going to do to us?'

'I dunno,' Danny said. Even at this stage, after all that had happened, it was still hard to believe that the man would really kill them. All the evidence to the contrary was there. He had shot at Danny and would have killed Corky as he had done Mole Hopkirk and the others, but even then the flare of hope and disbelief was in them. They were just boys.

'What's Corky doing?'

'He's asleep, I think.'

'Can he get through the wire?'

Danny shook his head, sending a negative vibration to Tom. 'Nobody can.'

Tom squirmed, a little shudder that Danny picked up by return. 'What's the matter?'

'I need . . . I have to have a pee.'

'Well, go.'

'I can't,' Tom said. 'Not here.'

'Sure you can,' Danny whispered, 'our hands aren't tied.'

'But I can't here. There's nowhere for it to go. I'll be in it. Sitting in it.'

'That's the least of your worries,' Danny whispered tightly. He didn't understand what Tom's problem was.

'No. I can't,' Tom insisted. His voice was rising above a whisper.

'Why the hell not?'

There was a silence. Tom gulped hard. Both of his hands were forced down on his crotch again, the way they'd been when they had all come down the valley at gunpoint.

'It's Maureen,' Tom said, and this time his voice did crack again into a half sob. 'My wee sister.' Danny nodded, remembering the thin little girl with thin arms and skin like quartz underlain with dull, cloudy bruises. Tom pushed his hand into his crotch, like a toddler holding in the need. He let out a little moan.

'When she . . .' he started. 'I mean. I was *there*.'

Danny didn't have to say anything. Everybody knew Tom had been there. His old man had been working up at Lochend on the new road, digging drains with the team of navvies, and Tom's mother, a small, spare woman with the same pale freckles Tom had and the same washed-out curly hair, she'd had to go out to the shops. Tom had been left in with Maureen and that was something he never minded at all, because she was his kid sister and she was sick and she liked him to read stories to her. Danny had been with him when he'd swiped the book from the library in the winter, stolen it so he wouldn't have to give it back, and he remembered it had been 'Billy Goat Gruff', the one about the troll under the bridge. He recalled Tom getting badly upset when somebody mentioned little Lucy Saunders under the bridge at Ladyburn Stream near the outlet at the Rough Drain.

'I was there, just me on my own,' Tom said. 'Mo, our Maureen, she was pretty sick. She'd been up in the night, but my mum had to go down town to get something. I think it was soup and the cough mixture for Mo because the thing she had, it made her cough all the time and she had a sore throat.'

Tom raised one hand to wipe away a tear. 'I was in with her, playing with my Dinky toys on the floor and she asked me to read the story again. Remember that book I nicked? She loved that one. She always said it made her go all squirmy and every time I read it, she squealed like she was scared, but she wasn't really. She loves the bit where the thing says: "Who's trip trap tapping on my bridge?"'

Danny picked up the slip of tenses. *She loves.* Little Mo had died before Christmas. Danny had experience of death, the whole town had by now, but it was all second-hand and at a distance, even counting Paulie down by the river. He had not lost anybody he loved. Not like a sister or anything.

'And I said, "Ok, I'll read a bit." I never minded, 'cause she really liked it and it made her laugh. She was all right, and that's why my ma went out. She had to get things, and it wasn't her fault she wasn't there. But I didn't know what to do.' Tom choked up a little and Danny sat silent. Tom sniffed and started again.

'I was reading and she was all scrunched up in the pillows, and I was just getting to the good bit when she said she had to go to the bathroom. It was dead quiet the way she said it, and I said, "Hold on a minute and I'll just finish this bit," and she looked up at me. She had these big dark bits under her eyes, like a panda, you know, like somebody had skelped her a couple of good ones. She said it was film-star's make-up and she was going to be like Audrey Hepburn when she grew up, except she said Audie Hebum 'cause she couldn't speak right with her front teeth out, and I said it would be Audie Murphy and she never knew what I was talking about. Only she wasn't going to grow up, was she?'

Danny heard the bitterness of loss and bleak hopelessness in Tom's voice.

'So I said, "Wait until I've finished the page," and she looked up at me and said: "I have to go to the bathroom, can you help me, Tommy?"'

'It was just like that. She was kind of smiling and kind of

frowning, like she was thinking hard, and her eyes were open and I got up to get the pot from the corner. She could only use the pot because she was too sore to get to the bathroom, you know? I went to get the pot and she was still staring like that. I never even knew. Honest to God, Danny, I never knew. I thought maybe if I hadn't finished the end of the page, maybe I could have . . .'

The tears were catching the last of the dying fire-glow.

'I lifted her up, and she had wet the bed. She was lying in her own pee. I could smell it and I never even knew then. She was still staring at me, that funny way, dead-still, and I was trying to lift her up. There was a puddle underneath her and it made a noise and I never even knew. Oh shit, Danny. She said she needed to go, but she'd already done it and she was lying in it. My wee sister. Maureen.'

Now Danny realized why Tom hadn't wanted to hear about little Lucy Saunders. She had died under the bridge, in the muck in the hollow of the concrete chamber, in a puddle of her own piss. The story had gone round the school like a brush-fire, the first killing, so far as was known at the time, at the hands of this twitchy-eyed killer who was now in the dark of the tent with Billy Harrison.

'I couldn't do anything,' Tom was saying. 'I never knew.'

He began to sob softly. Hand still pressed in hard. 'And I can't do it here. I don't want to sit in it. Not here. I don't want to die in my own piss.'

'Jeez, Tom, I never knew that's what happened.' Doug's voice was low, coming from his shadow on the far side. They hadn't realized he was awake. 'You should have said.'

'I couldn't say. Nobody should die in their own pee, nobody, especially a wee kid like Maureen. I told my ma I would die to bring her back. She was screaming blue murder and she hit me, but there was nothing I could do. I *would* have died to bring her back, you know. Honest I would. I can still hear her talking. Every night when I go to bed, I can hear her asking for that story and then I can hear her telling me she needs to go to the bathroom. And now I can't do it. Not here.'

'That's ok, Tommy,' Doug whispered. They heard him fumble in his pocket and then, a few moments later, the snick of something tearing. Danny smelt a peculiar odour on the air. Doug fumbled some more, then reached out. Something thin and floppy dangled from his hand.

'Piss into this,' he said. Danny stretched to see. Doug's teeth were glinting in the light. In his hand, Phil Corcoran's second condom dangled. Tom looked at it for several seconds before he realized what it was. He slowly reached his free hand and took it, unzipped his jeans. They all watched, though in the dark there was nothing to see. They heard a hiss of water spurting. The condom expanded very quickly and they smelt its odd scent mixed with the hot smell of urine. After about a minute, Tom let out a long sigh. He lifted the ballooning rubber by the neck. It wobbled a little. Very quickly he tied the neck to seal it, reached out beyond the little hollow and put it on the ground. It rolled several feet until it got halfway to the tent. There it hit something sharp and burst without a sound except for the sudden gurgle of water which drained into the dry grass.

'Thanks, Doug.'

'Don't mention it,' Doug said. 'I wasn't going to use it anyway. It's too bloody big.'

He was silent for a while and all three of them sat still while they listened to the night noises, the rustlings and the occasional distant cry of a wild bird far off in the gloom of the trees. Finally Doug spoke up again.

'You think he's all right? Billy, I mean.'

They knew who he meant.

'I think so,' Danny said, more in hope than in any certainty. They had listened to Billy's heartbreaking sobs for a long time after his squeals of pain had diminished. The man, Twitchy Eyes, he didn't seem to notice the noise or, if he did, it didn't bother him. Billy had been snuffling when the man had come out to hunker by the skulls and speak to a man who wasn't there.

'I never meant this to happen to him,' Doug said. 'I wish I never said he should have his neck wrung. I was just pissed off, know what I mean?'

They all knew what he meant. It had been a dreadful, brittle and dangerous moment.

'Christ a'mighty, I should never have told him about his old man. But he was always having a go at me. All the time. But honest to God, I never wanted this to happen to him. I mean, it was just because I was angry when he said that about Terry. That was a really rotten thing to say.'

'Yeah. And you were rotten to him,' Tom said. 'But it's finished. It doesn't matter.'

'I'd take it back if I could. No kidding. I don't want Billy to get hurt again. Not by that dirty bastard. If I could take it back I really would. It doesn't matter about Terry. He's my brother, isn't he? What difference does it make? Nothing! I still love the little creep, no matter what. And my mum and dad, they'll be ok, won't they? In Toronto?'

Danny and Tom could hear Doug was laying it out like a grid, wishing it to happen.

'Maybe they'll stop arguing all the time. It scares me sometimes. It used to be ok, but now it's not. I always knew there was something wrong, but it's not Terry's fault. He's a great kid. He always gives me a kiss every night when he goes to bed. Every night. I don't mind telling you that.'

He went silent for a while, then spoke again. 'Corky was right. We have to stick together while we can. It doesn't matter, does it? All the things that happen and we can't do anything about them? They don't matter. Corky was right, sure enough. See the way he looked in that bastard's eyes? I never saw anything like that in my life. If I get the chance, I want to be as brave as that.

'And when I get home, I'm going to hug my mum. Don't mind telling you that. I'm going to give her a hug and tell her I love her and my old man both.'

Tom sniffed in sympathy. Danny sat very silently, aware of pangs of loss inside him that he could not explain at all, even to himself. *Hugging* and *loving*.

The earth turned and the night got darker and colder, though it was still summer. Some time in the night, Corky woke up from his exhausted slumber and started working on the wire again, making that awful grinding noise with his teeth on the metal. Tom cried out in his sleep, just a wordless whimper that startled them all awake. Billy was silent the whole time through the long night.

Danny fell in and out of sleep, trying to keep awake, hoping against hope that Corky would make it through the wire. He was deadly afraid of what the morning would bring and in his mind, Corky's words kept getting mixed up with Mick Jagger's strutting rasp.

This could be the last time ... maybe ... maybe ... maybe ... I don't know.

Again, some time later, Danny dreamt of his father and heard him read from the prayer book, and he imagined himself crawling through pools of scalding custard while his father talked about the bad fire that would go on for ever. He saw John Corcoran's wasted face, one eye glaring at him and the other a red ruin. The wire was tight on Corky's neck and, when he opened his mouth to speak, his teeth were all chipped and broken.

'I tried, Danny Boy. I tried, honest to God. But there's no way out, even if you *can* talk posh.'

Somewhere in the shadows, a deep and echoing voice rumbled out: 'Defied me thrice. Defied me *thrice*.'

And Danny knew he was waiting in the dark in the Garden of Gethsemane in an agony of fearful expectation of a dreadful thing about to happen.

'Denied.' He insisted. 'It's not defied, it's *denied*.'

As soon as he said it a cold sensation of doom flowed into him. Before the cock crows twice ... It couldn't be thrice, because that would mean the cock would crow and it would be ...

CHAPTER THIRTY-TWO

. . . morning

Day was dawning and it was early morning. Danny Gillan jerked awake to the distant sound of the cockerel crowing far off down the slope of the moor in the direction of Blackwood Farm.

'Whassamatter?' Tom snuffled, almost incoherent, cringing in against Danny for warmth. Corky was slumped the other way, against the damp mound where the hawthorn roots twisted into the moss. The wire was across his throat, but not digging in the way it had in the dream. His eyes were closed and he was breathing shallowly.

The cock crowed, distant but still audible, a strange, fierce and challenging cry coming out of the mist which had gathered in the dark for the second time and now shrouded the world in a fuzzy blanket which blunted all the sharp edges which would later be honed by the rising sun.

'. . . *And the cock crew* . . .' The well-learnt words were ringing in Danny's head, in the shivery aftermath of the dream, fading now, but still powerful and ominous. Day was dawning, but it was still dark and the mist was almost solid downstream where the valley formed a scooped cup before the thick tangle of the forest. The trees were just a dark and impenetrable wall. It was still dark enough, but it was not night any more, and they had survived another one. They were still alive. Four of them, anyway. Across in the tent, there was no sound yet. Danny shivered again, feeling the damp of morning cold steal through him. His legs were stiff and his backside numb and wet from sitting hunkered in the moss and grass.

They had survived a second night, but what Corky had said sneaked in on him while he was trying to shake off the disabling drag of the dream. *It has to be tonight, because he won't give us another chance after this.*

And Corky had fallen asleep, tired and hurt and exhausted like the rest of them, and they'd missed their chance. Night had come and gone and they were still here, braided together with the fence-mending wire. Danny huddled still, trying to keep the instant panic down. For a moment, despite the closeness of the other three, his solitude was vast. Nothing moved in the valley except the near tendrils of mist which rose, wraith-like, from the pool in small, translucent columns to condense into the thick billows against the far wall, then flowed like some magical ecto-plasm around the roots of the alders and hawthorns, crept into the hollows behind the boulders and the narrow ravines which fed the tributaries into the main valley.

Far up on the moor, an early lark was singing into the morning sky. High up on the east, there was a tinge of opalescent pink to break up the grey, a promise of another hot summer day. Here in the valley, it was still shadowed, but bright enough to see the carpet of dew on the grass, like a frost. The air was clean and earthy, redolent of moss and heather roots and nearby uncurling ferns.

A soft morning.

Danny slowly raised his head to the far rim, on the west side where the bracken grew almost to the edge, fringed by tussocks. For a moment his eye was transfixed by the exotic border of glowing silk which undulated in the merest breeze, trailing like a white and lustrous banner across the edge of the canyon. He stared at it, puzzled, for a while longer and the sight of it, ethereal and magical on this cool and shrouded morning, helped damp down the rising tide of black fear.

The gossamer of a million tiny spiders, their gliding threads of silk-web, waved in the slow air, picking up the reflection of the roseate flush of dawn in the early sky. Danny gazed, mesmer-ized in a moment of rare beauty. The whole west rim of the valley, from the trees right on up past the hollow of rock, was limned with the slowly undulating silken tide. It was as if the world had been bedded in the cotton wool of mist and then wrapped in a cocoon of silk. The threads, rippling in glimmering sheets, seemed to bring a hush to the morning, giving an illusion of peace and harmony. As he watched, the top filaments caught the first sparkle of sun and up on the east edge, the sky flared in a spectacular flash of green and then pink, like an aurora, heralding the beginning of true day.

Way off, down at Blackwood, the cock crowed faint and far off again, to cut through the gossamer wrapping, and the moment of magic died as Corky's warning came suddenly back on the biblical echo of the dream.

He won't give us another chance after this.

Danny swivelled, nudging Tom, who gave a little shiver and tried to squeeze further in under his armpit, reluctant to come awake. He forced himself round towards Corky and sought the wire where he had tried to break through. A line of indentations roughened the metal about six inches from the loop around Corky's neck. In some places, the dull patina had been scraped away far enough to show the bright silver of metal underneath, showing how hard, how desperately Corky had worked and struggled in the dark of the night. Only the gouges and the shiny metal and the memory of the dreadful creaking sound remained.

Danny sighed slowly. Over to the right, the condom that Tom had filled was lying limp, like a shiny piece of intestine ripped from the raw fish. Doug sat frozen, head still cupped in his hands, elbows braced on his knees.

'I tried, Danny,' Corky's whispered voice jarred into the silence. For an awful moment Danny thought he was still dreaming. He jerked back, almost strangled himself on the wire, suddenly terrified in case Corky's teeth would be cracked stumps in bleeding gums.

'Couldn't get through,' he said. His face was pale, with his freckles standing out like sepia ink-spots. His eyes seemed grey in the light, and they looked bitterly forlorn. 'We're stuffed,' he added.

Danny shook his head. 'Don't say that,' he insisted.

'Say what?' Tom mumbled, coming awake. He shivered violently, strangled down a cough. Doug was blinking dopily. He sniffed and a thin trickle on his lip disappeared.

'Is Billy ok?' he asked. Danny shrugged.

'I think so. I haven't heard anything.'

'Doug, can you reach the end of the wire?' Corky asked. He couldn't see past Tom and Danny.

'No. I tried last night.' Doug's voice was just a soft hiss, barely above a whisper. In the silence of the valley, it sounded loud, too loud. 'It's out of reach.'

'Give it another go,' Corky said. He was stretching to see if his fingers could reach the root where the end of the baling twine was tied. His hand got to within six inches, but no amount of straining would expand the wire the way they'd been able to stretch the twine. It had been looped, right over left, then left over right, so even if they had risked trying to spin to unravel it, the turns around their necks would only have tightened with every turn. Doug tried once more, but couldn't get close. He was pulled away to the right, arm stretched out, face twisted into a toothy grimace. His outreaching fingers flexed in the air as he pulled as far as possible, reaching the very limit of give in the wire. He pulled further and his leg slipped on the wet grass, shooting right out in front of him. His toe hit the canvas sack which slid away with a tinny clank. Doug slipped back with a sudden, surprised gulp, pulling them all downwards with the drag on the wire. Tom gasped and tried to ease the stricture at his neck and Doug scrambled backwards to get to a sitting position before his air was cut off completely.

'Doug,' Danny hissed. 'Don't move.' This came out in a harsh rasp and, despite the discomfort, Doug immediately froze.

'What is it?' he managed to get out.

'Look,' Danny said urgently. 'At your feet.' Doug got to his elbows and looked down at his outstretched foot. The old, torn bag was only a foot or so from his toe.

'Can't see,' Corky said, straining to edge past Danny, who leant back just an inch or two, as much as he could. His breathing was now coming fast, excited.

'Bloody hell. It's been there all night,' Corky almost snarled, in an anger that boiled up on a sudden swell of hope.

'Can you get it?' Danny asked, hardly daring to speak, hardly daring to hope at all. Doug looked up at him, brows puckered up in a puzzled frown of incomprehension. Danny nodded at the bag.

'The tools!'

Light dawned. Doug's brows shot right up to disappear under his fringe of blond hair and his mouth dropped open. Tom started to shake again and suddenly the air was charged with that enormous, unbearable and brittle tension. Danny sensed time beginning to stretch out again on the surge of adrenaline and he felt all of his senses crystallize to glassy sharpness.

Doug lowered himself back down to the grass again and stretched his foot outwards. His toe touched the bag and he grinned hugely.

'Easy,' Corky hissed. Doug stretched and the bag moved.

'Can you hook it?' Danny asked, now feeling the panic rise up once more. Doug nodded, grunted, stretched until the wire was pulling right under his chin, digging in so far it was just a black line, as if his head had been cut off and stuck back again. A white bubble appeared from his nose, burst silently, and a lick of spittle flecked his lip where his teeth bit in tight. He concentrated on pushing and on ignoring the sudden hot strangle on his neck. They all watched in an agony of needing, each of them focused on that outstretched scuffed canvas boot that had seen plenty of better days. The toe got to the edge of the bag, barely to the corner. Doug made a low grunting sound that was all effort and concentration. The bag moved two inches, turning on the wet grass as it did so. Doug's foot slipped on the corner, came whipping across the side, and the bag slid away. Doug fell back heavily. They all heard the creak of the wire. Tom, still shaking with the wound-up tension, reached quickly and eased him up before he really did choke.

Danny's heart sank like a stone. The bag had been pushed out of reach, beyond Doug's ability to get his toe around it again and ease it backwards towards them.

'Shit,' Danny blurted. Corky said nothing. He was suddenly desperate to get the bag, to get a last chance, because he knew with complete conviction that this *would* be the last time, and that the crazy man with the twitchy eyes would do something terrible today. Today would be the end.

Just then, right at that moment, a movement downstream caught Danny's eye. He jerked his head and the others caught the sudden motion.

The heron came flapping down into the valley. It skirted the tall trees and swooped along the rim, stirring the silken gossamer spider webs with its passing. They sparkled and gleamed in the slanted rays of the rising sun, like filamented jewels. The big grey bird swerved, banked, then swooped low, over the top of the pooling mist close by the trees, then beat its wings slowly as it came flying upstream towards them.

'No,' Danny hushed. The heron followed the line of the stream, curving round at an angle at the point where Corky had been felled in the shallows of the lower pool. They all sat like stone, and all Danny could think about was that harsh alarm call. If it cried out it would wake the man, wake Twitchy Eyes, and they wouldn't have a chance.

The bird came flapping onwards. They could see the yellow of its eye, fixed and unblinking, and heard the low whoosh of its broad, slow wings. Danny waited, more acutely aware of the danger than the others. The heron had startled him and made him stumble up there on the high slope. His back still flared with the burn of the swollen skin.

'Shhhh.' He hushed at it, as if speaking to a child, as if he could will it to silence.

It came level with them, twisted in the air, as if suddenly aware of their presence, though none of them had moved a muscle. It veered sharply, pounding hard to gain height. Danny knew it would call out – *Kaark-kaaark* – knew that his bad luck would be back again, and final, too.

But it did not call out. The sweep of its wings trembled the three feathers of its dead mate in the mist at the waterfall, making them flutter like flags, and then it was gone, beyond their line of vision, beyond the low ridge where they sat under the roots. Corky breathed out.

'Try again,' he almost snarled. 'Go again, Doug.' All he could think about was the big pair of insulated pliers that Phil had jammed in with the rest of his stash. They could cut through mild steel. They could cut through fencing wire, no bother at all.

Doug tried again. He lowered himself back down again until he was lying almost flat, hands out to the side to brace himself. His foot went out to its full extent. He closed his eyes and gritted those teeth again. He made a little squeaking sound of effort and his long, bony frame seemed to elongate even further. Tom's eyes flicked from his foot to the wire around his neck, wondering how much more pressure Doug could take. Doug's face went red, then almost purple, shading down by degrees. He hooked his toe again, got it to the bag. Jerked. It slipped again.

Tom sighed in dismay. Corky said something under his breath

that sounded like a curse. Doug did not give up. He stretched even further, now making a gurgling sound in the back of his throat. His foot snicked the side of the bag and the old canvas handle flopped right down from the top side to land on top of his toe. Danny's heart was fluttering like a bird's, all out of control. He could feel the need to pant for breath, countered by the equally powerful compulsion to hold it in. Doug concentrated so hard his face was twisted as if it had been mashed. He eased his foot back and up. The loop of the handle followed, drew upwards, tight. Tom could see the wet canvas slipping over the rubber toe of the old baseball boot. Doug must have felt it and made a momentous decision. He kicked upwards. Something in the bag clunked again, muffled under the canvas, and the bag itself came right up off the ground.

For a heartbeat, it looked as if it would go tumbling off and land on top of the tent. Tom almost wailed in dismay. But at the very last moment, Doug managed to get enough purchase to flick it backwards. It took all of his strength and, as soon as that manoeuvre was finished, he flopped back, gasping for breath. Tom got his hands to the wire and slid his fingers between the metal and Doug's neck. Doug's face was suffused and swollen.

The bag came flipping backwards and hit Corky square on his chest with a heavy thud, hard enough to jar him backwards. Despite the sudden punch on his ribs, the joyful expression on Corky's face was incandescent. He raised his knees, almost reflexively, to prevent the bag from falling back, managing to cup it on his lap. He got a hand to the catch, loosened it with two blurring movements, dived his hand inside. For a scary split second, his mouth dropped open blankly as he fumbled inside, then lit up again. He drew his hand out, gripping the thick red pliers like a weapon.

Danny breathed out, sucked air back in again. 'You flippin' beauty,' he managed to mouth. He lifted the bag from Corky's lap and opened it out. A few tent-pegs remained, along with the ballpeen hammer they'd used to stick them into the turf. Doug's catapult lay in the bottom, along with Phil's old airgun. He took them out and laid them on the grass, searching for something else to cut the wire. There was nothing.

Corky raised the pliers up to the braid, gritting his teeth.

Before he even got a chance to squeeze, something shook the tent. A dull knocking sound came from inside, muffled by the fabric. The man snorted, as if just coming awake.

They all froze, nerves suddenly jangling, wound up tight as banjo strings.

The man's deep voice rolled out, though they couldn't make out the words. Corky's expression was suddenly stony and desolate; he was still sitting with both hands cocked up, gripping the inside jaws of the pliers against the twist of wire.

Bad luck, Danny thought, almost saying the words aloud. The heron had woken the man, somehow warning him of their escape attempt. Without thinking, he twisted his head round to look at the other heron's skull hanging in Billy's collection, what the man called his altar, half expecting the yellow eyes to be glaring at him mockingly. A flicker of white caught his eye. For an instant he couldn't make it out, then saw what it was. Pages of a book had been stuck to the spread of stag horns. Each page had been pierced with a sharp tine and left there like a pennant.

In that moment Danny realized it was the pages of the bible, pinned by horn, and in the same moment he realized that Corky would indeed be proved right. The man had torn pages of the bible and left them when he had killed people. He must have ripped them out last night in the dark, over by the skulls where he spoke to the shadows, talking to a man who wasn't there. If he'd torn the pages out, then he must be really going to do it.

'Oh, Jeez,' he muttered. Corky looked at him. Tom was cringing in again for heat or comfort or protection, and Danny felt he had none left to give. An emptiness yawned. Doug just stared at the tent, like that rabbit with the stoat.

Another rumble came out, very low. Billy said something. It sounded like a question. The man repeated whatever he said and Billy whimpered. Doug's teeth ground together like glass beads. A segment at the side of the tent bulged slowly and the whole thing shivered. The slit opened, expanding like a cat's eye and something white flashed in the interior darkness.

There will be weeping and gnashing of teeth . . . The words came back to Danny and he tried to shuck them away.

Doug jerked so hard that the wire creaked. Inside Danny the huge tidal wave of panic and utter dread was swelling to an enormous pressure. Both temples were pounding to the twisting beat of his heart. Tom was shaking once more, a human tuning-fork.

Corky put the pliers down on to the grass and for a moment the others wondered what he was doing. Very quickly he reached down, gripped the bottom of his shirt and hauled it up and over his head. A small green button flew off to the side and landed silently in the grass. Corky, working blind, placed the shirt up and over the braid of wire. He reached for the pliers, got them in under the bundled garment, wrapped the whole fabric tight around it so that both hands were hidden from view. The realization struck Danny and his surge of panic subsided under the fierce blast of admiration for Corky's practical thinking.

Corky closed his eyes, as if in prayer. His stocky shoulders flexed, tanned and muscular. Up under his shirt, a metallic click jarred out, very loud in their ears, too loud. As soon as the jaws of the pliers cut the wire and met, all Corky heard was the sound of the shotgun's firing pin slamming down on the empty chamber. The sounds were almost identical. A flare of anger suddenly seared inside him. Without any hesitation, he unrolled the shirt, put the pliers down and got his fingers to the braid of wire, working at the twists to unravel them. They jangled musically, but in only a few seconds, he had reached the braid at his neck, spun the wires and was free. The thin strands dropped away with a slight vibration.

There was no hesitation now. Danny was jittering, feet moving up and down on the turf in a frantic little dance that was close to hysteria. Corky got to his knees, twisted, brought his shirt up again. Danny could see he had two bruises on his ribs, the size of fists, where he had fallen when the man kicked him. His eyes were alight and alive and suddenly glittering with determination and anger.

He insulated the pliers again in the roll of shirt, squeezed hard. The metal snicked again, more quietly than before, right in against Danny's neck. He felt all the braids part in a snap. One of the edges stuck into the skin of his neck with a needle burn, but there was no pain and no blood.

Over in the tent, the man snored or snorted again, like a pig in a thicket.

Quickly yet very deliberately, Corky moved past Danny, did the same for Tom, moved on and snapped the cutting jaws down to free Doug, who raised his hands up to his neck. The bite of the metal had left a thin, fierce, red mark, exactly as if his head had been stuck on his body.

The tent vibrated. Maybe the man had rolled his weight against the nearest pole.

'What about Billy?' Tom asked in a tight little whisper.

Leave him! Danny's first, dreadful thought bubbled up before he had time to get a hold of it and stuff it back down. *We could get away!* Corky looked at them all, his eyes now more green than grey, his chest heaving. He put his cord shirt back on, pulling it fast over his head. Sweat was dripping from his brow and soaking his cow's-lick hair into little spikes.

'We have to get him,' Doug said, and it was probably the bravest, the most selfless thing, that any of them had ever heard. Billy and Doug had always been at loggerheads, were for ever sniping at each other. On the night before the twitchy-eyed stranger had appeared, they had savaged one another, stripping each of a protective coat, using a dreadful and devastating knowledge as a weapon. Now, in one short phrase, Doug Nicol redeemed himself from anything he had said in a display of the most noble and courageous altruism.

Danny bit down on the shameless little voice of unreasoning fear.

Corky raised a finger to his lips, quite superfluously demonstrating the need for silence. He moved like an Indian, feet making no sound, away from the little ridge where they'd sat all night, first towards the corner where Billy's old sheath knife had been thrown. He picked it up, jammed it into his belt, and then came halfway back again. The mist by the stream was almost gone, trailing its way downstream as the sun rose. Danny got a flash of iridescence from up on the east ridge where the gossamer sparkled in sunlight that was risen over on the moor. The morning grey was already melting to blue.

Without any hesitation, Corky moved, deliberately but stealthily, towards the pile of logs they'd hauled up from the trees.

Over in the tent, the noise came louder. A bulky shape of a shoulder pushed against the wall of the tent. The man was awake. Or he was waking.

Tom was still shaking, looking around them in confusion and fear, wondering what to do.

Corky lifted a thick spruce branch that had been pulled out from the trunk and had a heavy knot at the thick end. Most of the branches were that shape, because the limbs always split away like that when tall conifers fell. He hefted it like a club, which indeed it was. Danny realized what he intended and hurried across, denying and defying the creepy little voice that ordered him to run, to get up that slope and over the top and away home. He reached the firewood pile, selected a thick branch a yard long, pulled it out. The rest of the branches tumbled to the side in a scuffle of wood. Everybody froze yet again. Over in the tent, there was a silence, only for a few seconds. The man snorted again. A round shape, up from the shoulder, bulged the canvas, moving in slow rhythm.

Corky crept up again, holding the branch like a twisted baseball bat. He got to the side where the slit opened and close to the pushing of the shape inside. He bent down, suddenly tense, like a squat hunter facing a leery, spooked and dangerous beast that could charge out from a thicket. Inside, in the shadows, he saw movement. There was the red of Billy's T-shirt and beyond that the curve of a thick elbow. The one tattooed word stood out clearly, even in the shadow.

He stood up, turned to them. He nodded very solemnly across the short distance, and they saw his eyes were set like polished stones, glaring with a light of their own. His mouth drew back at the edges until his gritted teeth could be clearly seen. He eased the branch forward, head nodding a little to some beat only he could hear. Danny realized he was timing it with the motion inside the tent.

'Fucking bastard,' he grated in a low, hoarse voice, swinging the heavy branch up and then down in a fast arc, putting all of his strength into it. The heavy knot of wood at the club-end slammed against the rounded curve which pushed out against the fabric.

A noise like a pistol shot cracked out, a sharp shock in the charged air. Corky's club splintered and the thick end broke off and went spinning away towards the undergrowth, making a whirring sound, like dragonflies' wings, as it flew. On the other side of the canvas, a deep, somehow mindless groan rumbled out. The rounded hump in the fabric slid down towards the ground. Billy whimpered, high and quivering. Danny stepped past Corky who was standing there with only the shaft of his stick in his hands. He raised his own club, slammed it down on the shape. It was not as loud as the first whiplash crack, but duller, somehow deadly. Another groan, more a whoosh of expelled air, followed. Danny felt his club strike something hard, which moved only a little with the blow. Again he remembered the sound of the bullocks down in the slaughter-house chamber when the malletmen fired the bolt into their brains.

The tent quivered. A violent blow rocked it and then there was a thud and the sound of splintering wood. Something snapped the far upright and the whole thing tilted, caving in at one side, billowing at the side where Danny had cut the escape slit. Billy's hand reached out, palm down, then withdrew. He cried out. Two of the ropes snapped with sudden, high, almost musical notes and a tent-peg came shooting out of the ground to spin right over the tent and land by the circle of stones round the cold fire. The canvas pulled away from the groundsheet. The butt of the shotgun lay half exposed.

Tom grabbed the gun. He stood there, strange for a moment, baffled and undecided. The tent collapsed with a sudden snap of more ropes. The man was groaning now, *really groaning*, like an animal. The sound was deadly and awful, even more mindless than before. A large hand appeared under the frame of the bottom edge, fingers spread wide. A shape slumped against the billowing side. Billy's legs, feet still in his baseball boots, were sticking out on the front side, knees scrabbling for purchase. Tom spun the gun around, so that it was butt first, and ran in, now moving quickly and smoothly. He raised it up, swung it hard. The edge slammed the head-shape.

And the gun roared.

The noise was like sudden, catastrophic thunder, this close in and in the confines between the tent and the hollow. Tom felt an enormous punch jar through his arm. He felt the sear of fire from the end of the barrel as the shot belched scant inches away from his side. By a sheer miracle, when the butt connected, both barrels in his hands had not been pointing directly at him. The shot would have cut him in half.

The gun jumped out of his hands.

Less than twenty yards away, the rotten deer's skull and its decoration of bible pages exploded into fragments as the spread of shot knocked it straight out of the hawthorn branches. The white ram's head tumbled down and cracked against a hard rock, splitting into two halves. The heron's pointed head disappeared, along with half the foliage from the tree. The altar, in one cataclysmic blast, was gone.

The roar of the gun echoed on and on, as it had the first time, crackling in their ears. In the ruins of the tent, the twitchy-eyed stranger slumped down to the ground. Tom stood transfixed, face now white as the quartz. Corky ran in, grabbed the gun, turned it around and put the barrel down to the hidden head, jamming it right against where the ear would be.

Billy came out of the fallen tent, crawling fast. Danny saw his face. It was blank and awful. There was a streak of dark on his leg.

'See how you like it, you crazy fucking *bastard*!' Corky grated, not screaming, but low and straight and coldly feral. When he swore, he really meant it. He held steady, squeezed the trigger. All of them, except Billy, who was still stumbling to his feet, now dumbly trying to get into his jeans, braced themselves for the close blast.

Nothing happened. The hammer clicked again on the empty chamber. The metallic sound was not as loud as it had seemed the first time. The man was groaning loudly now, and rocking about under the canvas, blundering his way around. Corky looked at the gun as if he'd been betrayed, standing stock-still for several seconds. Then he moved, broke it open, looked into the empty chambers.

'Only had one shell,' he said. Danny felt a sudden seethe of resentment against Tom for wasting the last one, but it died instantly. Corky dropped the gun. The man groaned again, this time much louder and his head nodded up and down, jammed in against the corner. A stain of blood spread on the canvas. Danny could smell it. Billy was on his feet.

'Kill him,' he said in a shivery voice. 'Kill him, somebody. *Please*.'

The tent rolled to the side and the man's feet could be seen now, pushing against the trampled grass and ferns, scraping to get a purchase. He was struggling to get out, groaning and moaning wordlessly the whole time, like a wounded bull, trying to get free of the constraint. Doug ran to the fire, picked up a smooth rock in both hands, came striding back, straight towards the commotion inside the tent. He raised it up high, using his whole body, brought it down, crouching as he did. The rock hit something which snapped like a branch. This time the man roared, like a mad bull. His legs kicked out. One foot caught Doug on the shin and almost felled him. The stone rolled away.

'Kill him,' Billy quavered, very softly, but as powerful as any shriek. '*Kill him*.'

Doug backed off to stand beside Tom, who was holding on to Danny. Corky ran forward, tugging at the knife at his belt, leapt upon the humping shape. They could see his elbow jerk back. Once, twice, three times, each movement followed by a forward punch and a sudden, thudding sound. The canvas blossomed a flower of dark, wet sheen.

The man's roar stopped dead. He let out a long wavering moan that tailed away.

'Jesus, oh fuckin' Jesus God.' This from Doug who stood there, mouth agape. Corky backed off. Everything stopped for several seconds. The man's feet went still. His shape, rolled up in the bundle of canvas, lay long and prone. The blood formed a patch a hand-span wide at the far end. Halfway down, an even wider patch glistened and spread very quickly.

'Is he dead? Is he dead?' Billy was asking. He'd pulled his jeans up, but Danny could still smell the blood on him, and the cold, stale sweat of the stranger. His face was strangely slack, as if all the nerves had gone to sleep, but his eyes were dark and feral, almost the way the twitchy-eyed man's had been when he looked at the brightness in the water.

He spun, crossed to the bag, grabbed up the ballpeen hammer that lay on the grass and ran towards the prone man. He raised it up and slammed it down, not aiming, just hitting. It made meaty thuds where it landed. Billy's arm raised up and plunged down half a dozen times, before he stumbled back, panting very hard. He stood up, eyes fixed at first on the still shape.

Everybody turned to look at Billy. For a moment, he was fixed on the prostrate form, as if he wanted to continue, to keep on hitting with the hammer. A trickle of saliva drooled from his mouth and, in that moment, he looked completely mad. After a moment, he dropped the hammer. He backed off, and then realized they were all looking at him. An odd flicker crossed his face. Danny recognized it as deep and devastating shame, and his heart went out to him. Corky put a hand out and touched him on the shoulder, the way Tom had done to himself on the night of the big argument. It was just a touch, but it said a huge amount. In his other hand, Corky held the knife. Despite what he had done with it, the blade was surprisingly clean.

There was a silence for a long moment.

CHAPTER THIRTY-THREE

Corky stuck the knife in the loop of his belt. His chest was heaving up and down with the huge effort. They were all panting like wolves after a long chase and a desperate fight. They were stunned to immobility at the enormity of what they had done. The stain spread on the canvas. Some blood pooled where the grass had been flattened by the groundsheet. It was surprisingly dark.

'Jesus God,' Doug finally murmured, awestruck.

'Is he dead?' Billy whispered. His face was still white and bloodless. His hands were now trembling, fluttering like birds. Tom's mouth opened, closed, opened again. No sound came out.

'Hope so,' Corky said, with awful, grim finality. 'Come on. We'd better get out of here.'

'What about him?' Danny asked. 'We can't just leave him, can we?'

'Why not?' Doug said. 'He's going nowhere.' He went to the bag and picked up his slingshot and the gun. He handed the pistol to Tom, who took it soundlessly and let it dangle from his hand.

'We should burn him,' Billy said and they all stopped. 'We should make a fire and burn him. Nobody would ever know.' Danny looked at him and recognized the bleak and terrible shame at what the man had done to him in the tent.

'What do you think, Corky?' Doug asked, deferring now. They had all hit, all of them. But Corky had been the first, and then he'd gone in with the knife to make sure, right up close, *man to man*, where he could actually touch the twitchy-eyed madman, stabbing through the canvas sheet.

Corky turned and his face was still hard and set, bleaker even than Billy's. He was considering the best option. His eyes stared into the far distance, his mouth drawn down. After a while he nodded.

'That might be the best idea,' he said. 'Get all the gear together.'

Without hesitation, no arguing now, they started collecting their haversacks, trying not to look at the collapsed tent and the butterfly bloodstain on the fabric, but unable to keep their glances from straying. It pulled them like a magnet. Doug put the hammer back in the bag. 'What about the tent?'

'It stays. Burn it all. Phil can swipe another,' Corky said. His voice was distant and somehow coldly implacable. They'd never use the tent again.

Tom stuck the gun in his own belt-loop and gingerly approached the rumple of canvas where the pole had broken and speared right through the top. His own bag was lying half concealed by the old groundsheet, tucked on the grass that had been blanched by the four days without sunlight. He reached, got a hand to the strap, pulled, but the bag stayed where it was. He lifted a torn flap, found the strap was looped round the bottom of the broken spar and reached to free it, when the whole tent suddenly bucked. Tom's feet were pulled from under him and he fell on top of the pile.

A hellish roar boomed out, the huge bellow of a wild beast. Tom squawked in alarm and Billy got such a shock he stumbled backwards and tripped over the rock Doug had used as a weapon.

The man screamed, in anger or in pain, none of them could tell. A hand clawed out, clamped itself on the first thing it touched. It was Tom's leg. The fingers gripped like a vice and Tom yelled out in real pain and awful fright. His left leg kicked out at the wrist, trying to break free.

Corky ran forward on the far side, grabbed the gun, raised it up quickly and slammed it down on the bucking shape. He couldn't reach the hand that was holding Tom, otherwise the blow would easily have broken a wrist. The harsh and ragged roar cut off instantly and the fingers snapped open. The shape under the canvas rolled and Tom had to scramble out of the way. Both feet were now out from the encumbrance, digging into the ground as the man tried to force himself up to his knees. Despite the blood, he was twisting and turning with incredible strength.

He bellowed, a howl of fury, clawed his way out of the far end until his head pushed through the rent in the fabric. One eye was horribly *slumped* as if the whole eyebrow and half the cheek-bone had caved in. It made him seem to look in two different directions. Blood was streaming from both nostrils and his mouth was dripping both blood and saliva. He was snarling now, jerking from side to side to free himself from the restraint and he fixed his good eye on Corky, who backed away fast.

Doug and Tom had backed further and faster, right to the edge of the stream. Danny was helping Billy to his feet, scared almost witless, but still able to feel the jittery vibration that was making Billy's whole body quiver like a bowstring.

There were no words now, just the guttural, savage snarl of the man they'd thought was dead. The fact that he had come alive again was even more frightening. It made him, despite the appalling dent in his head and the pooling of the blood on the hard ground, somehow invincible and indestructible. He was fighting his way out, now halfway to his feet, one hand and arm completely free. He pushed violently and the canvas ripped with a high whine. Doug backed into Tom, who almost fell into the stream. The man pointed at Corky, still grunting and snarling, pointed straight at him. The threat was shockingly eloquent.

The other hand came up now, and in it was a large knife they had not seen before. Corky saw it flash in the morning light. It looked like a butcher's knife. The blade came down and slashed at the canvas, slitting it like paper.

Corky turned, pushed at Danny and Billy. 'Run,' he bawled. Tom and Doug needed no more urging. They went pattering across the stream, sending up spray. Danny and Billy followed, moving fast, crossed the water in four strides and got up the low bank on the far side. Behind them, the man was screeching now, his mad fury echoing from the high sides in a stuttering reverberation of noise.

Up the bank and along the low path on the far side they scrambled, now panicked into flight. The crazy man had the knife now and no matter what had happened, they were still just boys. Danny pushed at Billy, who was whimpering now. A dark stain had appeared on the seat of Billy's jeans and Danny realized it was blood. He urged him on and, behind him, Corky was trying to get them to go faster. He shoved him in the back, sending a howl of pain down the length of Danny's spine.

They got to the track that led up the narrow gully. Doug reached the broad part first and, despite his fear, he risked a look back. The man was right out of the ruined tent now, half naked, with his dirty jeans pooled around his feet. He hauled them up, still snarling, and somehow managed to fasten them without dropping the knife. As soon as he finished that motion, he was moving, running across the turf, over the ridge where he'd sat with Billy roped to the shotgun, down the shallow bank, and started across the stream. They all heard the splashing of his progress and Tom yelped in panic.

'Move!' Corky bawled. 'Come on. We can go faster than him.'

Whether he believed that was another matter, but he urged them all on, up the slope. He knew that if they couldn't kill the man with the hammer and the clubs and the stone while he was rolled up and trapped in the tent, or if he wouldn't die with a knife-blade stabbed three times into him, they had no chance when he was on his feet and crazier still with pain and anger. He sounded like a wounded tiger and Corky had read all the stories about wounded animals. He looked up at the top of the ridge, estimated the sounds of splashing behind him, gauged the distance.

They might make it. They just *might*.

Doug, followed by Tom, was on the broad turn into the gully where they'd discovered the backed-up lake behind the narrow cleft. Here the slope was very steep and the track narrowed to six inches, the kind of groove sheep make when they climb to the high pasture, or down to the stream for a drink. The grit was dry and powdery, occasionally broken by a line of pale, hard mudstone which gave firmer footing, but the surface still kept slipping from under their feet.

Billy made the flat and got to the track, Danny pushing him all the way, with Corky right on their heels. The man was about forty yards behind them, now snarling words which were all jammed together until they were totally incomprehensible. None of the fleeing boys mistook their content.

They scampered across the steepening slope, traversing it, moving like startled roe-deer. Even Billy was going at a rate. He was sobbing now, in fear and despair, and if Danny hadn't been at his back, goading him like a mule-driver, he would have collapsed in terror and waited for the end.

The gully took a turn here, allowing them a downhill run, first of all to scutter across the shallow rivulet and then up the far side, which was steeper than this one. They all went down in a tight line, panting for breath, using the momentum to get as far up the other side as they could. Shale and grit slid out from under them. Tom slid back two yards and Doug stopped in his flight, leant back, bracing his foot on a stone slab, to haul him back again.

The man came lumbering round the bend. Danny glanced back, saw the red stain on his side, just under the curve of ribs. Blood was soaking the waistband of the jeans. The caved-in face looked even more insane, like a monstrous gargoyle, but the man was still coming after them. Danny's heart tried to leap into his mouth and an awful pounding started up in his temples again. His foot slipped and he lost some height. Corky blocked him, preventing him sliding further, and pushed hard, getting him back up again.

They clambered up the slope, now so steep that one wrong step would tumble them down. The whole face was slipping and sliding with the vibration of their passage. Tiny avalanches of shale hissed and whispered, dislodged to trickle down towards the rivulet. By sheer luck and sheer determination, they got closer to the top. Beyond the fringe of bracken at the edge, there was a grassy corrie that went back for several yards to a hollow, rock-filled basin, before another much steeper climb up on to the moor.

Doug made it to the lip, clambered over, turned, hauled Tom up with one brutal and surprisingly strong heave that flipped him right up from the slope to land on his belly. Billy reached up. Doug clasped the hand in his own in a desperate handshake. He braced himself for Billy's weight, leant back, grunted, and dragged the heavy boy up to the flat. Corky pushed Danny up and Danny then turned, offered his hand. Corky took both it and Doug's. Together they heaved him over. Down the slope, just crossing the rivulet, the man came blundering on, still ranting at the top of his voice.

Corky quickly spun round, searched the flat turf. Over by the next steep wall he found a hand-sized piece of mudstone which he grabbed and hefted. Danny picked up a thick stick that had fallen from one of the trees that had managed to find root on the almost sheer face. He turned. Corky braced himself, pivoted on one foot in a movement just like a baseball pitcher, and lobbed the stone. It whirred audibly in the air, spinning as it flew.

It missed by a good yard and the man ignored it. Corky turned away, pushed Doug. 'Come on,' he yelled. Tom had crossed the flat and gone down into a little dip of a hollow at the base of the corrie and was just beginning to go up the slope. Small stones rolled out from under his feet. Danny crossed to the edge. The man was only thirty yards behind them now, almost vertically below them. He swung the curved branch in an easy loop and winged it downwards. It spun like a boomerang, whirled like the stick that had dropped the heron out of the sky.

It took the man right on the side of the head, where his eyebrow and cheekbones were caved in, and knocked him backwards. The man's hands shot out and the knife spun away. He peeled away from the shale face the way Danny had done, but he only fell backwards on to the soft scree of the lower slope, his shoulders digging into the gravel. Particles of shale dropped on top of him and glued themselves to the slick trail of blood on his side and on the top of his jeans.

'Great shot,' Corky gasped. He favoured Danny with a look of rueful admiration, gave him a quick, desperate grin. 'Come on, now. Let's go.' Danny backed away from the edge, still hoping that the man might have broken his back in the fall, but even before Corky hauled him back, across the level area of the little corrie towards the far face and the last climb, he saw the man shake himself and roll over, stumbling to his knees, to his feet. He scraped away the shale where the knife had landed, uncovered it, snarled even more ferally and came on, pushing his way up the slope. Danny had gained them maybe twenty yards.

The final climb was a killer, but it was the only way to the top. Here the slope was powdery soft, up at the height where there was no drain water to bind it. Pieces of mudstone flipped out and went rolling down under their feet, but there was no other way to go. This part of the climb narrowed in at an angle to the place where they'd played before. The rock on each side of the angle was sheer and offered no handholds save the gnarled and dead roots of old hawthorn trees that hadn't survived the impossibly precarious hold, but they were too far apart, and would probably pull out of the anchorages at the first tug. The only way up was the steep gravel slope where they could dig their feet in for purchase and push and haul at each other.

It was hard going. The first climb had tired them all out, and the fear and panic inside them was even more exhausting. Tom, smallest, weakest of them all, was beginning to flag. His knees were shaking so violently he was convinced he'd simply pitch off the side and go tumbling down to the scattered scree rocks in the corrie. He was breathing hard and fast, hauling for air. Behind him, Doug sounded like the old pair of bellows in the organ in the church hall. Some thick saliva had stuck at the back of his throat and was making a little musical monotone. He kept pushing at Tom, forcing him on, getting him higher.

Billy was struggling now because his heavier weight crushed the shale footholds to powder and made it easier for him to slip backwards, but Danny and Corky shoved at him, holding him up. Danny could smell the blood on him. Billy was whimpering in between breaths, loud and blubbery.

Up and over. Up and over. The litany was going through Danny's head, the way it had done when he tried to climb the last time, before the heron startled him and sent the rock crashing down to wake the man and wake the gun. His back was burning now, rasping with the scrape of his shirt across the skin, but it was only hot, not agony. He and Corky were almost level, clambering up as best they could while goading Billy on.

Tom got to the top. This time he made it over the high edge with a desperate shove from Doug. He turned to help Doug over, stopped and pointed straight down.

'Come on, Danny. *Move!*' His high-pitched cry was urgent and fearful. Danny couldn't risk looking back. He could hear the man's growling, ferocious snarling sounds in the back of his throat. If Tom could see him, that meant he was over the corrie edge and heading for the slope. Danny felt the unbearable urge to stop and look, just in case the man was *on* the slope. His muscles wanted to freeze solid. He felt like the rabbit hunted by the stoat.

'Move it, Danny Boy,' Corky said through gritted teeth. 'We can make it.'

Up at the top, Tom and Doug were bawling, jumping up and down, so close to the edge that one stumble would tumble them down to the corrie again, to land them right at the man's feet. They were yelling desperate encouragement. Billy was ten yards from the lip, almost completely exhausted. It was getting harder for the others to push him.

The sneaky little coward's voice tried to override the litany inside Danny's head.

Leave him! We can make it!

He tried to ignore it despite the huge surge of fear at the knowledge that Twitchy Eyes was right behind him with that big butcher's knife in his hand, ready to cut and slice the way he'd cut and sliced Don Whalen and that girl in the dark of the bomb-shelter. And underneath it all was the paralysing dread that the man was unstoppable; that he would not tire, that he'd keep on coming. Danny recalled the almighty crack of the club on the man's head, a devastating blow that should have felled anybody, and yet, despite the caved-in bone and the *slump* of his head, he was still after them, like a monster from some terrible myth.

Up and over. The top edge was ten yards away. *Leave him. We can make it.* He pushed on, felt Corky's hand on his back. *Up and over. Jesus, please us, oil and grease us.* Nine yards, eight. Corky slid back and Danny got him by the waistband. The knife wobbled in its makeshift holder, but stayed put. Danny pushed him hard and Corky gained a yard. The edge loomed. Behind him, the growling was getting louder as the man saw, with his one good eye, that they would reach it before he caught them. Tom and Doug could see him about a hundred feet behind. He had taken a run at the slope, slipped, fallen several feet and started up from a standstill just above the little scoop of the hollow.

Billy got to the top. Both boys dragged him over, with the other two pushing from behind. He got over, flopped and lay still, his feet sticking out over the drop. Danny made it, helped

Corky up, crawled forward through the couch grass, fingers snatching at the tussocks to pull himself along. His chest ached with the shale dust that had rasped his windpipe and lungs. He was panting like an animal. Corky fell beside him, retched violently, but brought nothing up.

'Come on,' Doug begged. 'Corky. Danny. Come *on*, now.'

'Get up, Billy,' Tom was cajoling on the other side. Billy was gabbling, unable to speak, arms flapped out on each side, as if all of his strength had gone. He looked finished. Tom hauled his exposed feet over the edge and on to the grass; Billy twisted, turning his face up to the sky.

The morning sun was just rising into the blue over the slope of the high moor and the whole sky was ablaze with light.

Corky got to his feet, pushing himself with his flagging strength. He went back to the ledge and peered down. The man was less than seventy feet below them, coming on with dreadful doggedness. He seemed to have huge reserves and they had drained theirs. Corky looked back at the long slope of the moor ahead. It was not a huge climb, but it was still a height, and uphill all the way to the shoulder before the long run down to the barwoods and the old bomb craters, and then down to the edge of town. If he kept on coming, he could catch them, one or two of them, before the brow.

'Why doesn't he stop?' he gasped.

Doug whipped out his catapult and loaded a small stone, pulled, fired, and hit Twitchy Eyes a glancing blow on the shoulder. He completely ignored it. Danny dragged Billy to his feet and pulled his arm round his own shoulder, doing his best to silence the creepy little voice in his head which told him Billy wasn't worth it. They staggered along the path towards the tree whose roots overhung the steep ravine where they'd played before.

Below them, the man was snarling again, forcing his way upwards. Doug could see that his eyes, at least the one eye that looked up at them, was flickering away with its madness. Fear and fury made Doug hawk and spit, but nothing came out of his dry mouth. They were going past the tree, moving as fast as they could, all in a line, with Danny still helping Billy, when Corky suddenly shouted at them to hold up.

'We'll never get away, not up there,' he said, pointing at the remorseless rise of the moor. 'He'll catch us for certain unless we stop him.'

'How can we stop him?' Doug wanted to know. 'He's got the knife.'

'What about this?' Tom said, pulling the gun from his waistband. It had stayed fixed there the whole time they'd climbed, despite slips and falls.

Doug grabbed it, pulled the lever which opened it. There was one slug in the slot, despite the fact that he couldn't remember anybody loading it since the time Billy had fired one at his backside and sparked off the big argument. He turned on his heel, with Corky beside him, and went back to the edge. The man had gained, clambering sideways to traverse the flat, steep face of the slope, getting right underneath them, the good eye still twitching madly.

'Let me,' Corky said.

'You couldn't hit a barn if you were inside it,' Doug said, biting down on his bottom lip. The low morning sun caught his big cupped ears and made them redly translucent. He closed one eye, took aim and fired.

A small crack, like a thin whip, and the gun bucked. The lead slug, slowed by the weak spring, flicked in the sunlight, just a blur, but it hit the man in the grotesque, damaged eye, and he screeched, clawing up with his free hand. The noise of his bellow echoed out from the cup of the corrie and right along the valley. He slid back five yards, and despite whatever pain the pellet had caused, he still dug in at the shale with the knife to brake his fall. He bellowed again, turned, and began traversing once more.

'Good shot, Doug,' Corky said. The gun was empty and there were no more slugs.

'We could make it up there,' Doug said.

'You and me and Dan,' Corky admitted. 'But not Billy or wee Tom. He'd cut them to bits.'

'Maybe he'll stop.'

'No,' Corky said, dreadfully convinced. 'This one won't ever stop. He's a fuckin' devil.'

He pulled back from the edge and went along the track, casting about for rocks to roll down, but here, the thick turf of the moorland grass covered everything. There were no rocks here. The others were at the tree now, where they'd been playing, the three of them, when the man had stepped across the stream and made Billy eat the fish. They scurried past, urging the others on, when Danny held up his hand and stopped them.

'What's that?' he asked, pointing at the tree.

The two black weights sat on the thick branches that had been pulled back from the forked double trunk and tied to the curving roots.

'It's the bombs,' Tom said. 'Come on. Come on.'

'Hells bells,' Doug said. Corky moved forward.

'We can use them,' he said. 'Brain the bastard.' The baling twine was looped round the branch, which had been pulled back so far it almost formed a complete circle, and several thick strands had been needed to lash it to the root. It was four inches thick and it had taken all their muscle to pull it back to the root. Corky drew the sheath knife from his belt and started hacking at the string.

'You go on,' he said, turning to Tom and Billy. The two of them turned away but, as soon as Corky started sawing at the thick twine, they stopped. Corky hacked and cut and, all the while, over the edge, they could hear the grunting breath of the man's progress. Danny could visualize him, covered in blood and shale dust, his caved eye looking down at his cheek, the knife glinting in the early morning sun. He could visualize him trailing after them up the moor, slashing and cutting, hacking away at them, snarling like a beast all the while.

'Come on!' he begged Corky, itching to be away, to be off and running.

Three strands parted with a machine-gun stutter and the branch uncoiled by about six inches. Corky cut again, got a fourth string to break, a fifth. The bomb rolled out of the fork where it had lain and tumbled to the ground. It started to roll down the gradient towards the edge.

'Get it, quick!' Corky yelled. Doug dived, got both hands to the rolling shape. It slipped, rolled more, and he caught it again, managing to stop it before it flipped uselessly over the side. He gasped with effort, heaved it back, and Corky went to help him. Together they lifted the heavy, deadly shape into their arms and together they carried it to the edge. Corky peered down.

'Where is he?' Doug tried to shrug, but with the weight in his arms, he failed in the attempt.

Just at that moment, the sixth and seventh strings broke with a sudden, unexpected crack and the bent-back branch lashed forward, so violently it smacked against another, thicker bough and the whole tree shuddered to its roots. Several stones dislodged by the vibration shot out from under the overhang and went tumbling down the face. Just then the stranger appeared in view, round the little, jutting point that had hidden him from up above. He looked up, saw the small avalanche, pulled back and waited until it was gone. He was crossing this part of the face, right under the tree, over the basin of the little corrie, maybe forty feet below them.

'I'll tell you when,' Corky said. This time Doug nodded. 'One, two, three and go?'

Another nod. Doug sniffed. Tom and Billy stood watching, unable to move.

The man was crossing the curve now. Corky gauged the distance, counted it out to himself, then looked at Doug. He counted it aloud this time, each number accompanied by a swing forward, each swing greater than the last.

'Go,' Corky bawled. They both grunted with the effort, and the heavy bomb sailed out, fins back. It turned in the air, fins up, dropped straight down.

The man looked up, saw the black shape plummet towards him. He jerked backwards and the bomb missed him by less than a foot. Had it connected, it would have slammed him right off the slope to tumble to the rocks below. It might even have killed him.

But it missed. The man spun, and began to slide slowly downwards, trying to grab for a hold, but gathering speed, losing almost all of the height he had gained. He came to rest in a little pile of accumulated shale, digging into its soft surface.

Corky said nothing. His disappointment was almost overwhelming. He spun away from the edge, hands balled into tight fists.

'Nothing's going to stop him,' he grated through teeth that were clenched into a straight line.

'Going to get you,' the man bellowed up. 'Going to get you all. The flies are going to get every one of you.' He laughed, high and manic, as insane as ever. Doug felt another shiver travel up and down his spine. Corky ignored the noise. He stormed over to the tree, raised a hand and slammed it against Billy's chest.

'I thought I told you to move?' he bawled. Billy took a step back. 'You want him to catch you? Get a bloody move on!'

Once again, Billy moved back. Corky looked at him, made a little motion of his head to let Billy know it was just the anger and the hurt and the madness of it all. He turned back to the tree. The second bomb was on its own branch, which was lashed the same way, to the thick loop of roots.

'The next one might work,' Corky said. 'Want to try it?'

Danny and Doug both nodded. The beast had slipped down the slope. They had gained yards. They had gained moments.

Corky took the knife and cut at the twine as before, sawing back and forth, peering down between the roots. Below him he could see the top of the man's head. He was moving on all fours, even more animal now than before, gabbling non-stop.

'*Kill you. Kill all of you. Nothing left. Not a thing.*'

He was right below the tree, gaining some height, close to the bottom of the slope. The other bomb was about twenty yards to the right, beyond the lip of the little corrie, lying on its side, two fins dug into the shale. It looked like a small, beached submarine. Corky sawed, and again, three strands stuttered apart. The jar as the branch jerked straighter by two inches shook the tree once more. This time, little stones bulleted out from underneath the overhang in a series of punchy little flicks. Corky cut again, reaching out over the drop. As he did so, his foot slipped, just enough to throw him off balance. Danny reached to grab him by the collar and stop him falling over the edge.

The motion altered Corky's swipe with the knife. It swung round in an arc and caught the pieces binding the branch to the root, slashing through more than half of them. There was another fast series of snaps, one after the other, as the thick twine parted in staccato, ripping sequence. Corky reached out for the bomb which sat on the branch, thinking he could pull it free.

Below them, Twitchy Eyes was coming, grunting and yammering. The tree creaked. They could see the branch, arm-thick and torqued, try to unbend in a slow-motion flex.

'Corky,' Danny bawled. 'Watch out. The whole thing's going . . . *it's going to . . .*'

CHAPTER THIRTY-FOUR

. . . It's going to . . .

The bindings parted with a savage crack. All of them gave at the same time and the thick branch whipped up, swiping through the air in a vicious whoop. It unleashed in a blur, uncoiling as all the latent tension punched upwards, like the arm of a siege catapult. The sudden violent motion threw Corky backwards.

'. . . Go!'

Danny blurted the word just as Corky slammed into him. Both of them landed beside Doug on the short, tough grass only inches from the drop-off. Danny instinctively grabbed a thick tuft to stop the pair of them rolling over the edge and tumbling down the scree.

The forked branch carried the bomb up, reached the end of its span, slammed against the cross-trunk, and once again the whole tree shook from the roots upwards in a seismic shudder. A scattering of leaves exploded outwards. The branch hit the trunk, rebounded, slammed in again and stopped dead, but the bomb simply kept on travelling, almost straight up into the air, thrown off its cradle with the huge and sudden acceleration.

It went on up, a black and heavy shape, soaring into the sky, wobbling just a little on its tail. The fins were clearly outlined against the cloudless blue of the morning.

'Christ on a bike, I thought it got you,' Doug gasped, but only Danny heard him, and he very faintly. His attention was fixed on the rising, black bomb. Corky was lying athwart him, face up, mouth agape. Over on the far side, beyond the tree, Billy and Tom stood, eyes wide, stunned by the catapult crack that had sounded so much like a pistol-shot, sounded too much like the sound of a club against a skull.

The bomb was travelling upwards, thick and massive, a solid black Zeppelin, defying gravity. Its ascension transfixed them all.

Danny's breathing stopped and the whole world seemed to freeze into a sludgy slow-motion. The bomb rose up and up.

'*It's going to . . . it's going to . . .*' His own words were still ringing in his ears, along with the air-shattering crack of the branch slamming the cross-trunk, and Doug's blurt, all of them jangled together, encapsulated in the focus of that single moment of time.

Billy Harrison saw the thing soar, unable for the moment to comprehend what had happened. Tom's body was in the act of turning, as if flinching from the whiplash of the tree. A deep vibration shivered in the ground, almost audible in a thrumming tremor. Hawthorn leaves floated in a wide, slow halo of green around the tree, and pieces of old bark scattered like shrapnel from the trunk. The bomb soared upwards and it snared Billy's eyes, a dark and powerful silhouette, shark fins jutting out from the tail.

'*What's happening?*' he heard his own voice ask, inside his head. The moment was somehow charged with an inexplicable and awesome energy. His heart was beating, still fast, squeezing inside his chest, but he felt it like a slow pulse, and the harsh whiplash of the tree seemed to stretch out and develop a bass thrum which matched the deep vibration under his feet.

'*Want to cross over? Eh, boy?*'

The monster had dragged him into the tent and broken him. *Tried to kill him!* He had lashed out with the ballpeen hammer, feeling it hit in meaty thuds, wanting to break and shatter and destroy.

The madman had taken him down to the water, he had gone down into the valley, into the shadow, and death had been hovering nearby. Pain throbbed up from the tender, torn skin and the bomb was going up and up, expanding rather than diminishing in his consciousness, powerful and mesmerizing. Billy stood slack-jawed, watching it, as if his life depended on it; unable to look away, despite the need to be up on the moor and gone.

Tom Tannahill was half turned, and his face tilted to the sky. The panic and exhaustion had squeezed at him so tightly that a little dribble of urine had spurted out to stain the front of his jeans. The bomb rose up . . .

'*Sorry, Tommy, just trying to say, ok?*'

Corky had looked over at him with eyes like fine glass, so fragile they could break and shatter, and they focused on him with such powerful regret and sorrow that it had reached and soothed a cooling balm into the raw, open wound of his hurt.

'*Read me the story, Tom, would you?*' Little Maureen's slow voice and the bruises under her eyes and the paunchy, sick swelling of her skin. '*I need to go to the bathroom, Tom. I need to go.*' And she had gone and everything in his life burst asunder.

Now the bomb was going up and it held him, held everything that he was, in that one brittle fragment of time. He held on to it, the fear magically numbed away.

Doug Nicol was on the grass, braced for balance, behind Danny and Corky. *Hells bells!* It was going up, heavy and thunderous, rising like a black stone.

The rock had gone up, raised high in his two hands, and then it had come slamming down and something had snapped with the sound of a branch cracking, like the sound of the string breaking, the noise of the hawthorn limb smashing upwards against the trunk. The bomb was up.

The first one had missed and they could have got him this time, but the knife had sliced wrong and their last weapon was gone. They could have used it like the camp-fire stone, just a weight to crush and break. Now the bomb was up, on its own course, not theirs, dragging his eyes with it.

Bugsylugs, Bugsylugs, Billy's voice taunted in the background of his mind and he ignored it. That had been then, before this *now*. The taunt was meaningless, its power gone.

There was a red pain across his neck, where the wire had bit into him. It had been worth it.

Did my best, honest to God. He had done his best. Together they had almost beaten him. Almost. Nearly. The bomb rose up and up, for that strange and unreal moment filling the entire sky.

John Corcoran watched it, sharp black against the light blue, black as the gaping barrel of the shotgun up against his eye. The crack of the branch had been like the crash of the pin against the empty chamber – world-shattering, devastating. Numbing.

Nothing happened. Nothing happened!

The air had whooped when the bough had uncoiled like the strike of some knotted, brown snake. He watched the bomb float up and away, heavy and blunt and somehow mindlessly vicious.

'*See how you like it, you crazy fucking bastard!*'

The pin had come down on an empty space again. *Nothing happened.*

'*Kill him.*' Somebody had said from far away. Under his back, the earth shuddered violently. The crack of the parting string and the crack of the shotgun's firing pin resounded inside him, with the jar of his teeth on wire, on and on and on, a mental ricochet that seemed as if it might go on for ever.

'*Kill him!*' Somebody had demanded and he had not hesitated, because the voice had really been his own and this could be the last time, this *would* be the last time, and Corky felt the quivering violence and he'd punched forward, felt the thud and then the fruity slide as the blade went in and the blood came out to make a butterfly pattern on the tent.

He'd done it again, twice, thrice.

And again he defied him. The voice had been mad and dreamy, black and rising, like the bomb soaring into the air.

You afraid, boy? You scared? Not of you, you creepy, mad cunt! But he was afraid. Really and truly. He could feel it in the grind of his teeth.

If thine eye offends me. Pluck it . . . And the black, rising shape held him now.

The bomb went up and Danny Gillan watched it, black as the valley of the shadow of death. Danny soared with it, numbed. *Up and over, up and over*, the litany that had kept him going up the slope while exhaustion and pain dragged at him and fear tried to paralyse him.

Denied me thrice. The night had been filled with the sounds of weeping and gnashing of teeth on a hard steel wire. *Bad luck, Danny Boy*. He had knocked the heron out of the air and brought bad luck down upon them all.

The bomb was floating there, huge in the sky above them. *Dung-fly!*

What did *that* mean? *What . . . ?*

The bomb found the reach of its trajectory, slowing down at the apex, the tail now beginning to rise up. It wobbled, seemed to stop still in the air, then, just as slowly, tilted, turned, began to drop.

The strange little bubble of time that had held them, it burst silently, threw them clear.

'Watch out,' Doug found his voice. A spittle of saliva spat out with the words. 'It's going to . . .'

He flinched back. The bomb fell straight down; all of two yards out from the edge. It had seemed to go straight up, but the uncoiling branch had thrown it forward too. It dropped like a stone, still wobbling a little, blunt end down. They turned to follow its progress. Down below, something pale fluttered; it was the man's face twisting upwards towards the sky and the black shape.

The bomb plummeted towards him. His mouth opened and he yelled something, jumped backwards with both arms outstretched, his skin white against the grey of the shale, streaked scarlet with blood. He missed his footing, rolled and skittered halfway down.

The bomb hit the soft slope, dug in a little, but its momentum ploughed it forward and it bounced out, somersaulting once, heading for the ledge of mudstone rubble twenty yards from where the first one had landed, but close to where the third bomb from the previous attempts had rolled in the shale. It hit the mudstone, tail first. A piece of tail-fin flicked off and it too spun, whirling, straight for the soft shale bank.

The man bellowed in lunatic triumph, despite the fact that he'd slid down the incline almost as far as the basin of the corrie.

The bomb bounced fast, straight towards where the other stubby black shape lay. They watched it, all five of them, high on the side of the gorge, unable to draw their eyes away.

It hit.

The whole world turned a brilliant, searing, blinding white.

CHAPTER THIRTY-FIVE

The whole world exploded..

The detonation was so vast, so colossal, that there was no sound, not at first. The narrow gorge erupted in a sea of searing light that turned everything white and burnt dark and cracking lines into the backs of their eyes. The very air slammed up at them, turned solid by the enormity of the explosion, catching them in a stunning body-blow that threw them right off their feet and into the air.

It was worse than they had imagined, more apocalyptic than anything they *could* have imagined. The whole earth leapt upwards under their feet at the same time as the searing, hardened air came punching up from down-slope.

In the first split second, there was no noise at all because the quality of the very air had changed in the instant of the explosion. The earth came up at them, shucked them off, and the blast carried them away. A monstrous hand reached up and snatched at Doug, who was lower down the slope, nearer the sharp edge toward which the man had been climbing. The hot hand grabbed at him, pressing against every inch of his skin, and squeezed so hard he felt his eyes popping outwards. The hand lifted and threw him and he went sailing through the blinding sky, arms and legs flailing.

Danny and Corky, lying in a heap beside the tree, were thrown up, along with the ledge of turf on which they sprawled, in a sudden reverse of gravity. They went rolling straight up the hill, one over the other in a tangle. Tom was slammed against Billy so hard that his nose burst against Billy's ribs and the two of them were punched over the low rise and dumped on to the thick heather.

The noise came then.

It was louder than anything they'd heard, louder than the explosions up in Drumbeck Quarry, or close thunder in a summer storm beating its way up the firth. It made the shotgun blast pale to a whisper. It was louder than anything in the world. It blasted into their heads in a sudden, excruciating blare that drove out all thought in a stunning, catastrophic concussion.

It was nothing like the movies at all. It was no fireworks. The earth itself simply exploded.

The blast wave drove under the roots of the hawthorn tree which had catapulted the bomb into the air and ripped it, roots and all, from where it clung to the edge of the gorge, lifted it straight into the air. Corky was tumbling upwards, landing on his shoulder, crashing on to his backside. His teeth crunched together and, up at the back, one of them cracked in a soundless, painless snap. The sky was white and the noise was crackling inside his head now, for he had gone deaf. All he could hear was the concussion and the glassy crackle inside the bones of his skull. There was no time to breathe, no time to yell, and every nerve in his body was slammed numb. He saw the hawthorn tree fly upwards like a jagged rocket, tumbling as it flew, the one trunk ripping away from the other, scattering leaves and twigs. He hit the heather with a thud which might have knocked his breath out, but he couldn't tell. Danny landed half on top of him, on his backside. His eyes were wide and unblinking and his pupils seemed to have disappeared so that only blue showed.

The blast went on and on, rocking through them, while the earth danced and jumped as if it was alive, and it seemed as if the explosion would never end. Corky managed to turn, found his breath, sucked in air that was hot and burning. The world smelt as if it was on fire.

Doug had landed over to the left, feet up, head down, flipped by the explosion up to the same level, but out from the protection of the heathery gradient. He was rolling back, trying to get a grip on the shale surface, sliding downwards as he did so, slipping straight towards the sheer drop.

'Doug!' Corky bellowed, but no sound at all came out, although he knew he had shouted. Doug didn't hear him. Danny was rolling over now, eyes trying to focus, a trickle of blood dripping from a burst lip. He saw Doug start to slide, saw the shale crumble under him. The lip was now closer than it had been before. Beyond it was the drop to the corrie below and the cauldron of white where the bomb had cracked the world.

Corky crawled over, forcing his numbed limbs to move. Danny

scrambled past, mouth working violently as if he too was shouting. Danny got a hand to Doug's ankle. Corky grabbed his other leg and Doug stopped slipping. He rolled quickly, grabbed Danny's shoulder and spun on to the relative safety of the turf.

All of this happened in bare seconds. The noise was still ripping inside their heads, and they were entirely unaware that each of them was bawling. Up the slope, Tom and Billy, further away from the blast and less concussed, had landed together on the low rise at the highest vantage over the main valley and all the runnels which fed it. They were both winded and numb.

The tree went on sailing upwards, even higher than where they sprawled. It was spinning and twirling and scattering its confetti of leaves and pieces of thorn into the white in a spectacular ballet.

Rocks and pieces of mudstone blasted upwards, some of them trailing dust or smoke, up and out, in a spectacular eruption, mixed in with red-hot pieces of metal which burnt through the sky like meteors in reverse. The rocks went up in a fountain and came back down as black hail.

Below the edge of the gorge, the face they had crawled up in panic, where Danny had slung the curved stick to knock the man off his feet, the whole slope shivered, shuddered, then all of it peeled away in an avalanche of rock and shale. The edge where Danny and Corky and Doug had sprawled slowly slipped away with a huge roar and Tom was surprised that he could actually hear it. It was not as loud as the percussion of the bomb, but the earth shivered even more violently. Corky and Danny held on to Doug as the ground began to slide from under them. They could feel the rumble of it moving, the bucking dance of ground in motion. Doug turned, crawled upwards, making his feet move faster than the sliding surface. Corky hauled on his collar.

From their vantage point, Tom and Billy could see the narrow ridge shatter and crack on the far side, the thin shoulder that separated this gorge from the next, where they had discovered the backed-up lake. The whole top end, a hump of volcanic basalt rock maybe some twelve feet high and six wide, was pushed outward by the enormity of the blast.

The three others scrabbled desperately to avoid being dragged down in the avalanche into the corrie below them. They got to solid earth, pushed themselves up on to the bracken, kept coming. Tom could hear them yelling frantically, but his eyes were fixed on the far side. Beside him, Billy stood like stone, legs braced, eyes wide, mouth even wider.

Corky reached them, his face grey with shale dust. He had Doug still by the collar as if he was unable to let it go. Blood was trickling from Danny's mouth. Tom's burst nose gave him no pain yet.

They all turned.

Down below, where the lip had started to slip and slide, the whole side of this gorge bulged outwards, undercut by the blast. The ringing in Corky's ears stopped suddenly. He saw Danny push his palms against his own ears as if trying to clear the pressure. For an instant there was an absolute silence and then something popped and Corky heard the bass, rumbling thunder.

The slope bulged, swelled as if a gigantic bubble were inflating underneath the ground. The lip where they'd been sliding just dropped from sight. Jagged, horizontal cracks, more or less parallel, appeared in steps above that and, almost instantly, in a jagged succession, they fell away in slices. The ground bucked again, almost hard enough to throw them off their feet.

'Back!' Tom bleated, and everybody heard this time except Doug, but Corky still had a hand to his collar and he simply dragged him further up into the heather.

Over on the far side of the defile, another series of horizontal cracks appeared, broken by vertical fissures that suddenly raced up the opposite face towards the ridge. The great boulder at the top shuddered and then rocked, not slowly, but surprisingly fast, twisting as it did.

Streamers of debris and shrapnel were falling down around them and there was no cover. The hawthorn tree was still tumbling through the air, both trunks in pirouette around each other. Rocks hit all around them. Further up the slope, behind them so they did not see it yet, a blazing piece of metal had set the dry, summer couch grass alight. It would eventually burn eastwards and blacken miles of the moorland. The five of them stood there, transfixed once more. Tom pulled a numb Billy down beside him. By a miracle, the outsplash hit none of them, though all around them it was rapping and thudding on the grass in a deadly hail, like shot from the gun.

On the far side, the rock shoulder slumped. A series of mudstone boulders shot out like squeezed pips, in a cannonade powerful enough to spit them across the gorge to smack into the other side, which was now a full-blown avalanche. The noise of grinding, rolling rock was unbelievable.

The ridge twisted under its own weight, then fell away, slowly at first, then falling into the next gully. Sharp cracks of broken stone came out like grenades and then the ridge just fell from sight.

'*Christ on a bike!*' Doug bawled, and his words were almost strangled by the death grip Corky had on his collar. Danny was speechless.

Below them the rockface slumped down into the corrie with a huge grinding. Over on the opposite side, the rock ridge toppled out of sight and slammed against something with such force that they felt the shock of it tremble under their feet from almost eighty yards away.

The shiver caused more of the ground on this side to slip. Danny pulled Corky, who dragged Doug without any ceremony. Tom and Billy followed on. They scurried, stiff, sore and numb, but miraculously alive, along the edge of the heather, gaining height on the curve of land which connected the twin, narrow gorges. From that distance they could turn and see what was happening.

'Look at that,' Danny yelled. Corky held a hand up to his ear. 'What?'

Danny pointed and everybody looked. The side of the valley, the one they had scrambled up in panic and fear, was sliding down in one huge sheet of shale and mudstone. Small pieces of rock were shooting out to tumble down to the little rivulet beyond the basin of the corrie.

Over on the other side of the ravine, they could now see from the vantage point of the high ground, the great rock on the ridge shoulder had rolled down to crash against the basalt walls which virtually bisected the valley. Behind it, Lonesome Lake stretched blackly, pocked by falling pieces of stone and twigs. The immense block of stone had rolled close to the top end of the wall where it bedded into the side of the valley, and now it was rocking massively back and forth.

'It's going to . . .' Corky bawled.

The huge stone swung forward, back, teetered, and then seemed to reach a point of equilibrium. Underneath its weight, the layer of mudstone began to crumble. Shards spat outwards on puffs of pulverized dust. The rock jarred, swung and then rolled. It all seemed to go in ponderous slow-motion, but it took only a couple of seconds for it to tumble down the steep slope.

It hit the wall where the trees and twigs and muddy peat had formed the natural dam, hit it with such a colossal, jarring blow that the basalt dyke shivered under the impact. One side of it, a foot back from the crevice cut by thousands of years of tumbling water, cracked and splintered, sending fissures growing up it like instant black branches. A squirt of fine water hosed out from the blockage, maybe ten feet up from the base. Lower down, where the new cracks spiderwebbed the rock wall, a fine spray hissed, almost invisible. Another spurted out, black and dirty, arcing out into the narrow gully. The edge of the wall bulged the way the side of the face had done. It seemed to breathe, stop, breathe again. Behind it, millions of gallons pushed with irresistible pressure. The cracks on the weakened wall close to the plug of twigs and branches, feathered out, flaked. There was a heartbeat of a pause when nothing happened.

Then the dam burst.

It exploded outwards, taking the barrier of logs and everything else with it. The thick trunk that had formed the main blockage went tumbling out like a caber, end over end. It smacked into a rock fifty feet down the gorge and snapped like a dead twig.

The water came out behind it in a roar that sounded somehow alive and ferocious. The wall of water came pushing out in a foaming cascade, taking rocks and sticks and everything with it. It shot straight out, hit the right-hand bend in the gully, where it turned to empty into the valley, and the bounding debris simply carved its own way through. Pieces of quartz and old red sandstone rolled along in blocks six feet high, carried by the enormous bore of water. The noise was cataclysmic.

The five of them watched, stunned once more to silence by the dam burst and the huge front of water rushing down the defile. The two halves of the jagged trunk which had blasted out were picked up again and thrown into the air, tumbling again. One thick section speared the shale on the far side, embedded into the ground before the water caught it again, plucked it free, and dragged it down into the valley. The avalanche of water, stone and silty mud came crashing out into the main valley of Blackwood Glen in a vast torrent that unleashed all the pent-up weight and power that had been the deeps of Lonesome Lake. Down there, they could see the little ridge where the hawthorn trees grew in a line, the place where the four of them had sat out the long night while Corky gnawed grimly at the wire. The front hit the hawthorns and simply swept them away. They could see the branches and the roots wave violently as they tumbled before it, then tumbled inside it. The next second, the flood swept over the camp-site, a wall of brown and white that was ten feet deep, surging with foam, the colour of mud. The tent flipped up. An enamel plate spun into the air like a Frisbee. In a split second the camp-site was gone. The circle of stones was scattered like billiard balls. A whole section of turf simply slid down, undercut by the sharp stones which were dragged and scraped along like a rasp-file.

The rampart of water reached the turn where Corky had been ambushed by the raggedy man, flinging stones ahead of it to embed themselves in the opposite slope, then the flood hit the trees, snapping the first ones like matchwood, great spruce trees, tall and straight, that had stood a hundred years and more, sending up a fusillade of gunshot over the roar of the devastation. The gully they had followed to reach the dam which held the backed-up lake was changed for ever, two of the turns, left and right, had simply been ground away to form a straight gash.

The camp-site was gone, taking with it the ruined tent and their old haversacks and the deer's rotted head, the gun, every shred of evidence that they had ever been there.

Over on the gorge to the left, where they had climbed the face, pursued by the madman, the geography had utterly changed.

The steep slope was no longer there. It had peeled and slid, taking with it the lip where the hawthorn tree had clung, and where Doug and Danny and Corky had fallen and tumbled before clambering for their lives after the blast. There was no slope, only a new, sheer face where the lines of mudstone sandwiched the thicker layers of gravel from the last ice age. It dropped almost a hundred feet into what once had been the little basin of the corrie that they'd reached after the scrambling, desperate climb up the shale slope.

The corrie was gone.

In its place, a huge mound of rubble and stone and gravel remained, hundreds, maybe thousands of tons of rock, still steaming and smoking and billowing dust. Trickles of rocks and stones ran down the flanks in miniature avalanches as the slip shuddered and settled under its own weight.

Above them, a vast cloud of smoke was roiling in the once blue, once white sky, turning it black, shrouding them in its shadow.

Below them, where the corrie basin had been, was a vast spoil heap of rock and shale, altered for ever from what it had been in the nightmare chase, the panicked, desperate dash for freedom.

The man with the twitchy eyes was underneath it. He was buried under this new hill.

For a long time they stood there, listening to the crackling in their ears, listening to the scouring roar of Lonesome Lake as it drained away, scraping the valley clean of everything that had been there, alive or dead, carrying it all down in a cataclysmic swathe of destruction downstream through the forest. In the distance, they could see the tops of the trees whipping back and forth as the torrent shook them to their roots.

After a while, the noise began to subside and the flow began to lessen. They still stood there, frozen, numb, rooted, hardly able to breathe, while around them the dust billowed and the smell of burning was hot on the air.

The grey, bare mound that now covered the corrie drew their eyes towards it like a magnet. They had buried him.

Far off, way down the slope on the other side, in the direction of Blackwood Farm, a cock crew. Closer in, but still some distance away, a big grey bird flapped into the sky above the trees, gaining height, obviously startled by the rushing torrent of water. Danny Gillan thought he could hear the hoarse cry of a heron.

Down in the depths, where the camp-site had been, there was nothing to show that anybody had been there, neither boy nor madman.

After a long time, as one, the boys turned to head for home. For an even longer time, nobody said a word.

Chapter Thirty-six

Reminiscence

For a long time, as we trudged up the moor, beyond the burning grass and heather which trailed white smoke into the now still air, nobody said a word. Nobody could. We breasted the hill and headed down the slope towards the distant barwoods, which formed the first barrier between the moor and the high farmland. Over the east, the sun had now risen well up beyond Langmuir Crags, soaring bright into a clear blue sky. Behind us, as we could see every time we turned around (and none of us could resist doing that), the pall of smoke had risen up in a huge column that flattened out at the top. We had seen clouds like that before, in newsreels in the old Regal cinema.

We had gone down into the valley five days before, and we had come out again, and life would never be the same again, not for any of us. Every now and again, one would turn back to look at the rising pillar of smoke, the black and transient marker of what had happened, but mostly we looked over our shoulders just in case the raggedy, bloodied and somehow unstoppable monster was clambering up the moor after us, waving that butcher's knife and repeating his own mad mantra.

Dung-fly . . . dung-fly . . .

We were all hurt and we were all bruised, both inside and out. Whatever Twitchy Eyes had done, he had reached inside each of us in one way or another and left his mark on our souls. *Jesus*, we were only thirteen years old.

Nobody said a word for a long time and that's how it stayed. We never, despite what happened after that, we never spoke about it to anybody else. Not ever. During that hot, crazy summer and the strangely bitter, unstable aftermath of the autumn which followed, we lived in the shadow of the man with the twitchy eyes. A few mothers in our town lived in this shadow too, and sisters and brothers and devastated families, but we had *seen* him. *We* had heard the sound of his voice, felt his touch.

We had looked into those eyes.

Back down the hill after those five days, carrying less in our hands than we had taken there, and weighed by so much more in our souls. We couldn't go home, not right away, so we stayed, huddled together for comfort in the heat of the afternoon, down in the damp shade of the Rough Drain, waiting until the old bus came back with the rest of the scouts, and mostly waiting until we could face another human being who was not one of us. Nobody knew.

Strange, isn't it? Nobody knew. Nobody suspected. Boys get away with murder, near enough. You come in with the knees torn out of your jeans and your furious ma wants to know where she'll get the money for another pair, never mind torn skin. She asks what you've been doing and you tell her you fell, and that's fine. You could have fallen off a cliff, but all she can see are holes in the jeans.

You get a scrape or a cut and you say you fell. A bloody nose? Fell. Mothers just don't look and most times they don't ask, and fathers don't notice at all unless it concerns other business. You get a scrape or bruise every other day. A torn shirt or ragged denims can hide a multitude of sins and plenty of damage. They can hide what Billy needed to hide. They can cover for ever the flaring then dying splashes of a shotgun blast. A kick from a madman's boot.

Scrapes and cuts are a boy's lot. Nobody really cares that much. Nobody sees. Boys hide it all, because that's the way boys are, and mostly that's the way men are too. We came back with the scouts and we took our knocks for damaged clothes and we hid our damaged souls.

The killings that had begun in the spring with the slaying of daft Mole Hopkirk, who would never, despite his stated ambition, have become the Greatest Cat Burglar in the History of Crime, those killings stopped. Some people, it seems, had their own theories as to why.

Little Lucy Saunders was long buried, laid to rest in a dry coffin, cleaned of the mud and her own mess. Don Whalen's mother spent two years in Barlane mental hospital, racked by the image of her son's gaping face and its covering of flies. Jeff McGuire, who found Mole's mutilated body, he was in and out of Barlane like a yo-yo, a strange and affected youth with an odd, distant look in his eyes.

Up at Blackwood Farm, where the cock had crowed, master of all it surveyed for two weeks one far-off summer, they cleared up the pieces that had been Ian McColl and his tiny, brave wife.

The killings stopped. After a while, the town tried to get back to normal, still looking over its collective shoulder, the way we had done on the strange, numbed trail down from the high moor that we'd climbed to get out from under, to find the dummy village of legend. Just in case. *Just in case.* ·

Nobody could really believe he was gone, but *we* knew. We knew why, and we never told a soul because we couldn't. Simple as that. There were five boys whose lives had been altered, infected by the touch of the man with the twitchy eyes. We tried to put it away, tuck it into a dark corner, but if you're reading this, you'll know that things that lurk in dark corners come out, and they always go for the throat. We could not tell anyone what had happened to Billy Harrison. We could all remember the deathliness in his voice when he stood there beside the crumpled tent.

Kill him!

We couldn't tell, not then. It's hard enough even now, after all this time.

Doug Nicol's father came home in the autumn and, a fortnight later, they had emptied the house along Braeside Street and gone off to Toronto. The last I saw of Doug, he was standing, blinking tears from his eyes, holding on to little Terry's hand, sniffing hard so that his big teeth showed. The sun was turning his ears pink. My throat was dry. He reached out and touched me on the shoulder and I put a hand on his, and I still remember that touch. I always will.

I remembered him, remember still, how he had turned to the rest of us, when we could all have got away clean, while the man was still grunting like an animal in the tent, and I can recall the words he said in that deadly low whisper.

We have to help him.

Skin-and bone, thirteen years old, and he would have laid down his life for his friend. Greater love has nobody, than that.

I remember Doug Nicol when he stretched out, choked by the wire, to get his foot to the bag, nearly killing himself for us all. He had run forward to snatch the shells away before the madman could load the shotgun. Then he had strode forward, raising that smooth stone up, to slam it down again. Doug Nicol. I never saw him again after he left town, never heard from him again, but I'll never forget him as long as I live. I hope he is happy. I really hope to God he is.

Billy Harrison's mother, who'd doted on her boy and filled his head with heroic tales of derring-do, myths of a hero father who did not exist, she met another sailor, not an American one, and moved to Portsmouth, met yet another, came back up north again and stayed, dragging Billy with her. They settled in Kirkland, a few miles along the Creggan Road, and she took to drink and died some time in the late seventies. Billy was never the same after that week in the valley. God, none of us were, for sure. Many years ago, I saw him coming out of a bar, in another place, another city, with another guy who was tall and black-haired, taller than Billy himself, and for a moment, my heart just stopped. Billy had a dog chain around his neck and the other man held the free end. Years after that, I hadn't heard but I found out later, he got a five-year stretch after a police raid on a child-porn ring. There was talk that some of the videos weren't just sex, but nothing of that was ever proved in court. Billy went down to Drumbain Jail. He hanged himself in his cell.

I only found this out after I'd come back myself, for my own personal reasons, and by then I'd seen what sparked all this off again, uncovering the memories I'd tried to bury down deep. I later discovered, from the records of the inquiry, that he'd hung himself with a tightening loop-noose made from baling twine from the prison farm's harvester.

I remember Billy Harrison on the ground, while the man hauled at him, trying to get the gun, a prostrate shape, flopped and flapping. I remember his heartrending cries of desperate terror in the dark of the night. I recall his triumphant return from the dummy village far up on that bleak moor with the sheep's skull paraded on top of his stave like a Roman standard. I remember the wet patch spreading on his jeans as he climbed up the hill. I can still see the dreadful, lost and barren look in his eyes down in the valley when he realized he had been singled out as the first special victim.

Whatever drove him on after all that, the man with the twitchy eyes was behind it and, for that alone, I hope he is burning in the everlasting fire. Billy Harrison was maybe a crazy kid, big in the mouth, tough in the talk, but he was never a bad one, just a bit troubled. Whatever else the man with the twitchy eyes had done, he'd touched Billy Harrison and passed on some of the infection of his own appalling sickness.

A year after Billy Harrison died, I met Tom Tannahill, by sheer coincidence. He was still small, still thin, and his curly hair was getting thinner still, but he was wiry and there was a toughness about him that was quiet and strong and it was good. He had been working in a hospital in Rwanda, right in the middle of the madness, all that killing. He had led a party of kids out, through the bush, through the wilds, past the marauding bands of bandits with machine-guns and Kalashnikovs and machetes, got them out to Zaire and to safety. He'd adopted one of them, a little girl, barely three years old, a girl he called Maureen. When he told me that, he looked me in the eye and something passed between us and that was enough. The next month he went back to Rwanda, where thousands were dying every day, and he was never heard of again.

Tom. Tiny Tom with his high voice and his shaking hands.

I remember him in the night, trying not to piss his pants because he did not want to die in his own mess. *Jesus*. He was thirteen, same age as me. I remember him swiping that book from the library so he could read a story to the little sister who was dying. 'Billy Goat Gruff'. I recall, like it was yesterday, how he swung the gun by the barrel, and I can still hear the thunder as the shot missed him by barely an inch. I remember him turning, despite his terror, at the top of the ledge, to reach down and help Billy up. Fixed in my memory is the picture of him facing up to the twitchy-eyed madman, raising the gun in his hands, trying to protect the rest of us.

Greater love hath no man than this.

And John Corcoran. Corky to his friends.

His old man, Paddy Corcoran, came out of jail even more crooked and a whole lot meaner, and within a year he was back in for a two-year stretch for an assault on Corky's mother. One prophecy came true. Corky's shoulder was dislocated and the court heard that had happened when he squared up to Paddy Corcoran, a big, blundering man with fists like hams who had thrown him around the room the way a terrier throws a rat. Corky told me about it later, grinning that slow, hard way of his, telling me it was worth it, because he'd got out from under. His mother was in hospital for a little while and when she got out, she left Paddy and abandoned Phil, who was just as much out of control. She and Corky and his aunt moved to a house up on Cargill Farm Road, only a couple along from the bungalow where Big John Fallon lived with his son and daughter.

Corky stayed on at school for an extra year to get the maths qualification he needed to become an engineer. He'd given up on the idea of making movies, though he was the natural, the one with all the imagination. When I walk by the canal at Barloan Harbour, I can still hear the *doom-doom*-doom echo up from the tunnels dug by those Racine rats. Corky never got to make movies, but he hauled himself out from under. And he was never going to be scared of anybody ever again.

The words '*Up and over*' somehow repeat themselves and maybe they're more appropriate. Corky got up and over. Big John, the police sergeant, gave him a solid recommendation to the shipyard at Barloan Harbour and he started his apprenticeship. He hauled himself up by the bootstraps, slogging away at night classes, determined to make something of himself. He got a good engineering degree, and he never bothered to learn to talk proper, the way the *toffs* did. Cargill Farm Road wasn't too far away and Corky and I stayed close in our teens. After a while, after the first few months, we never talked about what happened up in the valley, but it was something that held us together, something we had. Something private. We saved it for later.

A couple of years back, before my walk down on River Street, the first I'd taken in this town for a long time, a 'wheen of years', as we used to say, John Corcoran was the chief engineer on a big gas rig out in the North Sea. You'll recall it went up like a bomb, and remember, I know about bombs.

Corky stayed back, no surprise, getting men on to the lifeboats, waiting until the last minute, until the rest were safe. All of this is documented. It was in the middle of the night and a gale was blowing. The fireball had swept through the turnhouse and the sleeping quarters and Corky had been the one who got them out of there so that only four men, the ones caught in the blast, were killed.

A young Norwegian, one of the cooks, he was coming across the gantry, while behind him, the metal of the walls was buckling and twisting in the heat. The rungs had started to pop out and the boy was slipping, hanging over a hundred-foot drop. Corky turned away from the boat and crawled over the framework, risking his own life, grabbed the boy by the collar and dragged him back. Just then a stanchion higher up gave way and the whole side of the rig collapsed, taking John Corcoran and the boy with it, tangled in the safety rope. It slid down the leg and crumpled like a child's toy, dragging both men under the water. The young Norwegian says John Corcoran somehow got his knife out and cut the rope, still under the water, and pushed him to freedom. The lifeboat got to the scene a few minutes later, but it took them too long to shift the twist of metal and free John Corcoran, trapped just under the surface. When they brought him up, he was still alive, but lack of oxygen had caused dreadful and irreparable brain damage.

Those thirty long minutes under the freezing waters of the North Sea, they burnt out the flash and the fire and the brave determination that was our Corky.

Greater love hath no man than this. That he lay down his life.

I remember those eyes flashing with fear and anger, damned righteous anger, feet spread, knife out, challenging the crazy, twisted killer who was baptizing Billy in the pool in Blackwood Stream, preparing him for sacrifice. I remember him looking into that infinity of death and not flinching. I remember the awful grind of his teeth on the wire as he tried to free us all. I can still see his elbow jerking back twice, three times, to put the knife into the twitchy-eyed beast. In my mind I hear his soothing whisper as he pulled the damp T-shirt away from the searing skin of my back, taking the embedded pellets with it one by one.

John Corcoran. Corky to his friends. He had laid down his life many a time in that one summer.

I saw him, picking up litter on River Street, and his eyes looked into mine, through mine, with not a flicker of recognition and, of all the losses, that was the most painful of all. I could feel tears stinging in the back of my eyes and I suddenly could not swallow.

Hey arse-face. How's it hanging? The words stuck to the back of my throat and they still do. I remember those eyes flashing and I think of the dreadful waste of it all. The unfairness.

Some memories don't fade, no matter how you try to diminish them and push them down into tight little boxes with heavy lids. The memories have their own way of breaking free, beasts in the night, struggling to come back, because memories have a life of their own. I can still see the looks on their faces the day the man came clawing his way up the hill after us, roaring like a mad beast, madness in his eyes and murder in his mind.

For many years, I kept the memory right down and let it slumber fitfully, shying away from it, maybe hoping it would fragment and wither for lack of attention. For a while I succeeded, because you're supposed to go on, to grow up, to overcome. But then something would happen, a chance meeting, a record from those days, 'Red Rooster' or 'My Generation', played on good old Radio Clyde, a cutting from an old newspaper, even an old movie like *Deliverance*.

Or something like the eyes of John Corcoran, who sweeps the streets and doesn't now have the brains he was born with. Something like that would happen and in a second, in the twitch of an eye, I would be a thirteen-year-old boy again, with a faded sloppy-joe and torn jeans and scuffed canvas shoes. Memories come back.

Angus McNicol, the old policeman, he poured me a couple of whiskies and talked into the recorder, and probably exorcized a few of his own ghosts in the process. He asked me why I was asking all the questions and, while I spun him a yarn, by then I really thought I knew why.

I needed to know who he was, the gaunt man who had come across the stream while we were guddling for trout.

Twitchy Eyes.

On River Street, where the first killing had happened, the murder of Mole Hopkirk in the back room of old Cairn House, it had all come back, all of it in a rush, a crazy torrent like the one that had scoured the valley on the day the bombs exploded and burst the dam at Lonesome Lake. It came back clear as day, so powerful that I could smell the heather bloom and the sweat and the pine smoke from the fire. I could hear the flies buzzing over in the hollow where Billy had made his altar and the far-off crowing of the cock was still shrill. I could feel the searing burn of the pellets embedded in the swollen skin, the cold of the water, and I could see the parliament of crows judging me from the old swaying wire up in a deserted ghost village. It came back so powerfully I could feel panic rise in my chest and a hand squeeze in my belly and I had to know, to put a name to it. Now I have got a name, or at least I'm sure I do.

It hasn't made a blind bit of difference, knowing that. I know *who*, but I don't know *why*. Who the hell knows what madness is? Maybe we all have a little bit of it inside of us.

I know that I saw madness, absolute insanity in a killer's eyes, and I lived to tell the tale. Who knows how life would have been if we hadn't gone up there to find the dummy village. Or if the twitchy-eyed monster had picked another town to work his evil.

Late at night, or maybe in the dark and cold shallows of the morning when the light is murky, the colour of river water down at the old quayside, I wake up, heart pounding, from a dream, from *the* dream, the one where I see that grey and rotting hand come crawling like a diseased spider out of a bank of shale. Little trickles of gravel whisper down the steep slope and the fingers flex with a life of their own. The sifting granules are calling out to me.

Dung-fly . . . *dung-fly* . . . in the dream I understand what that whispering hiss means.

In the dream, my legs won't move and my feet won't climb and I can't move. I am nailed by my own dreadful fear.

On top of the ridge, a lone grey heron stands and fixes me with its staring, yellow eye.